MERCY

MERCY

by
Michelle Larkin

2018

MERCY

ISBN 13: 978-1-63555-202-7

This Trade Paperback Original Is Published By
Bold Strokes Books, Inc.
P.O. Box 249
Valley Falls, NY 12185

First Edition: April 2018

CREDITS
Editor: Ruth Sternglantz
Production Design: Susan Ramundo
Cover Design By Tammy Seidick

Acknowledgments

A special thank you to my editor, Ruth Sternglantz, whose edits, comments, and suggestions were like a torch of warm firelight along a snowy path in the woods after nightfall.

Another special thank you to Tammy Seidick for creating this beautiful cover design.

Immense gratitude to my babysitters, Erin Shea and Mary Shea, for taking such wonderful care of my sons and allowing me to cross the finish line with this book.

A long overdue thank you to Shar Coplen for her gentle enthusiasm as this story unfolded.

Heartfelt thanks to my mom, Ruthie, the Bean Town Medium, for being my biggest and most dedicated cheerleader, thank you.

And finally, my two sons, Levi and Jett, for making this journey through life incredibly worthwhile.

Dedication

To Sheila Loren—

You've read countless books.
It's time one was dedicated to you.

Warmly,
Michelle

CHAPTER ONE

Shadow blindfolded the girl with her father's favorite pinstriped tie and made her walk onto the balcony like the plank of a pirate's ship. Instead of a sword, he held scissors at her back. He withdrew a plastic bag from his pocket. Slowly, lovingly, he gave her bangs the trim they needed. Tears slipped from her chin as he cut, leaving tiny droplets of water along the metal railing. He kept every strand of her hair safe and sound inside the bag.

Amber was fourteen when she graduated valedictorian from Notre Dame Academy and seventeen when she graduated from Stanford at the head of her class. At the supple age of twenty-one, she was now just three weeks away from finishing medical school. There was no doubt in Shadow's mind that she'd contribute enormously to the medical and bioscience communities. Amber was well on her way to finding cures for a host of devastating diseases.

Fortunately, he was putting a stop to all her do-good nonsense. Thanks to him, she'd go down in the history books for blowing up the Golden Gate Bridge. During rush hour traffic, no less.

Shadow had already visited her parents' house and confiscated the album they'd kept of her accomplishments. He had scattered the newspaper clippings throughout Amber's apartment: between the pages of medical journals and textbooks, inside her coat pocket, underneath the silverware tray, taped to the bathroom mirror, and nailed to the bedroom wall. He'd taken the liberty of marring each article in angry, red marker. *Too much pressure. Do better next time. Not good enough. I'll show everyone!* The FBI would soon trace the bomb threat to her apartment where they would find all the evidence they needed for an open-and-shut case.

Satisfied that her bangs were evenly trimmed, Shadow removed the girl's blindfold and gave her a merciless shove. Her brilliant mind was freed from captivity ten floors later like a split watermelon on the sidewalk below. He peered over the banister and shook his head. Tragic, really. Her suicide would take a back seat to the thousands of lives she'd taken that very same day in San Francisco.

Stepping into the hallway, he tucked The Book under his arm and locked the door behind him. The jog down the ten flights of stairs was invigorating. By the time he reached the street, a crowd of nosy onlookers had already gathered around the body.

His shadow led him along the sidewalk, dark against the washed-out pavement. He looked up. Clouds loomed like sleeping giants in the distance. Sirens wailed a few streets over. Shadow withdrew his pocket watch and flipped it open. He had just enough time to pay tribute to the Golden Gate Bridge—or what was left of it—and grab a souvenir to add to his collection.

Mercy waited for the elevator at New York City's Jacob K. Javits Federal Building, her home away from home at the FBI. She glanced down at her gold wedding band and twirled it with her thumb. She just couldn't bring herself to take it off. Not yet. It had kept her company for nine years, a comforting reminder that Anna would be waiting for her at the end of the day.

This ring gave her the courage to face each new case. It had helped to keep her feelings of panic at bay countless times over the years. She hated to admit it, but she panicked at the thought of failing. Like the tide, this panic ebbed and flowed, sometimes gaining momentum and crashing ashore with startling fury.

Mercy's self-worth depended solely on her ability to do her job well. As lead special agent in the FBI's Unsolved Child Homicide Unit—UCH—she came to know the kids whose files crossed her desk as intimately as if they were her own.

She was well aware of the statistics. Thousands of children were abducted each year in the United States, but only a small percentage resulted in serious cases where they were held overnight, used for ransom, or murdered by the kidnapper. Out of those one hundred and twenty kids, about seventy survived.

The remaining fifty were the files that usually made it to her desk each year.

Ding. The elevator doors parted. Mercy stepped inside, checked her watch, and swallowed, unsure of the fate that awaited her. Tardiness was always a one-way ticket to hell.

Twenty-three floors later, she exited and flashed her badge to the posted security—an imposing man who wouldn't have looked out of place carrying his car to work instead of driving it. Mercy inserted her keycard and laid her hand across the black screen for her daily thermal fingerprint scan. A green light flashed as the door unlocked.

She marched down the hall, turned the corner, and stepped inside the steady room. Taking her seat at the head of an oblong table, she slid several files from her briefcase. Despite her conservative fashion style, no-makeup policy, and boyishly short hair, she was accustomed to lingering looks wherever she went. With her mixed-race heritage, it was as if Mercy's genes had been split right down the middle at conception. With the bronze skin tone of a professional surfer, she had her father's height, athletic build, and full lips. She had her mother's large eyes, petite nose, and silky dark blond hair. She had also inherited one brown eye from her father and one dazzling sky-blue eye from her mother. Whoever was upstairs calling the shots on the day she was conceived obviously had a sense of humor.

None of her colleagues seemed to notice as she discreetly eased into her chair, so she tried to relax and appear as though she'd been there for a while. It was customary to humiliate an agent in some fashion if they arrived late for a steady room meeting. As soon as the agent was settled in their chair, the meeting would come to a screeching halt. An antique wooden box would be retrieved from a locked cabinet and passed down along the table with a trail of heartfelt condolences.

"Oh, man…"

"Godspeed…"

"Glad it's not me…"

"Bummer, dude…"

"May God have mercy on your soul."

The wide-eyed offender was required to open The Box, remove a slip of paper, and read its contents aloud.

Mercy's personal favorite was the time she had to jog five miles in downtown Manhattan at the peak of rush hour traffic. That alone wouldn't have been so bad because she ran every day. It was the part about *while wearing a Red Sox jersey* that had made her wish she'd been on time. A devout Yankees fan, she was further humiliated when her wife had insisted on accompanying her. Anna jogged about twenty feet behind and periodically hyperventilated with fits of laughter as fellow New Yorkers cussed Mercy out and flipped her the bird more times than she could count.

The Box was replenished each month only by the agents who were subject to its humiliation. Mercy had learned the hard way never to underestimate the creative genius of this highly intelligent group.

Humor meant survival in this room. Laughing from time to time—or getting laughed at, as was so often the case—helped to keep her head above water most days. She suspected it was what kept all of them sane.

Her thoughts were interrupted by a knock at the door as an assistant poked his head inside and met her questioning gaze. "Turn on the TV," he whispered, his face ashen. "Someone just blew up the Golden Gate Bridge."

CHAPTER TWO

Shadow loved his name. Throughout the adventures of his unusually long life, he had never met anyone else who shared his name. It captured his essence perfectly. Indeed, he soldiered through life as humanity's shadow. That was his job.

He didn't work in an office crammed with file cabinets or even own a computer. On the contrary, his methods of organization were far more gratifying to the senses.

His favorite pastime was strolling down one of the aisles within his warehouse. He allowed himself the luxury of visiting an aisle a day. With each aisle measuring a quarter of a mile, there were fifty-four miles of aisles at his fingertips.

He doted over these aisles with affection, much like parents doted over their children. He'd chosen to name them after what he believed the letters in his own name stood for:

Sacrifice (Aisles 1–36)
Hatred (Aisles 37–72)
Aberrations (Aisles 73–108)
Destruction (Aisles 109–144)
Obsession (Aisles 145–180)
Wrath (Aisles 181–216)

Giant metal signs dangled on rusted chains that hung from the warehouse rafters. He'd often switch on the industrial fans overhead, creating a powerful draft that made the chains clink together in a cacophonous roar of metal. Flapping frantically to and fro at the fans' insistent urging, the signs made looming shadows on the concrete floor like pterodactyls circling their prey.

Today, he was scheduled to browse Destruction, Aisle 139. The first pearl that awaited him was no larger than a human thumb: the remains of a charred chalkboard from the Cleveland Rural Grade School in South Carolina. He'd set it afire one evening back in 1923. Sadly, a few had managed to escape the lapping flames. In the end, forty-one children and thirty-six adults were burned to death during a school performance.

Shadow ran his fingers over the blackened piece of chalkboard, brought his fingers to his nostrils, and inhaled deeply. Like Gianni Versace's eau de parfum lingering in the wake of a sensual woman, he could still detect the faint trace of children's hands as they fumbled with the chalk.

He strode farther down the aisle to rediscover other quaint treasures. Here was a dirtied work boot from a miner who'd perished from a methane gas explosion in Castle Gate, Utah, 1924. Shadow, of course, had triggered that explosion himself. He'd managed to collect each miner's left work boot after the bodies had been carried out, one by one, to be identified by friends and family.

One hundred and seventy-two work boots stood side by side on the shelf for his amusement. Few remained whole. Most peered back at him with gaping holes in their leathery skins. He chuckled. The miners had been blown right out of their shoes.

Many of the boots still held bits of dried blood and bone. He rubbed off some crusted blood from the tongue of a boot, brought it to his nose, and savored the faint metallic stench of decay. He was pleased that he'd had the foresight to remove each of these boots from their former tenants. Turned out it was well worth the tiresome chore.

When he flicked the dried blood away, it landed on the concrete in front of him. He made a point of crushing it under the sole of his red and black Forzieri Italian shoes.

Tap-tap, tap-tap. His footsteps echoed down the aisle as he sauntered past a frayed conductor's cap from a Quincy, Massachusetts, train wreck. Twenty-four passengers had died immediately or soon after the accident on August 19, 1890. Although Shadow was solely responsible for the wreck, authorities had cast blame on the innocent train supervisor. Poor, poor Joseph. He reached out to caress the cap's threadbare edges with slender fingers. This one was his favorite. He bent over and inhaled the cap's unique stench. Yes, there it was: the remnants of grief, shock, and panic that had oozed so freely from Joseph's balding scalp.

He owned three hundred and fifty conductor's caps and proudly displayed them here. The brim of each cap was lined up perfectly with its neighbors. He'd adjusted them so they were precisely one inch apart.

Shadow closed his eyes and edged forward, lightly fingering each cap's stiff black material. "All aboard!" he called out, to no one in particular. It pleased him just to hear the sound of his own voice.

"July 7, 1903—train wreck in Rockfish, Virginia, with twenty-two dead. August 7, 1904—train wreck in Eden, Colorado, with ninety-six dead and sixteen horribly mangled. What a pity." He paused and hung his head in mock prayer. "November 1, 1918— train wreck in Brooklyn, New York, with ninety-three dead and over a hundred injured." He opened his eyes, a vague smile forming at the corners of his mouth.

He surrendered to the buoyancy of joy welling up inside him and skipped along until he'd reached the very end of Aisle 139.

That went by much too quickly. It always did. He made a mental note to linger in tomorrow's aisle, to savor each morsel of Destruction as he would a perfectly aged cabernet sauvignon. He looked longingly over his shoulder, not allowing himself to turn and fully face the aisle. He knew better. Compulsion would overtake him, forcing him to snatch a second look at Aisle 139. Before he knew it, he'd be compelled to visit another aisle, then another, until day bled into night. One day would swallow the next for a week or more. He'd made that mistake in the past, but now he prided himself on discipline.

Shadow removed his pocket watch from its solid gold case— an original LeCoultre, circa 1890. Rubbing his thumb back and forth over the cool metal, he remembered pilfering this beloved timepiece in 1901 from the bullet-wounded President McKinley on his deathbed. Grinning, he unlatched the watch's cover. It was time to begin his workday anew.

He climbed inside his golf cart, inserted the key, and started her up. The motor hummed in celebration as he cruised past the mouth of each aisle. He'd already chosen the perfect spot for his new trophy.

He turned left on Aberrations, Aisle 108. He parked and hefted a sharpened chunk of steel that had twisted free from the Golden Gate Bridge in the explosion. Grunting with the effort, he shelved his piece of history, stepping back to admire the new addition to his family.

The bridge's original architect, Irving Morrow, would be saddened to learn that his masterpiece had just been ripped to shreds by a multitude of bombs strapped to its underbelly. It took construction workers nearly four and a half years to build the bridge back in the thirties. It took Shadow just one day to tear it down.

1.7 miles of orange vermilion painted steel, over 15,000 feet of cable, 128 lampposts, and 24 tower sidewalk lamps were ravaged beyond repair. 887,000 tons of raw building material were now rotting in the ocean. This disaster certainly made amends for the lack of human sacrifice in the bridge's early stages.

Foremen had estimated that thirty-five workers would suffer untimely deaths during the bridge's construction, but only eleven workers were killed during that time. Nineteen men were spared from falling to their deaths into the ocean, hundreds of feet below. All because of a disgustingly simple safety net.

Shadow had rectified the insufficient death toll by adding another five thousand lives to the list in just one day: vehicular passengers, bikers, pedestrians, boat tourists below. Rescuers were still frantically searching for bodies before they were consumed by hungering sea dwellers.

An intense jolt of pain in his head removed all coherent thought. Shadow brought his fingers to his temples and fell to his knees. He felt a door being pushed open inside his mind as his twin brother, Lucent, reached out to him.

Communicating telepathically had always made it difficult to keep things from his brother. He'd learned over the years that he could hide certain thoughts behind a steel door in the back of his mind but only with tremendous effort.

He remembered a time when he'd shared everything with Lucent, when their mind-to-mind communication was painless and easy. It had grown gradually more painful over the last few months, ever since he'd started devising his plan.

His brother's voice resounded in his mind, clear and full of homage. *It is time.* Lucent brought forth an image of Mercy Parker. *She is ready.*

Shadow stood, the pain in his head easing to a dull throb. *Yes, I concur. And her twin brother, Raze, shows great promise. I've been monitoring him closely.* He paused. He was loath to admit it, but he and Lucent were close to parting ways. *We're nearing the end, brother. Do you feel it?*

Yes, like heavy boulders on my spirit. It has been a long journey, and I am tired. Lucent sent the exaggerated image of a hunched old man trudging wearily up the side of a mountain, cane held tightly between gnarled fingers as a giant shadow trailed behind.

Shadow was glad to see that his brother had kept his sense of humor, poking fun at his birth name as he had when they were children. *You've worked hard,* Shadow assured him. *Your predecessor would be proud.* Although Lucent's job of working for The Other Side was in direct conflict with his own dark cloak, they were still blood brothers. Each had obediently fulfilled his destiny.

Lucent hesitated. *This is the last time that we will be able to speak.*

I know. Shadow sensed his brother's sadness. *We must prepare the next in line to assume their rightful places in the world...for humanity's benefit,* he lied, for he had no intention of adhering to tradition in any way. He was sweating and shaking now. The effort to keep his steel door locked and hidden was almost too great to bear.

It is our duty, Lucent agreed.

Without the need for words, they journeyed in their minds to a secluded cliff above the ocean. Stepping to the ledge, they peered down at the raging sea. Shadow felt the warmth of sunlight on his face. Fire danced in the sky. Their robes, one dark and one light, flapped wildly about in the wind. Long minutes stretched out in silence as each of them contemplated the future.

Finally, they turned to face one another. With blazing white hair, stone gray beards, and soft wrinkles in all the right places, they were the epitome of grandfatherly gentlemen. They looked to be about seventy but were actually much older.

Only a keen observer would be able to tell the two apart. Each brother had one blue eye and one brown eye. Lucent's right eye was brown, his left one blue. Shadow's were just the opposite.

Lucent was the first to break the silence. *We have traveled a clear path from the beginning. Let us leave a clear path for those who follow.* They hugged one another tightly. Lucent turned and shuffled away, his white cloak rippling behind him as he faded in the distance.

I will miss you, dear brother. Shadow hung his head. Their grassy cliff vanished as concrete floors reappeared beneath his feet. The link between them was severed.

He was sad to see his brother go, but it also came as a great relief. He no longer had to work so hard at concealing his plans. For the first time in over a century, his mind was his and his alone.

He seated himself in the golf cart and sped up the aisle. His days of souvenir collecting were drawing to a close. Finding Mercy Parker would be easy, but how was he going to get her attention?

Chapter Three

Mercy jerked awake and sat up in bed. The clock read 4:59 a.m. She reached up to scratch the side of her head. Her fingers slipped into something warm and gooey. "Aw, hell." She threw back the covers, swung her feet over the side of the bed, and switched the lamp on with her dry hand.

Bad Ass had barfed all over her pillow for the third time that month. Disgusted, she peered back at him over her shoulder. He was curled contentedly on top of the clean pillow on the opposite side, regarding her with hooded eyes through the white fluff of his tail.

"A dog would've had the decency to climb off the bed and throw up on the floor so I could step in it later." She stomped over to the bathroom sink, wiped the cat puke from her hair, and stomped back. One furry, six-toed paw poked out from underneath the bed skirt, daring her to wiggle her toes.

Even though she didn't have a dog, Mercy preferred to think of herself as a dog person. She'd probably brag about Bad Ass at work if he was a battle-scarred tomcat. Hell, if that were the case, she'd keep a picture of him on her desk like some of the other agents did with their pets. It just so happened that he was a feminine ball of white fluff. She'd be laughed right out of the office if anyone knew the truth.

Bad Ass came into her life when she was working the Lopez case—the nine-year-old who was kidnapped from her own birthday party at a neighborhood park. The girl's body was found three days later in a dumpster across town. Breaking the news to her parents had fallen to Mercy.

Turned out the girl's father had bought her a kitten for her birthday but never had the chance to give it to her. After learning of his daughter's murder, Mr. Lopez had pointed a finger at the kitten. "You have cursed my daughter!" he'd shouted. Mercy had watched as Mr. Lopez grasped the tiny kitten by the scruff of the neck and tossed it in the trash can. "It is evil," he'd whispered, his face wet with tears. "Please, take it from my home."

Against her better judgment, Mercy had grabbed the trash bag on her way out the door and set it on the sidewalk. She poked around inside until a fluffy head, no larger than a golf ball, popped up from an empty Folgers can. Covered in coffee grounds, he had reached out to her with one furry, six-toed paw and purred.

Needless to say, it was all downhill from there.

Her cell phone rang as she was stepping out of the shower. She slipped into a terry cloth bathrobe, walked to the nightstand, and unplugged her phone from the charger. She recognized the number at once and glanced at the clock. The chief never called this early.

"What's up, Chief?"

"I have a situation. I need you out here. Now."

As the chief of police in White Plains, New York, Chief Hamber was rock solid in every way. Mercy doubted if the chief had ever needed anything from anyone in his entire life.

"Someone broke into Captain Wilson's house and killed Sarah," the chief said, his voice cracking with emotion. "For Christ's sake, Mercy, she was only nine."

An awkward silence ensued. Mercy said nothing and waited for him to compose himself. She knew better than to try to console him. The chief was like an old grizzly with a soft heart that he didn't want anyone knowing about.

Other than Mercy's twin brother, Chief Hamber was the only family she'd ever really known. The chief had raised them both after their parents died in a train accident when they were six.

"I want you to handle this case, Mercy. Can you do that for me?"

"Wouldn't have it any other way." She was well aware that the chief and Captain Wilson were close. Young Sarah was the chief's godchild.

"I just faxed you the report. When can you be here?"

"Give me five, and I'm on my way."

"Good. I'll stay put till you get here." That was as close to a thank you as the chief had ever gotten.

With bare feet and long strides, Mercy jogged down the hall and plucked the fax from the printer. She left a message for Agent Carmichael to meet her at the crime scene and shrugged into her suit jacket. She slung her gun belt over one shoulder, grabbed the police report, and jogged down the stairs. There, waiting to see her off, was the furball hacker from hell. She gave him a quick scratch under the chin on her way out.

She pressed a button, and the garage door lifted. "Crap." She'd forgotten all about this stupid car. As punishment for showing up late to yesterday's meeting, she'd been forced to plunge into the depths of The Box. Thank God it wasn't another Red Sox run, but this really wasn't much better. The slip of paper had instructed her to leave her own car in the office parking lot and drive around in the Pooh Mobile for the next twenty-four hours.

The Pooh Mobile was aptly named because there were countless stickers of Winnie-the-Pooh stuck to the car from bumper to bumper. Special Agent Estes had given the 1987 Toyota Tercel hatchback to his daughter for her sixteenth birthday. According to her, the car had been forced upon her by her dad the minute she'd gotten her driver's license. "I used to park down the street and around the corner from school so no one would know this hunk of junk belonged to me," she'd confided to Mercy one day, kicking the rear tire in disgust.

The official story was that Estes kept the car in the FBI parking lot for undercover use after his daughter had tried her darnedest to abandon it in a junkyard. No agent had ever been even remotely tempted to use it in an undercover operation of any kind.

The truth was that Estes couldn't sell the car, and he was afraid his daughter would go behind his back and pay someone to steal it if he kept it at home. Anyone who knew Estes was aware of his little problem. The guy never threw *anything* out.

Mercy put her hands on her hips and gave old Pooh the evil eye. A crisis intervention team should have stepped in long ago to save Estes from himself. Regardless, she was instructed to drive this piece of crap until she could get her own car keys back at the next meeting. She sighed and climbed inside.

The car's interior door handle was broken in half. Someone had tied a rope to one end for the sole purpose of closing the door from the inside. She grabbed hold of the rope and gave it a good hard yank. The door didn't latch. Five more tries, and it finally shut.

Mercy's knees pressed painfully against the console because the seat was stuck in position for a much shorter driver. At five ten, she felt like a walnut trying to stuff itself into a peanut shell. She looked up. The roof lining hung down in tattered pieces above the passenger's seat. She tucked them in as best she could so as not to impede her view of the road.

To make matters worse, there was a bumper sticker on the rear windshield that read, *I Voted for Trump*. How thoughtful that her agents had slapped the sticker on the car just before handing her the keys on a shiny new Red Sox keychain. Seriously, were they trying to get her killed?

Despite these contingencies, Mercy persevered. She drove through the town of West Orange and hopped on Interstate 280. Just when she thought that she might have a real chance of surviving this ordeal, old Pooh wouldn't shift into fifth gear. No matter how hard she shoved, smacked, pushed, heaved, or cursed at the damn thing, the stick would not budge. Fourth gear was all the car would give her, allowing her to careen down the highway at an astounding—she glanced down at the speedometer—forty-five miles per hour. If she drove any faster, she risked overheating the engine.

Forty-five it was, then. Granny speed.

She checked the rearview mirror as the dreaded Grandma and Grandpa Motorist switched lanes and picked up speed in their cushy Lincoln Town Car. The old woman's tight gray curls poked out from a hat with tufts of peacock feathers along its brim. An older gentleman sat in the driver's seat beside her. Mercy thought they made a cute couple, so she smiled and waved hello. Instead of waving back with a delicate, white-gloved hand as she'd imagined, the old woman flipped her the bird with one gnarled, arthritic finger as Grandpa put the pedal to the metal and sped away. Mouth agape, Mercy realized she'd finally hit an all-time low.

The early morning traffic was starting to thicken. Cars were honking at her now, yelling political obscenities out their windows as they, too, picked up speed and flew past. "Please," she prayed, "someone take pity on us. Just crash into me and old Pooey here." She patted the dash. "For the love of God, just end our misery now."

She turned onto Captain Wilson's street an hour later. Sergeant Sloan was standing out front when Mercy tried to chug past. He stepped off the sidewalk and waved her down. "Hey, Parker!"

There went her plan to park down the street and around the corner from the captain's house to save her last tiny shred of dignity. She pulled up and rolled down her window. "Hey, Bug." Sloan had earned his nickname from eating a stink beetle on a dare when they were kids.

Bug pointed to the stripes on his uniform. "It's Sergeant Bug to you." He stepped back and grimaced at the car. "Nice wheels."

"Thanks." Mercy parked and wrestled her body from the car's evil clutches. Clipping her badge to her belt, she turned to face Bug. "How's everyone holding up?" She closed the car door. It didn't latch. After three more tries, Bug took pity on her and joined in.

"Cap was mad as hell," Bug said. "Put his fist through the wall when he found Sarah's body. Looks like he broke it. Won't let the medics check it out."

They opened the car door a sixth time and shoved up against it in unison. No luck. This car was taunting her.

"Wife's a mess," Bug went on. "I think the chief's pretty shaken, too"—he looked toward the house—"but it's hard to tell with him sometimes." They finally gave up on shutting the door and let it hang open like pants after a big meal. "You ever meet Sarah?" Bug asked, slightly out of breath.

Mercy nodded solemnly.

"Cap brought her around the station a lot. Great kid. Always smiling." Bug kicked at the dirt. "Come on, Chief's waitin' for you upstairs."

Bug led her through the house. Officers were everywhere, the steady pulse of support and loyalty to the captain coursing through the veins of each room. They ascended the stairs and found Chief Hamber standing in front of a door at the end of a long hallway. Arms crossed over a broad, muscular chest, his eyes were stone cold as he looked dead ahead.

"Hey, Chief." Bug threw his thumb over his shoulder. "Look what the dog dragged in."

"About time," the chief growled. "What took you so long?"

"Long story." Mercy pointed to the closed door. "Sarah's bedroom?"

Nodding, he stepped aside. "I'll leave the two of you alone then." He slapped Mercy on the shoulder. "Check in with me later."

Mercy had never seen the chief hug anyone, nor had she ever gotten hugged by him. It was widely known that Chief Hamber must really care about someone to bestow them with the honorable slap. Mercy had been getting slapped on that same shoulder since she was a kid. It often surprised her that she hadn't suffered permanent damage from a lifetime of shoulder slaps. They used to send her flying across the room back then, but now strong legs held her firmly in place.

Without waiting for a response, the chief turned and marched down the hall. He obviously couldn't bear to see Sarah's body. She'd meant a great deal to him, and he was silently suffering the loss of her.

Bug opened the bedroom door. "We've already dusted for prints," he whispered as they both stepped inside. Messy black powder coated the walls, windowsills, and pink furniture.

Mercy walked over to the body and slid the sheet aside. She was no medical examiner, but the telltale signs of asphyxiation were there: swollen face, ruptured blood vessels, bluish tinge to the face and neck. She replaced the sheet, stood, and looked around.

The bedroom was meticulous—each toy in its place, every stuffed animal posed to perfection. She ran a finger across the top of a pink bookshelf. Eight years in UCH and Mercy had never seen a child's room so neat. She thought back on her walk through the rest of the house: newspapers by the door, unfolded laundry on the sofa, dishes in the sink, a stray sock in the hallway. She turned to Bug. "Who cleaned up in here?"

"Nobody. Cap says he found it like this."

Something on the carpet in the corner caught Mercy's eye. The perp had arranged Sarah's Legos on the floor to spell two words. Her arms broke out in goose bumps as she read them aloud. *"Photo Psychic."*

Bug joined her and slid his hands in his pockets. They both stared down at the Legos. "Weird, huh?"

The message didn't make any sense, but Mercy couldn't shake the feeling that it was somehow meant just for her.

CHAPTER FOUR

The driver turned right on Forrest Avenue and pulled to the side of the road. Lucent reached for the pillow in the back seat, gently slid it beneath Jendy's head, and withdrew his wooden cane from the car. With nary a word, he left the sleeping girl in the capable and trusted hands of his driver.

Preferring to walk the last three blocks to Captain Wilson's house, he passed under the warm glow of antique streetlamps, smartly placed within the dark belly of an old New York road. Nighttime clouds cast a bone-chilling drizzle, spitting relentlessly on the citizens of White Plains. Lucent was neither cold nor wet. Without the need for an umbrella, he remained warm and dry all the way to the captain's front door.

He rang the doorbell and waited as tendrils of grief crept out from beneath the door and crawled up his pant leg like a kitten seeking refuge from the storm. The door opened to reveal Captain Wilson in an Irish green bathrobe and matching slippers. Lucent introduced himself and asked if he might come inside.

Thirty minutes later, he rose from their living room sofa, leaning heavily on his cane. He set a manila envelope on the coffee table and shook hands with the captain and his wife. Promising to return in one hour to hear of their decision, he walked humbly to the front door and let himself out. As he turned to leave, he glanced back long enough to see that his handshake was already kindling restorative sparks of color within each of them.

Lucent knew that he was akin to a living, breathing, walking box of crayons. With a simple touch, he could transform the withered pencil-gray edges of a spirit into vibrant hues of fiery red, sunset orange, and bumblebee yellow. Individual spirits were always tinged with different shades of green, purple, and blue, making each one as unique as a fingerprint. He liked to think of himself as a spiritual artist. Rather than painting with brushes made of horsehair, he painted with all his heart and soul.

He shut the Wilsons' door quietly behind him, and the night welcomed him back into its dark embrace. Following his own luminescent footprints down the steps, he peered ahead. Adjacent to his footprints was yet another set. Hard and lumpy like coagulated blood, they bordered the cobblestone walkway before veering off in the opposite direction from his path. Lucent took great care to step around them. Yes, Shadow had been here, too.

He'd found himself thinking more about Shadow over the last few months. They'd always been close, but something had changed between them that he couldn't quite put his finger on. It felt like his brother was hiding something whenever their minds linked. The more he tried to break through the barrier and find out what it was, the further it receded.

During their final conversation, Lucent caught bits and pieces of alarming images that he didn't yet understand, though he planned to ponder the matter until he did.

He retraced his steps all the way to the car, paused with his fingers curled around the door's handle, and watched as the hooded dog walker behind him crossed the street. Something shiny had caught the dog walker's eye.

Lucent knew that his footprints glowed, even from afar. Peripherally, they shone like brilliant oyster shells embedded in the pavement. Upon closer inspection, however, they had no real substance or definition, causing passersby to scratch their heads in confusion, just as the dog walker was doing now.

He opened the car door and silently seated himself beneath the sleeping bundle of child. Jendy's dark African complexion was striking against his cream colored slacks. The steady thrum of the car's engine had lulled her to sleep, thumb in mouth.

She'd slept fitfully on the plane ride from Nairobi to Johannesburg. From there, they'd boarded another plane to Georgia and flown on to LaGuardia Airport in New York. Memories of her family's senseless massacre lingered along the edges of her dreams whenever she closed her eyes.

As the sole survivor of a small village in Uganda, Jendy would be plagued with nightmares for many months to come. He looked down as he felt her tiny arms twitch in response to some unseen rebel soldier. Her breathing grew labored, and her small hands clenched in fright. Without touching her, he ran his hand along the length of her body. She quieted at once.

Fortunately, the East African government had agreed to expedite Jendy's adoption as a personal favor to Lucent. The only thing left to do was convince the captain and his wife to adopt her, despite the recent loss of their only child. He checked the time on the dash. All he could do now was wait.

Jendy stirred. She popped her thumb out of her mouth, blinked up at him, and reached out for reassurance. He spoke in her native Kenyi tongue. "Do not be afraid, little one. I am here." He lifted her into his lap, wrapped his arms around her, and held her close. "Would you like me to tell you a story?"

She nodded, popped her thumb back in her mouth, and laid her head on his shoulder. He felt her long eyelashes brush against his neck like butterfly wings.

"In a village somewhere far from here, there once lived a brave little girl named Jendyose. She was happy and very much loved by all her family. One day, the bad men came and took her family away." Lucent felt her small body tense within his arms. "Do not fear." He stroked her back. "I give you my word that this story has a happy ending, just like the stories your grandmother used to tell around the fire each night. Do you remember those stories, little one?"

She withdrew her thumb from her mouth, lifted her head, and stared into his eyes for long seconds. "I remember," she whispered, peering back at him with such sadness and strength.

He sighed, distressed at the true meaning of her words. "Yes, I know you do."

She laid her head back upon his shoulder, ready for the story to go on. Butterfly wings tickled his neck again as he spoke. "Little Jendy was so special that she was the only one left behind by the bad men. She remained in her village for five long and lonely nights when, finally, a young tribesman passed through and found her. The two journeyed on the strong back of a donkey all the way from Uganda to Kenya, where Jendy met many other brave children." He took a deep breath. "Do you know what happens next?"

"Little Jendy met the old man with magical eyes," she whispered.

"Yes, Jendy ran across the dirt road and reached up to the old man with strange eyes."

"No," she said firmly, lifting her head, her brow furrowed in all seriousness. He could smell the sweetness of oranges on her breath as she spoke. "*Magical* eyes," she corrected. Her hands were still sticky from orange peels as she reached out and petted the crow's feet he knew had gathered around his eyes. Fine lines on her forehead disappeared, replaced by an expression of awe as she concentrated on each of his eyes intently. "This one"—she gazed into his left eye—"is the color of sky. And this one"—she turned her attention to his right eye, thinking for several seconds before she finally whispered—"is the color of the fierce lion's mane."

"One day, many years from now, you will be a great storyteller." He kissed her proudly on the forehead as she settled on his shoulder once again.

"The old man with magical eyes knew that Jendy was special, so he invited the brave girl to fly like the birds in the sky to a far-off land where she could be happy once more. She took the old man's hand, and together they climbed inside the belly of a powerful bird with metal wings and wheels on its toes!"

She giggled.

"They flew toward a wonderful home in America where Jendy would find a new family to love her and keep her safe. Do you remember what I told you about your new family?"

"They cry today because their little girl has gone away." She placed her hand over the left side of her chest. "But I will make their hearts happy again."

"Would you like to know what they look like?"

She nodded.

From his mind to hers, he sent images of Captain Wilson and his wife. With most adults, communicating in this fashion was like pushing against a heavy door with rusted hinges. Children, on the other hand, were often eager to open the door, sensing his presence on the other side before he even had the chance to knock. Only on rare occasions did he go in without first asking permission.

"She has eyes dark like mine," Jendy observed of her new mom. "And he is very tall, but I am not afraid. He is gentle like…" She paused, searching for the right words. "Like a baby giraffe."

"They speak a different language, but you will learn quickly."

She sat up straight. "Will you teach me?"

"Of course." He gathered dozens of images with words, sowing them like seeds in a garden. As she sounded each one out, he thought back to the day they'd met in Kenya.

Jendy had spotted him from afar and was instantly drawn to him. She'd bolted across the dirt road, stood at his feet, and gazed up, captivated by his mismatched eyes.

An old woman had limped after Jendy, attempting to corral her back in line with the other children. The woman's face had been ravaged by fire. Pointy elbows and knees poked through filthy, paper-thin rags that hung like old skin. Self-conscious as Lucent followed her with his gaze, she kept trying in vain to gather the loose fabric around herself as she hurried after Jendy. Concern was stitched into every wrinkle as she shouted her name. That's when Jendy had reached her arms out, silently asking Lucent to pick her up.

Truth be told, Lucent was just as taken by Jendy as she was by him. She was an amazing little girl with splendorous colors peeling open within her spirit. Without a word, he'd bent over and lifted her into his arms.

Since Masaba was the old woman's native tongue, Jendy was shielded from understanding the painful truth of her circumstances.

She leaned in so close that Lucent was not spared her rank breath. "Jendyose does not reach her arms to anyone. You must have special magic." She bowed her gray head in humble request. "My heart breaks because I cannot afford to feed this child. If she does not eat soon, she will die. Please, find her a home."

Without the need for words, he knew that the old woman had lost her husband and all five of her children to the same fire that stole her face. Heartbroken and childless, she'd decided to become mother to the homeless children in her village. Word quickly spread, and soon everyone was bringing a child to her doorstep. The old woman did everything she could to make certain the children were well cared for. Often sacrificing her own meals so that the little ones could eat, she'd gradually frittered away to nothing more than skin on bones.

Moved by her love for the children, he'd laid a hand on her shoulder to heal her cancer-ridden hip. He'd also arranged for a month's supply of rice, bread, and fresh fruit and vegetables to be delivered to the orphanage. That was the least he could do, but his work was not yet finished.

He'd visited the captain and his wife to pick up where his brother had left off. Shadow had taken the life of the Wilsons' only child. Though he knew it to be necessary, Lucent grieved for their loss. Nevertheless, the path for the captain and his wife had been set.

Lucent took joy in bringing such steadfast purpose into their lives. It would give them the strength to go on and allow them, in turn, to change the lives of countless others.

He returned to the Wilsons' home exactly one hour later as promised. The captain and his wife had reviewed the envelope's contents to find the adoption papers in order. They had also watched the video of the old woman and her children as they struggled just to stay alive another day.

As Lucent had hoped, their hearts were now open. The captain and his wife intended to take action. Not only would they adopt Jendy, but they planned to make it their mission to grant the old woman's only wish: to find families for each of the children in her care.

Head bowed, Lucent retraced his steps from the captain's house to the car for the second time that night. Amidst the dirt and dead leaves on the moistened pavement, he glimpsed colorful footprints from a pair of very small sneakers.

Footprints from a particularly radiant spirit always lingered for a short time before fading completely. Unlike his own, Jendy's could not be seen by just anyone. Other than himself, there were only a handful of people in the entire world who were able to detect such things.

She was a glorious child, and he missed her sweet nature already. She had held his hand during the three block walk to her new home, skipping along the street with nervous excitement at the prospect of meeting her new parents. Like Halloween face paint, her colors had rubbed off into his palm. He studied the hummingbird blue and maple leaf green of her spirit as he strolled to the car.

He meant every word he had said to her. Indeed, Jendy would be a great storyteller one day, touching the hearts of millions of children across the world with words of pure magic.

Covering his own heart, he laid his hand upon the ivory cable-knit sweater he'd inherited from his father over a century ago and whispered in his Latin tongue, "Bless this child, Jendyose." He paused, considering his words carefully. "Let her bring good to the world and do many great things."

He watched the colors on his hand fade like the last glowing ember in a fire pit and felt as they were absorbed into the colors of his own spirit. Jendy was now a treasured part of him deep inside.

He lifted the car door handle, took one last look over his shoulder, and ducked inside to join his driver.

CHAPTER FIVE

Mercy leaned back in her office chair. It was the second most comforting possession in her life. The leather stretched and engulfed her familiar form. She'd devoted thousands of hours to breaking it in. But her greatest source of comfort still resided on the ring finger of her left hand, currently devoid of purpose, meaning, and mate.

She twirled her wedding band around with her thumb and rearranged the crime scene photos on her desk. Sarah Wilson stared back at her, her deathly pallor a sad reminder of the captain's loss.

Bug wasn't exaggerating. Everything Mercy had found out about Sarah in the last twenty-six hours confirmed that she was, in fact, a great kid. She opened the file on her desk and examined Sarah's school photo more closely. Her cheeks were plump with baby fat and freckles. One front tooth was missing.

There were times when the job really got to her. Mostly on nights like these when she was alone in the office. She'd stayed awake all night trying to get a handle on the case. She finally stood, stretched, and walked over to her bulletin board.

To the disappointment of many, Mercy wasn't compulsively neat or particularly obsessive about anything in her life—except for this bulletin board. She had made it after solving her very first case in UCH eight years ago.

She'd driven to a hardware store one Friday after work to buy the supplies and constructed the bulletin board in her garage over the weekend, making it collapsible so it could be easily transported. When she'd brought it to work the following Monday, she removed the boy's school photo from her case file—the seven-year-old who was sodomized then drowned in a nearby lake by his teenage babysitter—and hung it on the bulletin board with a blue pushpin. She'd told everyone that it would help her keep track of the caseload, both past and present. The only one who knew the real reason behind the bulletin board was Anna.

The truth was that she wanted to give each child a safe place to go where they would never be alone once their investigation concluded. She offered them protection in the only way she could, by keeping the photos of happier times—their freckled faces and toothless grins—close to her heart.

She sat on the edge of her desk and reviewed the crime scene one more time. Sighing, she picked up Sarah's school photo again. "I feel like I'm letting you down, kiddo. None of this is making any sense."

Mercy always made a point of talking to the photos of homicide victims when figuring a case. She got the harebrained idea from one of her instructors back at the Academy.

Lou, who'd insisted that his students address him by his first name, once told the class, *Talk to the photos of the deceased. Ask them questions. Then listen long and hard until you hear the answers they give you.*

The entire class had laughed out loud, thinking it a joke. But Mercy took his words to heart.

She rubbed her eyes. She'd been reviewing the photos, interviews, and lab reports for hours. The perp was meticulous. No hair, fibers, fingerprints, shoeprints, or tire treads had been left behind. According to the ME, the official cause of death was asphyxiation. Nine-year-old Sarah had been smothered to death with her own pillow.

She slid the Legos photo across her desk and studied it with a magnifying glass. "Photo Psychic," she read aloud, letting the words hang in the air and hoping for a revelation of some kind.

It didn't come.

The Legos were perfectly aligned, as if someone had used a level to measure their precise placement. Only the red Legos had been selected from Sarah's toy box to spell each word. She wondered if the color red was significant. It could represent so many things. Pain, anger, power...

"Photo psychic." She glanced down at her yellow notepad and tried spelling the two words backward until they became *cihcysp otohp*. Wondering if they might be a clue in another language, she researched the possibility, only to prove her theory wrong. She also tried rearranging the letters to spell other words. Unless the *topsy chic hop* was a new dance she hadn't heard about, or *pop hotsy chic* was symbolic of the perp's sinister intent—she couldn't come up with anything better—Mercy pretty much decided she had hit a dead end.

The only photo psychic who came to mind was Piper Vasey. She made a notation in the margin. *Vasey. Bureau psychic.*

There were rumors floating around that the former bureau profiler could communicate with a murder victim simply by studying their photograph. A colleague had once told her that Piper could solve a case in the time it took to pour a cup of coffee.

Mercy wasn't sure she believed in that mumbo jumbo, but the idea sounded attractive enough. The difference between them, she realized, was that the photos never answered any of *her* questions.

She knew Piper wasn't profiling anymore, but no one seemed to know why. She had resigned from the FBI three years ago and then just fell off the face of the earth.

In the past twenty-four hours, she'd discovered that none of Piper's colleagues had been successful at keeping in touch. Piper had dodged their phone calls, texts, emails, and letters expressing concern over her welfare. Christmas and birthday gifts were returned unopened. A few of her closer colleagues even drove out to her cabin in North Conway, New Hampshire, where they found her curtains drawn and her door locked. She'd finally came to the door in response to their insistent knocking though had refused to open it. One by one, she turned each of them away, making it clear she wanted to be left alone.

Mercy planned on pursuing her only lead with this former profiler, but she needed to find out more about her first. She scratched her head. How was she going to do that when nobody seemed to know a thing about this woman?

Realizing that her brain had probably short-circuited hours ago due to lack of movement, food, and sleep, she unlocked the exercise room. Forty minutes on the treadmill was enough to give her the jumpstart she needed.

Showered and dressed, she was just sitting back down at her desk when Agent Carmichael popped her head in the doorway at six forty-five a.m. Carmichael was the only other agent on the case since the San Francisco bombing.

She wrinkled her brow in true mother hen fashion. "Parker, you never went home last night, did you?"

Mercy shook her head. She adored Dana Carmichael. She imagined she felt about her the way she would've felt toward a kid sister, if she'd had one.

Armed with plastic containers full of homemade chicken noodle soup—it was the most delicious soup Mercy had ever tasted in her life—Carmichael made her weekly rounds through the office corridors to nurture flu sufferers back to health. Her motherly concern wasn't limited to their office. She made friends with flu fighters everywhere. All over the building. Every single winter. Her soup was legendary.

At the start of every flu season, Mercy found herself coughing a lot more in Carmichael's presence, secretly crossing her fingers that she'd bring some soup the next day. It worked. Carmichael had probably caught on to the scheme at some point, but she never said anything. She simply continued delivering soup in the same green container every Tuesday.

And today just happened to be chicken noodle soup day.

Carmichael went to the minifridge, opened the door, and tucked the sacred green container into a corner on the lower shelf—Mercy had already cleared some space for it. She leaned against the fridge and looked down, picking nubs of lint from the sleeve of her navy woolen blazer. "Where are you on the Wilson case?"

No lint was safe anywhere near Agent Carmichael. "Actually, I've been trying to get in touch with Dr. Vasey." Mercy leaned back in her chair, laced her fingers behind her head, and yawned. "Left her five voicemails and three emails in the last twenty-four hours. But…"

"Yeah?" Carmichael glanced up, flicking away another piece of lint.

Mercy unwittingly looked down at her own brown woolen blazer. It was her favorite blazer from college: leather elbow patches, intricately etched wooden buttons, perfectly sized pockets for her hands, comfy in all the right places. This was the one piece of clothing she had managed to hide from Anna when she donated half her wardrobe to the Salvation Army. "I think Piper would rather do a twenty-mile Red Sox run and drive around in the Pooh Mobile for a month before assisting us in any way with this case." Microscopic lint nubs that Mercy had never noticed before were suddenly larger than life on her blazer.

"That's not good." Carmichael moved on to the other sleeve.

"Nope." How could she not have noticed all this blazer lint before now?

"Why don't you give Lou a call?" *Pick, pick, flick.* "He and Piper were pretty tight."

Unable to hold herself back any longer, Mercy's fingers stealthily prowled to the first unsuspecting nub of enemy lint. "Where'd you hear that?" *Pluck. Pluck.*

"Estes had a major crush on Piper back at the Academy. Used to follow her around like a lovesick puppy. Guess he overheard part of their conversation after class one day. He got the feeling that Lou was kind of a father figure in her life."

"They still talk?"

"Probably. Why don't you give Lou a call and find out?" Carmichael asked.

"Maybe I'll do that."

Lint free, Carmichael stood and brushed lightly at her slacks. She glanced over. "Parker, what on earth are you doing?"

"What does it look like I'm doing?" She didn't even look up. "Picking lint off my blazer."

Carmichael inched closer, squinting. "Why don't you just change into a different blazer?"

"But I've spent all this time pruning *this* blazer." She stopped. "Why, what's wrong with my blazer?" She looked up and held out the sides of her blazer defensively.

Carmichael grimaced. "I just thought it might save you a little time, that's all."

"You don't like my blazer?" She was stunned. There was no better blazer to be found anywhere on the planet.

"Parker, that thing could win the Ugliest Blazer Award, hands down. Not to mention, I'll be ready to retire by the time you're finished picking out all that cat hair."

What cat hair? Mercy lowered her head and held up a sleeve for closer inspection. Woman enough to admit defeat, she stood and withdrew her arms from each sleeve.

She decided to take Carmichael's advice and called Lou at home. She could have conducted the interview on the phone, but Lou insisted that she come for a walk on the beach. "Come on, Parker. It won't kill you to keep an old retired bum company for a little while."

By the time Mercy hung up, she realized that she hadn't even told Lou why she'd called in the first place.

She booked a flight from LaGuardia to Logan Airport in Boston and rented a car for the hour-and-a-half drive to Cape Cod. Sand blew across the windshield as she parked in Lou's driveway. The smell of rain hung heavy in the air. She clutched at her trench coat and hurried to the front door.

Handing her a mug of coffee, Lou ushered her inside. "Since you're probably not getting many home-cooked meals these days, brunch is waiting for us in the kitchen. We'll eat, catch up, and take a walk on the beach after the storm blows over." He turned and headed toward the kitchen. "Then you can ask me all the questions you want about Piper."

Mercy trailed behind him, shrugging out of her coat one arm at a time, taking care not to spill the coffee. "What makes you think I have questions about Piper?"

"Well, isn't that why you came here?" Lou asked with one bristling salt-and-pepper eyebrow.

"You can't do that."

Lou knitted his eyebrows together and regarded her over spectacles that were perched on the very tip of his nose. "Do what?"

"You can't answer a question with another question. Everyone knows that." She laid her coat over the bar stool, took a sip of coffee, and set the mug down.

"Are you telling me you *didn't* come here to talk about Piper?"

"See?" Mercy threw her hands up. "You just asked three questions in a row."

"And you expect me to feed you a meal that I slaved over when *you* can't even give *me* a straightforward answer?" He set out two large plates, meticulously hand painted with tiny lighthouses along their borders.

"Fine. You made your point. You haven't lost your touch in interrogation tactics." Mercy turned. The ocean greeted her through enormous bay windows. Raindrops dotted the sand outside. "I always forget how great this view is."

"Trying to change the subject?" Lou poured orange juice into their glasses and set the pitcher on the glass tabletop.

"Five questions and counting, Lou. How about a truce if I grant you the title *Interrogation Master*?"

Lou unveiled home-cooked delicacies, peeling away the foil one dish at a time. Aromas rich in garlic, onions, and rosemary filled the kitchen.

Mercy tore her gaze from the view and stared at each unmasked dish. "Better yet, how about *Reigning King of Interrogation for All Time*?"

Lou peered at her over the rim of his glasses. "How about if I grant you the title *Full of Shit Agent Who Goes Home Hungry*?"

Her stomach growled. "You win. I came here to talk about Piper. Happy?"

"Yes." Lou smiled. "Let's eat."

She hadn't eaten a meal like this in ages. Pan-fried English muffins topped with Canadian bacon, poached eggs, and creamy hollandaise sauce. She took three helpings of fried potatoes with parmesan cheese, cracker crumbs, garlic, onions, and fresh herbs, and then left only skeletons of oranges and strawberry tops from the tower of fresh fruit. They took turns catching each other up while rain pelted the sand outside at the rate of a hummingbird's heartbeat.

They cleared the table in silence. Mercy heard the phantom voices of their wives and the excited clinking of dishes that had filled Lou's kitchen not so long ago. The four of them had shared many wonderful meals here together and were always reluctant to part ways at the end of weekend visits.

Despite the twenty year age gap, Jane and Anna had quickly become the best of friends. They connected the moment Mercy introduced them. It couldn't have worked out any better. She and Lou were like family.

Lou shouted to be heard above the blender. "This is delicious. I'm mixing orange juice, eggs, lime, and honey." He turned off the blender and lowered his voice. "It's called an Enchanted Sunset." He poured the blender's contents into both of their glasses and topped them off with a dash of nutmeg.

Clouds finally crept away as the sun reached through the bay windows, tugging on Mercy's shirtsleeve like an insistent child. A door off the kitchen led to a long stretch of private beach. They peeled off their shoes and socks and walked the first few minutes in silence, drinks in hand. She listened to the forlorn cries of seagulls overhead, the muffled sound of wet sand being pushed aside by bare feet, and the surf gurgling ashore, frothy with spraying spittle.

"Why haven't you ever mentioned Piper before?" Mercy asked, looking down at the sand as it squished between her toes. "I had no idea the two of you were close." She couldn't figure out why Lou had kept his relationship with Piper a secret. She wondered if they'd been having an affair but quickly admonished herself for the thought. Lou had adored his late wife, Jane.

Lou stopped walking and turned to face the ocean. "If what I suspect is true—that you need Piper's help with a case you're investigating—then there are two very important things you'll need to know. Never ask about her past, and do not, under any circumstances, ask her to explain her gift." He sipped his drink. "I'm the only person who's managed to keep my friendship with her intact because I never press for the details. As far as her past is concerned, I'm one of the few who knows about it. And as far as her gift is concerned, I haven't breathed a word about it to anyone in the last eighteen years. I'm doing so now only because I believe she needs you as much as you need her." He met Mercy's eyes with a fiery challenge. "If there's anyone who can get her to trust and open up again, Parker, it's you."

An hour later, Mercy was shrugging into her coat near the front door. Lou rounded the corner and handed her a thermos of coffee. "Here," he said, shoving a giant plastic bag of chopped fresh fruit in her hand. "It's a long drive to Piper's. And don't wait so long between visits. I miss having you around."

Mercy was driving south on Route 6 when she saw the voicemail message pop up on her cell. A new message had come in at ten fifty. She looked at the clock on the dash. It was already eleven forty-five. Cell service was spotty at best on many parts of the Cape.

Parker, it's Carmichael. Her voice sounded shaky. *Got a call from Madison PD in New Hampshire. Some bastard broke into my brother's house, beat him to death, and kidnapped my ten year-old niece, Emily. I think it's the same perp who killed Sarah Wilson in White Plains,* she went on. *Sounds crazy, I know, but he left something behind. Remember the Legos on Sarah's bedroom floor? Whoever kidnapped my niece left a red Lego on her pillow. I think she's still alive, Parker. I need you to help me find her. I'm the only family she has left.*

Mercy heard a booming voice in the background of the recording as someone made an announcement for passengers to start boarding.

I'm at LaGuardia, Carmichael said. *My plane lands at noon in Manchester, New Hampshire. I'll be heading over to the crime scene from there. Meet me as soon as you can.* Carmichael gave her the address and hung up the phone.

CHAPTER SIX

E mily knew the bad man had killed her father before he'd kidnapped her from her bedroom. She couldn't explain how she knew, but she knew for a fact that he was dead.

She'd watched the movie *Annie* last summer at her friend's sleepover. She remembered how bad she'd felt for poor Annie, being an orphan and all. After the movie, when her friends had finally fallen asleep, Emily had locked herself in the bathroom and quietly prayed for all the kids in the world who didn't have parents to tuck them in at night. She knew they must be out there, alone and afraid. Even though she didn't have her mom, at least she had her dad. After crawling back into her sleeping bag later that same night, she'd promised God that she would try and help as many orphaned kids as she could.

She'd talked with her dad and decided to start a fundraiser at her school for orphaned kids. It made her feel better to give hope to those kids, even though she hadn't met them in person.

Well, it looked like she was an orphan now, too.

A little part of her felt like it had died with her dad. Mostly though, she wanted to live. Even if it meant living without the one person she loved most in the world.

Her dad had always called her his little giant. She could still hear his proud voice telling the story of how she was born premature and how the doctors didn't think she would survive because she was so little. But her tiny body fought off infection, and she grew stronger with each passing day until she was healthy enough to be taken home. The doctors and nurses had nicknamed her Little Giant. They told her dad that she might look fragile on the outside, but not to be fooled because she was mighty on the inside.

He used to tell her that story whenever he tucked her in to bed at night. She never grew tired of listening. It made her feel strong.

Emily knew she was small for her age, but it didn't bother her. In fact, she considered it to be her secret weapon. She was only four feet tall and weighed fifty-one pounds, according to the scale in the garage. She knew she was cute only because that's what the grownups told her all the time. Sometimes she'd stand in front of the mirror and really look at herself. She had her mother's strawberry-blond hair, her father's brown eyes, and lots and lots of freckles. She tried to count them once, but *that* was impossible.

She knew that when people looked at her, they saw a cute little girl who needed to be protected. But she gave all the boys a run for their money in gym class. Despite her size, she was strong, fast, and athletic. She could pick up any sport quickly and do it well.

She was proud to be the only girl on the Little League baseball team, but being the only girl wasn't enough. She rode her bike down to the batting cages every day after school. The boys respected her because she was the best pitcher and hitter on the team. And she was *never* afraid of the ball.

She thought back to the fourth game of the season when she was hit by a line drive after she'd thrown a beautiful curveball. She didn't have time to put her glove up, so she took the ball right in the face. Even though it hurt a lot, she still bent over, picked the ball up, and threw it to her first baseman just in time for an out. Coach wanted to pull her from the game because her eye puffed up and she couldn't really see out of it anymore, but she told him she wanted to finish. She patiently explained that they were in the last inning. The score was tied. If she stepped down, that would mean Joey Fletchman had to pitch, and he *sucked*. She knew they'd lose for sure if Joey went in. Coach knew it, too. Eventually, she convinced him that she felt good enough to keep playing, so he let her.

They ended up winning that game by three runs.

She made herself stop thinking about baseball and start concentrating on where she was now. She wouldn't allow herself to panic because *that* never did any good. After taking some deep breaths, she decided to go over what had happened to try to make sense of it all.

She remembered waking up in the middle of the night to a noise. The big red numbers on her Batman clock read 3:52 a.m. She'd felt around for her Sheltie and realized she wasn't there. Bubbles always curled up at the foot of her bed and stayed put. Emily had gotten a bad feeling in her stomach, so she threw aside her Batman sheets and climbed out of bed to investigate. Before she made it through the door leading to the hallway, a man had stepped out in front of her and blocked the way. It was too dark to see his face, but she'd never forget his ugly, pointy red shoes. They were lit up by the night-light in the hallway.

Her first thought had been to turn and run for the window. Even though her bedroom was on the second floor, she would've rather broken her leg than let that creep get his hands on her.

In that instant, she'd bolted for the window, opened it with lightning speed, and jumped without looking back.

She recalled being yanked back through the window by the scruff of her X-Men pajamas. The bad man had knocked her head so hard against the window that she was surprised the glass didn't break. In that split second, she'd decided to pretend as though she'd passed out.

By pretending to be unconscious, she had hoped to catch the bad man off guard and escape when he wasn't paying attention. She thought it was a pretty smart plan, but it obviously hadn't worked. He set her down on the carpet, taped her ankles together, and then taped her wrists behind her back. After stuffing a rag inside her mouth, he put tape over that, too.

She had recognized the smell, sound, and feel of duck tape. She helped her dad around the house sometimes, and he used it to fix all kinds of broken stuff. What she didn't understand was why people called it duck tape in the first place. It didn't look anything like a duck. It wasn't even the same color. She hoped it wasn't made from a duck…She shook her head. What was she doing? She couldn't waste time thinking about this now. She promised herself that she'd look it up on the internet if she ever got out of this mess.

After she was all taped up like a FedEx package, the bad man had carried her to his van in the driveway. She had peeked, but there wasn't enough light to make out the van's color or license plate.

Now that she thought about it, she didn't know exactly why she needed to get the license plate. Wasn't she supposed to look for it? At least, that's what grownups did all the time in the movies whenever the bad guy drove the getaway car.

Anyway, all of that brought her to where she was now…lying on blue scratchy carpet in the back of a van. The bad man was driving, but she had no idea where he was taking her. She lifted her head to look around. A dark plastic curtain hung from the van's ceiling and separated the front from the back, which probably meant he couldn't see her from the driver's seat.

The sun was coming up. They'd been driving an awfully long time. All she could see through the windows were the tops of trees, an occasional telephone pole, and brief slices of sky. She scanned the interior but found nothing. Just the bare space of a cargo van. And she was probably the cargo.

The windows were tinted so dark that she didn't think anyone could see inside. She could just make out the edges of a sales sticker from the dealership. The interior smelled brand new, which would explain why it wasn't cluttered with stuff like their minivan.

Emily rested her cheek on the scratchy carpet. Her body was cramping up. Even though there didn't seem to be much hope right now, she refused to cry. Crying would only mean that she was feeling sorry for herself.

She shouldn't cry anyway because her mouth was taped shut. If she did cry, her nose would get all stuffed up, and then she'd suffocate to death on her own snot. What a gross way to die! She certainly wasn't going to do the bad man's work for him.

Her feet were cold, and her hands were pretty numb. Wiggling her fingers didn't do any good because she couldn't feel them enough to tell if they were actually wiggling. Then it dawned on her. She didn't know why she hadn't thought of it before now. All she had to do to get her hands in front of her was pull her legs to her chest and shimmy her arms underneath her backside.

Fortunately for her, she had long arms and a small backside. Her long arms always made up for being so short when it came to playing basketball.

She curled into a ball and squirmed around to free herself. Working hard for this small freedom, she thought about Wolverine, whose cartoon figure was printed on each leg of her green pajama bottoms. She imagined that he was giving her some of his brute strength, which helped her to finally free her arms. She bit down on the rag in her mouth as hundreds of pins and needles coursed through both hands, restoring the blood to her ice-cold fingers. Her wrists were still bound, but this was definitely a lot more comfortable.

She thought back to the day when she'd almost lost her right eye. She ran her fingertips over the scar's raised skin and made a point of remembering the important lesson she'd learned about playground bullies: they might be bigger and stronger, but she was faster and smarter.

Charles Benson was the biggest, toughest kid in the fifth-grade class, and he knew it. The fourth- and fifth-grade classes had recess together, so she saw him picking on the smaller kids all the time. Since she was popular on the baseball team, he pretty much left her alone.

Nobody ever stood up to him. Not even any boys in the sixth grade class because Charles was bigger than all of them, too. Fed up, she'd decided to take matters into her own hands.

For two whole months, all Emily thought about was boxing. She read books about boxing, looked up boxing on the internet, and watched countless videos of Muhammad Ali in the ring. She studied the way he balanced and shifted his feet, how he tucked his chin and ducked his head to keep from getting knocked out.

Imitating his movements, she'd practiced as she was getting dressed in the morning and before she went to sleep in the privacy of her bedroom. As soon as she felt that she had a pretty good chance of surviving a fight with Charles, she made up her mind to challenge him the next time he picked on someone at school. She didn't have to wait long. She saw Charles poking a little boy with a stick at recess the very next day.

Poor Jacob Hammond was pressed up against the chain-link fence, huddled in a ball with tears streaming down his cheeks. She'd run over as fast as she could, her heart thumping wildly in her ears. She'd wondered if she was crazy for what she was about to do, but then she heard Jake crying for his mommy. Instinct took over as she stepped in front of Jake to protect him from the sharp stick.

"Stop that," she'd hissed.

Charles didn't say anything at first. He just stood there looking totally stupid. She turned her head to make sure Jake was okay, and that's when Charles body slammed her into the chain-link fence. Something raked painfully against the skin above her right eye. Then her face was all wet, and she had to close her eye because it stung to keep it open.

She ducked, pivoted, and popped up right behind Charles. Not wasting any time, she took the opportunity to punch him hard in his side and landed three more jabs with both fists, one right after the other, before he even had the chance to turn around. Out of her good eye, she remembered seeing all of the school kids had gathered around. They started cheering her on.

Charles balled up his huge fist and came at her with pure rage on his face. She easily dodged the blow, shifted her feet like she'd practiced, and then delivered a solid jab to his gut. He bent over, red faced, clutching his stomach with one hand and reaching for her angrily with the other. She took one step back and delivered an uppercut to his face. Her small fist made perfect contact with his left eye.

Charles had just landed on the grass with a satisfying *thud* when Emily was picked up and whisked away by Mr. McVay, the sixth-grade teacher. He'd sprinted across the playground, carrying her in his arms like a baby all the way to the nurse's office. Totally embarrassing.

The next thing she remembered was waking up in the hospital with her dad. He was holding her hand through the cold metal bed rail.

Two days and eleven stitches later, she was back in school removing the bandage and showing off her battle scar to curious classmates.

Charles was suspended for a week. His eye was different shades of brown and purple by the time he returned. He pretty much kept to himself after that. The important thing was he didn't pick on anyone anymore.

Emily stared out the van's window. If she was strong enough to outsmart Charles Benson, then she thought she had a pretty good chance of outsmarting the bad man, too.

Since the tape covering her mouth was now within reach, she carefully peeled one corner aside and slowly pulled out the rag. She wiped the trail of saliva from her chin and pressed the tape back in place.

She glanced down to see what the bad man had stuffed inside her mouth and immediately wished she hadn't. It was her Sheltie's pink bandana. *Oh no...Bubbles.* Emily caught herself in a sob and muffled it with both hands. If she left the bandana out in plain sight, the bad man would figure out that she'd freed herself, so she hid it in her underpants.

She wasn't stupid. She knew what the scarf meant. Bubbles was dead, just like her dad. Her heart suddenly hurt so bad that she thought she'd die right there from having it break inside of her. Then she remembered her father's proud face and bellowing voice as he retold the story of her as his little giant.

She couldn't let him down. He believed she was strong, and she was. She would prove it.

CHAPTER SEVEN

Feeling quite pleased with himself, Shadow pulled the van to the side of the road. He needed to check on his package in the back. The package was uncannily quiet.

He slid the plastic curtain aside and got down on all fours. The package was bound and gagged as he had left her but still apparently unconscious. He watched her chest rise and fall evenly for several minutes before crawling over. He licked her cheek slowly. "What a tasty little snack. Are you awake?"

The package did not react. Satisfied that she was not in any shape to attempt an escape, he returned to the front, put the van in drive, and headed to a gas station up the road.

To his dismay, it was a full-service station, which meant he was at the mercy of the attendant. He rolled down his window as the attendant approached.

"Hiya, what can I get for you today?" he asked a little too cheerfully for someone who pumped gas for a living.

"Fill it with—" In the rearview mirror, Shadow watched as two small hands reached up to shove the plastic curtain aside.

A deafening scream reverberated off the van walls. "Help! He kidnapped me!"

Shadow sighed and shook his head at this little hiccup in the plan. The package was awake and had somehow managed to free herself from her restraints. She dove into the front and squeezed underneath the dash, kicking her legs wildly as Shadow reached for her.

Suddenly, the passenger's door was yanked open. The gas attendant was now taking Shadow's package out of the van without his permission. Gas guy was trying to be the hero of the hour. He had no business being a hero. He pumped gas for a living.

Shadow slid his gun out from the side of his seat, extended his arm, and blew gas guy's brains out. He brought the butt of the gun down on the girl's head just hard enough to knock her out and then returned her to the rear of the van.

He calmly opened his door, filled the gas tank with premium unleaded, and positioned the gas guy's lifeless body under the right front tire. Driving over the hero-wannabe with a four thousand pound vehicle was immensely gratifying. Shadow drove for another twenty miles before pulling off the road to inspect his package in the back.

He replaced the duct tape over her mouth. Studying her small body and freckled face, he shook his head. *Package* didn't suit her anymore. She was a fighter, which made the task of breaking her even more thrilling.

Thirty minutes passed. He spent the time meditating with his back against the van wall. Her eyelids finally fluttered open.

"Well, well. The brave little warrior awakes at long last." He scooted closer, overjoyed to see the dread in her eyes. "After your outburst this morning, I decided to get creative." He held up a shiny metal staple gun he had pilfered from her father's toolshed. "Do you know what this is, little warrior?"

She shook her head.

"Allow me to demonstrate." He pressed the staple gun against his forearm and squeezed the handle. She jerked at the loud *clap,* wincing as he pulled it away and tilted his arm in her direction. There, sticking up from his arm, was a large metal staple.

He grinned. "Keep your eyes open, little warrior. The show has just begun." He pushed the nose of the staple gun into his arm, squeezing the handle again and again, until his arm resembled some sort of bloodied biomechanical device. Finished, he set the staple gun on the floor and glared at her menacingly. "If you close your eyes, I'll be tempted to staple them shut."

She opened her eyes even wider.

Shadow dug into the bridge of each bloody staple with his fingertips. Rocking them back and forth, he popped them out one at a time and tossed them on the floor beside her. "Watch closely now." He waved his free hand over the top of his arm, whispering in his native Latin tongue.

The sound of dry, rustling leaves filled the van's interior as he slowly peeled back the outer layer of his forearm like snakeskin. Healed and whole again, he dangled the long strip of skin in front of her before lining it up neatly atop the duct tape over her mouth. "I'm trying to decide if I should remove this tape from your mouth." He traced his fingertips along its edges. "Would you like me to do that for you, little warrior?"

She nodded.

He held up the staple gun and turned it over in his hands. "One staple from this gun can burrow through multiple layers of human tissue and skewer the bone beneath." He studied her to savor the full sensation of her fear. "Sounds rather uncomfortable, wouldn't you say?"

She nodded in agreement, slowly this time.

He held the staple gun beside her ear and squeezed the handle, smiling broadly as she twitched in dread. He pressed it against the tape on her mouth and brought his face so close to hers that their noses touched. "I could remove this tape and just staple your lips together." He pressed the staple gun harder against her mouth, held it there for long seconds.

Deciding she'd had her fair share of terror for the moment—he didn't want to make her soil her pants and stink up the van—he slid the staple gun down the side of her face and pulled it away. He retrieved his strip of skin, balled it up, and casually tossed it in his mouth, chewing.

"If you're foolish enough to yell for help again," he said, still chewing, "I'll staple your lips together so tight that you'll be eating through a straw for the rest of your life." He swallowed and waved the staple gun in front of her face. "Do we understand each other, little warrior?"

She nodded vigorously.

He peeled the duct tape from her mouth, moved to the front of the van, and reached for the curtain, turning at the last moment to face her. "I don't think I have to remind you about what happens to innocent bystanders when a selfish little warrior like you tries to escape. You do remember the tragic fate that befell the man at the gas station?"

She shook her head.

"Oh, come now." He frowned in mock concern. "Suffice it to say he's dead now because of you." Shadow withdrew his gun from the front seat. "You forced me to put a big hole in his head," he said, pretending to aim and fire. "You should know there were five other people at the gas station during your little tantrum." He shook his head. "You may as well have killed them all yourself, little warrior. I pulled the trigger, yes, but you are the one who sealed their fate."

This, of course, was untrue. But he wanted the warrior to suffer.

She squeezed her eyes shut. Tears flowed freely down her freckled cheeks.

Satisfied, he slid the curtain back in place and started the engine.

❖

Mercy was driving fast, but it still took her almost four hours to reach Madison, New Hampshire. Fortunately, there weren't a lot of people on the road. She'd been calling Agent Carmichael's cell every twenty minutes since hearing her voicemail about Emily's kidnapping. She'd left three messages of her own and was starting to worry.

If the two cases were related like Carmichael thought, she had a theory. As far as she could tell, the only common thread between the two cases was Mercy. Each victim had a close relationship with an important person in her life. Sarah Wilson was the chief's goddaughter, and Emily was Carmichael's niece.

Since Mercy's life revolved around missing kids, wasn't murdering one child and kidnapping another the perfect way to grab her attention? If her theory was correct, she believed the killer had probably left something behind at the crime scene. A clue meant to entice her into an old-fashioned game of cat and mouse.

Mercy was forced to park the rental car a short distance from the house. Five cruisers crowded the driveway. Another six were lined up on the street.

With the ability to detect a drop of blood in the depths of human tragedy, the local media circled like ravenous sharks. Yellow crime scene tape marked the perimeter. Two police officers stood just beyond the barricade. Reporters and cameramen from every local news channel swarmed the area, vying for the officers' attention.

She waded through the feeding frenzy in search of Agent Carmichael, her badge clipped to the breast pocket of her trench coat. She scanned each room of the house. Carmichael was nowhere to be found.

She returned to the living room and introduced herself to the man in charge. "Commander, we spoke on the phone." She extended her hand. "Special Agent Parker, FBI."

Frowning, the commander sized her up. "Where's your partner?"

"Agent Carmichael isn't here?"

"Nope. Spoke with her on the phone about five hours ago. Said she was on her way."

"Maybe her flight was delayed." Mercy was reaching for her cell to call the Manchester airport when it rang. The caller ID read: *666.*

CHAPTER EIGHT

S hadow pulled his van into the McDonald's parking lot and waited. Gigantic George emerged a few minutes later— all six feet, ten inches of him—stuffing a Big Mac into his mouth and hugging several bags of food against his hulking torso with a tattooed and unnaturally muscular bicep. Acknowledging Shadow with an almost imperceptible nod, he loped across the parking lot. The van bounced in protest and lowered on one side as he climbed into the passenger's seat.

"You came," George said around a mouthful of burger, sounding surprised. He caught sight of the little warrior in the back and turned in his seat. Shadow had moved the curtain aside to keep an eye on her. "She for me?" he asked.

Shadow shook his head.

George studied her with a growing hunger in his eyes as he ravaged the burger. "I want her."

"I'd let you have her," he sighed, "but I need to get rid of her myself."

"Just give me ten minutes in the back with her," George pleaded.

Shadow considered granting his request, mentally calculating the time needed for the remaining tasks at hand: abduct Dr. Vasey as an offering to George, stash her in the woods behind her cabin, get George situated, and take the dog. "We're on a tight schedule. The answer is no." He withdrew a photo of Piper Vasey from his pocket and slid it across the dash. "This is the woman I promised."

George stuffed the last of the burger into his mouth and reached for the photo. A lustful grin tugged at the corners of his mouth. "Nice," he said, digging into the bag for a fistful of fries. "She'll do."

Shadow nodded at the glove compartment. "Keys to the black Suburban are in there. I'll lead you to her cabin."

❖

Piper felt a large, moist pink nose touching hers before she even opened her eyes. Her chocolate Labrador welcomed her into the day with a chin-to-forehead kiss that left her feeling sticky. "Morning, Bobby," she murmured, reaching out to give him a pat on the head. She knew from experience that if she didn't promptly acknowledge him, he would continue to assault her with dog slime.

After her husband's death three years ago, Bobby was promoted from sleeping in his dog bed on the floor to sleeping on Tim's side of the bed. She sensed that Bobby was careful not to disturb her each morning. It seemed he always woke first, waiting patiently there beside her, watching her intently for signs of consciousness and never moving a muscle. Sometimes she wondered if he ever really slept or just lay there staring at her all night. Regardless, she was comforted by his presence. She felt looked after, protected. In a way she couldn't describe—and wouldn't dare share with anyone for fear of being thought of as crazy—she sensed that Bobby was more than just a dog.

She heard the *swish, swish* of his tail on the blanket as he rolled over for his morning belly rub, tongue dangling lazily from one side of his mouth. She obliged him with his usual ten minute rubdown before getting up to prepare for their morning jog. Dressed in Nike running gear, she pulled her long hair into a ponytail, threw on her favorite Adidas cap, and turned to face Bobby. "Ready?"

He eagerly led her downstairs to the front door, tail wagging the entire way. Their breath exhaled in plumes of smoke from their warm bodies into the frigid morning air as they ran for miles on the quiet country roads of North Conway, New Hampshire. Piper never bothered with the leash anymore. Bobby was a puppy the last time

he'd worn one. They'd been running together every day for the past
three years. He matched her pace and stride perfectly.

It was early spring, and New Hampshire was just waking up
from an icy winter slumber. Despite the cold, Bobby was panting by
the time they rounded the last bend an hour later. They ended with
a brisk walk to help cool down and continued up the driveway as
Piper stroked the top of his head. "Good job today, boy." She was
glad he enjoyed their runs as much as she did.

He trotted over to the newspaper, picked it up carefully by the
elastic, and carried it inside while she held the door ajar for him.
Setting the paper down on a kitchen chair, he padded over to his
food and water bowls and sat beside them, ready for breakfast.

She fed him boiled chicken, chopped veggies, and one raw egg,
and then settled down at the kitchen table to sip her coffee and read
the paper. Belly round and full, Bobby soon joined her. He nudged
Piper's hand, curled up at her feet, and fell fast asleep.

The remainder of the morning slipped past as Piper showered,
dressed, and tinkered around the cabin. When she finally grabbed a
thermos to fill it with water for their hike, Bobby magically awoke.
Taking his cue, he dashed off to his toy box in the living room and
returned to meet her at the door with two tennis balls stuffed in his
cheeks like a chipmunk gathering food for the winter.

"We only need one ball, Bobby," she said, reaching for the
other. But he ducked and backed away, defiantly keeping two balls
securely in his mouth. She laughed, remembering that she had
refused to continue yesterday's game of fetch after the tennis ball
rolled into a big pile of bear poop. Did Bobby actually remember
that, too? Was he bringing a spare in case it happened again? As far
as she knew, dogs weren't smart enough to plan that far ahead. Then
again, she reminded herself that Bobby was no ordinary dog.

"Fine, we'll take it." She shrugged out of her backpack,
unzipped the front pocket, and extended her hand. "I'll carry one for
you." As if in understanding, he deposited one ball in her palm but
selfishly kept the second for himself.

Tail wagging, ball in mouth, he led the way to their favorite
clearing in the woods for an invigorating game of fetch. Piper set

her backpack on the ground and threw the ball as far as she could. Bobby gave her a lingering look of gratitude before bounding off after his prey.

Many throws later, she could see he was beginning to tire. She hid the tennis ball behind her back. "Look at me, fur face."

Panting, he reluctantly shifted his eyes from her arm to her face.

"Last throw," she told him. "On your mark…"

He pranced backward.

"Get set…"

She tried not to laugh as he nearly tripped over himself in frenzied anticipation.

"Go!"

With one final retrieve and a look of pure pride, he galloped back. When she bent over to take the ball from his mouth, he released his grip at the last moment and hit her with his trademark kiss from chin to forehead.

"You're welcome," she said, wiping the pine-needled slime from her face. She squirted Bobby with some water as they started on their hike back home.

Dead leaves from winter's embrace crunched underfoot. Springtime was truly breathtaking in these woods. The air felt different on her skin, not only due to the warmer temperature, but because new life existed within it. The woods were full of aromas, green and rich in texture. Piper could feel the new life all around her just by closing her eyes, inhaling, and letting it saturate her senses. The buzz of excitement in the air, the sweet songs of enthusiasm in the branches overhead, and the scampering of renewed purpose underfoot. All converging in whispers to let her know that Mother Nature was busily working tiny miracles, one after another. Spending time outdoors with Bobby on a day like this was a welcome distraction to the void that Tim's death had left inside her.

Deep in thought, she strolled right past the oak tree when Bobby's *chuff* from behind halted her in her tracks. She turned. Bobby was already sitting in his usual spot. He snorted and looked from the tree to her as if to say, *We're here, you dummy.*

He followed her with his eyes as she unzipped the backpack and removed a small purple flower that she had clipped from one of her houseplants. "Miss you, Mary Beth," she whispered. "Here, your favorite color." She kissed the flower before tossing it into the pile to join its fellow fallen comrades.

Fifteen minutes later, they were crossing into the backyard when Bobby halted in midstride. He sniffed at the air, raised his hackles, and growled deep in his throat.

This wasn't like him. She shivered. "What's wrong, boy?"

He looked up at her, tucked his tail, and whined.

Something was wrong. Piper felt it, too.

Chapter Nine

Mercy's cell rang a second time. She removed her Bluetooth earpiece from the inside pocket of her trench coat, slid it over her ear, and answered in her usual tone. "Parker."

"Listen closely, Agent Parker. Follow what I say precisely or I'll hang up and the girl dies."

Wondering how on earth this lunatic had gotten her number, Mercy decided to follow her instincts and cooperate. She took a deep breath. "I'm listening."

"There's a toolshed in the far northwest corner of the backyard. Go to it. Quickly."

She signaled for the commander to follow and let the screen door bang shut behind them as proof that she was following orders. "I'm in the backyard now," Mercy said, letting the caller believe he was the one in control. She led the commander through ankle-high weeds and brown sunflower stalks that were nearly as tall as she was.

"Are we there yet?" the caller asked in a childlike voice.

"Almost." As they approached, Mercy spotted the shiny new combination lock on the shed door. She didn't like this at all. "You plan on telling me what's inside the shed?"

The caller sighed dramatically. "As you so eloquently explained to Lou this morning, you're not allowed to answer a question with another question. As punishment for your own hypocrisy, I'm not going to give you the combination to the lock on that shed door as

I'd originally intended. You have exactly thirty seconds to puzzle it out for yourself." His voice dropped to an ominous timbre. "If you fail this exercise, Agent Parker, the girl dies. Let the countdown begin. Thirty…"

Mercy thought back. She was in Lou's kitchen when they'd had that conversation. Was Lou's house bugged?

"Twenty-eight…"

Her mind raced. Was Lou okay? Maybe this psycho had mentioned Lou as a clue to the combination.

"Twenty-seven…"

She cradled the phone against her shoulder and turned the combination dial to the right, mentally reciting the month, day, and year of Lou's retirement. Finished, she pulled down on the lock. It didn't open.

"Twenty-four…"

She tried Sarah Wilson's birthday. Nothing.

"Nineteen…eighteen…"

Mercy could see her breath like barroom smoke. Despite the cold, she felt sweat beading on her lip. *Think, Parker, think.* She needed to stall for more time. "Wait a minute. You never told me your name."

"My name is Shadow. You're wasting time, Agent Parker. Sixteen, fifteen, fourteen…"

She tried her own birthday…no. The date that Sarah was killed…no. Today's date…not that, either.

"Six…"

Mercy thought back to the caller ID.

"Five…four…"

She frantically turned the dial to the right until it reached the number six.

"Three…"

Turned the dial to the left until it reached the number six.

"Two…"

And then turned it to the right again until it reached six.

"One."

She yanked down hard on the lock. *Click.*

"Your time has expired. Shall I sharpen my blade?" Shadow sounded sickeningly hopeful.

"No, I opened it. Don't you dare hurt Emily." She wiped the sweat from her forehead with the sleeve of her trench coat. "What do you want me to do now?" The answer seemed obvious, but going inside that shed ranked last on her bucket list of things to do before she hit forty. It reeked of a bad setup.

"Step inside, close the door, and try not to worry so much, Agent Parker. Nothing inside that shed will harm you." His tone was jovial. "Where's the fun in ending the game before it has even begun?"

Mercy signaled for the commander to stay outside before crossing the threshold and closing the door behind her. She stood in place, letting her eyes adjust to the darkness. There was a sliver of light—its source a small oval window. The glass was riddled with cracks and covered in a thick film of grime.

The smell of death suddenly hit her. A small dog dangled from a metal hook.

She felt a surge of righteous anger over the dog's suffering that she fought to keep under control. She had to stay focused. There was nothing she could do for the dog. Emily, on the other hand, could still be alive. She wasn't about to jeopardize Emily's safety by saying something stupid.

Holding the collar of her trench coat over her nose and mouth, she stepped forward to take a closer look. A large white envelope was wedged between the dog's teeth.

"Have you spoken with Dr. Vasey yet?" Shadow asked.

"No. I left her a few messages, but she hasn't called back." She reached up and gently loosened the envelope, tooth by tooth.

"I'd like to place a little wager, Agent Parker."

She didn't like where this was going. "I'm not a betting woman, Shadow."

"I'll wager the lives of all those people inside the house behind you that I get to Dr. Vasey before you do."

Her stomach dropped.

"Too late. You lose." The phone clicked. The line went dead.

Tearing the envelope free from the last tooth, she spun around. Her trench coat wheeled behind her like a cape as the bomb exploded.

The explosion was deafening. Mercy had never heard anything as loud before in her life. Flying debris smacked the shed's roof and walls in rapid succession. She threw open the shed door and held an arm in front of her face, shielding her eyes from the fireball of heat that had stood as a home just seconds before.

Engulfed in flames, the guts of the house were ravaged. Her heart raced as she tried to remember how many officers had been inside.

"Commander!" she shouted, stuffing the envelope inside her coat pocket. Something sharp grazed against her cheek. She felt a trickle of blood.

Pang, pang, pang! Objects from the house's innards pelted against boulders and tall pines. They ricocheted off rocks and gouged big chunks of bark from the trees behind her. She knew it was only a matter of time before the tree line lit up in flames. She squinted ahead into the tall weeds and heard the unmistakable crackle of fire. She had to find the commander.

"Commander!" She kept low to the ground. The smoke was thick. It stung her eyes. She tripped over something in her haste to dodge a spiraling plank of wood and fell to her knees.

The commander was stretched out on the ground. Mercy felt for a pulse—his heartbeat was strong. She brought her ear to the commander's mouth. He was breathing, too. Judging from the gash on his forehead, he was probably just knocked unconscious by debris from the blast.

Mercy scanned the area, trying to gauge the best path of escape. Half of the backyard had already been devoured by flames. She hooked her arms underneath the commander's body and began dragging him along the ground as a second explosion assaulted the house.

She ducked behind the shed to avoid another whizzing piece of debris and looked back as a toilet bowl thudded to the ground, decapitated of its lid and seat cover. That would've hurt. It was also an extremely undignified way to go. Being blown to smithereens was one thing, but crushed to death by the porcelain throne? No, thanks.

She adjusted the commander's body and headed west, mapping her route as she went. She should cut through the woods, then head south toward the front of the house.

Sidestepping rocks, fallen trees, and twisted roots, she was making good time when she spotted an officer's severed arm and torso. A beetle scurried out from the officer's torn sleeve. She released the commander, unclipped the officer's badge, and said a silent prayer before moving on.

Her mind kept returning to Shadow's threat. The more she thought about it, the more ominous it sounded. *I'll wager the lives of all those people inside the house behind you that I get to Dr. Vasey before you do. Too late. You lose.*

Did that mean Shadow had already found Piper? What did Piper have to do with this case? She switched her Bluetooth on and instructed it to call Piper Vasey.

It came as no surprise when she didn't answer. Either she was ignoring the phone like a pain in the ass...or Shadow had already gotten to her.

When her voicemail kicked on, Mercy left another message. "Don't have much time to explain what's going on. A house just exploded, I'm dragging an unconscious man on the ground who's eaten a few too many potato chips, and I'm trying to find my way out of a burning forest...but I'm pretty sure your life is in danger. I'll be heading to your house as soon as I can." Not that she'll welcome the company, Mercy thought. "This is Agent Parker, by the way. Calling *again*." She recited her cell number. Twice.

She was almost to the street when she felt the commander tense under her grip. She released him, helped him to his feet, and kept a steadying hand on his elbow. She pointed to the gash on his head. "That'll need stitches."

He explored the wound with the tips of his fingers before wiping them on the front of his uniform. He looked despairingly toward the house. "My men..."

"No one inside could've survived that blast. I'm sorry." She let go of the commander's arm. "Call in for backup and fire. I'll check on the civilians out front. Meet me there. We'll recruit some bodies to help us move those cruisers."

The commander's jaw muscles flexed. "I don't care about the cruisers! I won't leave my men behind!" Low hanging branches prevented him from seeing the house like a mother shielding the eyes of her child after finding the family cat in the road. He darted off to a clearing in the trees. Mercy hurried after him.

The commander halted at the tree line and dropped to his knees when he saw what remained of the house. The stench of burning bodies filled the air. Fresh blood pumped out of the gash in his forehead as he turned and threw up in a bush.

"Here, I found this," Mercy said, handing him the officer's badge. "Back there in the woods."

He stared down at the badge. "Sergeant Flynn. Dead?"

Mercy nodded. "Listen, each of those cruisers in the driveway has a tank full of gasoline. You know as well as I do that gas and fire don't mix. A lot more people could get hurt if we don't do something to keep those tanks from exploding." She laid a hand on the commander's shoulder. "Those are the people we can help right now."

The commander looked past her to the unseen ghosts of fellow officers and tightened his grip around the badge. "Meet you around front."

She heard his solemn words to dispatch fading behind her as she jogged toward the street. By the time she arrived, the sharks were in full feeding frenzy. Every news channel was present, hungrily filming footage of the burning house. At least three times as many people had gathered behind the police barricade.

She checked her watch. Just fifteen minutes had passed since she'd arrived on scene, and she still hadn't found Agent Carmichael. Something told her Carmichael had never even made it there.

The two officers stationed at the barricade earlier were nowhere in sight. She picked five volunteers from the crowd and held them off to one side to await further instruction. Excited voices filled the air, more suffocating than the smoke as she held up her badge. "FBI. I need all of you to step back to that corner curb." She pointed to a spot just behind them. Heads turned in unison to follow her finger. "This gentleman right here"—she gestured to the man with the crewcut on her left—"will be in charge of making sure you stay there. Now, let's go! Move!"

With ramrod-straight posture, the man with the crewcut surveyed the crowd, herding the stragglers along with a militant bite in his voice.

Mercy studied the driveway, turned to the other four men, and instructed them to climb behind the steering wheels of the first four cruisers in the driveway. She put herself in charge of the vehicle closest to the fire. "Just drive to the end of the block and park along the curb."

The commander jogged over to their circle.

"Take the keys," Mercy went on, "lock the doors, and meet me—" Her cell phone rang. Everyone's eyes darted simultaneously to the pocket of her trench coat. She reached in and read the caller ID. "Same bad guy," she said under her breath.

CHAPTER TEN

Childless, Lucent sat in the passenger's seat as Neshera studied him intently. "You miss her, don't you?" After fourteen years in America, her Nigerian accent still resonated in every word.

He studied his hands in his lap and answered softly. "Yes, like a worried father bidding his child farewell on the first day of school." He met her gaze and felt his throat tighten a little as he spoke. "And yet I am blessed with the gift of knowing that her life will be sacred."

She reached for his hand and squeezed it reassuringly. "You are still permitted to grieve, old man."

"I suppose I am," he said. "But now is not the time. There is still work to be done."

Neshera wrapped long, well-manicured fingers around the steering wheel. He smelled cinnamon chewing gum as she spoke. "Where would you like me to drive?"

Intending to trade places with her, he opened his door. The car's interior light blinked on. "It is generous of you to offer, Neshera, but you need your sleep. I will take over from here." He managed to set just one golden shoe on the wet pavement before thinking to glance back over his shoulder. She made no move to exit the car.

He watched as she slid her hands down the steering wheel and started the ignition. Lips pursed determinedly, she focused on the darkened road ahead. "No need to worry about me." She clicked on the headlights. "It is you, old man, who needs the rest." Withdrawing something from her lap, she raised her hand to reveal a white foam cup. Steamy tendrils rose from the lid's sipping hole.

With his right foot firmly planted on the ground and his left foot hovering in midair, Lucent hesitated. He sank his eyes into the colors around her and tried to decipher whether she required sleep. Reading her colors in the same amount of time it took to check his watch, he concluded that she was, in fact, feeling weary.

She sipped her coffee and regarded him. Hazel, catlike eyes narrowed as she realized what he was up to. "I thought I told you not to do that anymore," she said calmly, tucking the cup in her lap.

"My apologies." He lowered his gaze. "It is a difficult habit to break." Neshera had been with him for so long that he couldn't read her anymore without her knowing about it.

A woman of great pride, the thought of being looked after in any way by Lucent greatly unnerved her. No matter how accurate his readings were, she always objected to being read at all and demanded that he simply take her at her word.

Neshera had not changed much over the last fourteen years. She was just as stubborn now as when they'd first met. It was hard to believe that fourteen years had passed since he'd aided in her escape from Nigeria.

Lucent had journeyed there to counsel Neshera's mother, a dear and trusted friend. She'd sought his guidance over a tragic situation with her eldest daughter, Safiya.

Devoted wife and mother of two small boys, Safiya had been beaten and raped by the village merchant. She'd staggered back to her family's home after the attack, her two young sons in tow.

The burden of proving that Safiya was raped rested solely with her family. The court insisted they provide four male witnesses to testify on her behalf or slander charges would be filed against her. In addition to eighty lashings for the crime of slander, the court announced that she'd be sentenced to death by stoning for the crime of adultery. Five days later, beautiful Safiya was stoned to death in the village square with her entire family in helpless attendance.

Lucent would never forget that terrible day. He'd galloped in on horseback as villagers were carrying Safiya's broken body through the streets of Sokoto shouting, "Look upon Safiya! Do you see what happens when you are not faithful to your husband?"

Lucent wept alongside Safiya's parents in their home later that night. Sickeningly close, he'd arrived twenty minutes after the final stone was heaved. Five minutes earlier and he could have saved her life with one touch of his hand.

At the request of both her parents, he smuggled their one remaining child over the Nigerian border the very next day.

Even then, Neshera's spiral of colors twirled and danced, often reaching out to give him a defiant poke in the gut. At eleven years old, her young spirit had the strength equivalent to an army of well-trained soldiers.

She'd insisted on staying with him throughout the years, claiming he needed an assistant for the overwhelming workload. Lucent knew she would never leave him. Truth be told, he was deeply grateful for her company. Not only had he grown to care for her like a daughter, but she had proven herself indispensable over the years. The personal sacrifices that she made on humanity's behalf were humbling, to say the least. He suspected that Neshera would continue her work undaunted, even after his death.

Mercy Parker would soon have the opportunity to see for herself that Neshera's contributions to The Greater Good were deserving of praise. She would do everything in her power to help make the burdensome transition a little easier on Mercy.

Lucent shut the car door and buckled his seat belt. Neshera blatantly refused all gifts, favors, compliments, or niceties of any kind. Over the years, he'd learned the only thing he could give her was the belief that he needed to be taken care of. That, alone, was his gift to her.

"You know me too well, Neshera. I am tired. Thank you for noticing." He sighed, rubbing his eyes in feigned exhaustion. "It is easy to forget that my resources are now limited. I cannot afford to drain them this close to the finish line, now can I?"

"That would be foolish." She reached into the back seat, lifted a foam cup identical to the one in her lap, and handed it to him. "I thought you might see it my way. Here's some of that tea you like so much. The one that makes you snore. How do you say?" She paused, biting her lip. "Camel tea?"

He smiled and took the warm cup from her hands. "Chamomile. It is an herb that helps one to relax." Now that he thought about it, he was feeling weary and suddenly found himself looking forward to a nap. What he'd told Neshera was true. There had been a time when his resources were inexhaustible. But now, with the end so near, he had to conserve his strength.

She reached behind him once more and withdrew a small pillow and blanket, both the color of honey. She unfolded the blanket and draped it over his legs. "I want you to rest and gather your strength, old man." She sipped her coffee, switched on the windshield wipers, and put the car in gear. "Where would you like me to drive?"

Lucent gazed into the night. He closed his eyes and reached out with his mind. Mercy Parker had already arrived in Madison. "North, Neshera. Our destination lies in New Hampshire."

CHAPTER ELEVEN

Mercy's cell phone rang again as sirens sounded in the distance. She brought it to her ear and tried not to sound as tired as she felt. "Parker."

Shadow was singing an old nursery rhyme, twisting the sweet lyrics of "Bingo" into something much more sinister. "There was a woman who had a dog and Bobby was his name-o! *B-O-B-B-Y, B-O-B-B-Y, B-O-B-B-Y*, and Bobby was his name-o!"

The little dog dangling from the hook in the shed flashed through Mercy's mind, but the nametag on its collar said Bubbles, not Bobby. Shadow seemed too meticulous with details to have made such an obvious error. Who was Bobby? She was tired of playing this game. "How about you and I talk like normal people instead of speaking in riddles?"

"Because normal is *bor*-ing, Agent Parker. I suggest you make better use of your time and ask more pertinent questions."

She dreaded the thought of putting Carmichael through the horror of losing her niece. "Is Emily still alive?"

"Emily-schmemily. Is she all you can think about? She's trivial in this matter, but if you must know..." He sighed. "Yes, our little warrior is very much alive and kicking." He laughed. "Come now, don't you have something better for me?"

Mercy was afraid to hear the answer to her next question. She hadn't heard from Carmichael in several hours. "How'd you get my number?"

"It was programmed into Agent Carmichael's cell. Speed dial three, if I'm not mistaken."

She felt her face, neck, and chest filling up with red-hot rage. "Where is she?" she asked through clenched teeth.

"Why don't you try giving her a call? I have a feeling someone will actually answer this time. Let me prepare you, Agent Parker." He paused. "The news isn't good, I'm afraid."

Mercy said nothing. She didn't trust herself to speak.

"Which brings me to my next point. From this moment on, I want you to handle the investigation on your own. The only exception I'll make to this rule is Dr. Vasey. That is, *if* you can find her. I've hidden her well. I suggest you sever ties immediately with whomever you've enlisted at the bureau to assist you in this investigation." Shadow cleared his throat. "And Agent Parker, if I find out you've allowed anyone to assist you with this case—all branches of law enforcement included—I'll see to it that he or she suffers a fate similar to Agent Carmichael's."

The line went dead. Mercy had been dismissed. Sick to her stomach, she dialed Carmichael's cell.

A woman answered on the third ring. "Hello?"

"I'm calling for Dana Carmichael. Who is this?" Mercy asked, bracing herself.

"Your name, please?"

She paced the sidewalk. "Agent Parker, FBI. I need to speak with Dana immediately."

"What did you say your name was?" The woman's tone changed.

"Special Agent Parker. I work with Dana." She ran a hand through her hair. "Is she okay?"

"I just spoke with Agent Parker a few minutes ago. A man."

Shadow had obviously beaten her to the punch, using her identity to fish around for information. "No, that obviously wasn't me. Listen, I don't have time for this right now. Just tell me, is she okay?"

"Please hold."

Voices shuffled like paperwork in the background. She heard the phone being handed off. "This is Dr. Lewis. How can I help you?"

"This is Agent Parker calling on behalf of the FBI. I've been trying to reach Agent Carmichael all day."

The doctor cleared his throat. "I just spoke with someone else who claimed to be you. Just how many Agent Parkers are there?"

She stopped pacing. "The man you spoke with falsely identified himself. Do me a favor and check the caller ID on Dana's cell. She has my number saved under *Parker*. Since I'm calling from my cell right now, my name should appear in that window and confirm my identity."

A brief silence hung on the line before the doctor cleared his throat. "Dana was brought in by ambulance earlier this afternoon with severe head trauma from a car accident. I was the attending physician. We did everything we could to save her, but she coded about ten minutes ago. I'm sorry, Agent Parker. She didn't make it."

She sat on the curb and put her head in her hands as he inquired about next of kin. Mercy was quiet for a long time. "Dana doesn't have any family left," she said finally, "so I'll take care of everything." She provided her contact information, assured him that she'd follow up with the morgue to make the necessary arrangements, and disconnected the call.

Despite the bustling aftermath of firefighters, EMTs, police, news reporters, and neighbors watching from the safety of their front lawns, she sat on the curb feeling very much alone. Dana's death hit close to home, punching her in the gut as Anna's death had done not so long ago. There was a part of her that wished she could trade places with Dana. It just wasn't fair.

She looked up at the sky. Storm clouds settled overhead. The corners of her trench coat flapped in a futile attempt to fly away. Hugging the coat close to her body, she saw the corner of a white envelope sticking out from her pocket. With everything that had happened, she'd forgotten all about Shadow's note.

Ordinarily, she would have covered both hands with latex gloves before handling this type of evidence, taking care to unseal it in a sterile environment so the lab could examine it for fingerprints and fibers. Her instincts told her she didn't have time for all that. Throwing years of training and old habits aside, she tore the envelope open.

Inside was a photograph of a Caucasian male in his fifties. The corners of his mouth were lifted into a smile, but his eyes were soulless and hungry.

Scrawled across the bottom in red ink were the words, *Guess who?* She turned the photo over and read the newspaper clipping taped to the back:

George Edward Ball was released yesterday after serving twenty-three years in the New Hampshire State Penitentiary for sixteen counts of rape in the first degree.

Mercy had a bad feeling about this. She read the next slip of paper, written in red ink in the same hand as on the front of the photo:

After twenty-three years in prison, George was excited to learn of my charitable donation to his worthy cause. A beautiful woman awaits him. I've already taken the liberty of undressing her for the benefit of George's probing eyes.

They're both tied up right now, so to speak. George is chained— at least for the time being—with a preprogrammed lock. This lock is set to release at precisely seven o'clock, after which George will be free to commit whatever perversions most suit him. Any guess as to who this woman might be?

Mercy stood, stuffed the contents of the envelope back inside her pocket, and checked her watch: 5:05 p.m.

Thunder boomed overhead. Her trench coat fanned out behind her as she jogged down the street to her rental car. Fat raindrops began slapping the windshield and roof as she ducked inside. She turned the windshield wipers on high, gunned the engine, and sped through the darkening neighborhood.

Shadow was really starting to get on her nerves.

Mercy was a little surprised at how protective she felt of a woman she'd never even met. Scanning the note as she drove, she searched for a clue that would direct her to Piper's whereabouts. She jumped when her cell rang on the seat beside her. She didn't bother checking the caller ID this time. "Parker."

"Agent Parker, this is Captain Wilson." The captain sounded out of breath. "You told me to call you if anything came up with my daughter's case."

She set the letter down and gave the captain her full attention. "Did something happen?"

"A man showed up at our door last night asking to speak with me and my wife. He told us how sorry he was to hear about our Sarah and said that you were working hard to bring her killer to justice. Somehow, this man knew we couldn't have any more children because of my wife's condition. That's when he told us about Jendy." The captain paused to catch his breath.

"Who's Jendy?" Mercy asked, wondering if Shadow had claimed yet another victim.

"She's four years old. She lost her entire family when rebel soldiers attacked her village in Uganda. Sounds crazy, doesn't it?"

"I'm not following you, Captain."

"I know, I know. When I hear myself trying to explain all this, it sounds like crazy talk." He took a deep breath. "This man said Jendy needed us because she has nobody else. He said he'd already made arrangements for the adoption and handed us a folder full of papers. When he got up to leave, he asked us to watch a video and said he'd come back in an hour to hear our decision. Just like you, my wife and I were confused. Nothing made sense until we opened the folder." He stopped to catch his breath again.

"Inside, we found Jendy's birth certificate, medical records, and adoption papers. Everything was there. Then we watched the video of the orphanage she was living in. God knows she didn't stand a chance in a place like that. There wasn't even enough food to go around. But this little old lady—God love her—she was doing the best she could. There were lots of other kids there, too. Kids who need help from families like ours. My wife and I talked about it," he went on. "We decided to let Sarah's death mark a new beginning in our lives. We want her death to mean something, Agent Parker. I have twenty-two years in with the department. I've decided to retire, start a new career. My wife and I have made it our mission to find families for every kid in that orphanage." He breathed excitedly into the phone. "Because Sarah would've liked that."

Mercy was stunned. She couldn't think of a thing to say.

"Agent Parker?"

She cleared her throat. "Did this man come back later like he said he would?"

"Yes, and he brought Jendy with him. Said he was confident that my wife and I had made the right decision. He hugged Jendy, then turned right around and left. I've spent all day today verifying the documents in this folder. Turns out they're legit. My wife and I are heading down to the courthouse tomorrow to legalize the adoption"—his voice cracked—"and become parents again."

"Can you tell me anything more about this man?"

"Actually, he never introduced himself. With everything going on, it didn't even occur to me to ask. He was about six feet tall, mid to late sixties, and he had eyes like yours—one blue and one brown."

"You're sure about that?" Mercy asked.

"Positive."

They were both silent.

"I know this whole thing sounds crazy," the captain admitted. "It's like this guy just walked into our lives and…now everything makes sense again. In fact, he asked me to give you a message. He said to tell you that he won't be far behind. My wife and I got the feeling that he's trying to help you somehow with our case. He's a good man, Agent Parker. Someone you'd definitely want on your side, if you ask me."

CHAPTER TWELVE

5:30 p.m.

According to the rental car's GPS, it should have taken Mercy thirty-four minutes to drive from Madison, New Hampshire, to Piper's cabin in North Conway. She made it in twenty-two.

She parked on the street and slid the keys from the ignition, halting the windshield wipers in midsweep. A veil of blurry raindrops blanketed the glass within seconds. She turned up her coat collar, climbed out of the car, and sprinted up the driveway to Piper's cabin.

Wind shrieked through the trees all around her, rattling their naked branches like the hollowed-out bones of a skeleton. She jogged around the cabin, cupping her eyes against each window for a better view inside as she wound her way to the front porch steps. Eager to escape the battering rain, she climbed massive, square-cut logs. Streams of water wrung from her hair. There, nailed to the door, was a poem in Shadow's neat script.

"I've always wanted a pup!" she said,
As he wiggled and squiggled around.
He had soft brown fur and oversized ears,
His belly all pink and round.

Then her husband died on his way home from work,
And the dog was all she had left.
She withdrew from the world, a coward,
All semblance of life, bereft.

If you get to her before George does,
Tell her that I am the one to blame
For stealing the thing she cares about most
And condemning Bobby's sweet name!

5:33 p.m.

Mercy slid the paper over the nailhead and added it to the envelope in her pocket. Studying the door, she recognized the manufacturer at once. This had to be a Cressman Woodworks door. Individually crafted and made to order.

She couldn't help but be reminded of her wife's insistence on finding the perfect door for their new home. Anna's standards were high. She believed the door to a home said everything about the occupants inside. A flimsy door was code for a frugal homeowner who probably shaved on expenses in other important areas. A glass door indicated the dwellers were open and honest. Conversely, a security storm door meant the residents were just plain paranoid. The list went on and on.

A tower of rejected catalogs had grown by the day until Mercy was convinced they'd have a gaping hole in front of their house for all time. But Anna never lost faith. She insisted the perfect door was out there. Somewhere. Just waiting to be found.

Coincidentally, it happened to be this very one. The Byzantine Door. Well, there went Anna's theory right out the window. According to her, Piper should have fallen into the storm door category of paranoid homeowners. Hell, when she pulled up to the cabin, she'd half expected to see a moat with thrashing crocodiles and a rickety wooden plank leading to a drawbridge.

She knew from months of forced research that the Byzantine Door was made from knotty alder, solidly veneered over a multidimensional fiber core. Warp resistant and dimensionally stable, it was one and three-quarter inches thick, three feet wide, and stood a respectable six feet, eight inches tall. All the stiles and rails were married with mortise and tenon joints and then glued with polyurethane adhesive to maximize the door's integrity.

She tried her luck and jiggled the latch. Locked. Despite being trained in the fine art of breaking down a door with either a swift kick or a shoulder tackle, she refrained from employing either method. First, she had too much respect for such a finely crafted door to subject it to the unnecessary assault. Second, and maybe more important, she didn't think she'd be able to barrel through this formidable door without the entire New York Giants football team behind her.

So Mercy did the only respectable thing she could do. She walked to the side of the cabin and busted the living room window, instead.

She poked her head inside and scanned the furniture, floor, and ceiling. She was unsure whether the booby traps she was looking for would've been left behind by Shadow, introducing a new element of risk to the game, or Piper, teaching some poor, nosy neighbor a lesson they would never forget. Either way, she wanted to make damn sure nothing plummeted from the ceiling or spiked her in the chest like a vampire at an inopportune moment. She scratched her chin. Come to think of it, there was really no good time for something like that to happen. *Any* moment would be inopportune.

Satisfied that no surprises awaited her, she cleared away the broken glass, shrugged out of her trench coat, and set it over the windowsill. She launched herself headfirst into a vanilla-scented candle. Resting on the trunk of a birch tree, the honey-colored candle held bits of twigs and flower petals in its wax. It smelled *really* good.

She teetered like a human seesaw, balancing her body on the window's ledge as she took one last, lingering whiff before moving the candle off to one side. She slid in the rest of the way, stood, and looked around.

5:36 p.m.

An L-shaped cranberry sofa with horses stitched into the pillows faced a stone fireplace. The pinewood coffee table had three galloping horses carved into its face. Herds of wild mustangs raced along the golden border of an area rug. Antique snowshoes, old rock climbing gear, and one red kayak adorned the wall space. Baskets filled with fragrant pinecones flanked every nook and cranny.

Mercy had never been inside a home where she instantly felt so comfortable. Taking in her surroundings one detail at a time, she continued to scan the room for a clue as to Piper's whereabouts. She checked her watch. One hour and twenty-three minutes to go.

The dining room was separated from the living room by ancient cypress beams. Contrary to the barn wood siding in the living room, the walls here were made of red heart pine. Hand-hewn logs crisscrossed a domed ceiling. A large bay window overlooked the backyard where dozens of tall, furry pines stood guard. Overhanging the dining table was a simple wagon wheel chandelier. The table was mammoth, the top a single plank from a beast of a tree. Nicks, scratches, and hairline cracks in the dark wood lent the table an unspoken history of quiet purpose.

She passed through a weathered barn wood door to the kitchen. Goose bumps suddenly broke out on her arms. She couldn't shake the feeling that someone was watching.

She slid her blazer aside, felt for her 9 mm, and stood, listening. The refrigerator hummed. Winds outside rattled a loosened windowpane in the dining room. She turned to look behind her. She could've sworn somebody was standing right there...but there was no one.

She loosened her grip on the gun, letting her hand slip away a little self-consciously. Okay, so she was feeling a little jumpy. Totally normal, given the circumstances. The last house she'd set foot in exploded, so she cut herself a little slack.

She'd also been awake for over thirty-six hours and hadn't eaten anything since breakfast. A bad combination for someone faced with the imminent rescue of a damsel in distress.

Okay, so maybe Piper wasn't *exactly* a damsel in distress. More like a tied-up, naked ex-profiler who was probably hoping for a miracle right about now. But it helped to think of her that other way. Shaking her head, Mercy continued with her search of the cabin.

Barn wood cabinets, granite countertops, and heart pine floors in the kitchen. Twin giant cypress beams decorated with antique cast-iron skillets flanked both sides of a long island. A five foot by three foot etching of a Labrador retriever had been burned into the wood floor. She bent down to take a closer look. Underneath were the initials *PV*.

Impressed with Piper's artistic talents, she stood and walked over to a timber-lined hallway off the kitchen. Another barn wood door offered access to a full-size bathroom with an old farmhouse sink, claw-foot tub, and stone shower. She opened the door to the basement and switched on the light.

5:40 p.m.

Mercy looked around the basement in awe. Western saddles, English saddles, trail saddles, and pack saddles were individually seated on wall racks in rows of three. A dusty film dulled their once shiny luster. Dust-covered leather reins, stirrups, bits, leads, halters, bridles, breast collars, and lunging lines dangled from steel tack racks. Dust-covered manure forks, stall mats, and muck carts lined the opposite wall.

Good thing she wasn't allergic to dust.

She felt a tickle inside her nose and sneezed. Still scouting for a clue, she stepped forward with her hands in her pockets.

Fleece-lined saddle pads and horse blankets with colorful Southwestern designs were folded in open-mouthed storage bins and stacked floor to ceiling—all of them covered in dust. Dust-covered water troughs, feedbags, and grain bins were neatly arranged on large wooden shelves in the corner. Spiderwebs, old and new, clung to just about everything. She sneezed three more times.

Photographs—dusty ones—of quarter horses, palominos, Arabians, American saddle horses, pintos, Appaloosas, Tennessee walkers, Thoroughbreds, and several other breeds she didn't recognize adorned every inch of wall space. The same man posed with each horse. A handsome, wholesome-looking guy.

She felt her eyelids begin to swell. Still no closer to finding Piper, she turned and headed back. She stopped to run a finger along one of the saddles, leaving a distinct line in the accumulated dust. Piper obviously hadn't been down here in quite some time. If Shadow's poem rang true, it was probably too painful to be reminded of her husband in this way. Unable to cope with his death, she'd forsaken his belongings to the darkest, loneliest place in the house.

There were times when Mercy wanted to do just that with Anna's things. Remaining in the house they'd dreamt about and built together was a difficult decision. She was especially reminded of Anna whenever she walked down the hall past her office. The way she'd furrow her brow as she was crafting the chapters of a new novel. She'd linger in the doorway and watch as Anna busily tapped at the keyboard, feeling profoundly grateful that Anna had chosen to spend her life with her.

That room was the very essence of Anna. In many ways, it *was* Anna. Mercy had slept on the living room sofa and showered in the first floor bathroom for months following her death just to avoid walking down the hallway past *that* door. Eventually, though, she missed Anna so much that she finally gathered the courage to leave the office door ajar, even daring to poke her head inside from time to time.

She decided it was better to have Anna in that way than in no way at all. It didn't take Mercy long to realize that she honored her wife more by embracing her memory than by trying to push it away. Every so often, she made a point of leaning up against the doorway like she used to. She'd imagine Anna sitting there as she talked to her. Sometimes she talked for hours, telling Anna everything she'd neglected to mention while she was still alive. All those unimportant things that she'd grown quiet about over the years.

The featherlight tickle in her nose and throat triggered four more sneezes. Barely able to see through the tiny slits that were now her eyes, she looked down, rubbing the dust between her thumb and forefinger. She had a feeling that Piper's resignation from the bureau coincided with her husband's death, which would mean that he'd been dead for more than three years.

She climbed the basement stairs and went to the kitchen sink. Splashing cold water on her face always helped to minimize the itching and burning. She didn't have to look in the mirror to know that angry red blotches covered her face and neck, making her look like she had a bad case of poison ivy.

All she had to do now was try not to scratch. That was very important.

She grabbed some paper towels and retraced her steps to make sure she hadn't missed anything. Cold air blew in through the broken living room window. The downpour had finally abated. A mild drizzle reached in from outside and clutched at the windowsill with damp fingers.

Scratching her neck, Mercy scanned the living room one last time and looked up. Rhododendron branches and aged tobacco poles made up the staircase leading to the second floor. The wood creaked noisily under her feet in protest to the intrusion.

A reading loft greeted her. Hundreds of books were neatly arranged on pinewood shelves that were built into the walls in seamless perfection. A handcrafted wooden love seat with miniature pine trees rested between giant log support beams. Twig furniture, candles of all sizes, and a throw rug in the shape of a black bear made her want to sprawl out with a good Western adventure novel and take a nap.

To the right of the reading loft lay an exercise room with enough equipment to work every major muscle group. Another room down the same short hallway served as an office. Heart pine bookshelves lined two walls from floor to ceiling. Green plaid curtains adorned the only window in the room. Aside from the plants—several of which were now budding with brightly colored flowers—this room spoke all work and no play.

Scratching, Mercy sat at the desk and swiveled the chair around. The window provided an unobstructed view of the street. She would've bet anything that this lonely square of glass served as Piper's only connection with the outside world. She imagined her sitting there busy with work, glancing from time to time at her neighbors as they strolled past on the street below. No doubt, there was a part of her that longed for the companionship she so adamantly denied herself.

5:43 p.m.

Mercy stood from the chair, walked the short hallway, and passed through the reading loft to take a peek at the master bedroom on the other side.

Chunky wooden furniture, an old hope chest, and a king-sized lodge pole canopy bed furnished spacious sleeping quarters. A mountain stone fireplace rose into vaulted ceilings where support posts with ancient mortises converged with hand-hewn logs. Exposed stone, square-cut timber, and heart pine floorboards combined to make the master bedroom the most skillfully constructed room in any house that Mercy had ever seen.

Finding nothing of use in the master bath, she scratched as she made her way to the nightstand. There, lying facedown, was a framed photo. She picked it up.

A man and woman smiled back at the camera with a horse standing between them. It was the same man who'd posed for the pictures in the basement. Deductive reasoning suggested that the woman in the photo was Piper.

She was stunning. With long raven hair and haunting gray eyes, she smiled back at the camera with a look of expectation.

Those eyes...something about them reminded Mercy of brooding summer thunderstorms—the storms that came out of nowhere and put an end to her street hockey games as a kid. All the neighborhood moms would yell to their kids from the front porch steps, called to motherly action by the lightning in the sky. From the age of six, Mercy had no mom to worry and fuss over her like the other kids did. Once her friends went home, she was free to linger in the street and tempt fate. She remembered it like it was yesterday.

She would hold her hockey stick up high and stand like a statue in the middle of the street. The sizzle in the air always made her arms and legs break out in goose bumps. She'd point the stick at the sky, daring a lightning bolt to strike her dead as the other kids looked on from their bedroom windows. Little did they know that a terrified part of her wanted to flee from the storm and seek shelter in her own house, but she forced herself to swallow her fear, remaining in plain view of the storm clouds until they finally moved on to some other kid's neighborhood, no match for the small, white-knuckled fists of a tomboy holding on to her hockey stick for dear life.

She studied the photo. There it was. Piper had that same look of stubborn fear in her eyes. Something about her called to Mercy. Not only did she need to find her for the sake of this case, but she suddenly found herself *wanting* to find her, yearning just to have the chance to look into those eyes.

She tore her eyes away from Piper's face and scanned the rest of the photo. Impossibly, the horse standing beside Piper was a carbon copy of a horse Mercy once knew—the same horse assigned to her by the FBI eight years ago.

As the final step in the hiring process for UCH, each agent was given a feral mustang with instructions to gentle the horse until it could be ridden. Agents were required to train alone with their horse, quarantined from family and friends for however much time they needed to complete the exercise.

The theory behind the taming exercise employed by UCH was simple. If the agent succeeded, it told UCH everything they needed to know about that person. Not only could the agent work alone, but they also possessed enough fortitude to see a difficult task through to the end.

Since UCH was challenging in every way imaginable, the FBI wanted to make certain that its agents had the necessary tools to make it through physically, psychologically, and emotionally intact. The words *Whoa, steady now* brought each agent back to that place of self-discipline, giving them a solid foundation on which to rest when cases got under the skin, as certain cases inevitably did.

By the end of their first month of active duty, each fledgling UCH agent intuitively understood the reason behind the label *the steady room*. As far as Mercy knew, no one had ever felt the need to ask what it stood for.

Mercy's assigned horse, Nutcase, hadn't made the exercise easy. Since each agent was strictly forbidden to seek outside help from trainers of any kind, she was left to her own devices. And what did she know about horses? The only pet she'd had growing up was a turtle named Smelly. Aptly named after a trip to the vet, she'd learned that Smelly had a fungus underneath his shell that made him smell really, really bad.

Nutcase's name came about in a similar fashion. Not only couldn't she get within fifty feet of him before he'd bolt in the opposite direction, but he blatantly refused to eat anything—hay, grains, oats—that Mercy had touched with her bare hands. Afraid that the bureau would think she was starving her horse as a means of training, she was forced to start wearing gloves when handling his feed.

When she read that apples were a horse's favorite snack, she thought she'd hit the jackpot. She didn't bother wearing gloves. Nutcase would find the apples irresistible, right? Then Mercy would climb on his back, ride off into the sunset, and land the job with UCH. Cakewalk.

Mercy crept outside later that night to leave an apple near his favorite maple tree. She scratched her head in confusion when she awoke to the same unbitten apple on her doorstep the very next morning. Convinced that someone from the bureau was playing a joke, she ran surveillance one night. Sure enough, Nutcase came trotting around the corner at about two in the morning, apple in mouth. He deposited it, unscathed, on the ground outside the door. Dumbfounded, she realized that Nutcase was playing a game with her.

Mercy began hiding the apples in a new spot every day. Nutcase would find them and leave them at her doorstep in the middle of the night. After two weeks of Hide the Apple, Mercy decided it was time to call a truce. She sliced an apple into sections, took them outside, and casually began eating them where Nutcase could see her. He approached and nudged Mercy from behind with his big head, asking for a piece of the apple. Pretty soon, they were standing there together and sharing the apple like old friends.

She studied the horse in Piper's photo, half convinced it was her apple-retrieving friend from years past. Same roan coloring. Same white ticking on the face. "Nah, couldn't be," she said finally, replacing the frame facedown.

She jogged down the stairs, opened the Byzantine Door, and kept jogging down the driveway until she reached the rental car. Her hands shook a little as she called Lou.

5:47 p.m.

Mercy let it ring once and hung up. She looked at her watch and called three more times with ten second intervals in between. She scratched while she waited for Lou to call back.

She and Lou had devised a plan long ago to warn one another of an impending threat. To date, no circumstances had emerged to necessitate its implementation. One ring every ten seconds meant, *Get your ass moving and find a pay phone fast.*

She closed her swollen eyelids and tried to recall Shadow's exact words. She could still hear the echo of arrogance in his voice. *As you so eloquently explained to Lou this morning, you're not allowed to answer a question with another question.*

There was no way Shadow could have known about their private conversation. Unless Lou's house was bugged.

Fishing the envelope from her pocket, she smoothed out each note, held them side by side, and thought back to Piper's kitchen.

The etching of the Labrador on the floor was probably Bobby—the same dog that Shadow had referenced in his poem. Bobby was obviously nowhere to be found because Shadow had already taken him. His motive for doing so was a matter of simple deductive reasoning. Shadow was banking on the fact that Mercy would find Piper before the seven o'clock deadline, and Bobby was the bait to ensure Piper's cooperation in the investigation thereafter.

The question she didn't have the answer to was *why*. Why in the world did Shadow want them working together?

She didn't know enough about Piper or the surrounding geography to make an educated guess as to where Shadow had hidden her. She twirled her wedding band around, thinking as she scratched some more. It would be somewhere secluded. Probably a place that held sentimental value for Piper. She slid a pen from her pocket and opened the glove compartment. No paper. She turned her hand over and listed the questions she wanted to ask Lou about Piper's personal life.

They had discussed Piper's psychic ability earlier that afternoon during their walk on the beach. Lou cited countless cases where the FBI had utilized her to solve dead-end homicides. Turned out the rumors had been true all along. Piper could study a victim's photo and provide a fully detailed account of what had happened. Lou admitted that he'd seen it firsthand.

Even though Mercy thought herself a skeptic, she trusted Lou's judgment implicitly. If Lou was convinced Piper was the real deal, then that was good enough for her.

She rolled down the window to let the rain chill the fire on her face. Maybe Shadow was giving her too much credit. Her heart raced. What if she wasn't able to find Piper in time?

5:49 p.m.

Her cell phone rang. "Parker," she answered.

"I'm standing in the freezing, pouring rain at the only pay phone in town right now. No umbrella," Lou complained.

"And I'm sitting toasty warm, though slightly itchy, inside my rental car. But if it makes that much of a difference, I'll open the door and stand outside in the rain, too."

"Better not. It's best if only one of us perishes from hypothermia." Lou's voice trailed away as wind exhaled into the receiver like a prank caller. "Itchy, you say?"

"Yup."

"Been cavorting with those dust bunnies again, I take it?"

"Can't get enough of 'em." The car shook as Mercy scratched.

"Then I guess we're even. One pay phone popsicle for the dust bunny blotches sounds like a pretty fair trade."

"Hardly." Wishing her nails were just a little longer, she inserted the key and started the engine. "Wanted to give you a heads-up... You should probably call an exterminator."

"You think I have bugs?" Lou asked, sounding genuinely surprised.

"It's a good idea to rent a room for the night and get a doggie sweep." *Doggie sweep* was code for the K-9 bomb squad.

Lou was silent on the other end. "You in trouble?" he finally asked.

Mercy gave him the abbreviated version of everything that had happened since Sarah's murder, giving special mention to Shadow's threat against any outsiders on the case. She wanted to be sure that Lou was aware of the risks.

"You really expect me to bail on you just to save my own sorry ass? Think again, my friend. I may be retired, but I'm as tough as a rhino's rear end."

Scratching, she checked her watch. "We have exactly seventy minutes to find her. I'm open to suggestions."

"Don't have any."

She stopped scratching long enough to read the notes from her palm. "How'd her husband die?"

"Tim was stabbed to death three years ago at an ATM in Bartlett. It's a small town just outside North Conway."

"Too public. Looking for someplace private. Where'd she get the dog?"

"Tim brought Bobby home for Christmas about five"—Lou shouted to be heard above the wind and rain—"maybe six months before he was killed. Not sure where he got him."

"I found a picture of Piper and Tim with a horse. They do a lot of riding?" With a rising panic to start looking *somewhere*, she put the car in gear.

"She did her fair share, but it was Tim who had the passion for horses. They owned a stable. She took me there once a couple years back. Said she needed to check on a sick horse."

"What was the name of the place?" She pulled into Piper's driveway, put the car in reverse, and backed out so she was facing the opposite direction.

"Twin Stables...something or other. I'll remember, just give me a sec."

She drove down Piper's street and hesitated at the stop sign, wondering which way to turn.

"Twin Horse Stables. No, Twin Farm. Twin...let me think here." Lou was quiet for a moment. "Twin Gate Farms. That's it. In fact, I think she still boards one of her horses there."

They hung up with the understanding that Lou would purchase a new cell phone and call back as soon as possible.

6:04 p.m.

Piper's vision swam into focus. The first thing she became aware of was the explosive headache that made her instantly nauseous. She had never experienced a migraine before, but she figured this would definitely qualify as one. The second thing she realized was that she was very, very cold...due in large part to the fact that she was outside—she glanced down at her body—without any clothes on. Outdoors? In the buff? Now why would she go and do a thing like that?

She tried to call out, but there was something holding her mouth shut. She squinted against the fading daylight at the looming form above her. A tree. She tried to bring her hands to her temples to massage them and realized she couldn't move her arms. She looked down at herself again and saw the ropes crisscrossing her chest and stomach. Hard to think. Felt like there was a toxic spill in her brain, and each neuron was now coated in thick black oil. She squeezed her eyes shut, trying to will the confusion away. Took her a few moments to realize that she was tied to...a tree?

6:06 p.m.

Mercy looked up the address to Twin Gate Farms and entered it into the rental car's navigation system. The stables were just over two miles from Piper's cabin. She pulled onto a dirt drive and parked in the farm's muddy lot.

A fine drizzle coated the windshield. It felt like the temperature had dropped twenty degrees in the last hour. According to NHPR, there was a chance of snow flurries later.

She climbed out of the car as the mother of all puddles swallowed her feet to her ankles. Her shoes suctioned noisily as she pried them from the mud. She felt ridiculous in her blazer and dress slacks. With all hope of maintaining a professional image lost, she slipped and slid her way to the farmhouse, wishing she had dressed in more suitable attire.

The screen door that greeted her was battered, yet warmly inviting. Red paint chips were flaking off to reveal a second layer of dull tree-bark brown. The sign above the door read *Office*, its letters carved into the wood by a child's unsteady hand. Women's voices drifted out. She stomped the mud off to announce her presence, opened the screen door, and stepped inside.

A woman in a blue raincoat and black rubber boots was bent over, adding a log to the woodstove. A second, younger woman with a long braid down her back was hanging leather reins over a wooden peg on the wall. They both turned to face her.

Mercy held up her badge. She walked over and reached out to introduce herself. "Agent Parker, FBI."

With a wordless gasp, the younger woman took a step back and folded her arms protectively across her chest.

The older woman shut the door to the woodstove, straightened, and marched right up to Mercy. Making no move to return the handshake, she narrowed her eyes and studied her face. "The FBI actually let you out lookin' like that?"

The two women—Sandy and Jill—turned out to be the farm's owner and manager. Mercy interviewed them as the woodstove behind her crackled with warmth. Aromas of hay, manure, and burning logs filled the office. Neither of the women had noticed any unusual activity, nor did they remember seeing anyone other than the regular boarders during the past few days.

She requested a tour of the property just to be safe. Sandy tossed her a raincoat and met her out front in a green tractor-like machine. She called it the Gator. "Hop in"—she winked—"unless you'd rather cover the land on foot."

Mercy shook her head and climbed in.

"Good." She patted the Gator's dash. "'Cause I don't want you out there without these wheels under your tush."

"Why's that?" Mercy asked.

Sandy pulled a tattered Patriots hat out of her pocket and nestled it on top of an unruly mound of gray hair. "'Cause that ugly mug of yours is apt to startle my horses. And when they come chargin', you won't be able to run fast enough." Sandy looked over as Mercy took a seat beside her. "Holy Clydesdale, your mug's as red as a baboon's ass."

Shrugging into the borrowed raincoat, Mercy laughed at her own expense. She didn't bother pulling the hood over her head. The rain felt good on her face.

They found nothing out of the ordinary. Back inside the office, she gave each of the women her card and asked that they call immediately if anything changed. She started to peel off the raincoat when Sandy slapped her on the shoulder. "Keep it," she said. "You can return it to me later after you find whatever it is you're lookin' for. Then we can talk about a horse I got for sale you might be interested in buyin'."

Mercy stared at her. "What makes you think I'm interested in buying a horse?"

"I don't claim to know a whole lot in life, Ms. Parker, but I do know two things: horses and people." She reached out to shake Mercy's hand. "I could tell by your body language out there in the Gator, you got a kinship for horses. I'll let you in on a little secret." She leaned in close and whispered, "A horse can heal your heart."

Mercy was halfway to the car when Jill, the young manager, called out from the porch steps. "Agent Parker, wait!" Her long braid slapped against her back as she jogged over. She handed Mercy a tin jar and looked shyly at the ground. "This will help reduce the inflammation in your face. We use it on the horses all the time, but it's safe for people, too."

6:18 p.m.

Lou rang as she was making her way back to the rental car. "No luck, Lou. Time's running out."

"Wish I was there. We could split up and save some time."

She climbed behind the steering wheel, started the engine, and blasted the heater. "I think Shadow expects me to figure this one out myself. What I don't understand is why he wants me working this case with Piper in the first place."

"Well, he obviously knows about her gift. He spelled at least that much out for you on the victim's bedroom floor."

"Sarah," Mercy corrected, turning the dial on the heater to high. She hated it when people referred to one of her kids as *the victim*. "Which raises another question. How'd he find out Piper was psychic to begin with?"

"Maybe he dug into her background a little, found it there."

She popped the lid on the tin jar, adjusted the rearview mirror, and peered at her face...or, to be more accurate, what was *formerly* her face. "Has anything ever been written about her?" she asked, carefully applying the salve.

"Piper has always been intensely private about her gift. She'd never give an interview, if that's what you're thinking."

Silence crept on the line. "Although..." Lou was the first to break it.

The car heater blew steady as pins and needles attacked Mercy's feet. "What?"

"She made me promise never to share this with anyone."

She replaced the lid on the jar and tossed it in the glove compartment. The burning sensation in her face was finally starting to subside. "Spit it out already."

Lou hesitated. "Piper was twelve when her best friend, Mary Beth, was reported missing. Search parties were formed, but no one found anything. She rode her bike down to the police station one afternoon and told them she knew where Mary Beth's body was. She also told them she knew exactly who had killed her. She described everything that had happened to Mary Beth before the investigators even arrived at the crime scene. They found her naked and bound to a tree in precisely the way Piper had described."

Wherever that little girl had been murdered was where she'd find Piper. Mercy was sure of it. "Where'd they find Mary Beth's body?"

"In the woods. Somewhere in North Conway, I think."

Rain slapped hard against the rental car's roof. "The case was probably in the papers. I passed a library a few miles back. Bet they have it on microfiche." She floored it. The front tires kicked up a thick paste of mud and pebbles against the car's undercarriage. "What happened after they found her?"

Lou cleared his throat. "When detectives asked Piper how she knew what had happened, she told them that Mary Beth had spoken to her from a photograph. After hearing that, they hardly looked at the guy she fingered for the murder. Get this. Not only was he the city mayor, but he also had an airtight alibi with his wife. It didn't take long for detectives to start looking at Piper as the most likely suspect. Even her parents turned their backs on her."

"That's awful," Mercy said.

"She was subsequently committed to a state psychiatric institution. I came on staff as the institution's consulting psychiatrist about four years later, which is when I met Piper. I was assigned to oversee her psychiatric treatment, but there was just something about her that made me believe her story. I tried repeatedly to approach the assistant DA who prosecuted the case. He wouldn't even hear me out.

"Then, a year later, another girl was murdered in Cambridge, Massachusetts. Same MO. I started poking around and found that the mayor was visiting Cambridge on business during the time in question. I contacted the local papers and leaked the story anonymously. I told them that a gifted young girl had been wrongly convicted while the real monster was still at large. The media ate it up, and the DA reopened Mary Beth's case at once. They were able to trace the DNA found underneath both victims' fingernails back to the mayor.

"Piper was released just after her seventeenth birthday," Lou went on. "Her parents still didn't want anything to do with her. Since she was like a daughter to me by that time, Jane and I decided to take her into our home. She finished high school a year later, then went off to college and grad school. After that, she followed in my footsteps and applied to the bureau.

"We all agreed early on that it was best to have her name legally changed since the media was still buzzing about the local Photo Psychic. For obvious reasons, she's fiercely private about her gift. That's why we made every attempt to keep her work at the bureau under wraps. Sounds like Shadow may have found those newspaper articles from years ago and somehow traced them back to her. Aside from the media, no one has ever referred to her as the Photo Psychic. I think that's more than mere coincidence."

"Could be," Mercy agreed. "Do you remember the month and year of Mary Beth's murder?"

"Let's see. Piper was admitted in June of 1994. Mary Beth's murder would've fallen somewhere between March and May of that same year."

She assured Lou that she'd call back as soon as she could. She tossed the cell on the seat, threw open the car door, and ran up the library's cement steps.

6:21 p.m.

Piper's memory was fuzzy but starting to return. She and Bobby had just stepped into the backyard from their morning game of fetch. Bobby halted in his tracks and growled, looking up at her as if in warning. He knew something wasn't right before she did. Seconds later, she felt a sharp pain in her stomach. She looked down in time to see the red-tipped syringe that had pierced through her sweater and skin. It delivered a knockout blow to her nervous system. Her legs gave out almost instantly. Bobby was whining and licking her face when she saw an identical syringe land in his shoulder. He went down quickly, too. Before she knew it, they were both on the ground, nose to nose—just the way she had woken up with him earlier that same morning.

She had stayed conscious for as long as she could, peering into Bobby's eyes the whole time. After that, she remembered nothing. She woke up here. And Bobby was gone.

6:28 p.m.

The North Conway Public Library had already closed for the night. Mercy withdrew her badge and rapped on the door with its beveled metal face until two librarians came out of hiding. The smaller woman fretted nervously, unsure of what to do, but the older woman held her ground like a seasoned bullfighter.

Hands on hips, she marched straight toward Mercy. Bifocals swung from her generous bosom in rhythm with her step. Her stone-gray hair was pinned tightly on top of her head. It was the most perfectly rolled bun Mercy had ever seen. "Agent Parker, FBI." She shouted to be heard through the glass. "This is an emergency. Open the door."

Lips pursed, the librarian unfolded her glasses and perched them on the very tip of her nose to examine the badge more closely. "You will answer two questions before I open this door," she said. She removed her glasses and folded them neatly. "What's wrong with your face, and is it contagious?"

Mercy revealed her unfortunate allergy to dust. She considered coming up with something more creative but was fairly certain this woman wouldn't let her in unless she told the absolute truth.

The woman finally unlocked the door and held it open in outright defiance.

"This won't take long. Where's your microfiche viewer?"

"We open our doors at eight o'clock tomorrow. Why don't you come back then?" Her speech was clipped, as if she took great care to pronounce everything with rigid accuracy. "I'd be happy to give you a microfiche tutorial in the morning."

Mercy stepped inside and flicked the light switch on the wall to her left. "Afraid this can't wait until morning, ma'am." She turned to the smaller woman. Her head swiveled back and forth like a nervous sparrow's as she looked from Mercy to her superior. Mercy finally stepped between the two women, barring her view of the older woman's intimidating gaze. "Where's the microfiche? I don't have much time."

The nervous sparrow led her to the reference section in the far corner of the library and pointed to the covered viewer. "Well, here it is." She shrugged, glancing uneasily over her shoulder.

Mercy slid the viewer's cover off, pressed the power button, and took a seat. The ancient wooden chair creaked noisily. "What's the name of the local newspaper?"

"It's, uh…" The sparrow opened her little beak and froze. "*The Conway Daily Sun*," she finally blurted.

A tall gray file cabinet stood to her right. Mercy scanned its labels and opened the drawer with microfilmed issues of the *Conway Daily Sun* from 1994–2003. She extracted a roll from 1994 and clicked it into place on the viewer.

Mercy fast-forwarded to March 1, but found nothing on Mary Beth's murder. Since her death was sure to have made front-page headlines, she skipped ahead to the first page of every issue for the month of March. No luck.

She did the same for the month of April while the librarian wrung her hands beside her chair. *Bingo.* She zoomed in.

Exactly twenty-two years ago to the day, authorities found Mary Beth's body. She skimmed the article.

Missing Girl Found Dead

The body of Mary Beth McCarthy was discovered by the North Conway Police Department yesterday afternoon on Twin Fox Hiking Trail. According to the medical examiner, the official cause of death was hypothermia. The twelve-year-old was reportedly last seen walking home from the bus stop with a classmate. She was subsequently abducted and sexually assaulted by an unknown assailant. There are no suspects at this time.

Mercy printed a copy, grabbed it as it came sliding out, and stood. She turned to the nervous sparrow. "I need to see a detailed map of hiking trails in North Conway. Specifically"—she studied the printout—"Twin Fox Trail."

The senior librarian poked her bobby-pinned bun around the corner. "You don't need a map," she said matter-of-factly. "I can tell you exactly where Twin Fox Trail is located." Her wrinkled scowl softened some as she pulled up a chair. "My husband and I used to walk that trail in the nicer weather before it became private property."

She sketched a map of the two-mile trail, providing Mercy with directions to the trailhead from the library. Mercy had no doubt that the librarian's directions were just as accurate as those that any satellite would have provided. She replaced the cap on her pen and handed Mercy the map. "Does this have anything to do with Mary Beth? I'm her grandmother, you know."

6:44 p.m.

Mercy sped out of the library's paved lot. Infuriated, she realized that Piper had been right under her nose the entire time. Twin Fox Trail was nestled in the woods directly behind her cabin.

She cruised through the stop sign at the end of Piper's street and drove past Tudors, Colonials, Capes, and Victorians. Living room windows were aglow with mysterious family gatherings in which Mercy had never taken part. It was times like these when she felt an ache in her chest, a longing for Anna to be restored to life and returned to her so they could start a family of their own.

Following six miscarriages after nine years of marriage, they'd finally started the adoption process for a little boy in Ethiopia. The Ethiopian government put their application on an indefinite hold when they learned of Anna's death.

She parked in Piper's driveway and walked in through a side door that she had unlocked before leaving. Grabbing a backpack from the hallway closet, she bolted up the stairs to the master bedroom. Assuming she would find Piper naked as Shadow had implied in his letter, she intended to do the kind thing and bring her a change of clothes. She threw the backpack on the bed and hurried to the walk-in closet.

Faint traces of silky perfume still hung in the air. Tucking a pair of sneakers under her arm, she turned to face the closet's inset wooden drawers. She opened them one after another until she found some underwear and socks. She yanked a pair of maroon sweats and a gray sweatshirt off the shelf, stuffed everything inside the backpack, and fled down the stairs two at a time.

She stood at the kitchen window and peered into the woods. Night had already staked claim to the forest. It would be difficult, if not impossible, to find her way in the dark. She jogged down the hallway, opened the door to the basement, and snatched a utility flashlight from the hook above the light switch. She grabbed a water bottle from a nearby shelf and left through the rear door in the kitchen.

6:53 p.m.

Piper saw movement. Chained to a tree about thirty feet away, an enormous man with a bald, tattooed head sat up from the ground. "Son of a bitch! He darted me, too," he growled, shaking and pulling at the chain furiously. He continued to heave and tug at the chain with huge tattooed arms, profanity like nothing she'd ever heard before spewing from his lips. Piper remained silent and just watched him. The man had apparently been darted and was being held against his will just as she was, but something about him felt... wrong. Her instincts warned her he was dangerous.

He suddenly grew very still and met her gaze with eyes devoid of humanity. Chills broke out all over her body.

6:54 p.m.

Mercy crossed the backyard and jogged along the perimeter until she found the trailhead tucked behind a small storage shed. According to her watch, she had exactly five and a half minutes to find Piper before the seven o'clock deadline.

She ran as fast as she dared, sweeping the tree line with the flashlight on both sides as she moved. She strained to hear past her own heavy breathing, past the sound of rain smacking against the trees, past the thumping of her own feet upon the frozen earth. Her shoulders started cramping from the backpack. She hadn't bothered to adjust the straps, and it was sized for a smaller frame, probably Piper's.

She was soaked to the bone in no time at all. Frigid air singed her lungs with each inhalation. But she didn't allow her body the luxury of slowing down. It was simply a case of mind over matter. Raw, achy, exhausted, her lungs desperate for warm oxygen, she forced herself to maintain a fast and steady sprint the entire way.

CHAPTER THIRTEEN

With the tranquilized dog on his shoulder, Shadow threw open the van's rear door. The little warrior was curled up in a ball in the corner exactly where he had left her. She knew the consequences would be dire if she disobeyed. He'd left her unattended to finish his work with Dr. Vasey and gigantic George. The dog was just a loose end.

He knew this dog had already been touched with magic by his twin brother, Lucent, several years before when he was a puppy. Part of working for The Other Side meant Lucent had the laborious and menial task of easing someone's grief. Knowing ahead of time that Dr. Vasey's husband would die, Lucent had arranged for the puppy to land in their home before that happened. He'd probably wanted to give the doctor a warm, furry shoulder on which to cry. What a ridiculous waste of time and talent.

Shadow wasn't sure exactly how Lucent had used his magic to change the dog, but he wasn't taking any chances. He lowered the dog's limp body from his shoulder and tossed him in the back with the little warrior. He would drive them both to his warehouse and properly dispose of them there.

❖

7:02 p.m.

Gasping, Mercy paused at the fork in the trail. She hooded the flashlight with one hand and wiped the rain and allergy cream out of her eyes with the other. Her smoky breath hovered in front of her as she withdrew the map from her pocket.

According to the map, she should bear left at the fork. She shined the flashlight on her watch. It had taken her just under seven minutes to cover the 1.2 mile distance. The seven o'clock deadline had already passed, but she was only about two hundred yards from the tree where Mary Beth's body was found. She shoved the map back inside her pocket.

Since Shadow might have given George a heads-up on her impending arrival, she decided to tread the rest of the way in darkness. She doused the flashlight, unsnapped her holster, and slid out her 9 mm.

Every man-sized tree and jutting branch posed a threat as her eyes tried to puzzle out strange shapes on both sides. When she'd covered more than half the distance to the tree, she slowed from a jog to a fast walk. The salve dripped down her forehead, and her vision blurred. She wiped at both eyes with the back of her sleeve.

An exposed tree root in the middle of the trail brought her to her knees in the slippery mud. She grabbed the flashlight as it went rolling away and stood.

Swathed in rain clouds, the moon withheld its glow. Twenty yards to go. She crouched down and walked the last sixty feet in stealthy silence, barring the noise that her squishy shoes, labored breathing, and pounding heart were making. Other than that, she figured she was nearly undetectable. She stood still and strained to hear past the sounds of the forest on a freezing, rain-soaked night.

The scraping of metal first caught her attention. Its source was just a few feet ahead on the right. She ducked, hugging the tree line as she felt her way along the trail. *Clang, clang, scraaaaape. Clang, clang, scraaaaape.* Chains. Reminded of the classic ghost story, she inched closer. Instead of being dragged behind on the attic floor by vengeful spirits, these chains were being dragged over the ground by strong human legs.

Suddenly, the chains ceased clinking. All was still in the night.

She squatted, carefully set the flashlight on the ground beside her, and shrugged out of the backpack. She leaned against a tree trunk, the bark damp and jagged under her palms. Resting on the balls of her feet, she took shallow breaths and wondered if anything had given her away.

Clouds peeled away from the moon long enough to illuminate the shapes around her. Something shiny reflected in the moon's glow about five feet in front of her, suspended in the air just below eye level. It took her a few seconds to realize that it was a piece of jewelry—a necklace. Relief washed over her as she saw that the necklace was dangling from the bare neck of a woman. Her arms were tied around the tree behind her, knees drawn tightly against her chest. She was shivering uncontrollably. But there she was so close that Mercy could reach out and touch her. She followed the graceful lines of Piper's neck to her feminine jawline and lips, and then...those eyes. Gray thunderstorms returned Mercy's gaze. She felt things begin to shift inside her—old doors closing, new ones opening—as they held eye contact for interminable seconds.

"Hey there, gorgeous." A gravelly voice gushed out of the darkness from somewhere above.

Piper didn't take her eyes from Mercy's. Mercy was the first to break contact. From her position, all she could see was the breath steaming from George's nostrils like an angry dragon. One thing she knew for sure was that George was tall. Six eight? She couldn't tell for sure. Even more pressing was the issue of George's hands. For her safety and Piper's, she needed to find out if good old George was holding a weapon.

She shifted and looked over just in time to see a size sixteen work boot rocketing straight toward her face. Instinctively, she ducked and rolled away, the boot just barely grazing the side of her cheek. She was still rolling onto her back when she pointed the gun in George's direction and shouted, "FBI! Get down on the ground! Now!"

The moon deserted her. Darkness reclaimed the forest. She squinted, trying to pinpoint George's exact location. Rain beat down so hard that it stung the exposed skin on her hands, face, and neck. She had to keep blinking to make out anything at all.

She pushed herself up with her elbows, rolled onto her knees in the mud, and proceeded to stand. Before she was fully erect, George's work boot smashed into her left hand and knocked the gun from her grasp. Sharp waves of pain coursed down the inside of her wrist as her finger bent back. The bone finally gave way with an audible crack. Another powerful kick to her ribs made her crumple to her knees. The good news, Mercy thought as she clutched at her side— because there had to be a silver lining to every bad situation—was it appeared as though George's only weapons were his steel-toed work boots. Which, incidentally, packed quite a punch.

A second kick to her ribs on the opposite side was even harder than the first. She felt one of her ribs snap on impact.

Something wasn't right. How could George see well enough to target specific areas of her body when Mercy could barely make out her own hand in front of her face? George's eyes couldn't have adjusted to the darkness *that* much.

Night-vision goggles. That had to be it. George was probably armed with a pair of NVGs to level the playing field, and Mercy suspected she knew exactly who had made that generous contribution. No fair. Shadow should have consulted with her first instead of just assuming that she would've chosen the gun. Frankly, she preferred the NVGs over the 9 mm. She wondered if George would consider a trade.

Thrown face-first into the mud with a swift kick between the shoulder blades, she guessed this wasn't the time to ask. The pain was so excruciating that she wondered if he had fractured her back. She had no choice but to keep fighting. No matter what. Piper and Emily were counting on her. She was all they had.

Almost as soon as she hit the ground, she pushed herself up and rocked back on her knees. She couldn't hear anything beyond the pounding of the rain, couldn't see anything but shadows. She closed her eyes and focused. Patient, she waited for the next strike.

She felt George circle around her like a predator toying with its kill. She clutched at her side, drawing in short, raspy breaths. She wanted George to think that one of her lungs had been punctured with that last kick. Believing victory was imminent, he would feel confident, grow careless.

Mercy slowly brought her right knee up and planted her foot on the ground for better leverage. She knew where the next kick was going to land.

Just as she expected, George struck from the front and went for Mercy's jaw with his size sixteens. She deflected the kick, grabbed George's leg, and held it aloft in one fluid motion. Lunging forward to put all her body weight behind the blow, she jabbed the heel of her hand against the inside of George's kneecap. With a resounding crunch, George howled in pain and toppled to the ground.

She rose just as George was reaching for the gun on the ground beside him. The gun's barrel was suddenly pointing at Mercy's chest. Without thinking, she leaned into the gun and swept George's hand off to one side as it fired.

Tunnel vision set in. All that mattered was retrieving her 9 mm. Straddling George's body, she smashed the back of his hand against a rock, two times…three times…four times. Plump fingers finally unfurled. Now growling with rage, the giant began to rise beneath her.

Mercy grabbed for the gun. George bucked like an angry bull and flung Mercy onto her back. Searing pain flashed between her shoulder blades. George plucked a rock from the trail and clambered over her body. He raised both arms high in the air, obviously intending to finish off his quarry with a bludgeoning strike. Mercy gritted her teeth against the pain in her back, pointed the gun at George's heart, and fired.

The giant's body sagged with the impact of the bullet. At some point during the struggle, the NVGs had been knocked off, exposing George's pockmarked face. Mercy watched as the giant's expression went from anger to surprise as he parted ways from the living, an unwitting perpetrator of his own fate.

She rolled George aside, sat up, and checked for a pulse. Nothing. Despite his massive structure, George proved no different than most when it came to matters of the heart.

She couldn't even summon the energy to laugh at her own joke. Flashes of pain trailed each intake of breath. She knew at least one of her ribs was broken. Her back and shoulders felt like they'd been run over by the six o'clock subway. The nerve endings in her damaged hand now fired off continuously, making her acutely aware of the torn ligaments and tendons around her broken finger.

She put on her best poker face, limped over to Piper, and knelt down in front of her. "Agent Parker, at your service. I'd shake your hand, but you seem a little tied-up right now."

She looked at Piper who was guarded and stiff with cold. A blindfold hung loosely around her neck. She peeled the tape from Piper's lips and slid the rag out from her mouth.

Mercy knew what it felt like to be gagged. As part of her training, she was gagged and bound for several hours. Not a pleasant experience. A rag soaked up most of the mouth's saliva, leaving one's throat as dry and brittle as the Sahara.

Piper swallowed and started to choke. Mercy reached for the backpack with her good hand, withdrew the water bottle from an outer mesh pocket, and popped the top. "Little sips," she said, tilting it upward. "That dryness in your throat will pass. "

Piper took turns sipping and choking. Drenched from the rain, clumps of long, dark hair dipped sluggishly in front of her face. "Agent Parker...the lesbian FBI agent?"

"I wasn't aware that was my official title at the bureau," Mercy replied, amused.

"Sorry, I've just heard about you for years. The entire male population has been complaining that you're...off limits." Piper shivered with cold. "Now I see why."

Mercy smiled at the compliment, relieved to know the salve had finally kicked in and restored her face to its normal proportions. "If we'd met an hour ago, you wouldn't be saying that."

"I'm naked," Piper blurted.

"Hi, Naked. Nice to meet you." Mercy reached out, gently brushing Piper's dark hair to one side.

"Very funny."

"Thank you."

"You already knew, didn't you?" It sounded more like an accusation than a question.

"That I was funny?"

"No, that I was sitting here"—Piper hesitated—"in the buff."

"Oh, that. Sure, though it turned out to be a minor detail in the big scheme of things." Piper was positioned with her back to the tree, her arms fanned out to either side. From what Mercy could see, it looked like several layers of rope had been wrapped around her stomach, chest, and arms, anchoring her securely to the base of the tree. She followed the tree's giant girth with her eyes and craned her neck to see exactly where the ropes met on the other side, but it was too dark to see much of anything.

"How?"

"How what?" Mercy asked, preoccupied with freeing her.

"How'd you know I was naked?" Piper's voice had a pleasant, natural throatiness.

She shrugged, crawling over to the flashlight. "Lucky guess?"

"I can't believe it!"

Mercy crawled back to her side. "What?"

"Here I am, tied to a tree in the middle of the woods in the freezing cold, soaked to the bone, and you *sneak a peek*?"

"Did not."

"Did too," Piper insisted through chattering teeth.

Mercy stopped what she was doing, careful to focus only on Piper's face.

Piper averted eye contact, seemingly embarrassed.

"Listen, even if I wanted to sneak a peek, it's not like I can see anything out here." Mercy's left shoulder was throbbing like crazy. She felt the warmth of her own blood trickling down her back and chest and wondered if her tattoo was still intact. Better be. That yin-yang tattoo had been with her a long time. Kind of a security blanket.

"You admit it, then."

"I'm not answering anything further until my lawyer is present." Then, for the first time, she looked at Piper. Really looked at her. She saw how tenuously this woman was holding on to consciousness. She reached out and cupped Piper's cheek with the palm of her hand. It was like touching ice. She realized then that Piper's words were empty of any real challenge. She was simply using the debate to keep herself from slipping into a tempting slumber of hypothermia.

And she was no longer shivering. A bad sign. Piper had gone from mildly hypothermic to moderately hypothermic.

Mercy unzipped the backpack, dug out the sweatshirt, and draped it over Piper. "I brought you a change of clothes. Just give me a minute to get these ropes untied, and we'll have you warmed up in no time."

"You can't do that," she objected.

"What did I do this time?"

"You can't be nice when I'm trying to pick a fight with you."

"Fine, then let me give you something more to work with." Mercy looked away, trying to find just the right words. "I busted your living room window, broke into your cabin, and rifled through your personal belongings. There's more, but I'll leave you to stew on that for now." She turned and crawled away.

"Did you go through my underwear drawer?" she called out.

Mercy reached the far side of the tree, clicked the flashlight on, and stopped cold. "I was trained to do whatever the circumstances necessitate," she shouted back, trying to sound relaxed. "Actually, I pegged you for a cotton girl, but the silk was a nice surprise." Well, untying the ropes was definitely out of the question. Dozens of granny knots encased a black box. Large red numbers were counting down from within a tangled mass of rock-climbing rope. She dug into her pocket for her Swiss Army knife and came up empty-handed. Her knife was on the other keychain. She'd taken the rental car keys and left her own set behind. *Shit.*

Piper continued, "And to think I was actually sitting here, considering whether or not I should help you with this case." Her voice was shaky with cold. "I could probably forgive you for the broken window. I could even overlook the illegal breaking and entering into the privacy of my home. But you rifled through my undergarments, and *that's* where I draw the line."

It stopped raining. Winds picked up, lashing icy fingers through Mercy's hair and clothes. Her heart raced. Blood oozed from the hole in her shoulder. The pain was getting worse. She was starting to feel dizzy. Her mistake now loomed larger than life: she hadn't brought anything with which to cut the ropes.

Fifteen minutes remained on the timer. She crawled around the tree, flashlight in tow.

Piper opened her eyes. "Mighty underwear woman to the resh...cue. Back so shoon?" she said dreamily.

Telltale slurring invaded her speech—the second sign that she had entered phase two of hypothermia. Mercy shrugged out of her raincoat, draped it over Piper, and peeled off her blazer. The entire right side of her own shirt was saturated with blood. She stripped it off, tore it in half, and made a tourniquet for her shoulder. She wound the material as tightly as she could, studying Piper as she spoke. "I know you think I'm only in this for the underwear, but I'm not. There's a little girl out there who needs our help, and the only way we're going to find her is if we work together. In order for that to happen, you need to stay alive."

"Why?" Piper closed her eyes. "You going somewhere?"

"Wake up," she shouted.

"I'm so tired."

"You have to stay awake, Piper. Bobby needs you."

"Bobby," she repeated, trancelike. "He's all I have." She wrinkled her forehead. "Well, I guess I have the underwear, too."

Mercy laughed, reigniting the pain in her ribs. She tucked in the last of the tourniquet and reached for the backpack. "I'm going back to the cabin." She draped the sweatpants around Piper's head and shoulders for added insulation.

The winds raged, blowing the legs of the sweatpants up like a frantic, flapping bird. Mercy wrestled them out of the air and tucked the sweatpants around Piper more securely. Piper had been exposed to the cold for so long, but there was nothing more she could do for her right now.

The first few snowflakes started to fall. She reached out and lifted Piper's chin. Piper blinked repeatedly as gray thunderstorms swam into focus. There it was. A flicker of coherency. "You hang in there. I promise—I'll make it back in time." Mercy let go of her chin and stood.

CHAPTER FOURTEEN

Emily held her breath when she heard the bad man approaching. He opened the door at the back of the van and looked in at her. There with something draped over his shoulder...a dead dog? He set the dead dog down, slammed the door shut, and walked around to the driver's seat.

Feeling a little grossed out, she scooted farther away from the dog's body before she realized it was still breathing. She waited for the bad man to start driving, and then crawled over to examine the dog more closely. She set her hand on its furry chest, feeling it rise and fall with each breath. Very much alive, it was a chocolate Labrador that appeared to be sleeping. But how could it stay asleep through all this? Maybe the bad man had knocked it unconscious. She felt around on its head but didn't find a lump like the one she had. Taking a deep breath to steady her hands, she cautiously felt along the dog's body for injuries and found nothing. She shook it gently to see if she could wake it up. It was sound asleep.

She had no idea why the bad man had brought the dog along, and she didn't dare ask. A bunch of explanations ran through her head. Was this his dog? Did he bring a vicious attack dog to keep her in line? Chocolate Labs were usually pretty nice, but maybe this one was different. The more Emily thought about it, the more nervous she got. What was going to happen when it woke up?

❖

Mercy wound to the other side of the tree and took one last look at the timer. Thirteen minutes, eleven seconds remained. She picked up the NVGs from the ground near George's body and fitted them over her head. The forest suddenly unveiled in fuzzy greenish hues. She'd have to be sure and thank Shadow for this handy gadget.

She looked down at her watch and mentally calculated how much time she had before the bomb exploded. She'd need to return for Piper no later than 7:27 p.m. That gave her twelve minutes to get to the cabin, grab some scissors, and run back like an Olympic sprinter. Leaving her with one minute to free Piper from the ropes and clear the area.

She could do this. She had to.

She tore down the trail without looking back. The NVGs bobbled as she ran. Every step jolted the pain in her shoulder, back, and ribs. Chewed up by the bullet, her flesh throbbed with a ferocity that surprised her. She didn't remember it hurting this much the last time she got shot.

She had just graduated from the FBI Academy and was assigned to the Criminal Investigative Division. One of her very first cases involved a young woman by the name of Holly Angelini. She stole rare and expensive sports cars and had been getting away with it for the better part of a decade. Not only was Holly skilled at planning and executing intricate grand larceny operations all over the country, but she was also a master of disguise, changing identities to elude capture as easily as someone changed their clothes. Known as Holly Houdini, she was a real nuisance to law enforcement everywhere.

The real zinger was when Holly lifted the deputy director's beloved candy-apple-red 1988 Porsche 944. She drove it to the Virginia governor's mansion, switched cars, and then drove back to the deputy director's home, depositing the governor's prized 1989 Aston Martin Zagato Volante convertible in the deputy director's parking garage. After that, the FBI wanted her so badly that multiple task forces were formed, devoted entirely to her capture.

At that time, Mercy was paired with Drawers, her rookie partner. His real name was Jeff Glibbins, but everyone called him

Drawers because he could never get his pants to stay up. He was always pulling, tugging, and fighting with them. Always at war with his pants.

Determined to make a name for themselves, she and Drawers worked day and night to find the elusive Holly Houdini. They interviewed and re-interviewed past acquaintances, staked surveillance in different parts of the country where she was recently sighted, and worked with a sketch artist to portray her in every imaginable disguise. They even implored psychics to help shed light on the case, but none of those leads proved fruitful.

They sacrificed food, sleep, beer, sex, and anything that remotely resembled a personal life, focused solely on bringing Holly Houdini to justice. They did everything they could think of, short of airing a national broadcast in which they'd beg Holly to turn herself in—a strategy they seriously contemplated during one particularly low point in the investigation.

Until one day, they had a break in the case. They flew off to California and staked surveillance on a flashy nightclub reputed to be one of Holly's recent hot spots. Drawers posed as a bouncer at the nightclub's entrance while Mercy guarded the rear. They maintained communication via radio.

Disguised as an alley wino, Mercy could hardly believe her eyes when Holly strutted out from the back door in red stilettos at about four a.m. that first night. Mercy's scruffy, store-bought beard and paper bag of bottled water didn't fool Holly for one second. She spotted Mercy immediately and fled down the alley like a gazelle.

Holly was surprisingly fast in heels. Mercy gave chase, shrugging off layers of filthy clothing as she went until her FBI vest was prominently displayed. She notified Drawers by radio, who also left his post to join in the pursuit.

Mercy quickly closed the gap. She reached out to grab the back of Holly's pearl white blouse, the tips of her fingers just barely skimming the surface of the silky material. She had played this moment over and over again in her mind. She knew *exactly* what she was going to do. Throw Holly to the ground, make the arrest, give Drawers a high five, and go down in FBI history.

Then, out of nowhere, came a fire in her backside. Mercy stumbled to the ground, scraping her hands and elbows raw as she skidded across the pavement. Confused, she craned her neck to peer down at her own backside. Lo and behold, there was a bullet in her buttock.

She'd watched helplessly as the red stilettos galloped away and vanished around the corner, forever just beyond her reach.

She was carted away by ambulance and woke up later in the hospital with a bandaged heinie hanging in the air. For several weeks following the…*accident*, she was forced to rest her rump on a stuffed doughnut whenever she sat down.

Turned out her own partner had shot her in the ass. Drawers humbly explained that his pants had come loose and dropped around his ankles as he was tearing down the alleyway, gun in hand.

As soon as Mercy was discharged from the hospital and resting uncomfortably at home, she ordered Drawers a pair of suspenders and had them shipped to the office. Express.

Instead of going down in FBI history as the two rookie agents who captured the most elusive perpetrator of grand larceny in US history, they became known as Butt and Jeff.

It took Mercy a long time to shake that name.

Every year for Christmas, she still sent Drawers a nicely wrapped box with a brand new pair of suspenders inside. One year, she had little butts embroidered up and down both sides. Another year, she glued miniature sports cars to the suspenders and ironed on tiny patches of red high heels. In return, she received a comparably decorated stuffed doughnut.

Like the scarlet letter, Drawers wore his suspenders. Faithfully. To this day.

Before Mercy knew it, she was crossing over into Piper's backyard. The toolshed was a passing blur as she made for the cabin. She'd left the kitchen door ajar on her way out to find the trailhead. The winds had blown the door wide open, repeatedly banging it against the side of the kitchen counter with a stuttering *knock-knock, knock-knock* as if a ghost was waiting at the door's interior, demanding to be let out of the house.

A nagging suspicion that someone was near fell over her as soon as she stepped inside. Chills ran up and down her arms. She lifted the NVGs, set them on top of her head, and glanced around. The coast was clear.

She tore through the kitchen drawers in search of scissors, yanking a few open so hard that they skidded to the floor. Nothing. Her last resort would be to settle for a knife with a serrated blade, but she preferred scissors over a knife. It would eat up too much time if she had to saw through each of the ropes individually. A box cutter was her first choice as it would slice through the ropes like paper, though she couldn't afford to go scavenging through the house in search of one.

Mercy had just decided to settle for the serrated knife when she had that feeling again. This time, she *knew* someone was standing in the kitchen.

Directly behind her.

Damn, she didn't have time for this now. She plucked a knife from the wooden block on top of the counter, prepared to confront the intruder with a quick jab and then make a break for the trailhead. She'd free Piper first and worry about the intruder later.

Knife at the ready, she spun around. There, standing before her, was the man in the photo on the nightstand—the same man who had posed with all those horses in the basement. It didn't make any sense. The man in the photos was Piper's husband, Tim.

Tim was dead.

All sorts of crazy ideas raced through her mind at that moment. Maybe Tim wasn't dead. Maybe he worked for the CIA and was forced to fake his own death for reasons of international espionage. Or maybe Tim was really Shadow, returning to the forefront after three long years to exact revenge on...She paused, thinking. To exact revenge on whom? Okay, scratch that one.

"What do you want?" she finally asked. Tim's form flickered like fuzzy TV reception, which was when Mercy realized she could actually see *through* him to the refrigerator on the other side.

Tim stared back, his eyes dark and wide and full of urgency. *Follow me.*

Had she really heard that, or was the blood loss finally starting to take its toll? Tim's mouth hadn't even moved. The snowy form turned and loped away. She followed Tim to the living room where they stopped beside a pine armoire with moose and black bear stenciled on its doors.

Tim turned to face her. *Open it.*

Mercy did. Hundreds of CDs flanked a state-of-the-art stereo system. One small drawer lay in the center. She wrapped her fingers around the wrought-iron handle and slid the drawer out. Tea light candles, incense, and matches filled the drawer. A bright orange box cutter was tucked along the right side.

She threw the knife to the floor and lifted the box cutter out of the drawer carefully, reverently, the pain in her shoulder receding... as if she were suddenly King Arthur sliding Excalibur out of stone. She held it in her hand, the metal casing cool against her palm.

Go.

That single word floated across her mind like a sailboat on a windless afternoon.

Now!

That one packed more of a punch, reverberating through her with such force that it left her with a headache. When she finally looked up again, Tim was gone.

She slipped the box cutter in her pocket, glanced at her watch, and bolted out of the cabin. Just over six minutes remained. She lowered the NVGs and ducked behind the shed to find footing on the trailhead once again.

The winds had died down a bit, but not by much. Snowflakes marched down from the sky, obstructing her view of the uneven trail. Looked like spring was going to be late again this year.

She ran, bleeding, dizzy, exhausted, and totally depleted of reserves. Her mouth was so dry, she couldn't even work up enough saliva to spit. Her shoes kept slipping out from underneath her on the thin layer of slush.

She passed the time rehearsing exactly what she was going to do when she arrived at the tree. Something told her she couldn't afford to waste one second. Not a moment's hesitation was allowed when it came to cutting the ropes and getting Piper out of there. She probably wouldn't be able to walk. Mercy would have to carry her and put as much distance between them and the bomb as possible.

She didn't bother checking her watch anymore. Doing that would force her to take her eyes from the trail, and that could cost Piper dearly. From here on out, she wouldn't allow herself the luxury of keeping time. It didn't matter anyway. If she made it to the tree with just two seconds to spare, then she would spend those last two seconds at Piper's side. Fighting like hell to free her.

CHAPTER FIFTEEN

Emily heard the *tick, tick* of the turn signal as the van changed lanes. An eighteen-wheeler roared past like a grumbling dinosaur. They'd been traveling on a highway for a while now. Her bare feet tingled with the engine's vibrations. The dog lay curled at her side, still sleeping.

The van's speed dropped. Emily climbed to her knees and peered out the window. She caught a glimpse of a green rest stop sign with the words *Gas & Food*. Her stomach growled. Maybe the bad man had taken her request for food and water seriously.

He pulled into the rest stop and sped past a restaurant, past a gas station, and kept driving all the way to the end of the lot. He parked the van in the very last space. No cars or people were in sight. She scooted away from the window and sank back down to the floor.

He cut the engine and slid the curtain aside. "Will you behave while I'm gone, little warrior?"

She nodded.

"Do you know what will happen if you try to escape?" he asked, sliding the gun from the holster on his shoulder.

She glanced down at his pointy red shoes. He was wearing black slacks with red pinstripes, a matching vest, and a white shirt with long, puffy sleeves. A black Charlie Chaplin hat sat on top of his head. Hair as white as the walls in her bedroom poked out from both sides of the hat, making his neatly trimmed beard and moustache look dark by comparison. Mismatched eyes—one blue and one brown—stared back at her, strange and wild.

She lowered her eyes. "You'll hurt more people," she whispered.
"I'll shoot and kill everyone who tries to help you."

Something shiny caught her eye as he slid his gun back inside
the holster: gold cuff links with a symbol she'd seen somewhere
before.

He shut the curtain and climbed out of the van. She was listening
to the tapping of his shoes grow more distant on the pavement
outside when she remembered where she had seen the symbol. She
turned her wrist over and looked down. It was the same symbol as
the one on her bracelet.

Her dad had given her the bracelet for her tenth birthday. She
didn't usually wear jewelry because it got in the way of playing
sports, but there was something about the bracelet that she just
couldn't resist. The symbol that was stitched into the center with
black and white thread had stirred something inside her.

At first, she'd kept the bracelet in her pocket, taking it out from
time to time to show her classmates. She swore she felt it burning
against her thigh one day during math class, so she went to the
bathroom, emptied her pockets, and pulled down her pants. There,
burned into her freckles, was the bracelet's mysterious symbol.

Curious about what the symbol meant, she'd looked it up in her
school library. It turned out to be an ancient Chinese symbol, more
commonly known as the yin-yang: a perfect circle filled with two
rounded teardrops.

The symbol on the bad man's cuff links was the same, but the
colors were different. The yin-yang's traditional colors of black and
white had been replaced with red and gold. A red teardrop filled one
half of the circle, and a gold teardrop filled the other. Each half had
one dot of the other's color in its middle. According to the Chinese,
those dots meant that each half contained the seeds of its opposite.
She remembered reading that the interaction of yin and yang allowed
change to take place in the world. She didn't know why, but she had
a feeling the symbol on the cuff links was somehow important.

The dog suddenly jerked awake and sat up beside her. It looked
around, confused, until its eyes met Emily's.

"Oh, hi. You're awake." She backed away a little, hoping it
wasn't going to bite her.

The dog tucked its tail, went to the window, and whined.

"I don't know where the bad man took you from, but you're here now. I don't know where we are exactly. He kidnapped me, too. What's your name? I don't even know if you're a girl dog or a boy dog." She knew she had a tendency to babble when she was nervous, but talking to the dog like it was a person was taking it to a whole new level. So far, so good, though. It wasn't biting her face off or anything. Yet.

The dog turned away from the window, stepped over to her, and lowered its head. She saw the name *Bobby* stitched into the red collar. It was almost as if he understood what she had said and was now showing her the collar. But that was impossible.

"Your name is Bobby?"

He lifted his head, peered into her eyes, and wagged his tail at the mention of his name.

"So you're a boy dog. It's nice to meet you, Bobby. I'm Emily."

He licked her on the chin.

"I think the bad man—that's what I call him because he didn't tell me his real name and I'm too afraid to ask—I think he went to get some food for me. I hope that's what he's doing because I'm really hungry. I'll share with you if he brings me something."

She wanted to reach out to Bobby, but she didn't want to startle him. It felt so good to have him there and not be alone anymore. "I'd really like to pet you, but you don't know me. I don't want to scare you."

As if on cue, he lowered his body and nudged her hand with his muzzle.

She stroked his head and back. "You're soft. And you smell good. Whoever had you must've taken really good care of you," she went on. "My dad takes good care of me, too." Then she remembered her dad wasn't alive anymore. And neither was Bubbles. For the first time, she realized that she'd never, ever see them again. She buried her face in her hands and started to cry.

She felt as Bobby pressed his warm body against hers. When he laid his head on her shoulder like a hug, she wrapped her arms around him and cried into his fur.

❖

Breathing hard and numb with cold, Mercy skidded to a stop and dropped to her knees in front of Piper. She didn't even bother checking the timer on the bomb. She preferred not to know how close she was to having her body parts catapulted through these woods.

Piper was leaning back against the tree. Her eyes were closed. Strands of wet hair clung to her face and neck. She looked so pale. "Piper? Still with me?" But she was unconscious.

Mercy's hands shook as she started cutting through the ropes around Piper's chest and stomach. Snowflakes gathered on the surface of the NVGs, obstructing her vision. She couldn't afford to waste precious seconds cleaning them off, so she relied mostly on touch.

She reached out and felt for the ropes around Piper's right wrist, cutting through them one by one. Her fingers were nearly frozen, but the razor blade sliced through each rope easily. "You better not die after dragging me all the way out here." Mercy leaned over her and started cutting through the ropes on the other side, relieved to feel Piper's warm breath against her neck. "Just for the record"— Mercy's teeth chattered—"all you've been so far is a royal pain in my ass." She sliced through the last rope and felt around to make certain that nothing else was attached.

Couldn't be more than a few seconds left on the timer. Mercy wrapped one arm behind Piper's shoulders and the other underneath her legs. Her shoulder throbbed as she stood. Everything went black. She held Piper in her arms and fought to stay conscious, angrily shaking her head, waiting for the blood to catch up.

Time moved slowly. She turned and ran from the tree as fast as she dared. The slush-covered ground spat up at her with each footfall. Her toe caught on an exposed tree root. She compensated by transferring the bulk of her weight to her other foot, but the trail was just too slippery. She held Piper against her chest as they both went down, her own elbows taking the brunt of the impact.

Searing pain shot across her ribcage. The edges of her vision grew fuzzy. "*No!* Not now," she growled, willing herself to stay alert. She tore off the NVGs and grabbed for Piper. She felt warm breath against her neck as she cradled her. Piper was ice cold. She would die if Mercy allowed herself to lose consciousness now.

She was rising to her knees when the bomb exploded. It sounded like a rocket launching. She hit the ground and shielded Piper's body.

The ground trembled. Debris rained down all around them. The tree peeled apart with an audible crack, like a giant splitting wood with his bare hands. Mercy looked up into the nighttime sky. An ancient oak staggered in the air as it scanned the forest floor in search of a place to land.

Then slowly, lazily, it began to topple. She wrapped her arms around Piper and rolled her body aside. The sound of snapping branches and cracking wood filled the night as the oak wiped out every other tree in its path. Several thundered to the ground, one right after the other. She kept her body over Piper's, half expecting a tree to land in the middle of her back and break her in two.

Mercy opened her eyes. The forest was silent, the moon bright. It had stopped snowing. She lifted her head and looked around. Dozens of pine trees littered the forest floor on both sides. If she had rolled just six inches to the left or a foot to the right, they both would have been crushed.

She put her ear to Piper's lips. She wasn't breathing. Mercy checked for a pulse and found none. "Don't you dare!" she yelled, rising to her knees. She locked her hands together and started chest compressions. "One, two, three, four, five..." She counted aloud until she reached thirty. "Breathe."

Blood dripped from the tourniquet on her shoulder. She tilted Piper's head back, pinched her nose, and gave her two breaths. She knelt over Piper's body, repeating the cycle. Her lips met Piper's as she exhaled into her mouth. Mercy slid two fingers from Piper's throat to her carotid artery and felt for a pulse. There it was. A heartbeat. She brought her ear to Piper's lips and watched her chest rise with each inhalation.

All she had to do now was get Piper back to the cabin and warm her up. Without passing out during the mile trek to get there. "Cakewalk," she told herself.

She lifted Piper in her arms and eased her way to a standing position. The forest was aglow with moonlit shadows. She carefully sidestepped fallen trees until she found the trail once again. A cold breeze urged her along from behind.

On the move, she studied Piper. She was toned and lithe, her muscles softly defined under creamy white skin. Piper's body felt good in her arms. It was then that Mercy realized she was attracted to this beautiful woman. In fact, since she had a nasty habit of being honest with herself, she had felt that attraction building from the moment she'd set eyes on her in that photo.

Mercy looked away as pangs of guilt superseded the pain in her body. For the last ten years, the only woman she'd ever thought about was Anna.

She would never forget Carmichael's expression as she'd stepped inside her office that fateful day two years ago. As soon as she'd closed the door, Mercy *knew*.

Anna was buying a pastrami sandwich at the deli on the corner of Tenth and Second when an armed man strutted in and started shooting up the place. Standing in line behind her was a pregnant woman, a stranger. Anna turned, threw her to the ground, and shielded her from gunfire with her own body. In testament to Anna's quick thinking, both mother and baby survived.

Anna, however, wasn't quite so fortunate. She died at the deli that day from a single .40 caliber bullet that had lodged in her spine. The worst part about it was they never even caught the son of a bitch who did it.

Tears blurred Mercy's vision as she passed the shed and jogged to the kitchen door. She didn't stop until she reached Piper's bedroom. She set her on the bed, covered her with a comforter, and checked to make sure she was still breathing. Piper's lips and eyelids were blue, her skin like ice to the touch.

She decided against calling for an ambulance. The local authorities would get involved and ask questions that Mercy couldn't answer. There was also the matter of George's body to explain—or what was left of it after the bomb exploded. Shadow's threat was clear. He would kill anyone who helped in the investigation. Mercy refused to put anyone else at risk.

She stacked some logs in the fireplace and started a fire. The heat felt good on her body. She grabbed a sleeping bag off the closet shelf, unzipped it, and set it on the floor in front of the fire. The room already felt warmer.

Piper's breathing was shallow, her pulse steady but slow. She lifted her from the bed, carried her to the sleeping bag, and laid her inside.

Too exhausted to do anything but lie down, Mercy stretched out on her back and held Piper in the crook of her arm, manipulating her body so they had maximum contact for warmth. Her hair smelled like raspberries. It had been a long time since she'd felt a woman against her. Piper fit perfectly.

She felt Piper's heart beating against her own chest, felt her warm breath against the sensitive skin on her neck. It was almost like their bodies were made for each other. She could lie here forever, breathing Piper in as she slept.

Mercy's entire body ached from the recent battle with George. Logs hissed and crackled in the fireplace. The heat from the flames made her eyelids heavy. She couldn't let herself fall asleep. She needed to stay awake...stay alert...keep checking on Piper.

Shadows danced on the ceiling. The smell of burning wood filled the room. She could almost imagine the past two years had been nothing but a terrible dream, and it was actually Anna snuggled there beside her. Maybe she'd close her eyes, after all. Just for a little while...

CHAPTER SIXTEEN

Mercy awoke to the sound of a familiar voice. Lou was leaning over her. Salt-and-pepper eyebrows, unkempt and wild, bristled behind wire-rimmed glasses. They reminded her of giant furry caterpillars—the weird ones in Africa with outrageous hairdos to ward off predators. She tried to laugh, but it came out as a series of wet coughs.

Lou was talking, his brow creased with worry. "…lost a lot of blood…weak pulse…Stay with me, Parker."

Everything went black.

When Mercy came to, Anna was sitting on the edge of the bed in a long white nightgown. Golden locks spilled over her shoulders. She was smiling. A leather-bound book sat in her lap, the cover cracked and threadbare.

"Anna?" This must be a dream, but she'd never had one that felt so real. "I'm dreaming, aren't I?"

Anna took Mercy's hand and held it between her own. "No, Mercy. It's really me."

Anna looked exactly the way she remembered her. Mercy reached out and touched her cheek. Her skin felt warm. "I've missed you, Anna."

"I've missed you, too. There were so many times I wanted you to know that I was still close by."

"It's been hard without you," Mercy said. "I always thought we'd grow old and wrinkly together."

"Speak for yourself. I would have aged gracefully." Anna turned and looked behind her. "How's Lou?"

"He misses Jane, but he's getting along." She squeezed Anna's hand. "Have you seen her?" Jane had died of a stroke just three months before Anna was killed.

"Yes. Jane was waiting for me at the deli that day. In fact, she made me promise to pass along a message."

"Let me guess." She thought about Lou's eyebrows. "She wants me to get him a pair of tweezers for his birthday." Mercy smiled as Anna threw her head back and laughed. She would give anything to hear that laugh every day for the rest of her life.

Anna tilted her head sideways, the way she used to when she was about to say something serious. "Lou's been thinking about opening a restaurant. Jane wants him to know it's a wonderful idea."

"A restaurant? Hmm, I didn't know."

"Well"—she slapped Mercy upside the head—"he might have mentioned something if you'd visited more often."

"Okay, okay. Point taken. Isn't there a rule in the afterlife about being nice to the loved ones you left behind?"

Anna grinned. "Just be thankful I'm coming to you like this instead of haunting your ass."

There were so many questions Mercy wanted to ask her. She could hardly think straight. "That woman and her baby would have died if it hadn't been for you." She sat up. "What in the world were you thinking, babe?"

"When that man came in and started shooting, I just asked myself what you would've done." She shrugged. "That's the answer I came up with. Everything happened so fast, Mercy." Anna reached over to caress her cheek. "I didn't feel any pain."

"That woman went into labor a few days later and gave birth to a healthy baby girl." She looked down, feeling the lump in her throat. "She named her after you."

"I know." Anna squeezed her hand.

"How come I get the feeling I can't come with you?"

Anna took a long moment to answer. "It's your choice, Mercy. No one will force you to stay if you don't want to." She glanced at the book in her lap and opened it to the first page. "I'm here to make you aware of what will happen if you choose to leave, so listen closely." The urgency in her voice made the hair on the back of Mercy's neck stand up. "These are things you'll want to remember."

Anna read for hours. Mercy watched her lips move as solemn green eyes shifted from one page to the next. Anna told her things she didn't want to hear. The more she read, the more obvious the choice became. So many people were depending on her. Finished, Anna closed the book. The silence grew heavy.

"Will I ever see you again?" Mercy finally asked.

Almond shaped eyes returned her gaze, forthright and strong. "Someday." She turned her head suddenly, as if someone had called to her. "It's time for me to go."

"Not yet. Stay with me a little longer." Never taking her eyes from Anna's, she scooted over to make room on the bed. "Please."

Anna stretched out alongside her and nestled into the crook of her arm. She lifted her head and whispered in her ear. "There's a woman who needs you, Mercy. Don't push her away because of me. Loving another woman won't ever change what you and I shared."

Mercy held her against her chest, running her fingers through Anna's hair like she used to. Tears ran down her cheeks as she closed her eyes and drifted off.

When Mercy came to, her chest felt heavy, and every part of her body hurt like hell. The room lay mostly in shadow, lit only by a meager fire in the fireplace. It took her a moment to realize she was in Piper's bed. She could still smell faint traces of her on the blankets under her chin.

Lou straightened in the chair beside the bed.

Mercy licked her lips, tasting blood. "How long have I been asleep?" she whispered.

"Three days." Lou seemed distracted as he reached for the glass on the nightstand and held the straw to Mercy's lips. "You've lost a lot of blood. You have a high fever. Truth is, you're not doing well."

She took small sips. "Could've fooled me. Never felt better."

Lou looked away, silent. That, more than the pain in her body, told Mercy everything she needed to know. It was bad.

"I've been treating you myself," Lou said.

Pill bottles, bandages, creams, and towels filled every inch of the nightstand. Mercy heard herself wheezing. Her lungs burned viciously.

"Shadow called," Lou went on. "Told me if I took you to the hospital, I could kiss Emily and Bobby good-bye. It was a tough decision, Parker. I knew what *I* wanted to do, but then I asked myself what *you* would want." He reached over and plucked a tissue from the box on the nightstand. "I started you on an antibiotic as soon as I got here, but it doesn't seem to be doing much good. Your shoulder is badly infected." He took off his glasses and wiped at each lens.

Mercy said nothing. She laid her hand over Lou's and squeezed. "Is it time to send for Dr. Kevorkian?"

"Glad you find this funny." Lou frowned. "Can't you be serious for one damn minute? This is your life we're talking about!" He shot up from the chair.

Mercy grabbed his arm before he could storm off. "Hang on a sec," she said, remembering her dream about Anna. "Something I need to ask you."

"Anything," Lou said, taking her hand.

"Are you thinking about opening a restaurant?"

"What? Why are you asking me that?"

"I saw Anna," she whispered. "She gave me a message to pass along. Jane thinks the restaurant is a good idea."

Lou's mouth hung open as he lowered himself to the chair.

"Oh, and I'm not going to die," she added.

"She said that, too?"

"Not exactly." Mercy wheezed. "I don't remember much else, but I do know that I'm not going anywhere for a good long time."

"Then why am I sitting here holding your hand?"

"You were just about to confess your love to me?"

Lou let go, stood, and shoved both hands in his pockets.

A soft knock sounded at the door as Piper poked her head inside. "Thought I heard voices. Is she awake?"

"Affirmative." Lou frowned down at Mercy. "Despite my efforts to the contrary."

The doorbell rang. Lou reached for his holster on the corner of the chair, slipped it over one shoulder, and moved toward the door. "Stay with Parker," he said to Piper. "I'll go see who it is."

Nodding, she followed Lou, locking the door behind him. She withdrew the gun from her holster and moved to Mercy's side.

A series of wet coughs erupted from Mercy's chest. She hated being stuck in bed, useless to everyone if Lou was in trouble downstairs. She pointed to the chair beside the bed. "Please, sit. You're making me nervous."

Piper sat but kept her eyes on the door. She set the gun in her lap and tied her hair in a ponytail. Her jeans looked faded and comfortable. A charcoal sweater accentuated the gray in her eyes, and a small silver locket hung just above the V-neck. It was the symbol of yin and yang.

"Where'd you get that?" Mercy asked, pointing to the necklace.

Piper's hand moved to the locket. She rubbed it between thumb and forefinger. "My grandmother gave this to me when I was a little girl. She said it had magical powers."

"Yeah?" Mercy raised an eyebrow. "What kinds of magical powers?"

"She said it would bring me great adventure and change my life forever." Piper smiled, her gaze far away. "She also told me that my soul mate would have the same symbol."

A knock at the door made her rise to her feet. Mercy didn't get the chance to tell her about the yin-yang tattoo on her own shoulder.

"It's okay." Lou's voice drifted in from the other side of the door. "Open up."

Piper fumbled with the lock and stepped back.

"Don't be alarmed," Lou said. "There's someone here who wants to help. He says he knows Parker."

An old man limped across the room. "Hello, Mercy." He hung his hat on one corner of the chair, leaned his cane up against the nightstand, and sat primly. "My apologies for not coming sooner. I was forced to wait until your choice was made." He studied Mercy with one blue eye and one brown eye. "I know it was a difficult decision to let her go. You have my deepest respect and sympathy." The old man bowed his head.

This was a little on the weird side. Made even weirder by their matching mismatched eyes. Other than her brother, she had never met anyone who shared the condition. "Do I know you?"

"My name is Lucent." He touched Mercy's arm and closed his eyes. "An infection has spread from the bullet wound to your lungs. You have two fractured ribs, one dislocated vertebra, and a broken finger." He opened his eyes.

This guy could just be blowing smoke up her ass, but something told her he wasn't. Sure hurt like hell in all those places. "You forgot the headache."

Lucent glanced over his shoulder at Lou. "We must get started soon. Where is the brother?"

"Raze should be back any minute now. He left to get some supplies."

"Raze is here, too?" Mercy asked, throwing daggers around the room. She hated the thought of people fussing over her like this.

"You were on your deathbed." Lou shrugged. "So I called him."

The doorbell rang, followed by pounding on the door and Raze's familiar voice shouting, "Hey, open up! I'm freezing my ass off out here!"

"Speak of the devil." Piper rolled her eyes. "I'll get it."

Mercy turned her attention back to the old man. "What is it exactly that we need to get started on?"

Lucent cupped his hands and blew into them. "Why, healing your injuries, of course."

"Oh, right. Of course." She raised an eyebrow at Lou. "Don't know what I was thinking."

Raze's booted feet thundered up the stairs. The metal zipper on his leather jacket clanged against the doorknob when he stopped short in the doorway and peered into the bedroom. "Sis? You awake?" He looked like hell. He obviously hadn't shaved or changed his clothes in a while. He strolled over to the foot of the bed. "How ya feeling?"

"Better than you look," Mercy said, wrinkling her nose, "and I definitely smell better than you."

"Love you, too, sis." Raze flipped her the bird, turning to Lou. "She gonna be okay?"

Lou nodded at the old man. "I suspect she will now, yes."

"Who're you?" Raze asked rudely.

The old man stood. "Forgive me. My name is Lucent." He looked from Lou to Raze to Piper, and then finally down at Mercy. "Everyone is here," he said with a satisfied smile. "We can begin."

CHAPTER SEVENTEEN

Emily let go of Bobby and wiped her face with the shirt of her pajamas. She felt like a big crybaby. "Thanks, Bobby. I'm not usually like that."

He peered into her eyes, whined, and gave her a lick on her chin.

"I'm okay. Just a little sad, that's all."

Something at the front of the van suddenly caught his interest. Sniffing excitedly at the air, he trotted over and nudged the plastic curtain aside with his muzzle.

"Bobby, no!"

He withdrew his nose, looked back at her, and snorted. He poked his head through to the front again and disappeared behind the curtain.

Maybe he smelled some food. "Bobby, come back!" She didn't want him to do anything that would make the bad man angry.

Tail wagging, he returned and sat in front of her with a book sticking out of his mouth. He set it in her lap and looked up at her.

"Where'd you find this?" The book's brown leather cover was worn. She thumbed through the pages. Everything was written in a combination of numbers and letters. Looked like some kind of secret code. The name *Amber* was written on the inside back cover. "We need to return this before the bad man comes back and sees that it's missing." She didn't know what the consequences would be for

Bobby if the bad man discovered the missing book. She decided she didn't want to find out. She couldn't stand the thought of the bad man hurting Bobby. She'd confess to taking the book herself if it came to that.

Book in hand, she started making her way to the front of the van when she heard the bad man's shoes tapping on the pavement outside. He was close. Her only choice now was to hide the book. She looked around. But where?

As if reading her thoughts, Bobby plucked the book from her hands with his mouth, set it on the floor, and curled up on top of it in the blink of an eye. It was completely hidden from view.

No way! she thought silently. *Did you just hear what I was thinking?*

Keeping the rest of his body as still as a statue, Bobby wagged his tail.

The bad man opened the back door and threw a McDonald's bag at her, along with several bottles of water. "Thanks," Emily said, surprised he'd brought her some food and water. One of the bottles struck Bobby on the head, but he didn't budge from his perch on top of the book.

Without a word, the bad man slammed the door shut, and they were on the road again before she knew it.

She gathered the water bottles and turned her attention back to Bobby. *Can you really hear what I'm thinking?* she wondered.

Bobby rose and sat in front of her, as if waiting for her to go on.

Emily could hardly believe what she was about to do. She covered her mouth with her hands to make sure she didn't say anything out loud. *Lie down*, she commanded.

Never taking his eyes from hers, he wagged his tail and lowered his body to the ground.

Coincidence, she thought. *Do you know how to roll over?*

Bobby rolled over for her, exposing his belly like a goof.

All the way over, showoff.

He righted himself and looked at her expectantly.

❖

Lou, Raze, and Piper stood around the bed. Mercy studied each of their faces as they listened to the old man.

Lucent sat in the chair beside the bed, his hands folded neatly in his lap. "I am older than any of you would believe and nearing the end of my time here. My power to heal is at its weakest. For the first time in my life, I am unable to perform this task alone—"

"You're gonna heal my sister?" Raze snorted. "You actually expect us to believe that?"

"No, Raze," the old man replied. "*We* will heal your sister."

"Just like that, huh? *Poof*, and she's all better. Don't we need some magic fairy dust or something?"

The old man took so long to answer that Mercy wondered if he was ignoring the question altogether. He finally stood from the chair and met Raze eye to eye. "Will you do me the favor of lifting your shirt, young man? I'd like you to show everyone that laceration on your abdomen."

Raze looked down and examined his own shirt—probably for telltale bloodstains—but the shirt was clean. "How'd you know that?"

"There are tiny bits of glass embedded in your skin from the neck of the beer bottle. That fight at the bar was unnecessary, but I understand why you felt the need to come to your friend's defense."

For the first time ever, Mercy saw her brother rendered speechless.

"That wound needs to be cleaned and sutured. Please, lift your shirt and remove the bandage."

Raze did. Fresh blood trickled down as he peeled the bandage away. The cut was definitely deep enough to require stitches.

The old man reached across the bed. "Give me your hand, Raze."

Raze glanced around self-consciously. "Just as long as you don't start singing 'Kumbaya.'"

The wound began knitting itself up the second their hands touched. Mercy watched in amazement as the edges of Raze's skin melded together until all that remained was a faint pink line.

The old man released his grip. "There. That should feel better." Everyone watched as he opened his hand and emptied tiny shards of glass into a Styrofoam cup on the nightstand.

Raze looked up, a new respect in his eyes. "You can do that for my sister?"

The old man laid a hand on Mercy's shoulder. "With the help of everyone here, yes."

Without another word, Lou held Piper's hand, Piper took Raze's, and Raze reached out for Lucent.

Mercy felt a rush of energy course through her body the moment their hands connected. The throbbing in her finger ceased, the shooting pains down her neck and back subsided, and the heaviness in her chest floated away like a hot air balloon. She took a deep breath. Her cracked ribs felt whole again. The constant ache in her shoulder where the bullet had pierced her gradually diminished. It felt like microscopic robots were hard at work beneath her skin, knitting her cells back together again.

The old man slid his hand from Mercy's shoulder. New energy coursed through her veins. It was a powerful feeling. Mercy sensed she would never be the same.

Lucent watched her, a knowing look in his eye. "You may feel some tenderness for the next few hours." He reached for his cane. "But that should subside by daybreak—"

Without warning, the old man crumpled to the floor. Raze bent over, scooped him up, and carried him to the sofa in the corner.

Mercy pushed the covers aside and stepped across the room. Still a little stiff, she knelt. "Lucent? Can you hear me?"

The old man finally opened his eyes. "That drained me more than I'd imagined." He chuckled, patting Mercy's cheek with one bony, trembling hand. "It is good to see the color back in your face, young woman." He struggled to sit up. "My assistant, Neshera, is waiting outside in the car. Will someone fetch her for me?"

"I'll go." Piper turned and headed out of the room. Lou followed after her.

"There is no need to worry. I simply need time to recover." The old man looked from Mercy to Raze. "You two have many questions, I'm sure. We can discuss the coming events over a cup of tea before the warmth of a fire. Your friends are welcome to join us."

Raze helped the old man downstairs while Mercy showered. She was drying off when she heard a soft knock at the bedroom door. She wrapped the towel around herself, still trying to process what had happened. "Come in."

Piper stepped inside with a pile of clothes. "Thought you might want something to wear." She walked to the bed, dropped a pair of hiking boots on the floor, and set out jeans, shirts, sweaters, and socks. "I figured you'd wake up sooner or later, so I guessed your size and had fun shopping." She withdrew a pair of scissors from her back pocket and started clipping off the tags.

"Well, there goes my plan to make a toga out of the bedsheet."

"Everything should fit," Piper said, tucking a loose strand of raven hair behind her ear. "If not, I'll get the special pink flowered sheets and fashion the toga myself. Underwear and sports bras are in there." She pointed to a shopping bag on the bed. Tags in hand, she turned to face Mercy with a look of surprise. "Wow, that's amazing!"

"I know. Lucent patched me up pretty good, huh?"

"That's not what I meant." She stepped over to examine her skin more closely. "Parker, look at your scar. It's the yin-yang symbol." She held out her necklace. "They're the same."

Mercy had forgotten all about the tattoo. When she looked down, she realized the bullet wound had overlapped the tattoo exactly. No trace of the tattoo remained. In its place was a raised pink scar in the shape of yin and yang.

"What do you make of that?" Piper asked.

"I must be the soul mate your grandmother was talking about."

Piper swatted her on the arm.

Maybe the bullet had reacted with the ink in her skin and somehow reconfigured the tattoo into a permanent scar...except the scar she was left with was much larger than the tattoo. She looked at Piper's necklace. She was right. The scar was an exact replica of the symbol on her pendant. They stared at one another in silence.

"I haven't had a chance to thank you," Piper said finally, "for saving me. What you did in the woods, risking your life like that—"

"Did he touch you?" For her own sanity, Mercy needed to know if George had gotten the chance to rape Piper. "Did he assault you at all before I got there?"

"No, not that I remember. I went down fast after he darted me with what I'm assuming was a pretty potent sedative. Then I saw

Bobby get darted. He went down fast, too." Her eyes teared up at the thought of Bobby. "Lou and Raze looked everywhere for Bobby but never found him. I just hope he's okay."

"Me, too," was all Mercy could think to say. She was relieved beyond measure that she had gotten to Piper before George did.

"Next thing I remember," Piper went on, "was waking up tied to a tree. But now for the important question." She crossed her arms and sat down on the bed. "Did you rescue me just because you knew I was naked?"

"We all need a little motivation now and then to get the job done," Mercy conceded, still standing there in nothing but a towel. She eyed the clothes on the bed longingly. She had a feeling Piper wasn't leaving anytime soon. "How about we continue this little chat later…when I'm fully clothed?"

"Now works better for me."

"But I'm standing here in a towel."

"Right, you are," Piper said with a satisfied smirk.

"I see. You're trying to make me uncomfortable because I saw you naked. Well, it won't work because I'm completely comfortable with my body," she said, trying to get one up on Piper. She dropped the towel. "There, we even?"

Undaunted, Piper let her eyes roam freely over Mercy's body.

Lou gave a quick knock and opened the bedroom door, catching full view of Mercy's backside. "Ah, my eyes!" was all she heard from behind her before the door slammed shut again.

Piper bent down to pick up the towel and handed it to Mercy. "Now we're even." With one last, lingering look at the scar on Mercy's shoulder, she left the room and closed the door softly behind her.

Mercy had her work cut out with that one. Shaking her head, she went to the mirror and examined her scar. She felt branded. Raze had the same symbol tattooed on his shoulder. They'd gotten them together on their eighteenth birthday.

She plucked a long-sleeved shirt, jeans, and a forest green sweater from the pile on the bed, grateful to be wearing clothes instead of a pink flowered toga.

"You want coffee or tea?" Lou asked as soon as she set foot in the kitchen.

"Load me up with the hard stuff."

"Coffee it is." Lou readied the coffeemaker while Piper set out six identical cranberry-colored mugs.

Lucent watched from the comfort of the kitchen table, cane in hand. Still looking a bit unsteady, he caught Mercy's eye and winked.

A woman stood at the table, unwrapping each tea bag. She glanced over her shoulder at Mercy. Intense hazel eyes regarded her. "My name's Neshera, assistant to this foolish old man." She nodded in Lucent's direction. "I'm glad you're feeling better, but *he* should be more careful," she said, clearly for the old man's benefit.

Raze stepped out from the bathroom in the hallway, the legs of his torn jeans wet from where he'd dried his hands. "Sis, we ordered Chinese. You must be starving, huh?" He opened a cabinet and took down some plates.

Mercy looked around the kitchen in awe. She felt as though she belonged here with these people, like she'd been waiting for this moment her entire life. They were a united front, a family. These five people had come together and saved her life—a debt she could never repay.

She had the uncanny feeling they were readying themselves for some kind of battle. She suspected the old man felt it, too. Mercy tried to push the rest of what she sensed aside, but she couldn't. It had already surfaced like some dark and terrible secret.

She didn't know who, but one of the people in this room would not survive. And the thought of losing someone else she cared about scared the hell out of her.

CHAPTER EIGHTEEN

Empty cartons of Chinese food littered the kitchen table. Everyone ate in silence. Mercy knew she needed the nourishment to regain her strength, but she didn't have much of an appetite. She pushed the food around on her plate, her mind on Emily for the duration of the meal. It had been three days since Shadow's phone call. She wondered if Emily was still alive.

She and Piper cleared the table, Raze started a fire, and Lou and Neshera filled each of their mugs with coffee or tea. They all settled on the huge L-shaped sofa in the living room.

Lucent cleared his throat. "What I'm about to share with you is humanity's deepest, darkest secret. I trust that each of you will take great care to guard this secret, just as I have throughout my life." He reached for his cane, stood, and paced in front of the fire. "My twin brother and I were born in 1867—over one hundred and fifty years ago. In fact, we were about your age"—he turned to Mercy and Raze—"when we learned of our destiny. Our predecessors, Cozen and Candor, took us from the lives we once knew and burdened us with what I am about to tell you. All I can offer you now is my most sincere apology, as this is sure to weigh heavy on your souls." He rubbed his cane with his thumb and resumed pacing.

"Every one hundred and fifty years, a new pair of twins is called upon for the benefit of humanity. These twins work closely together, striving toward the accomplishment of one goal: to contribute good to the world with as little suffering as possible. Traditionally, one twin paves the way to bring about change through…rather tragic circumstances. The other continues the work from there, bestowing healing and goodness to as many lives as possible."

Piper and Lou turned their eyes on Mercy and Raze. They all shifted uncomfortably.

"My brother and I have had to make some very difficult decisions over the years," the old man went on. "What sustained us was the knowledge that The Greater Good far outweighs the individual." He looked at each of their faces. "Unfortunately, the callousness behind those words does not alter their truth. Before you pass judgment, allow me to share our latest endeavor.

"My brother's final mission of change was to take the life of a little girl so that children in another part of the world could be saved."

Piper set her mug back down on the coffee table without taking a sip. "Your brother *murdered* an innocent child?" she asked, looking just as shocked as Mercy felt.

The old man stopped pacing and looked at Piper solemnly. "Please, before you pass judgment, allow me to share the story in its entirety."

Piper shook her head. "If you're going to stand there and try to justify what your brother did—"

Lou reached over and put a hand on her shoulder. "You saw how he healed Parker. Let's just hear what he has to say."

The old man furrowed his brow. "My brother took this little girl's life in the most humane way possible. I assure you, she did not feel any pain." He stroked his neatly trimmed beard. "I was visiting a small Ugandan village at the time, where I met a four-year-old girl by the name of Jendy."

Mercy's head snapped up. She thought back on her phone conversation with Captain Wilson. The Wilsons were in the process of adopting a little girl with the same name.

Over the course of the next twenty minutes, Lucent told them what the captain had confided to Mercy just days before. The old man explained how Jendy had ended up in the care of a woman who couldn't afford to feed her. He told them of the other thirty-five orphans in her care and how she often sacrificed her own meals to feed as many children as she could. "I took Jendy away with me that day, secure in the knowledge that I would find her a home with the couple who had just lost their only child. Not only did they adopt little Jendy, but they promised to make it their mission to find loving families for each of those orphans—twenty-three of whom would have died within the year from malnutrition." The old man looked around the room. "I ask you now, if you were in my shoes, what would you have done? Allow a single child to go on living at the expense of so many others?"

"You could have gotten another couple to adopt Jendy and found families for the other children yourself," Piper said. "That way, *no one* had to die."

"Unfortunately, the world we live in forces us to choose one over the other." He bowed his head. "The situation is made even clearer since I am privy to...certain information."

Lou stared into his coffee mug. "Can you be more specific?"

"There are things I know that I cannot explain—"

"Like how you knew about the fight at the bar," Raze volunteered.

"Precisely." The old man perched on the arm of the sofa. "Every living thing in this world is surrounded by an aura of color. These colors speak to me. Sometimes they tell me of things past. Other times, they tell me of things to come. Often they are quiet, saying nothing at all." He smiled. "When I met Jendy, she was surrounded by color. I knew at once she was destined to become a great storyteller, touching the hearts and minds of millions of children across the world. I could not, in all good conscience, let that gift to the world go unrealized. You see"—he stood again—"it is like a chain. If Jendy does not grow up, then she cannot reach countless others who haven't yet been born.

"At this very moment, a newlywed man beats his young wife. Years from now, this couple will conceive a son who will read one of Jendy's books and learn about the importance of CPR. This son will save his mother's life after a particularly brutal beating. He will later go on to become a skilled surgeon, developing new techniques to be utilized in medical institutions all over the world.

"I could also tell you of a baby girl who will be born in poverty. One of Jendy's books will unleash her imagination. This girl will grow up to become a famous artist. Rather than using her great wealth to improve her own quality of life, she will establish better school systems in her community, thereby altering the lives of countless generations of children." He paused. "There are many other such stories. I would be happy to go on, but I hope that I have made my point."

Neshera rose and handed the old man a mug of tea. She squeezed his arm and smiled reassuringly before taking her seat beside Piper.

Aside from the crackling fire, the room was silent. Mercy stood and walked to the fireplace. She picked up the poker and shifted the logs. "So are you telling us that Raze and I are the next twins in line?"

"That is correct."

It all sounded so ridiculous. Like a fairy tale gone wrong. Part of her wondered if she was dreaming. The other part knew—had always known somewhere deep inside—that she and Raze were different from other people. But there was no way either of them would ever commit murder. She released the poker and spun around. "And what if we refuse?"

Lucent's gaze was steady. "In the beginning, that is what my brother and I tried to do, as well. I was a physician with my own family medical practice. I gave care to those who could not have otherwise afforded it. My brother owned a racetrack. He donated money every month so I could keep my clinic open. After meeting with Cozen and Candor, we rejected the very notion of our destiny and insisted on living normal lives.

"My brother and I learned quickly that the consequences to humanity were dire." He averted his mismatched gaze. "Our own guilt followed us around like unshakeable shadows. Knowing the lives we had stolen due to our selfishness bore down on us until it became difficult even to breathe."

Lou leaned forward, lacing his fingers together. "Why not find another way to achieve the same results? Surely, there are a number of alternative strategies you could employ." He raised one bristled eyebrow. "Say, one that doesn't involve murder?"

"Yes, my brother and I thought of that, too. Once we accepted our destiny, we tried everything we could think of to avoid carrying out the required sacrifice. But by circumventing that sacrifice, we unwittingly triggered further tragedy, which in turn yielded devastatingly different results."

"In other words, you're damned if you do, and you're damned if you don't," Lou said, shaking his head.

Piper looked doubtful. "I don't get it. How can *not* killing somebody cause bad things to happen?"

"We were just as puzzled then as you are now." Lucent stroked his beard and stared off into the distance. "It was 1901. My brother's first sacrifice was a twelve-year-old boy by the name of Mathew. He and his father had emigrated from Ireland after losing their family to typhus fever. My brother just could not bring himself to take the man's one remaining child, so he chose to let him live. Three months later, we learned that Mathew had contracted tuberculosis. He transmitted the disease to others while working alongside his father at a factory in Boston. The factory workers brought it home to their wives, children, neighbors. Sadly, Mathew and his father passed away." He looked at Mercy. "As did hundreds of others."

"What would've happened if you or your brother had died back then, too?" Piper asked. "There'd be no one to take your place. Mercy and Raze weren't even born yet. Would the cycle finally stop?"

The old man shook his head and frowned. "As soon as my brother had taken life for the first time, pain and remorse of unspeakable proportions ate at his sanity. He tried repeatedly to take his own life, which was when it became clear to us that we were shielded somehow from sickness, injury, even death."

Raze rubbed at the stubble on his face. "How does your brother know who's supposed to die?"

"As I mentioned before, every living thing in this world has an aura. Colors speak to me. They speak to my brother, as well. They just tell him different things...such as what will happen if he does *not* complete his half of the work."

Piper sat back and crossed her arms. "That's what your brother does? He just goes around killing innocent people?"

"Death isn't always necessary to bring about change for the betterment of humanity," replied Lucent. "A little girl fell from her tree house a few years ago and broke her neck. My brother had loosened the wooden rung near the top of that tree the day before the accident. The girl was rushed to the hospital where doctors informed her family that she would be paralyzed for the remainder of her life.

"Over the next year, little by little, this girl regained sensation and movement in her limbs. After a year and a half, she was able to walk with crutches. After two years, she was running and playing with children her age like nothing had ever happened. The girl approached her father one day and told him she wanted to find other paralyzed children. When her father asked why, she said that she wanted to share her own story to give them hope of getting better, too."

The old man pierced Piper with a gentle, steady gaze. "Today, she is a very healthy ten-year-old girl. She and her family travel throughout the country year-round. They visit with paraplegics and quadriplegics, encouraging them to believe that anything is possible."

Raze lowered his booted feet from the coffee table and sat up. "Sounds like you got to go out and play nice while your brother did all the dirty work. Why didn't the two of you just split the work, fifty-fifty?"

Mercy saw pity in the old man's face as he regarded Raze. "I am incapable of taking life or creating tragedy of any kind. It is how I was made." He held out his hands and looked down at them. "My touch transmits healing, vitality, *life*. Although I desperately wanted to, I could not share my brother's burden. He was left to carry out his work alone."

"Shadow is your brother," Mercy said, appalled.

Lucent nodded.

"Do you have any idea what he's done? He killed a man, kidnapped his daughter, and blew up a house with about a dozen police officers inside. He also murdered my colleague, tied Piper to a tree in the middle of the woods until she almost froze to death, and then tried to blow us both up with a rigged explosive." She felt her face and neck flush with anger. "Tell me, Lucent, how does all of that contribute to the greater good?"

"It may be difficult for you to understand, but Shadow was once a decent man—"

"Just answer the damn question!" She hadn't meant to shout. It felt like everything was spinning out of control.

Neshera stood and moved to Lucent's side. "He may be old," she said defiantly, "but he can hear as well as anyone in this room."

Lucent touched her arm. "It is all right, Neshera."

"No. I will not allow her to speak to you like that." She turned to Mercy. "Can you not see he's trying to help?"

Mercy looked at the old man on the arm of the sofa, gaze cast down at the floor. She couldn't deny it. There was something inherently good about Lucent. Shadow, however, was a different story. She had never hated anyone so much in her life. Lucent couldn't be held accountable for his brother's actions. Mercy, above anyone, should understand that. How many times had she been blamed for something Raze did when they were kids?

She stepped closer and laid a hand on the old man's shoulder. "I'm sorry, Lucent. It's your brother I'm angry with, not you."

"And you have every right to feel as you do." Lucent reached up and patted Mercy's hand reassuringly. "My brother's recent behavior *is* perplexing, which is why I came here alone. Tradition dictates that we both meet with you and Raze to mentor you to the best of our abilities for the journey ahead." He gazed at the fire. "As far as I know, no one has ever broken tradition in quite this way before."

Mercy turned to pick up the fireplace poker. The symbol of yin and yang loomed in the fire before her. All of a sudden, it felt like someone was holding a match to the scar on her shoulder. Out of the corner of her eye, she saw that Raze had brought a hand to his own shoulder.

Stenciled in flames along the charred surface of a log, the yin-yang symbol split in half and then, like walking fingers, crept back into the fire. The burning in Mercy's skin eased to a dull, raw ache.

Raze stood, his hand still pressed against his shoulder, his eyes locked on Mercy's. "What do we do now?"

"That is why you have all gathered here tonight." Lucent's jaw tightened as he looked around the room at each of them. "My brother has to be stopped."

CHAPTER NINETEEN

Shadow turned onto the dirt road. Pebbles pinged off the van's metal undercarriage. A dust cloud drifted up and seeped into his open window, as if welcoming him back home.

He rounded the last bend in the road, and his warehouse finally came into view. Dozens of grimy windows lined the first floor. Most were either cracked or broken. The warehouse had been painted dark brown at one time. A few brown patches lingered here and there, but most had been rubbed away by the sun. Part of the roof was caved in, and chunks of wood were gouged from one corner. He likened himself to this warehouse. The wear and tear and broken outer shell created a new identity within, thereby unveiling its true purpose and beauty.

"We're here, little warrior!" He parked, cut the engine, and climbed out. Throwing open the van's rear doors in a flamboyant gesture, he stood off to one side. "Come, it's time to show you your new home."

She obediently scooted over, holding the plastic bag with all the remaining food and water in her lap. He smiled, knowing that she wouldn't be alive long enough to require further sustenance.

Rocks poked up at her bare feet as he led her and the dog to the side of the building. Shadow knew the dirt and rocks must be uncomfortably warm under the scorching Arizona sun. Her bare, tender feet were no doubt feeling it right now. He took pleasure in her pain, taking his time and making her stand on the hot earth for long minutes. To her credit, she didn't complain. She simply kept shifting her weight from one foot to the other.

Her amusing little dance lifted his spirits even more. It was important to take time to appreciate the little things in life.

Buoyed by her pain and the reunion with his beloved warehouse, he began whistling the tune to "Bingo." He took a deep breath and, with much anticipation, finally rolled the rusty metal door aside. Filthy, scarred walls and rotted-out wooden beams stretched as far as the eye could see. A fat black scorpion scurried across the threshold.

Home sweet home. His perfect space. His canvas. The stark beauty of this place was intoxicating. And all of it was his.

Suddenly impatient to get his plans under way, he motioned for the dog and the little warrior to step inside.

The old man went on to explain how he communicated with his brother telepathically, just as all the twins before them had done. He turned to Mercy and Raze. "It is much easier than it sounds—"

"Whoa, hold up," Raze said. "You expect me to talk to *her*"— he directed his thumb over his shoulder at Mercy—"with my *mind*?"

The old man looked amused. "Forgive me, Raze. I've been living this way far too long. Sometimes I forget how strange this all must seem."

"Strange ain't the word for it," Raze muttered.

"All you have to do is envision a door inside your mind. You can open and close this door at will. Whenever one of you needs to contact the other, simply stand outside the door and knock." The old man looked at them expectantly.

"What, you want us to do that now?" Raze asked, wide-eyed.

Lucent picked up his cane, limped over to Raze, and sat in the chair beside him. "Go on, son. Give it a try."

Mercy shook her head. She didn't buy it, either. She was still trying to wrap her brain around the fact that Lucent had healed her.

Lou cleared his throat. "May I make a suggestion?"

Mercy looked from her deer-in-the-headlights brother to Lou.

"I propose recording the data so the rest of us simple folk can see the results of this experiment for ourselves."

Piper rose from the sofa and started toward the kitchen.

"Where are you going?" Mercy asked.

"I think I know what Lou has in mind." She winked. "No pun intended." She returned a minute later with a pad of paper and two pens.

Raze looked up. "What's that for?"

"The point of this exercise," Lou explained as Piper handed each of them a pen and paper, "is to prove that mental telepathy is actually occurring. You'll write down what you're thinking, and then Mercy will write whatever she hears in her mind." He patted the sofa. "Come over and sit with me, Raze. Piper, you stay there with Mercy."

Raze stared blankly at his sheet of paper on the opposite side of the room. He finally shrugged and scribbled something down.

Mercy closed her eyes, imagined the door the old man had described, and opened it without waiting for the knock. Words floated in the air across the door's threshold. She wrote them down as they appeared, one at a time.

This...is...bullshit.

Mercy opened her eyes and laughed out loud at what she'd written. "I don't think it's working," she said, holding up her paper for everyone to see. But she could tell by the way Raze's mouth dropped open that it *had* worked.

"Interesting." Lou held up Raze's paper with the same words scribbled across the top. He adjusted his glasses and peered at Raze. "Try another."

Grinning, Raze leaned over his paper and jotted something down.

The words came through the door faster this time, and Mercy swore she even heard the faint echo of her brother's voice. *Piper has the hots for you, sis.*

She'd already finished copying the message by the time she realized what she'd written. She opened her eyes and tried shielding the paper from Piper, but it was too late. Piper grabbed it and held it up.

"If his says something different," Piper whispered, "then you have a serious ego problem, Parker."

Mercy sighed with relief when she saw identical words scrawled across the page in her brother's handwriting. This time, she decided to send her own message back. *Let's stay focused. We have to find Emily.*

Raze didn't bother with the pen and paper. Once Mercy was finished writing, he simply spoke the words aloud.

"Amazing," Lou said, removing his glasses as soon as Mercy's paper was revealed. "You're right, though. We can appreciate the rarity of the situation later when we have more time. Right now, we need to stay focused on finding Emily. And Bobby," he added, throwing a glance at Piper.

"Unfortunately, Emily and Bobby are secondary to the issue at hand. Another more pressing issue demands our immediate attention." Lucent stood and paced around the room with his cane.

"There have been times during the past few months when I was convinced Shadow was hiding something from me. It was tucked away in the farthest recess of his mind. Every attempt I made to uncover it was thwarted until I questioned whether or not I was simply imagining things. You see, when two people link, it is difficult to keep anything from one another. Since my brother and I have always been forthcoming, I was not immediately alarmed as I should have been."

Lucent told them of the images he saw inside his brother's mind when last they spoke. A vial. Doctors in protective suits. Mass graves. "Men, women, children—" He covered his mouth. "So many bodies piled in the earth's belly. At first, I assumed my brother had glimpsed the future and was only trying to shield me from seeing it. It was not until a few days ago that I came to understand his true intentions. If he is allowed to carry out his plan, he will obliterate humankind. I do not know the specifics"—he shook his head—"but he has clearly gone mad."

They were all silent. The full horror of the situation drifted up and hung over the room like a giant thundercloud. Mercy twirled her wedding band with her thumb. "Sounds like he's planning to release some kind of plague."

"Either that or a chemical agent," Lou said.

The old man shook his head. "What I saw in that vial was not a chemical agent. It was most definitely bacterial or viral in nature."

"What makes you so sure?" Mercy asked.

"As I mentioned earlier, every living thing is surrounded by an aura of color. Viruses and bacteria have distinct color patterns."

"We've been cooped up here for three days." Raze ran a hand across his stubble. "How do we know he hasn't turned this thing loose already?"

"Good point. Let's turn on the news." Mercy turned to Piper. "Where's the TV?"

Piper stood and pushed a button on the wall. A sixty-five inch curved Samsung Smart TV descended from the ceiling. She tuned to CNN, and they all watched the latest reporting on the investigation into the Golden Gate Bridge explosion. A photo of the only suspect appeared on the screen: a smiling and very harmless-looking young woman in a cap and gown, diploma in hand. Authorities had traced the bomb threat to her residence and found evidence there connecting her to the massacre.

Mercy breathed a sigh of relief. "Looks like it—whatever it is—hasn't started yet."

Piper edged forward, eyeing the photo of the young woman on the screen. She rose from the sofa, hurried to the dining room, and disappeared around the corner. Mercy and Lou followed after her.

They found Piper sitting on the floor with her back against the wall, her eyes squeezed shut. "Please, just go away," she pleaded.

"She's not talking to us," Lou whispered, kneeling in front of her. "Just give her a minute. She'll come out of it."

Mercy crouched down. "If she's not talking to us, then who's she talking to?"

"That photo on the TV…"

"What about it?"

"I presume the young lady in that photo is deceased, Parker, and she's probably trying to communicate." Lou stared at Mercy like she was an idiot. "Does the term *Photo Psychic* ring a bell?"

"Right. Sorry." She turned her attention back to Piper. "Can she hear us?"

"Depends on how insistent the person on the other end is. If they're yelling, then no. She won't be able to hear anything we say."

"Does she see them or just hear them?"

"Both. But they usually give up and leave if she ignores them long enough."

Piper opened her eyes and looked straight ahead at something just over Lou's shoulder. Mercy turned but saw nothing.

"She must have found someone of particular interest." Lou adjusted his glasses. "I can't imagine what they said to capture her attention so quickly."

A few minutes later, Piper finally blinked and looked up. "You're not going to believe this," she said. "I just met a young woman who says she was pushed from her balcony by the same man who took Emily and Bobby."

CHAPTER TWENTY

L ou helped Piper to her feet. "Are you okay?"

"I will be." She started massaging her temples. "Can you turn off the TV?"

"Consider it done," Lou said. He headed off, leaving Mercy alone with Piper.

Piper crossed her arms and gazed toward the living room. "I can't go back in there."

"Why not?" She was standing so close that Mercy could smell her perfume.

"How do I explain all this? They'll think I'm crazy."

"After everything we've seen and heard tonight? Sorry to break it to you, but talking to dead people is small potatoes compared to *my* new ability."

"You saying I'm yesterday's news, Parker?"

Lou stuck his head in the archway. "Coast is clear. I turned the TV off and hid the remote inside my magic briefcase."

Mercy couldn't help herself. "What's so magic about your briefcase?"

Lou ducked behind the wall, lifted a pot-bellied briefcase, and proudly held it aloft. "I'm convinced it's bottomless. It's a wonder it hasn't exploded yet."

With Piper's permission, Lou stood in front of the others and told them about her gift. Mercy watched as Piper busied herself with picking dog hair from the arm of the sofa, a permanent shade of red in her cheeks.

She couldn't stop thinking about how awful it must have been for Piper, being blamed for her best friend's murder and then locked up in an institution as punishment for a crime she didn't commit. According to Lou, Piper's entire family had shunned her. The experience had obviously left her scarred, and now she was afraid of what people might think if they discovered her secret. Mercy wondered how she had managed to keep it from her husband for as long as she did.

Neshera refilled Piper's coffee mug. "It must be scary hearing from people who have already moved on from this world."

Piper took a sip. "Amber is the young woman who came to me just now. The authorities believe she committed suicide after blowing up the Golden Gate Bridge."

Mercy leaned forward in her chair.

"But she didn't kill herself," Piper went on. "She was framed for the bombing and then pushed from her balcony. Amber said she was murdered"—she looked up at Lucent—"by a man who looks like you."

"Amber." The old man wrinkled his forehead in thought. "I do not know her. She was not a part of our plan, which can mean only one thing. She was to be left alone."

"What else did she tell you?" Mercy asked, curiosity getting the best of her.

"Well, Amber was twenty-one when she died. She was getting ready to graduate from medical school and—"

"How could she be graduating from med school at twenty-one?" Raze asked.

"Amber had a brilliant mind," Piper replied, sadness evident in her tone. "She was a gifted young woman who wanted to make a real difference in the world."

They were all quiet. Lou got up to throw another log on the fire.

"I know my brother. He must have taken Amber's life for a reason." Lucent frowned. "You say she was getting ready to graduate from medical school?"

Piper nodded.

"Did she happen to mention which type of medicine she had decided to practice?" Lucent asked.

"No, but Amber did show me a picture of where she was going to work. She said she had already started working there on weekends the year prior. The place was called Galveston National... something. There was a third word that started with an *L*, but I couldn't make it out."

"Laboratory," Lou said. "Galveston National Laboratory. It's located at the University of Texas Medical Branch. It makes sense that she'd be working there. Assuming what she told you is true— that she was graduating from medical school so young—then GNL would have actively recruited her as a research doctor on staff." He leaned forward on the sofa. "UTMB is a giant complex with four schools, six hospitals, several research institutes, and the largest library of medicine in the Southwest." He looked around at everyone. "GNL is a National Biocontainment Laboratory. There's a Level Four facility on the premises."

"Which means they're authorized to handle highly infectious, frequently fatal diseases with no known vaccine or treatment," Mercy finished. "Now we're getting somewhere."

Lucent rubbed his thumb back and forth over the top of his cane. "Yes, I believe I understand now why my brother took Amber's life." Everyone watched as he rose to his feet. "She was probably the only one alive who could have found a cure for whatever was in that vial."

"Are you saying he killed the only person who could've helped us?" Raze asked. His question was greeted with silence. "That blows."

"Wait a minute." Piper looked over at Lou. "Amber said something that didn't make sense to me at the time. She kept saying *my research, my research* over and over. I just assumed she was upset because she'd never be able to finish her research." She glanced around the room, briefly meeting everyone's gaze. "A spirit can have difficulty moving on if they feel something has been left unfinished." Piper stared off into the distance. "But Amber wants to help us."

"Help us how?" Raze asked. "She's dead."

Piper rubbed the pendant on her necklace. "With her research."

Mercy was trying her best to follow along. "You think Amber knows what Shadow has planned?"

"I have a feeling she does. The more I think about it, the more sense it makes." The deep flush in Piper's cheeks had finally faded. "Amber showed me a book with a brown leather cover and said that Emily has it."

Raze shrugged. "So?"

"I think her book has the formula for the cure to whatever it is we're dealing with here." Piper narrowed her eyes. "We need to find that book."

"Not that I don't believe you—because I do—but we're all just speculating on what Amber was trying to communicate." Mercy thought for a moment. "Is there any way you can contact her again to confirm our theory?"

"It doesn't really work that way." Piper started picking at the dog hair on the arm of the sofa again.

Raze stared at Lou's overstuffed briefcase in the corner. "But if you saw her picture again, could you...hell, I don't know, summon her or something?"

"Yes, I could if I had to. The thing is, if I did that, I'd be using up the last clear channel." Piper sighed and looked over at Lou. "How can I explain this so they'll understand?"

Lou adjusted his glasses. "Think of it as a television with only three channels," he said. "You can watch each channel only once. The first channel comes in the clearest. The second has more static. With the third, you're lucky if you catch anything at all."

"But if I'm right about Amber wanting to help us," Piper added, "then she'll come to me when we need her, and I won't have to use up one of those channels."

"So it's a crapshoot.'" Raze put his boots up on the coffee table. "What if you're wrong and we waste all this time looking for a book that ends up meaning squat? Then we're screwed, right?"

Piper's color rose again. She said nothing and just stared at the floor.

Mercy imagined the door in her mind and sent her brother a message. *Come on, Raze. Try to be a little more sensitive. And get your feet off the table.*

Raze looked over at her, his lips parted in surprise as he lowered his booted feet to the floor.

She turned to Piper. "What do your instincts tell you?"

Piper thought for a moment and finally looked up. "I think Amber will find me when the time is right."

"Then we'll wait until that happens. In the meantime, we need to find that book." She turned to Lucent. "Do you have any idea how much time we have before your brother releases this...plague?"

The old man thumped his cane on the floor. "I fear it is soon," he growled.

"Any ideas about where we should start looking for him?"

"I saw one thing more during my final conversation with Shadow. This particular image was less guarded than the others. There were concrete floors, high ceilings, long aisles with metal signs, monstrous overhead fans—"

"Sounds like a warehouse," Lou said.

"Yes, I believe it is where he is taking the child. A flagpole stands outside the entrance, its wood bleached white by the sun. The surrounding land is barren and flat and riddled with flowering prickly pear."

"That's a type of cactus, isn't it?" Piper asked.

"Yeah, and it's all over the Southwest." Raze's expression turned to one of painful memory. "Ran my Harley into a bunch of those when I was driving through Arizona a few years back."

Mercy stood and began pacing. "Okay, so we know Shadow probably has Emily and Bobby stashed inside a warehouse in the desert somewhere. We should start searching online for abandoned warehouses in the southwestern states." She turned to Piper. "Can we use your computer?"

Piper nodded. "Upstairs."

Mercy had one more question for the group. "We know Shadow has Emily and Bobby. What we don't know is why he took them in the first place."

Lucent stepped over to Mercy, piercing her with a steady gaze. "Because a small part of my brother hopes you will stop him. Even though you do not wish to believe it, Agent Parker, there is still decency and goodness in his heart."

Mercy shook her head and turned away. "Let's get cracking on that search."

Piper led the way to her office. She unzipped her laptop from a black carrying case, flipped it open, and turned it on. Mercy sat on the corner of the desk as Piper initiated the search. Lucent and Neshera looked on from the futon in the corner, and Raze and Lou brought chairs in from the other room, monitoring the progress over her shoulder.

"There are hundreds of vacant warehouses in the Southwest." Piper tucked her hair behind one ear. "Can we narrow it down a little?"

They ended up discarding all the warehouses in or near a populated area, which brought the number of possibilities down substantially. From there, they selected only those in the remotest of locations. Crossing off warehouses that had been renovated, demolished, burned, or flooded, they cut the list to eight: three in Texas, three in Arizona, and two in New Mexico.

Lou sighed. "Now that's a more manageable number." He looked over at Mercy. "How about we break into pairs, fly out, and visit these places in person? That way, no one else gets involved and we don't put anyone at risk."

Mercy nodded and directed her next question at the old man. "You up for one last adventure?"

Lucent ran his fingers along the length of his cane. "I would not have it any other way."

It was closing in on two a.m., but they decided not to wait until morning. Mercy made the flight reservations from Logan Airport in Boston.

Piper grabbed her car keys off the pegboard and tossed them in the air. "You drive," she said to Mercy on her way out the door. "I'm a little rusty with this *cops chase evil guy to save the world* thing."

They all piled into Piper's Land Rover. With nothing but the clothes on their backs, they sped down the driveway and out into the night.

CHAPTER TWENTY-ONE

Emily was sweating. The sun beat down on them through the gaping hole in the roof. She and Bobby were pressed against the wall in the corner, trying to fit into a tiny sliver of shade from the shelf overhead. The plastic bag with their food and water lay on the floor between them. She took small sips from the water bottle, trying to save what little they had.

The room was about the size of her classroom at school. There was one broken window set high in the wall. A white golf cart sat in the center of the room, its black roof faded gray by the sun. An old, broken-down refrigerator rested up against the wall to their right. Spiderwebs with little insect shells rounded out all the corners along the wooden baseboards. A scarred file cabinet stood in one corner, all the drawers missing but one. Yellowed receipts were stuffed inside a cardboard box that Bobby was resting his head on. Other trinkets lined the walls: a basket with some of the weave missing, a bag of dirty rags, several pieces of rope, and a splintered baseball bat.

Emily didn't have a watch, but she figured at least a couple of hours had passed since the bad man had locked them inside. She gazed up at the hole in the roof. The sun had moved a little. Hopefully, it would start cooling down soon.

Bobby was sprawled out on the concrete floor, panting. He lifted his head and peered up at her, looking pretty miserable.

I'm hot, too. She stroked his fur. *It's hotter here than it is back home, that's for sure.*

He stopped panting and tilted his head.

She followed his gaze and looked up at the only window in the room. About twelve feet off the ground sat a tiny square in the wall without any glass. She might be able to squeeze through if she sucked in her stomach and stretched out her body. But how in the world was she going to get all the way up there? There was nothing tall enough for her to stand on…except the refrigerator, which she'd never be able to move in a million years.

Even if she managed to get the golf cart over to the window and stood on its roof, she *still* wouldn't be able to reach. She went to the file cabinet. It was a little taller than the golf cart and probably a lot easier to move. All but one of the drawers were missing. Maybe she could use it like a ladder.

Bobby was eagerly trailing behind her thoughts. He stood in front of her and wagged his tail.

Thanks, I'm glad you approve of my idea. I just hope it works. She pulled out the only drawer, set it aside, and started pushing the metal cabinet along the concrete, inch by inch. By the time she had it centered underneath the window, beads of sweat were running down both sides of her face. She took a long drink from the water bottle, cupped her hand, and offered some to Bobby, telling him her plan as he drank. *I'll lay the drawer on top of the file cabinet, and then I'll try to stand on it. Hopefully, it'll make me tall enough to reach that window.*

He finished lapping from her hand and peered up at her, concern in his eyes.

Don't worry. I'll be careful. She picked up the drawer, stood on tiptoe, and slid it on top of the file cabinet. Using the drawer holes as rungs, she climbed to the top, turned the drawer on its side, and balanced herself in the center. As soon as she felt the metal starting to bend underneath her, she shifted her feet to the outer edges where the metal was stronger. She reached up and barely grazed the window's metal frame. It was no good. She still wasn't tall enough. If only she could get her hands on the windowsill, she could scramble up from there with no problem. She climbed trees all the time with the boys in her neighborhood, and she was usually the one who got to the top first.

She climbed back down to the floor. *I can't reach, Bobby. I just need a few more inches.* She looked around the room. The cardboard box was too old and soft to be useful, and there was nothing else she could stand on to give her the extra height she needed.

Bobby nudged her hand.

She stroked his head, trying to come up with a new plan. *I'm not ignoring you, Bobby. Just thinking, that's all.*

He nudged her again.

She looked down at him, confused.

She saw an image in her mind of Bobby standing on top of the file cabinet with her balanced on his back.

Actually, it wasn't a bad idea. *I'm pretty heavy,* she said doubtfully. *What if I hurt you?*

Bobby nudged her hand again, puffing out his chest a little.

Well—she shrugged—*I guess it's worth a try.* She studied the file cabinet. *Now we just have to find a way to get you up there.* She'd never be able to lift him. He was bigger and weighed more than she did. He'd have to get to the top by himself. If she tilted the file cabinet and leaned it against the wall, maybe he could use the drawer holes like ladder rungs, just as she had. But she'd need to wedge something underneath the file cabinet to keep it from sliding on the concrete floor.

She scanned the room, pausing when she spied the wooden shelf they'd been using for shade. She could probably pry it off the wall, but it was too high for her to reach. And she'd rather not drag the file cabinet all the way over to the other side of the room. *Okay, Bobby. Let's try your idea on the ground first.*

He stood underneath the shelf and leaned the side of his body against the wall. Emily put one foot on his shoulders and the other on his hips. She hugged the wall to keep from falling backward. *You okay, Bobby?*

He wagged his tail and she almost lost her balance. The shelf was right above her head, its left side already loose. She gave it a good hard yank and loosened it the rest of the way. Bits of drywall spilled from the hole. She worked the right side next. It pulled free after a few tries, taking a big chunk of the wall with it. Shelf in hand, she climbed down from Bobby's back and wiped the drywall and paint chips from his fur. *Good job, Bobby. You're really strong.* She bent down and hugged him.

She set the metal drawer aside and pulled the file cabinet away from the wall. *Have you ever climbed a ladder?* She sent him an image of her dad climbing their ladder at home.

Bobby stopped panting for a second and perked his ears.

She tilted the file cabinet so it was snug against the wall. *Climbing a ladder isn't much different than climbing stairs.* She wedged the wood underneath the base and then tested it to make sure it was safe. Wiping her hands on her pajama bottoms, she turned to him. *I'll spot you from behind. Ready?*

When he set his paw on the first rung, she supported his back end from below. His legs trembled as he tried to find solid footing on the metal file cabinet. He finally reached the top and peered down at her, his forehead creased with worry.

Even though he was trying hard to be brave, she sensed how scared he was of heights. *You did great! I'll be up in a sec.* She tested the file cabinet one last time to make sure it would hold both of them and climbed up slowly. *Can you make some room for me?*

He stood sideways and leaned his body against the wall.

Perfect. Stay just like that, she told him.

When she reached the top, he looked up at her with chocolate-brown eyes.

She placed her right foot on his shoulders and her left foot on his hips, then reached up and grabbed hold of the windowsill. "Ouch!" She jerked away and almost fell backward. The metal windowsill had been fried by the sun.

Bobby whined.

She blew on her fingertips to cool them. *I'm okay.* She shrugged out of her pajama shirt and threw it over the windowsill as a barrier against the hot metal. Lifting one foot at a time from Bobby's back, she dug her toes into the wooden planks on the wall and scrambled up.

Her hair clung to the sides of her face as she hooked her forearms over the windowsill and pulled herself up. The metal burned through her shirt, making her squirm as it heated the skin on her belly.

An old wooden flagpole stood about five feet in front of her. Too bad it wasn't a little closer. She could've slid down like a fireman.

She studied the ground below. It was a good twelve-foot drop. She definitely wasn't going headfirst. She glanced to either side of the window. A large metal ring stuck out from the wall to her right, and when she reached for it, she felt the heat from the sun graze her fingertips.

Emily balanced on her belly, wriggled out of her pajama bottoms, and fed them through the metal ring. She pulled down as hard as she could to make sure the ring was firmly anchored to the wall. Feeling like Tarzan, she slid out the rest of the way and held on tight to the pajamas. To her relief, the metal ring stayed put.

She swung back and forth, trying to work up the nerve to grab her shirt from the windowsill. Aside from the fact that she would have been embarrassed to walk around half naked, the shirt would help protect her skin from the sun.

She held on to her pajama bottoms with one hand, released her grip with the other, grabbed the shirt, and then dropped to the ground. The landing stung her feet a little, but she shook it off. *Bobby, can you still hear me?*

She heard him scratching in response on the other side of the wall.

I'll go find the door we came in and get you out of there. She pushed her hands through the shirt's armholes. *I won't be gone long. Don't climb down until I'm there with you.* She stepped into the legs of her pajama bottoms and pulled them up. *I don't want you to fall.*

More scratching.

Dressed, she looked toward the road to make sure the bad man wasn't coming and then ran around to the metal door. She rolled it aside and sprinted as fast as she could. Her footfalls echoed through the building. She lifted the chair, unlatched the deadbolt, and opened the door to find Bobby standing exactly where she had left him.

He looked at her and wagged his tail so hard he nearly fell off the top of the file cabinet.

She laughed. *I'm happy to see you, too.* He climbed back down with shaky legs while she spotted him from below. She felt relief wash over him as soon as all four of his paws touched the ground.

We should pack a few things to take with us. She grabbed the dirty rags, pieces of rope, baseball bat, and their plastic bag of food and water. When she turned around, Bobby was standing in front of the door with the leather book in his mouth. Amber's book.

She walked over and slid the book out from between his teeth. *Okay.* She still didn't know why they needed it, but she dropped it in the bag anyway. *This place must have a faucet somewhere. We should fill our water bottles before we go.*

Bobby sniffed the air and led her to a sink in the next room. A brownish liquid came out when she turned on the faucet, so she let it run until it was clear. Altogether, they had six bottles of water. She hoped that would be enough to get them through.

They turned and headed back the way they had come. Emily hesitated in front of the door to their room. *Wait a minute, Bobby.* She closed the door, wedged the chair underneath the knob, and locked the deadbolt. In case the bad man came back, she wanted him to think they were still locked inside.

They passed through a long hallway and came to the entrance. She glanced over her shoulder at an archway that led to another huge room. *Hold on a minute,* she said. *I'd like to take a quick look around.* Bobby followed at her heels.

Endless aisles stretched out as far as she could see. The shelves on her right were stacked with burned clothing. Leather boots lined the shelves to her left. It looked like they were standing in the middle of a warehouse. A huge metal sign was bolted to the wall behind her. She read it to herself and shivered. "Weird."

When she looked over at Bobby, she noticed that his tail was tucked between his legs. *You okay, Bobby?*

He hung his head.

Yeah. I feel it, too. This place is bad. She reached down to stroke the top of his head. *We should probably go.* She was tempted to search the rest of the warehouse, but she didn't want to waste time and risk getting caught. Even if she found a phone, she doubted there'd be any service in a place like this. With Bobby at her side, she hurried back to the metal door and rolled it shut.

They both looked toward the road and then jogged around to the back of the building. Still no sign of the bad man.

Her mouth dropped open when they stopped to take in their surroundings. She could see for miles in every direction. Tall cactuses and short, weird-looking plants with needle-sharp points dotted the land. Except for Bobby's panting, the world around them was silent.

She looked up. The sky was huge...much bigger than it had ever seemed back home. Puffy white clouds drifted across a blue sky while darker clouds churned in the distance like a witch's brew.

Bobby kept shifting his paws on the sand. The ground was hot. Emily sat down and reached inside the plastic bag for the rags and pieces of rope. *I'll make us some shoes so we don't burn our feet.* She wrapped a rag around each of his paws, tied them on with rope, and did the same for herself. Finally, she stood and turned to Bobby. *Well, which way should we go?*

He raised his muzzle, sniffed at the air, and turned in a full circle.

The winds picked up. Dust devils swirled all around them. She watched the darkening sky as Bobby led her out into the desert.

CHAPTER TWENTY-TWO

Mercy glanced in the rearview mirror. Lou, Neshera, and Lucent were sound asleep in the back seat. Raze was wide awake, watching the passing blur of houses in silence. Her brother had always been a night owl.

Mercy felt wide awake, too. She had inhaled four cups of coffee during their online search and couldn't keep from tapping her fingers on the steering wheel to give herself something to do.

"When does our flight leave?" Piper asked, glancing at the dashboard clock.

"Five a.m." She kept her voice down.

"It takes three hours just to get to the airport from my house."

"Which leaves us plenty of time to spare." Mercy coasted through a red light and looked both ways before crossing the intersection.

"Parker, we'll have ten minutes to check in, get through security, *and* find our terminal." She shook her head. "There's no way we'll make it."

"Ye of little faith." They'd better make it. There wasn't another flight to Phoenix until 7:20 a.m. With Shadow making plans to unleash the next plague on the world, the thought of sitting in an airport for any length of time made Mercy fidgety.

Lou and Raze had seats on the 6:00 a.m. flight to New Mexico. Lucent and Neshera would be boarding the 7:10 to Texas. They paired up in that order at the old man's urging. His reasoning made sense. Lou and Mercy were the only two with cell phones. Since they didn't have time to buy phones for everyone else, the old man pointed out that they could stay in touch with their minds. Mercy, Raze, and Lucent would communicate telepathically, thereby keeping everyone linked and updated on one another's progress during the search for Emily and Bobby.

She hopped on I-93 and headed south toward Manchester. Aside from the eighteen-wheeler she'd just passed, there were no other cars on the road. She intended to shave several minutes off their travel time by putting the pedal to the metal the rest of the way.

An orange construction sign up ahead indicated that the highway narrowed to one lane. A second sign farther along warned of a steep downward slope.

She saw the eighteen-wheeler fast approaching in her rearview mirror. The trucker honked his horn and started passing on the left as the road grew dangerously narrow. The trucker honked a second time. He was gaining speed by the second and obviously out of control.

Mercy slammed on the brakes, but the car didn't slow.

"Parker!" Piper shouted over the truck's blaring horn.

She pushed the brake pedal all the way to the floor. "Brakes are gone!" she shouted back.

Concrete dividers lined the left side of the highway and merged two lanes into one. A metal guardrail bordered the right. There was nowhere for them to go.

The hill was steep and the Land Rover continued to accelerate. Horn blaring, the eighteen-wheeler careened past as the road narrowed.

The smell of burning rubber filled the air. Smoke rose from the rear of the truck as one of its tires exploded. Shredded rubber bounced off the windshield and thumped underfoot, repeatedly slapping against the Rover's metal undercarriage.

Mercy yanked on the emergency brake as hard as she could and heard the screech of tires. To avoid striking the concrete divider, the truck veered in front of them, clipping the front of their bumper in the process. The steering wheel was ripped from her grasp as the car spun out of control.

They struck the guardrail first and then smashed into the concrete barricade. Mercy tried to remember if everyone was wearing a seat belt. The car bounced back and forth like a pinball as she mentally checked off each passenger. Everyone in the car was belted in...except Raze.

Her heart dive-bombed to her stomach. She extended her arm and held it protectively against Piper in the passenger's seat as the car flipped over the guardrail, landed on the embankment, and rolled too many times for her to count. Crunching metal and shattering glass assaulted her ears. The Rover made a feeble attempt to right itself but finally gave up and came to rest on its roof.

An unnatural stillness filled the air as she struggled to unbuckle her seat belt upside down. A streetlamp overhead illuminated the interior just enough for her to see. "Everyone okay?"

"Next time, I'm driving." Piper freed herself from her seat belt, somersaulted, and helped Mercy with hers.

Lucent spoke up from the back seat. "Neshera and I fared well, considering." He cleared his throat. "But Lou appears to be unconscious, I'm afraid."

Mercy slid down to her shoulders, somersaulted, and crawled along the roof until she came nose to nose with Lou.

Lou hung like a bat from the rafters. His glasses dangled from one ear. He opened his eyes, adjusted the glasses. "If I'm dead, and yours is the first mug I'm seeing here in heaven, then I demand to talk to whoever's in charge to file a complaint."

"Not if I file one first for having to be the angel who greets your sorry ass." Mercy glanced at the empty seat on Lou's left. "Where's Raze?"

"Lost track." Lou fumbled with his seat belt. "We'll find him."

Mercy stuck her hand in something wet and brought it to her nose. Gasoline. Lucent was already crawling out the window with Neshera close behind and Piper pulling up the rear. She leaned closer to Lou and looked up. "What's taking you so long?"

"Seat belt's stuck."

Lou raised his arms above his head to brace himself on the roof while Mercy pushed the seat belt's orange release button. It was jammed.

Piper crawled back inside to grab the old man's cane. "Why's Lou still hanging upside down?"

"Everything's fine, Piper," Lou said, a tone of relaxed confidence in his voice. "But Raze isn't back here. Check around the car. See if you can find him. We'll be out in a minute."

"Don't worry, Parker. He's probably just off peeing in the woods somewhere." Piper turned and crawled out the window.

Lou's glasses slid from his nose. His face was as red as a maraschino cherry. "This is giving me a headache. Any chance you could hurry it up a little?"

Mercy kept battling with the seat belt. "You're probably the first person in history to get a hangover without alcohol." The smell of gasoline was much stronger now. "Think you could slide out of there if you sucked in that gut a little?"

"There *is* no gut to suck in," Lou said indignantly. "Besides, the seat belt's locked up too tight for me to move."

"Then we'll have to cut you out." She crawled to the front seat and yanked open the glove compartment. A flashlight, tire gauge, and several trail maps spilled out. No jackknife. She picked up the flashlight and switched it on. Smoke was billowing in from the gas and brake pedals overhead. Not good. She hurried back to Lou's side.

"What's wrong?" Lou asked.

Mercy ignored the question, held the flashlight between her teeth, and focused on the orange button.

"Is that smoke?" Lou put his hand over Mercy's. "Get out of here, Parker."

"Dammit, Lou." She spit out the flashlight. "Get your hand out of the way so I can see what the hell I'm doing."

"Are you crazy? Get out of here," Lou shouted. "Leave me!" Then he shoved Mercy away so hard that she knocked her head against the door frame.

Mercy rolled to her knees, balled her fist, and struck Lou on the side of the head just hard enough to knock him out. Lou's arms unfolded and hung limply in the air. There was no way in hell she'd ever leave her friend behind in a burning car.

She grabbed the flashlight, held it between her teeth, and focused on the seat belt. Gasoline fumes made her lightheaded as she pushed, pried, and cursed at the orange button to no avail.

Piper stuck her head in the window. "Hey, need some help?"

"Find something I can use to cut the seat belt." Her lungs burned from the gasoline. "And tell everyone to get away from the car."

Piper disappeared only to return seconds later with a pair of manicure scissors. "Here," she said, handing the scissors through the window.

"Gas leak," Mercy wheezed. "Car could blow any second."

She tried sliding her thumb and forefinger through the tiny holes of the scissor handles, but they were too small for her fingers and slipped from her grasp. She readjusted them. Tried again.

Every fume-filled breath made her lungs burn hotter. Her stomach felt queasy. A thick layer of smoke crept into the back seat. When she looked up again, Piper was hovering over her. She plucked the scissors from Mercy's grasp and began cutting at the seat belt.

Part of her wanted to order Piper out of the car for her own safety. Another part was just grateful that Piper had small fingers.

She could barely think straight. All her body wanted was clean air. The queasiness in her stomach intensified to full-blown nausea. Damn, felt like she had swallowed a live octopus. Vomiting in front of a beautiful woman was simply out of the question. She'd rather do a dozen Red Sox runs in downtown Manhattan than puke her guts out with Piper right there beside her. All hope of being seen as an attractive, single lesbian woman would be lost forever.

Inch by inch, Piper chopped at the seat belt as Mercy's insides churned. It was simply a case of mind over matter. Under no circumstances would she ever allow herself the indignity—

She turned and threw up in the corner. A chow mein noodle slid from her nose.

"Now that you're finished soiling my upholstery, can you hold Lou up while I cut this last bit?"

Humbly, she braced Lou's torso. "We're getting to know each other on pretty intimate terms." She grinned when Piper looked over at her. "I figure retching in front of you like that is an even exchange for seeing you in the buff."

"And just who do you think gave you your sponge bath when you were laid up in bed?" Piper asked with a final snip.

Mercy's grin quickly died.

Piper dragged Lou by the back of his collar while Mercy grabbed hold of his legs and shoved from behind. Flames erupted overhead. Out of the corner of her eye, she spotted the metal toe of Raze's boot just outside the window. Her brother bent down, lifted Lou's body, and carried him away from the car.

Mercy crawled out after them but stayed kneeling on the ground, unable to do anything but replenish her lungs with clean oxygen. Lucent shuffled over with his cane and reached down to help her to her feet. Her stomach settled at once.

Blood trickled down the old man's cheek as he nodded toward the car. "This is my brother's work, I'm afraid." He withdrew a golden handkerchief from his pocket and dabbed at the blood on his face. "Shadow must have interfered with the brakes days ago."

"I'm liking your brother more and more by the minute, old man." She gave Lucent's shoulder a gentle squeeze.

Flames devoured the car's interior. Fiery specks of foam and upholstery drifted up from the broken windows and floated away into the nighttime sky.

She thought back to waking up in Piper's bed and remembered smelling something sweet on the sheets. At least, she'd *thought* it was on the sheets. Reflecting on her comment about the sponge bath, however, Mercy finally put two and two together. "So *that's* why I smelled so good when I woke up."

"Raspberry Delight body shampoo," Piper said, bending down to check Lou's pulse. "It nourishes and revitalizes the skin."

She looked around for her brother. "Where'd Raze go?"

Neshera pointed toward the woods.

"That trucker must have seen what happened," Piper said, indignant, hands on hips. "I can't believe he didn't stop."

Lou sat up. "And I can't believe Parker has such a decent left hook." He climbed unsteadily to his feet. "Don't mean to sound ungrateful for the blow to the head, but has anyone seen my glasses?"

"Here you go, Lou." Piper unclipped them from the front of her sweater. "Parker feels really bad about that, by the way."

"No I don't."

"Yes, you do."

"That's okay." Lou wiped each lens with the tail of his untucked shirt. "She's still trying to get even with me for locking her in my classroom at the Academy."

Mercy would never forget that fateful day. Nine years ago, she had fallen asleep smack in the middle of Lou's lecture and awoke several hours later to an empty classroom. Since the door was locked, she had been forced to stay overnight. His class filed in the next morning behind Lou, where they found Mercy hungry and achy from a restless night of sleeping on the cold tile.

"I know you're fast approaching those senile years, old friend"—she slapped Lou on the back—"but has my parting graduation gift already slipped your mind?"

To get even, Mercy had enlisted the help of a few classmates and broken into Lou's off-campus apartment the day before graduation. They'd covered all of Lou's belongings in aluminum foil, taking great care to wrap everything individually: plates, silverware, toiletries, books, clothing. Not even the furniture was spared. It had cost her a small fortune in foil, but it was money well spent. In the end, Lou's apartment looked like the inside of an alien spaceship.

Lou laughed. "I *still* have nightmares about being abducted by foil-crazed extraterrestrials." His smile faltered as he looked past Mercy toward the highway. "We have company."

They all turned and watched as a dark van parked in the only lane on the road above. A man climbed out, stepped over the metal guardrail, and started down the embankment.

It took Mercy a few tense seconds to realize it was her brother.

Raze strutted over and gestured over his shoulder. "Found us another set of wheels."

"What exactly do you mean by *found*?" Piper asked.

"Just what I said." Raze hooked his thumbs in his pockets and stared at the ground.

"Was someone driving it?" she prompted.

"Nope, passed that van on the highway a little ways back. It was just sitting there waiting to be towed, so I popped the hood and made a few repairs." He shrugged. "She started right up for me."

"The owner left the keys inside?" Neshera asked, sounding very surprised. Her naïveté made Mercy smile.

"Not exactly." Raze glanced around at everyone with a wry grin. "She just needed a little rewiring."

Piper crossed her arms. "In other words, you stole it."

"Man, why do you have to focus so much on the negative? I found us a way to get to the airport, didn't I?" Raze bent over and scooped up a handful of dirt. "I'm good with cars, but ain't no way I'm gonna be able to fix *that*." He tossed the dirt on the growing ball of fire.

Lou followed his gaze. "He makes a good case. Maybe this isn't the time to look a gift horse in the mouth."

Mercy nodded. "If we don't leave soon, we'll have to explain everything to the police. We can't afford to miss our flights." Decision made, she led the way up the embankment to the road.

Raze hopped behind the steering wheel, touched two wires together, and started the ignition. Mercy felt a little like a fugitive as she and Piper slid into the front seat.

"The only way to enjoy a late night drive," Raze said as he reached for the radio knob, "is with some good old-fashioned…rock 'n' roll!" Speakers blaring, he belted out the lyrics to "Jeremiah Was a Bullfrog." Lucent, Neshera, and Lou sat passively in the back seat as Raze sped down the highway.

The late night drizzle abated. For the moment, theirs was the only car on the road. Piper's leg was pressed against Mercy's. As Piper's perfume settled over her, Mercy was tempted to reach out and take her hand. Although they'd met only days ago—and in less than desirable circumstances, she reminded herself—holding her hand seemed like the most natural thing in the world. Piper was wedged between her and her brother, but it didn't escape Mercy's attention that she had scooted closer to her side without touching Raze at all.

They arrived at Logan Airport and parked the van in an uncovered lot just outside the main entrance. Mercy left a napkin on the dash that read, *This van was stolen. Please call the Conway Police Department. P.S. My brother says it needs a new timing belt.*

By the time they checked in, passed through security, and found their gate, the plane was already pulling away from the terminal. Mercy jogged up to the counter and pulled out her badge. "FBI. My partner and I need to board that plane."

The gate attendant alerted the pilot immediately. His hands shook as he handed the headset to Mercy. "Here, she wants to talk to you."

Mercy reassured the pilot that there was nothing wrong with the plane. She was vague with the details of their travels, informing her only that official business awaited them in Arizona.

Lucent, Neshera, Lou, Raze, and Piper stood near giant windows and looked on as the 747 halted outside. Mercy handed the headset back to the attendant. "Pilot says we're good to go."

"Wait here," the attendant said, disappearing behind a security door.

Mercy watched from a distance as Piper hugged everyone good-bye. From afar, they appeared an unlikely bunch: an impeccably dressed old man with a cane, a black woman clad in bright colors, a man whose bushy eyebrows and plaid sweater screamed of retirement, an unshaven biker with torn jeans and leather boots, and a woman whose mere presence in a room made everyone turn and stare.

Shaking her head, Mercy walked over to join this circle of misfits that had so quickly become her family.

Lou hugged Piper. "You two, be careful. Stick together. Don't go anywhere alone."

"Same goes for all of you," Mercy said. "We're on the buddy system from here on out. Agreed?"

Everyone nodded.

Mercy turned to Raze and Lucent. "We should check in with each other every few hours." The thought of communicating telepathically was still so foreign to her. Unsure if she would ever see these people again, she went down the line and gave each of them a hug.

The gate attendant finally grew impatient enough to step forward. "We need to go," he whined, bouncing from one foot to the other in an anxious little jig. "Maintenance is attaching the portable staircase so you can board."

With one last glance good-bye, Mercy and Piper let the attendant lead the way. They stepped outside, climbed into a motorized cart, and sped to the hulking 747.

CHAPTER TWENTY-THREE

Mercy and Piper boarded the plane. The flight attendant offered to seat them in first class, but Mercy shook her head. "If it's not too much trouble, we'd prefer to sit in the back."

The flight attendant nodded. "We're not even close to full capacity," she said, a lazy, Southern drawl rising to the surface of each word. "You're welcome to sit wherever you like." She winked and leaned in conspiratorially. "With the world the way it is these days, I'm just glad to have an officer of the law aboard." Then she turned and led them down the aisle. She stepped to one side near the end of the aisle and waved at all the empty seats around them. "Take your pick."

They settled on the second to last row in the middle. The closest passenger was four rows up, which gave them all the privacy they needed.

"By the way, my name's Marla. Feel free to let me know if there's anything else you need." She opened a storage compartment above their heads and handed them pillows and blankets.

The plane started toward the runway, and Marla retreated to the back as the pilot's voice came over the intercom. "Ladies and gentlemen, we'll be taking off momentarily, due to land at Sky Harbor Airport in Phoenix at nine a.m. local time. Takeoff may be a little bumpy, but we should be in for a pretty smooth ride as soon as we clear this storm at about fifteen thousand feet."

Mercy took a deep breath. "Does flying make you nervous?"

Piper tucked a rogue raven hair behind her ear and regarded her. "Not at all."

"Must be nice." She laughed. "I'm scared as hell."

"I used to be afraid of flying," Piper admitted, "until Lou shared a little secret with me. He ever tell you about Frank?"

"Nope." Butterflies took flight in her stomach as the plane revved its engines and sped down the runway. She grabbed the armrests with moist palms.

"There's this elephant, Frank. He's thirty-five thousand feet tall. He carries the plane on his back."

"Is that why they hand out peanuts on the plane?" Mercy asked, holding on to the armrests for dear life. "All this time, I've been eating those peanuts and letting poor Frank go hungry?"

"Sorry to break it to you, but Frank is actually *my* elephant. You'll have to find your own."

Mercy felt all the blood drain from her face as the plane lifted off the ground. "Can't you share Frank…at least temporarily?"

"Hmm." Piper frowned. "Well, I guess I could."

"That's very kind of you." Violent tremors shook the plane. She looked across the aisle to the window, but the clouds blocked her view of the city lights below.

"Don't worry about the bumps." Piper set her hand over the top of Mercy's. "Frank's pretty clumsy. He probably just stepped in a pothole."

She shifted her attention from the window to Piper as the turbulence abated. Goose bumps traveled up her arm from Piper's touch. Mercy loosened her grip from the armrest to give her hand a gentle squeeze.

"Do me a favor?" Piper said.

"Sure." She didn't think there was anything she wouldn't do for this woman.

"There's an open magazine…" Piper nodded at the seat in front of them. "I can see it through the gap. Can you close it for me?"

Nodding, Mercy unbuckled her lap belt and stood.

Last month's copy of *National Geographic* was opened to an article about a tribe in West New Guinea. There was a photo of a black man with bamboo sticks in each earlobe and a boar tusk through his nose. He was standing with a wooden spear, buck naked, his lithe body decorated with white feathers and red paint.

Mercy closed the magazine and sat back down.

"Thanks." Piper squeezed her eyes shut. "He was really starting to get on my nerves."

"The man with the nose ring?"

Piper nodded.

"I came close to getting a nose ring once." Mercy paused as the plane muscled its way through another series of bumps. "But I gave up on that dream when I found out the bureau would've made me wear a Band-Aid over it during office hours."

Piper kept her eyes closed and smiled.

"Is Nose Ring Man here?" Mercy asked. "Now?"

"Sitting in the seat to your left."

She hesitated, but just slightly, before casting a glance over her shoulder. Thankfully, the seat was empty. "He's dead?"

"Yup. Killed by a crocodile while out fishing for his village."

"Ooh." Mercy grimaced. "Poor guy." Without a doubt, Piper's eyes were the most captivating feature on her face. Even with her eyes closed, Mercy was still awed by her beauty. "How long will he stay?"

"Depends."

She waited for her to elaborate. "On what?" she finally asked.

"On whether or not he finds you…appealing."

Mercy thought about that for a moment. "I don't understand."

"Put it this way." Piper opened her eyes. "His tribe is one of the last remaining tribes in the world that still practices cannibalism."

She felt a momentary panic rising in her chest at the thought of being eaten by a ghost she couldn't see. Then she saw the impish grin on Piper's face. "Funny." She smiled. "You almost had me there."

Piper leaned forward and gazed past her to the seat on the other side.

"Still there?" she asked.

She shook her head and leaned back.

An awkward silence filled the space between them. "Must be something you never quite get used to," she said.

"I used to handle these visits a lot better." Piper fingered the pendant around her neck. "But I've been cooped up by myself for so long that I'm just really out of practice."

"When I talked to your old colleagues, they said you'd pretty much sentenced yourself to solitary confinement." Her instincts told her she was broaching a sensitive topic. "I figured you were just tired of talking to dead people."

Piper studied the wedding band on her finger. "My husband was murdered." She shrugged. "Guess I kind of…fell apart."

"They ever find who did it?"

"They didn't." Piper met her gaze with haunted eyes. "I did."

She waited as Piper seemed to gather her thoughts.

Piper took a deep breath. "Tim was stabbed to death at an ATM about two miles from our home. The security camera in that particular location was malfunctioning at the time, so the police had little to go on. When they came back to me a month later still scratching their heads, I decided to take matters into my own hands. I dug out a picture of Tim and called to him. He showed me exactly what happened that night.

"An old farm truck had pulled up alongside him as he was getting money from the machine. Tim said he knew as soon as he saw the guy's face that something wasn't right, but the knife was already in his chest by the time he realized what was happening.

"It didn't take me long to find the guy. He lived on the first floor of this really scummy apartment building. I drove down late one night, found him smoking a joint on his patio. He was talking to one of his buddies over the phone about some drug deal. Even from a distance, I could smell his sour sweat from crystal meth. His T-shirt had these yellow armpit stains and streaks of dirt from where he'd smeared his hands across the front. Looked like he hadn't shaved or showered in weeks. Dirt was caked under his fingernails, and he had this long, greasy hair. When he finished his joint, I climbed over the patio railing and watched him through the sliding glass doors for a while.

"I felt completely calm inside. I took my gun out, clicked the safety off, and aimed at his chest. As luck would have it, at that very moment, a little girl wandered out of a back bedroom. She reached up to this guy, called him Daddy." Piper sighed. "Talk about bad timing. I was just about to kill a man right in front of his daughter." She stared down at her hands. "The really frightening part was I still wanted to, even with her there."

"So what did you do?"

"What else *could* I do? I left."

Mercy searched Piper's face to see if she was telling the truth.

"Even though I didn't go through with it, the fact that I went as far as I did scared me to death. If that little girl hadn't walked out, I would have pulled the trigger, Parker. I had no idea that I was capable of killing someone in cold blood. After learning something like that about myself, how could I ever trust myself again? I realized then that I was no good to anyone anymore and nothing but a liability to the bureau. I figured it was best for everyone if I just...went away." Her chin quivered. "I turned in my resignation the next morning and haven't looked back since."

Mercy raised the armrest to remove the barrier between them and gathered Piper in her arms. Holding her, Mercy couldn't help but wonder what she would do if she ever came face-to-face with the man who killed her wife.

Piper's body eventually relaxed. Her breathing grew steady and deep as she slept.

The plane ride was smooth, just as the pilot had promised. A steady thrum from the engines vibrated underfoot. She rearranged Piper's body slightly—her arm had fallen asleep—and, with Frank in mind, waved Marla down for some peanuts.

She thought of Emily while she snacked. It occurred to her that she didn't know all that much about Emily. Hell, she had no idea what this little girl even looked like. The only useful information she had was the presumption that she was traveling with a chocolate Lab. If their search of the warehouses turned up squat in all three states, how on earth was she going to locate a child based on that?

The image of a rattlesnake slithering along the floorboards of the plane interrupted her thoughts. In fact, if Mercy didn't know any better, she'd swear she could even hear the snake's tail as it rattled in warning. Funny how the mind could play tricks on you like that. She was no shrink, but this one was pretty easy to figure out.

A few weeks ago, Raze had hijacked her TV and ordered that ridiculous movie, *Snakes on a Plane*. Mercy had obviously managed to tame her fear of flying only to have her subconscious mind replace it with a new one just as stupid. Determined not to give in to irrational fears, she didn't even bother looking down when she felt something brush against her pant leg.

Chapter Twenty-four

S hadow couldn't help himself. He was on his way to watch the passengers from the first plane disembark. Even though it meant leaving the little warrior alone in his warehouse, he just had to see the effects of the virus for himself. Months of hard work were about to be realized.

He would never receive due credit for this latest accomplishment, but that didn't deter him in the least. It was payment enough just to witness the extermination of the human race. Careful research had promised him that the world's population would be shaved in half within five days. The remaining half would be clinging to false hope for the next five days until they, too, slowly succumbed to the virus.

Sure, there might be a handful of survivors here and there with unusually strong immune systems, but depression would soon take its toll as the stench of rotting bodies filled every city. Suicide rates would inevitably climb.

Shadow grinned. He only hoped he'd still be alive to see the devastation unfold in its entirety.

It was a nasty little bugger. The government had christened it BCV-114. A biochemical virus programmed to target every major organ system in the body. During the first twenty-four hours of infection, the patient would exhibit a rash, generally limited to the neck and hands and accompanied by periodic nosebleeds. Intense headaches would plague them on the second day. The patient's esophagus would constrict on the third day, disallowing the passage of food and water. By the fourth day, partial paralysis in the lower limbs would reduce the spring in someone's step to nothing more than the elderly shuffle. Severe stomach cramps and bloody diarrhea would render the patient grotesquely incontinent by the fifth day, precipitating the shutdown of all major organs until the body could no longer sustain itself and death commenced.

What a glorious disease! Shame on the government for not putting their research funds to better use and finding a cure for their own deadly creation. He was just teaching them a little lesson. Fortunately, they wouldn't be alive long enough to learn from it.

He sauntered up to the two uniformed guards posted at the airport entrance and handed over his false DOD identification. The guard examined the ID, looked him over, and handed it back. "No one's allowed inside without protection. You can get PPEs in there." He adjusted the strap of his M16 and pointed to a makeshift enclosure.

Shadow knew PPE stood for personal protective equipment. From the looks of it, the military wasn't taking any risks. Level A PPEs—fully encapsulated chemical and vapor-resistant suits, each one affixed with a self-contained breathing apparatus—were being issued to all DOD and CDC employees on-site.

Even though the gear wasn't necessary for *his* safety, he nodded to the guard and strolled over to suit himself up. He fought hard not to smile as he walked. This was the most thrilling day of his life, after all. He ducked inside the tent, whistling.

A young man was sitting on an army-green military cot, partially suited. His tanned, freckled face and golden highlights made Shadow long for a walk on the beach. The laminated identification card that hung from his neck had *Mark Zamoida* printed across the front.

"I remember that song from when I was a kid," beach boy said. "That's 'Bingo,' right?"

Shadow turned to him and smiled. "My granddaughter keeps singing it over and over," he lied. "Must be contagious." No pun intended. A military officer took his false DOD card and handed him a suit. Shadow withdrew a second ID from his pocket, untangled the nylon cord, and looped it around his neck.

Beach boy shook his head. "Wish I had something to whistle about. Things are looking pretty bleak right about now." He reached into the suit's armholes until Shadow saw his fingers wiggling inside the chemical-resistant gloves at the end of each sleeve.

"Do not make the mistake of losing hope, young man." Shadow frowned. The suit felt heavy and bulky in his hands. It definitely wouldn't allow him to move as gracefully as he usually did. And bumblebee yellow didn't do his complexion justice.

"Similar reports are coming in from flights all over the world," beach boy went on. "We've never seen anything like this before." He stood and wiped the sweat from his forehead with the back of one glove. "Aren't you worried?"

Shadow placed his hand in his pocket and slid the gold ring over his finger. He felt along its band for two spikes with needle-point edges. "Whether or not I'm worried is irrelevant." Rotating the spikes in toward his palm, he withdrew his hand from his pocket. "Our fellow countrymen are depending on us to keep them safe." He slapped beach boy's shoulder in a gesture of reassurance, compromising the suit's integrity with two tiny pinpricks. "Now's the time to keep your wits about you for the sake of the American people, son."

"You're right. I have a job to do." Beach boy fitted the face mask over his head, adjusted the respirator hose, and gave Shadow a thumbs-up. "See you inside," he said, his words muffled behind the glass.

Shadow watched as beach boy turned and marched to his doom in an oblivious haze of courage.

Well, one down. Six and a half billion to go.

Seconds before, Mercy had been eating peanuts in the plane as Piper slept beside her. But she suddenly found herself standing in the middle of the desert. Her instincts told her she was in danger.

Clouds loomed overhead. The smell of rain was in the air. A rattlesnake lay coiled on the rock in front of her, poised to strike.

Mercy looked down and saw her foot hovering just inches from the snake's head. To her astonishment, her size nine feet had shrunken to those of a child.

She tried to back away, but her body wouldn't listen. The rattlesnake lashed out and struck her big toe. She felt her body jerk back in surprise and falter to the ground. The realization slowly dawned on her that someone else was controlling this body. Mercy was simply along for the ride.

A chocolate Labrador appeared at her side. The dog leaned down to sniff her child-sized foot. She felt the dog's anger boil over as he turned to confront the snake and heard the voice of a child scream aloud, "Bobby, no!" But the dog ignored the warning and growled, antagonizing the snake by circling it repeatedly. Fangs bared in self-defense, the snake lashed out. Mercy heard the girl's voice inside her own head. A message passed along from one mind to another. *Watch out!*

The dog heeded the warning and ducked to avoid the bite. The girl pleaded with the dog in her mind. *Don't do this, Bobby. Please. Just back away.*

But Bobby paid little attention to her words. He snapped at the air and goaded the snake into striking again. In one fluid movement, he lunged forward, pinned the snake's head to the ground, and tore into its flesh with his teeth until all that remained was a bloodied stump.

Finished, the dog lifted his head. He walked over, his head lowered in shame.

Mercy finally realized what was happening. She wasn't dreaming. She was actually witnessing events as they unfolded between Emily and Bobby. She wanted to separate from Emily—to step outside of her and get a physical description for later use—but she was fearful of breaking the connection.

She heard Emily's voice inside her head. *Are you okay? Did that snake bite you anywhere?*

The dog wagged his tail, ducking out of reach. He stared down at her foot, pawed at the ground, and whined.

Although Mercy could feel her rising panic, Emily willed herself to remain focused, calm. *It's okay. I just need a minute to think.*

A gentle shake on Mercy's shoulder snapped her out of the magical body swap. She opened her eyes and saw Piper peering back at her. "You okay, Parker?"

"Yeah, I'm fine." She rubbed her eyes. "Why?"

"I was getting ready to put in a request for the pilot to do a loop-the-loop. Are you always that hard to wake up?"

"Bobby's a chocolate Lab, right?"

Piper blinked. "Yeah."

"Brown eyes? Pink nose?" she asked.

"Yup," Piper nodded, "that's him."

"Does he have a red collar with his name stitched into the fabric?"

"This is getting weird, Parker." Piper fingered the pendant around her neck. "How'd you know that?"

She shook her head, sighed. "You wouldn't believe me if I told you."

"Try me."

Mercy explained her impromptu trip to the desert as best she could. "It was like someone shrunk me down to fit inside this little girl's body. I was seeing everything she was seeing, hearing everything she was hearing. Hell, I even felt the rattlesnake's fangs in my foot." Now that she thought about it, her big toe was throbbing. She untied her hiking boot and removed her sock. Two bloody holes stared up at her.

Piper shot a glance from Mercy's foot to the floor, pulled up her own feet, and curled them securely underneath her. "Looks like you were bitten, all right."

Mercy plucked her boot off the seat beside her and examined it. "But I've had my shoes on since we boarded. And look"—she handed the boot to Piper—"no holes."

Piper studied the boot before handing it back. "You're right. Do you feel funny at all? Lightheaded, nauseous, disoriented?"

"Toe hurts like hell. Rest of me feels fine."

"Let's just keep our fingers crossed that you don't go into shock. Antivenin might be hard to find at this altitude."

She slipped her sock back on and tried wedging her foot back inside the boot, but her toe had already swollen to twice the size. It wouldn't fit.

Piper reached inside her pocket and pulled out a tiny pill case. "Here, take some Ibuprofen. It'll help with the swelling so you don't have to go around looking like somebody stole your shoes."

Mercy popped two in her mouth and swallowed them dry. "I haven't even mentioned the craziest part." How could she say this without coming off like she'd completely lost her mind? "Emily and Bobby were…communicating."

"Hate to burst your bubble, Parker, but dogs don't talk." Piper frowned. "You sure you're feeling okay?"

"They weren't talking like you and I are talking," she whispered. "Emily was talking to Bobby in her mind, and he understood everything she was telling him." Mercy heard herself and realized she did, indeed, sound crazy. "Geez, listen to me." She ran her fingers through her hair. "I don't even believe what I hear myself saying."

They sat in silence as the morning sun reached in to settle on their laps. Murmurs from waking passengers overlapped the steady thrum of the engines.

Did she actually believe she had teleported to the middle of the desert and witnessed some kind of telepathic communication between a girl and a dog? Mercy wondered if she had completely lost her mind.

Piper rubbed her pendant. "I believe Bobby came into my life to help me cope with the loss of my husband. I've been so grateful for his companionship. He's been there for me every step of the way." She tucked her hands in her lap and looked at Mercy. "But there's also this nagging little part of me that knows Bobby's special. These may sound like the rantings of a lonely hermit, but there were times I actually felt he was more human than dog. Deep down, I've always known he had more of a purpose than just being with me. Sounds

like he's helping a little girl who's fighting for her life right now."
She met Mercy's gaze with watery eyes. "I'm so proud of him."

Mercy's ears popped as the plane started to descend. The
pilot's voice came over the intercom. "Ladies and gentlemen, we're
beginning our descent into Sky Harbor Airport in Phoenix, Arizona.
We'll be touching down in about thirty minutes. We're just missing
a large storm front to the east. We'll be landing without delay."

She turned to Piper. "That's it," she gasped, digging into her
back pocket. Piper looked on as she unfolded three warehouse maps
that they had found online. "Out there in the desert, I saw dark
clouds in the sky. Felt like a big storm was approaching. The pilot
just mentioned a storm front to the east. There." She pointed to the
warehouse in Mesa, Arizona. "I'd bet anything that's where they
are."

A bright crimson drop landed on the map an inch above Mercy's
finger. She looked up at Piper. "You're bleeding." Three more drops
fell on eastern Arizona before Piper pinched her nose.

"Must be the change in altitude." Piper unbuckled her seat belt
and made a hasty retreat to the bathroom.

If what she had witnessed in the desert really happened, then
there was a little girl out there who was just bitten by a rattlesnake.
Emily's chances of survival diminished with every passing hour.
Mercy had to get her some antivenin. Fast. Map in hand, she decided
on the best route to the warehouse from the airport. It looked to be
about a forty minute trip.

Piper returned a few minutes later with balls of tissue stuffed
up her nose. She sat and buckled her seat belt, staring straight ahead
while Mercy studied her with a smirk.

"Make one wisecrack," Piper whispered, "and I'll announce to
the whole plane that you voted for Trump."

"But I didn't vote for Trump."

"I know that," Piper grinned, "but *they* don't."

Mercy glanced up as a pregnant woman hurried past, bloodied
tissue in hand. Seconds later, a middle-aged man in a tailored suit
fled to the restroom on the opposite side, the cuffs of his white
starched shirt stained with bright red smears. Lines began to form

at each bathroom door as passengers of all ages awaited their turn. Conspicuous red stains dotted sleeves, collars, and the bosoms of several well-endowed women. Piper handed some spare tissue to an older gentleman on her left before turning to Mercy. "What's going on here?"

Mercy wiped at her own nose. Dry. "I don't know." She stood and looked toward the front of the plane. There were two long lines at the bathrooms on the opposite end.

Her heart pounded inside her chest. She took a deep breath. Every seat was empty.

CHAPTER TWENTY-FIVE

Mercy sat back down and pointed to the bloodied tissue in Piper's lap. "Mind if I borrow that?"

"You're not bleeding, Parker."

"I know that, and you know that, but they don't," she whispered, nodding at the line for the bathroom.

Voices rose as passengers started to panic. A middle-aged man pointed to a woman wearing a dark blue hijab. "What the hell did you do to us?" He looked to the others in line. "Those Muslims are letting these women with the head scarves do their dirty work now. She must've brought something on board that made us all sick." He balled his hand into a fist. "And now we're all gonna die up here!"

Mercy grabbed Piper's bloodied tissue and stood, shouldering the ignorant son of a bitch aside. "FBI." She took out her badge and waved it in the air. "All of you, return to your seats right now. A flight attendant will come around with some tissues."

The man begrudgingly lowered his fist. "How come everyone here has a bloody nose but you?"

Mercy knew better than to single herself out as the only healthy person aboard, so she held up the bloodied tissue and lied. "Because I've already stopped the bleeding."

Everyone obediently filed back to their seats.

The flight attendant hurried down the aisle handing out travel-sized packets of Kleenex. She stopped in front of Mercy and leaned in. "Pilot wants a word with you."

Passengers hushed as she walked past and proceeded to the cockpit. The copilot was busy staunching the flow of blood from his own nose. The pilot, on the other hand, had adopted Piper's method of stuffing tissues up each nostril to keep her hands free. She turned and nodded when Mercy stepped inside.

"Thought you might want to know," she said, "we have a situation."

"Okay." Mercy crouched beside her chair and tried to keep a straight face—what with the tissue and all. "Fill me in."

"Seems that passengers from flights all over the country are experiencing similar symptoms."

Oh no. It was happening already. "You said *symptoms*. More than just the bloody nose?"

The pilot unbuttoned her collar and held it aside. An angry red rash was visible on her neck. "Nosebleeds and rashes are the only reported symptoms so far." She adjusted her headset. "Air traffic control, this is Flight two-two-nine. That's affirmative." She returned her attention to Mercy. "Is your presence here a coincidence, or did the government have a heads-up on this thing?"

"I assure you, the FBI had no prior knowledge."

She studied her gauges. "We're within twenty-five minutes of Sky Harbor Airport. The CDC and DOD are already on-site. They've put all incoming and outgoing flights under quarantine. The entire airport is sealed. No one goes anywhere. There's a news blackout on this story and we've cut off the plane's Wi-Fi, but it's just a matter of time before this gets out."

Mercy stood. "There's an angry Islamophobic man in the back who'll be especially pleased to hear that." All eyes were upon her as she stepped from the cockpit and shut the door. She tried to appear relaxed as she walked to the center of the plane.

"Can I have your attention, please?" She put her hands on her hips. "I want to assure you that everything is under control. We'll be landing at Sky Harbor in about thirty minutes. Trained medical professionals are already waiting there to address your concerns."

A woman with multiple facial piercings and fuchsia hair stood up near the back and pointed at her tattooed neck. "What about this rash?"

A young man with long hair and a goatee stood a few rows over. He pulled the collar of his black Fall Out Boy T-shirt away from his neck to reveal his own rash. "Yeah, how come some of us have it and some of us don't?"

Mercy couldn't let on to the severity of the situation until the plane was safely on the ground. It would be too easy for passengers to draw their own conclusions and panic. "My guess is that it's something faulty in the plane's ventilation system. Nothing to get too worried about."

A shaky voice called out from somewhere behind her. "Could this be another terrorist attack?"

"Let me make this clear." Mercy paused for effect. "The FBI does *not* believe this is the work of a terrorist. Just sit tight and try to relax until we're safely on the ground."

As if on cue, the pilot came over the intercom and requested that passengers prepare for landing. Mercy returned to her seat.

"How's your toe?" Piper asked.

"Better." She looked over. "How's your nose?"

"Bleeding stopped."

She noticed angry red splotches on the side of Piper's neck, nearly identical in size and color to the pilot's rash. "You look much better without that tissue stuffed up your nose," she said, wondering what the hell they were dealing with here.

"Thanks. Did they actually take you seriously up there?"

"Yeah. Why?"

Piper picked up Mercy's hiking boot from the seat and handed it to her. "No reason."

When Mercy glanced down at her foot, one argyle sock stared up at her. "The CDC and DOD have already quarantined the airport," she whispered, wedging her still-swollen foot inside the boot. "Reports of passengers with the same symptoms are coming in from all over the country."

"I liked your problems-with-the-ventilation story better," Piper said.

"Me, too." She double knotted her laces and sat up. "You ever do any running?"

"We're in the middle of a national health crisis, and you're asking about my exercise habits?"

"I need to make sure you can keep up when the DOD is chasing us."

"Oh. Well, then." Piper frowned. "I guess it depends."

"On what?"

"Will they be shooting at us?"

Mercy scratched her chin as she pondered the question. "Probably."

"Then I'll keep up just fine." Piper looked at her and shrugged. "What? I work better under pressure."

By the time the plane touched down, Mercy had already discarded a number of half-baked ideas on how to escape from the airport. In the end, she decided it was best just to fly by the seat of her pants.

She turned to Piper as their plane was approaching the terminal and pointed to the knapsack at her feet. "Have any makeup in there?"

Piper held the collar of her shirt to one side while Mercy applied some concealer to the rash. She intended to make it appear as though they were both symptom-free. They'd still be required to comply with the quarantine, but being the only two uninfected passengers might just give them the advantage they needed.

"Okay," Mercy stood, "let's go." They made their way to the front of the plane. She turned to face the rows behind them. "Everyone, please stay in your seats for another few minutes. My partner and I will brief the medical team so they can better assist you."

A flight attendant opened the door. Two DOD security guards were already waiting outside with rifles and fully encapsulated bright yellow PPE suits. They raised their rifles as Mercy held out her badge and stepped forward.

"Stay where you are. Lay your weapon on the ground, ma'am."

Mercy looked down. Damn, the bulge of the holster underneath her sweater had given her away. She held up her hands. "FBI. Here's my badge." She tossed the badge at their feet. It landed on the floor with a slap.

Rifles at the ready, neither of them made a move to pick it up. "Still need you to hand over your weapon, ma'am."

Reluctant to part with her gun, she lifted her sweater, unsnapped her holster, and slid out her 9 mm.

"Slowly," the first guard cautioned. "Now, lay it on the floor and then kick it over here."

"My partner and I are asymptomatic. We have vital information that concerns the security and welfare of this country." She kicked the gun away. "We need to speak with someone in charge immediately."

The guards exchanged looks. One of them bent over to pick up the badge. He straightened and looked to Piper. "Where's yours?"

"I don't have it with me." Piper opened her wallet, withdrew her driver's license, and handed it to him. "Piper Vasey, FBI profiler."

"Wait here." The guard stepped away to consult with someone at the other end of his headset.

Seconds later, a third DOD guard came marching down the terminal. He spoke briefly with the other two and strode over, a confident swagger in each step. He tossed Mercy her badge and handed Piper her driver's license. "Follow me." Without another word, he turned and led them through the airport.

Mercy looked around in awe. The CDC had sealed the entire airport inside an airtight plastic biosphere. She had to give it to them—they were obviously going to great lengths to keep this thing, whatever it was, from getting out to the general population.

Most of the second floor had been closed off. Only a handful of terminals were accepting incoming aircraft. The escalators had also been shut down, forcing everyone to use the stairs. Suited in bright yellow PPEs, formidable-looking guards with M16s were posted at every exit.

Passengers were grouped according to their flights, sectioned off in various corners of the airport with yellow crime scene tape. Men and women of all ages were slumped over in chairs or balled up on the floor, clutching their stomachs and writhing in pain. Young mothers were struggling in vain to console crying infants and screaming children, their own eyes glassy with fever, their necks and faces speckled with rash.

As they wound their way through the airport, Mercy fought off a feeling of doom that threatened to suck the very breath from her lungs. Looks of desperation and panic pierced her from every direction. The overwhelming stench of body odor, vomit, urine, and feces clawed at the back of her throat, making her gag involuntarily. Flashes of pale faces assaulted her—some already tinged with the bluish hue of death's embrace.

Every single passenger here, she suddenly knew, was going to die. She hated to admit it, but she felt their imminent demise as tangibly as if she were holding their printed obituaries in her hands.

They made their way to a tentlike structure on the first floor. With a slight nod of his head, the guard peeled back the tent flap and held it aside. "Step inside. Colonel Dougo's expecting you."

The colonel stood as Mercy and Piper stepped inside. Even with his baggy suit and face mask, he was a petite man. He knocked on the plastic face mask with his knuckles. "Christ, I hate this thing. You two hear me all right?"

Mercy nodded. "Loud and clear."

"Good." The colonel perched on the edge of the desk. "Anyone who knows me will tell you I'm not one for small talk, so let's cut to the chase. It's unfortunate that you were both on that plane. Turns out, it's a piss-poor time to be traveling. You've been exposed to something we haven't identified yet. Precautions had to be taken to minimize contagion." He studied them intently. "My lieutenant informed me that neither of you have exhibited any symptoms. Is that true?"

"Yes, sir."

"Interesting." The colonel rose and began pacing in front of the desk. "You understand that the quarantine is still in effect. No one's allowed to leave the airport." He looked up. "You do know that you and your partner are no exception."

"We understand that, Colonel."

"Glad we're on the same page." He cracked a humorless grin on the other side of his mask. "My lieutenant also said you might have some information about what's going on here."

Mercy needed to stall for more time. She cleared her throat. "Unfortunately, we can't share that information until we run it by our superior first."

"This isn't FBI territory, Agent Parker. It's DOD jurisdiction now."

"I'm sure you understand, Colonel"—Mercy withdrew her cell phone—"that we're still required to follow protocol." She didn't flinch as the Colonel stared her down. "And if you don't mind, we'll need some privacy," she said, waving her phone in the air.

"Fine, but I'm not in the habit of sharing my office." Colonel Dougo shouldered past. "Make it quick." He pushed the tent flap aside and disappeared in a hurry.

"Okay." Mercy sighed, putting her phone away. "We need an escape plan like yesterday."

"There are *dozens* of guards out there," Piper said, pacing the perimeter of the tent. "And in case you haven't noticed, they're armed."

Mercy reached underneath her sweater and touched the empty holster. "We'd have a better shot at sneaking out of here if we could get our hands on a couple of those PPEs."

"True." Piper stopped pacing. "But even if I ask real nice, I have a feeling the colonel won't want to share."

"He must have been an only child."

They both turned as Colonel Dougo lifted the tent flap and stuck his masked head inside. He pointed to where his watch would've been beneath the bulky suit sleeve.

Mercy tried to think on her feet. They still didn't have a plan. "I spoke with the director's executive assistant. He's calling us back in the next few minutes."

"Colonel!" One of the guards raced in and nearly tripped over himself in the process.

The colonel reached out to steady him by the shoulders. "For Christ's sake, what's the matter with you, son? You're gonna tear your goddamn suit!"

"Sorry, sir." The young guard paused to catch his breath. "Some of the men from flight two-two-nine took Donati hostage. They got his weapon and sealed the plane's door. Pilot's still inside."

"Shit." The colonel turned to Mercy and Piper. "You two, stay here." He spun on his heels and charged from the tent like an angry bull from the starting pen.

"Angry Islamophobe strikes again." Mercy shook her head. "How much do you wanna bet that taking a hostage was *his* brilliant idea?"

Piper nodded and resumed pacing. She pointed at the tent flap. "Think there's a guard posted outside?"

"Probably." Mercy walked over and folded the tent flap aside.

"How many guards?" Piper asked, joining her. She stood on her toes to see for herself. "Two guards," she whispered.

"With machine guns," Mercy added.

"How in the world are we going to get past them?"

She grinned. "I have an idea."

CHAPTER TWENTY-SIX

No way!" Piper was adamant. "I am *not* taking my clothes off."

"Not everything. You can leave your underthings on." Mercy sighed. "Come on. I'd do it, but somehow I don't think it'd have the same affect."

Piper crossed her arms. "No."

"Fine, you asked for it." Mercy kicked off her boots. "Time for plan B." She pulled her sweater over her head and shrugged out of her shirt.

"Parker, what are you doing?"

She unbuttoned her jeans. "Stripping down to my birthday suit."

"And what good is *that* gonna do?"

"Maybe one of the guards"—she peeled off her jeans and threw them over a chair—"thinks athletic lesbians are unbelievably sexy." Standing there in nothing but her sports bra, underwear, and socks, she practiced flexing and posing. "All I need you to do is knock him unconscious and confiscate his weapon while he's busy gawking at me."

"Parker, put your clothes back on."

"Can't." She felt Piper's eyes on her body. "The very future of the world hangs in the balance. These"—she flexed well-defined biceps—"could be mankind's only hope for survival."

"Then we may as well give up now." Piper threw her hands in the air and sighed. "Fine. I'll do it," she said, already unbuttoning her jeans.

Mercy was tying her laces as Piper slipped out of the last of her clothing. Wearing nothing but a black bra and panties, she sat on the desk a little self-consciously.

She could barely think straight with Piper sitting so close. She. Was. Gorgeous.

"We're rehearsing, right?" Piper crossed her legs. "Let me guess…You're playing the role of the gawking guard?"

Aware she'd been caught, Mercy looked away guiltily and felt the heat crawling from her chest all the way to her ears. "I'll take a rain check on the witty comeback until further notice." Turning, she ducked outside to retrieve the first hapless victim.

The guard to the left was busily checking ID cards from incoming personnel, so Mercy held up her badge and approached the guard to the right. She gave him a story about an intoxicated, sex-crazed, gorgeous FBI agent just around the corner inside the colonel's tent. "I mean, I'm trying to be respectful and everything, but between you and me, she's totally lost it." She leaned in with a conspiratorial whisper. "You definitely don't want the colonel coming back to find her naked and sprawled out on his desk like that."

The guard's eyes widened.

"Maybe you can cover her up and move her someplace private?" Mercy suggested.

The guard nodded, following her to the tent without question.

When they stepped inside, Piper was lying on the desk, eyes closed, just as she'd promised. Mercy's breath caught in her throat. One bra strap was pulled down, daringly close to exposing her left breast.

The guard adjusted his M16 until it was safely out of reach and resting on the small of his back. "Holy shit," he said through the face mask without taking his eyes from Piper. With one gloved hand, he reached out for her left shoulder—presumably to help her bra loosen the rest of the way.

Mercy stepped behind him and ripped off his face mask, dismantling the tiny microphone inside and severing all communications. She wrapped her bicep around the guard's neck and squeezed until his body went limp. "Men are pigs," she said as the guard's body sagged to the floor. "How can you stand them?"

"Some of them aren't so bad." Piper was already pulling up her jeans. "But I do like women." She straightened, buttoned her jeans, and kissed Mercy softly on the lips.

It was the first kiss she'd had from a woman in two years. Strangely, she felt no guilt. Only excitement at the attraction that existed between them.

Piper reached for her shirt. "Better go round up guard number two."

Mercy bent down to replace the guard's face mask. He should be unconscious for at least another few minutes. Badge in hand, she stepped outside and jogged over to the second guard. "One of your men went down in the colonel's tent," she said, feigning panic.

They both hurried inside as Piper was kneeling next to the body. "He just passed out, but I'm afraid to take off his mask." She waved the second guard over. "Hurry!"

Guard number two adjusted his weapon and knelt down. Mercy slipped behind him, pulled off his face mask, and squeezed. Yellow-gloved hands scratched at her arm to no avail.

She and Piper worked in silence, stripping the guards of their PPEs. They threw the suits over their clothes and shouldered the M16s. "Can't forget these," she said, tossing Piper her ID card.

Piper slid the cord over her head and read the name on the other side. "Great. I get to be Harold Walker." She looked down at herself and shrugged, her feminine curves still visible through the loose-fitting suit. "Just call me Harry. Dad must have wanted a boy."

"We'll exit to the right and walk out of here like we know where we're going."

"Ten-four." Piper nestled the bulky headgear over her face and neck and nodded toward the tent flap. "I'll follow your lead."

They marched from the tent and exited the building, nodding to the guards outside as they hurried past. They moved like they had a deadline. Which they did, Mercy reminded herself. A little girl was waiting for a miracle in the middle of the Arizona desert. She couldn't let her down.

Plus, there was this other saving-humanity-from-extinction thing. But no pressure.

They removed their face masks and crossed the sidewalk to the parking garage. Once inside, they ducked behind a corner and let out a sigh of relief.

Piper grinned. "You look like a giant sunflower."

"There are some things you should feel free to keep to yourself."

She nodded toward the rental car office. "It's closed." She turned in a full circle. "They're all closed. Please tell me we have a way to get out of here, Parker."

"Of course we do." Mercy gestured at the cars all around them. "We just have to be creative, think outside the box a little." She hesitated. "You don't know how to hot-wire a car by any chance?"

"Must have skipped that class at the Academy, though I do vaguely remember them teaching us something about blending in with our surroundings. Forgive my ignorance, but is neon yellow the new camouflage?"

"Good point," Mercy said. "Ditch the sunflowers."

They peeled out of their suits and listened for signs of approaching guards. The coast was clear.

She imagined the door that Lucent had taught her about and knocked. *Raze? Can you hear me?*

The door opened and Raze stared back at her, thumbs hooked inside the pockets of his jeans. *Hey, sis.*

Mercy briefed him on everything that had happened. The great part about communicating telepathically, she found, was that it saved a lot of time. It was like talking in warp speed. *I need you to help me hot-wire a car.*

Cakewalk, Raze said. *First rule of grand larceny: the older the car, the easier to hot-wire.*

Mercy scanned the first floor of the garage. She spotted a rusty black Honda near the end of the first row. *Okay. Got it. What now?*

See if it's unlocked.

Right. Hoping an alarm wouldn't sound, she lifted the driver's side handle. Bingo. *I'm in.*

Pull off the panel under the steering column. Find the ignition circuit wires. They're probably red.

Probably?

Piper pointed at the cement wall surrounding the garage. "I'll see if they've started searching for us yet." She jogged away, staying low to the ground.

Mercy smacked the panel with the heel of her hand until it came loose. A tangle of multicolored wires stared back at her. *Now what?*

Take the ends of the red wires from the ignition and touch them together.

Just like that, the engine started. *We're in business.*

Raze gave her a thumbs-up. *Catch you later, sis.*

Based on the information they'd traded, Mercy knew Lou and Raze were still in the air. Following in the footsteps of her own flight, every single passenger had been stricken with a rash and bloody nose. The only symptom-free passenger aboard was Raze.

Same as Mercy.

Piper jogged back to the car, climbed inside, and slammed the door. "I don't think they realize we're missing."

Mercy put the car in gear and backed out of the parking space. Exiting from the south side would force her to drive past the airport entrance. Luck had been with them so far, but passing the DOD and waving out the window with a big cat-ate-the-canary grin *might* be pushing it a little.

If she exited on the north side, she'd be driving in the wrong direction on a one-way road. They'd still hit a military blockade before reaching the Route 202 access ramp, but maybe they could talk their way out of that one.

"Buckle up." She pulled forward, half expecting the rear windshield to explode from machine gun fire, but nothing happened.

Mercy considered crashing through the barricade but thought better of it when she spotted a small red cooler on the backseat. Perfect. "Let's play this like I'm FBI—"

"You *are* FBI."

"And you're Dr. Volkova," she went on, "world-renowned Russian bacteriologist."

"Bacteria-what?" Piper looked over at her. "I can't even pronounce that."

She eased the car to a stop. "No pressure, but you have about three seconds to come up with a convincing Russian accent." She rolled down the window and held out her badge to the approaching guard.

Their discarded yellow PPEs were plainly visible on the back seat, lending just enough credibility to her story. "We're transporting a specimen to a lab in Phoenix." She pointed to the red cooler behind her. "Need to get this there ASAP."

The guard glanced in the back. Three crisply starched chevrons decorated the sleeve of his uniform.

Mercy looked at her watch. "Clock is ticking."

The sergeant peered across the seat at Piper. "I need to see some identification, ma'am."

"Dr. Volkova's from Russia," Mercy explained. "She speaks very little English."

The guard straightened. "Shut the engine off," he ordered.

"Can't," Mercy said, indicating the tangle of wires at her knee. "Had to confiscate this vehicle for undercover purposes." She met the guard's eyes. "Your security clearance isn't high enough to warrant further explanation, Sergeant."

The guard stepped away and spoke into his radio. Mercy watched the tension in his shoulders as he waited for a response. Long seconds passed. He pressed the radio's button, spoke again, and waited some more. Eyeing Mercy suspiciously, he finally gave up on the radio and consulted with the second guard.

Both guards cautiously approached the car. "This is Corporal Yakovlev." The sergeant gestured to the guard just outside Piper's window. "He speaks fluent Russian. He'd like a word with Dr. Volkova. Tell her to roll down her window. Now."

Mercy nodded and discreetly shifted the car into first gear. Looked like they were going to have to do this the hard way, after all.

CHAPTER TWENTY-SEVEN

Piper slowly rolled down the car window as Corporal Yakovlev laid his giant paw over the door frame and addressed her, presumably in Russian. All Mercy heard were a bunch of consonants running together. She shook her head, marveling at the blatant omission of vowels.

Time ticked by as the corporal awaited an answer. He plucked his canteen from the notch on his belt and took a long, slow drink. A wallet-sized photo of an old woman was taped to the bottom of the canteen. She was smiling and waving at the camera, a colorful shawl draped around her shoulders.

Mercy prepared to accelerate. She held her breath and sized up the barricade. A couple of wooden sawhorses shouldn't pose a problem. If they were lucky, maybe they'd run over the guards' toes and gain a head start by a few seconds. If they were really lucky, maybe the old Honda would suddenly grow a bulletproof shell.

She was just about to burn rubber when she heard Piper answer the corporal in the same long-winded rush of consonants. Flabbergasted, Mercy stared at her. She was no expert on languages, but it sure sounded like Piper was speaking Russian. She loosened her grip on the steering wheel and breathed a sigh of relief.

They talked excitedly. It was like watching a Ping-Pong match, Mercy decided. Now the corporal was nodding and smiling. She cleared her throat. "Dr. Volkova."

Piper paused in midsentence and turned to look at her.

She pointed to her watch. "Tick-tock."

Piper nodded, throwing one last smile at the corporal. "*Spasibo*," she said.

That was the only word Mercy understood out of the entire conversation—*thank you*. A good sign they would soon be on their way.

Both guards met near the front bumper and talked briefly. Still smiling, the corporal sauntered away to clear the wooden sawhorse from their path.

The sergeant stepped to the window and handed Mercy her badge. "You're free to go."

Mercy eased the car forward and waved out the window. She watched the smiling Russian disappear from her rearview mirror as she rounded the corner to Interstate 202. Glancing repeatedly in the rearview mirror, she picked up speed as soon as they hit the highway. Part of her couldn't believe they weren't being shot at and chased.

She cast a quick glance at Piper. Her eyes were closed, and she was resting her head against the window. "So tell me," Mercy said, breaking the silence, "what other hidden talents do you have?"

Piper opened her eyes and straightened.

There it was…that faraway look again. The same one she'd had on the plane after seeing the spirit of the man from New Guinea. "You okay?" she asked.

"I'm fine." Piper tucked a loose strand of hair behind her ear.

"Since when do you speak Russian? I don't recall reading that in your file."

Piper rubbed the pendant on her necklace between thumb and forefinger. "Just got a crash course in Russian from Corporal Yakovlev's nana. She passed away in her sleep a few years ago. Very nice lady, by the way." She shook her head. "But she sure does keep a close eye on her grandson."

Mercy decided it might be best to save her questions for later. "This talent of yours just keeps catching me by surprise."

Piper turned away, red faced. In the blink of an eye, Mercy saw the shame that had wrapped itself around her like barbed wire. It was then that she realized how deeply Piper's shame was embedded. Piper assumed that her gift had made Mercy uncomfortable, which was far from the truth. She felt genuinely awed by her talent. Grateful, too. Without it, they never would have made it this far. "You're an extraordinary woman, Piper Vasey," she said. "But there's just one little thing I'd change about you if I could." She watched as Piper braced herself for another blow. "I wish you saw your gift the way I do. It's not something to be ashamed of." She reached out and took her hand. "It's something to be proud of."

Piper wiped a tear from her cheek and met her gaze. "You're not getting all sappy on me now, Parker, are you?"

"Yes, and it's just one of my many endearing qualities you'll come to love over time."

Piper squeezed her hand and looked out the rear window at the empty road behind them. "Shouldn't we find another car in case they start looking for us?"

She was right. It was only a matter of time before the colonel noticed they were missing. "There's a hospital up ahead. We'll switch cars there."

They exited from I-202 and pulled into the hospital parking lot. Since they still didn't know what Piper had been exposed to on the plane, they agreed she should wait in the car.

Although the weight of the world rested on Mercy's shoulders—literally, she knew the survival of the entire human race was depending on her—her heart had been swallowed whole by the two new women in her life. A ten-year-old girl and a psychic she'd met just seventy-two hours ago.

Deep down, Mercy sensed they were already a family. Her first real family. She felt a lump in her throat as she jogged to the emergency room entrance. Somewhere in the desert, there was a scared little kid fighting to stay alive, and she couldn't let herself dwell on the fact that the woman she was falling in love with was sick—possibly dying.

She would do whatever was necessary to save them. It scared the hell out of her to admit that saving Emily and Piper mattered more to her than saving the entire rest of the planet.

She darted past the check-in window and followed a nurse down a long hallway to several curtained exam rooms. The nurse spun around, startled. "Ma'am, you can't come back here."

Mercy brushed past her without a word.

A young doctor was leaning against the wall behind the main desk, focused intently on her clipboard. Mercy held up her badge. "Parker, FBI." Everyone stopped what they were doing and stared at her. "Doc, I need some antivenin. Like, yesterday."

She jogged out to the parking lot, antivenin in hand. Piper was sitting on the hood of the car. "There's an SUV a few rows over." She pointed. "Doors are unlocked, keys inside."

"Our days of crime are over." Mercy grinned. "Got us something better."

The hospital paramedic pulled an ambulance around front, climbed out, and tossed her the keys. Mercy drove to the old Honda, waited as Piper collected the M16s, and then peeled out of the parking lot.

Piper turned to her and frowned. "How come you get to drive?"

"Need you to run lights and sirens."

Piper's face lit up. "Lights and sirens coming right up."

Cars pulled aside to let them pass. What an adrenaline rush! Mercy never tired of weaving through traffic with flashing lights and wailing sirens. Never grew tired of chasing the bad guys, either.

Piper leaned forward, squinting at the intersection ahead. "There it is." They didn't know how far Emily and Bobby had traveled into the desert, so they'd decided to make a pit stop at an outdoor sports store to pick up some supplies. She parked at the curb and hopped out.

The store's interior was dark. Mercy checked her watch. It was only nine thirty, and the store didn't open until ten. She stepped around to the back of the ambulance, grabbed the fire extinguisher, and chucked it through the plate-glass window.

The sound of shattering glass echoed through the parking lot. They were already climbing through the hole in the window as the last of the glass was falling away. Shards crunched underfoot.

"Probably tripped a silent alarm," she called over her shoulder. "Grab what we talked about. Make it fast."

Right behind her, Piper hurried off to the rear of the store.

Mercy hit the backpacks first and plucked a pair of hundred-ounce CamelBaks from the shelf. A locked display case stood in the middle of the store, polished and pristine...but not for long. It shattered when she pushed it over, spilling jackknives in assorted colors and sizes onto the tile. She bent down and selected two. Winding her way back through the aisles, she tossed the rest of their gear into the CamelBaks: flashlights, binoculars, sunglasses, lighters, protein bars, and bottled water.

She returned to the front as Piper was rounding the corner with an armful of clothing. They stepped onto the sidewalk, jogged to the back of the ambulance, and tossed everything inside. Sirens sounded nearby as they slammed the doors shut.

"I've never stolen anything in my life," Piper wheezed, buckling her seat belt. "In less than twenty-four hours, I've stolen two cars, an ugly yellow suit that I'll never wear again, a machine gun, and expensive hiking attire." She paused. "And I don't even feel guilty about any of it." She looked over at Mercy, worry lines etched into her forehead. "I've turned into a hardened criminal."

Mercy couldn't help but laugh as she sped from the parking lot and pulled onto the main road. She handed Piper the wrinkled map from her pocket as two police cruisers darted past. "Quit browbeating yourself and navigate before I arrest you myself."

They found their way back to I-202 and headed out to the first warehouse. Ten minutes later, they spotted their exit and started across a long uninhabited stretch of Mesa, Arizona.

There wasn't a single car, house, or person in sight. They doused the lights and sirens, traveling the rest of the way in silence.

Piper crawled into the back to ready their hiking gear. Mercy heard water pouring into the CamelBaks, heard pockets unzipping as she stuffed things inside. Piper's bare shoulder caught her eye in the rearview mirror. She was changing in the back. It was difficult to keep her eyes on the road, but she managed somehow.

Piper reemerged minutes later, sporting khaki pants that unzipped into shorts, a purple moisture-wicking shirt, and a navy blue *Life Is Good* baseball cap. She looked good enough to hike the cover of *Cosmo*.

"Wow, is there anything you *don't* look good in?"

"Put your eyes back in your head and pull over." She grinned. "You change. I'll drive."

Mercy stopped on the side of the road and brushed against Piper as they traded seats. Clothes were already set out and tag-free on the stretcher in the back. She undressed and threw on a royal-blue tank top, a red long-sleeved shirt, and gray hiking pants. She nestled the matching *Life Is Good* cap on her head before returning to the front.

"Wow." Piper whistled like a true New York City construction worker. "Is there anything *you* don't look good in?"

"Put your eyes back in your head and pay attention to the road." She crossed her arms and did her best to look offended. "There's more to me than just my body, you know."

Mercy rolled down her window as the day started to warm. The desert smelled moist from last night's storm, but today the sun ruled proudly from its blue throne in the sky. Saguaro cactuses were in bloom all over the desert, their tiny flowers held up like golden offerings to the heavens. She studied the map and pointed to the dirt road ahead. "There, that's it."

Piper made the turn as Mercy reached behind her seat for the M16s. The ambulance bucked and kicked underneath them, protesting against the uneven dirt road. Overgrown weeds surrounded them on both sides. A perfect setup for an ambush.

CHAPTER TWENTY-EIGHT

With his hands in his pockets, Shadow strolled out of the airport, exhilarated. Not only was every passenger at Sky Harbor infected, but a handful of people were actually accelerating through the different phases of the virus. BCV-114 was everything he had hoped for and more.

Of course, he had inserted the appropriate amounts of concern and scientific bewilderment in all the right places when addressing the afflicted. A difficult challenge, to say the least. He'd had to bite down on his tongue to keep himself from breaking into song as the chaos unfolded around him.

The highlight of the morning was when one of the passengers took a guard hostage and re-boarded the plane. The fanatic ended up shooting said guard and one pilot to death before taking his own life. Shadow was almost certain the psychotic episode had been triggered by some internal reaction to the virus.

He looked down and smiled. The shooter's red *Make America Great Again* ball cap was resting comfortably on the seat beside him. Blood and gray matter still clung to the brim.

It pleased him to know that similar acts of violence were no doubt occurring in airports throughout the country, which meant the military would soon tighten its leash on incoming passengers. It was only a matter of time before airports started operating like high-security prisons, where people would be held against their will and forced to spend their last days with guns shoved in their faces. They'd be shot trying to escape. Riots would ensue—face masks ripped from guards' faces, respirator hoses disconnected, PPE suits intentionally compromised by sharp objects—forcing the guards to come down even harder. With military forces spread so thin in airports around the country, civilians were bound to break free, taking the virus along with them.

Sooner or later, it would be every man for himself.

If there was one thing Shadow knew about the human species, it was that they'd do just about anything to stay alive. He planned to stick around for as long as he could and watch the city streets with binoculars from the tops of high-rise buildings. The entertainment value would be immeasurable.

He stopped by the store, bought some popcorn and Milk Duds for the upcoming show, and climbed inside the van. Anxious to add the cap to his collection, he started back to the warehouse.

❖

Mercy realized that she could be just moments away from coming face-to-face with Shadow. She was so focused on finding Emily that she had pushed Shadow to the very back of her mind. What if Shadow was already waiting for them at the warehouse? She looked down at the machine gun in her hands and almost laughed out loud. According to Lucent, they were both indestructible. Where was the justice in that?

They came to a clearing where weeds gave way to flat desert scrub. She glimpsed a building in the distance before the road curved and took it from sight again. "Pull over."

Piper pulled to the side of the road. "What's wrong?"

"Something I need to check out." Mercy grabbed the binoculars and jogged back along the road. Piper hurried after her. Their boots crunched on the gravel. She stopped at the clearing and raised the binoculars.

Lucent's voice rang clear inside her mind as she recalled the old man's words. *A wooden flagpole stands outside the entrance, its wood bleached white by the sun. The surrounding land is barren and flat and riddled with flowering prickly pear.*

She couldn't have described it any better. "This is definitely the place." She lowered the binoculars and handed them to Piper.

Piper took her time studying the warehouse. "I don't see any movement. No car, either." She handed the binoculars back. "Unless Shadow parked his vehicle somewhere inside, it looks to me like he probably isn't here."

"Still, we need to be careful." Mercy scanned the area one final time before returning to the ambulance.

As they traveled the dirt road, she reached out to Raze and Lucent with her mind. *We found the warehouse.*

Lucent was the first to respond. *Good work, Mercy. You must find that little girl, and quickly.* He sighed. *Neshera has fallen ill. The virus is killing healthy cells within her body at an astounding rate. She is showing symptoms much faster than the others.* He hesitated. *I am afraid there is nothing I can do for her.*

Lou got it, too, Raze said, *but he seems to be holding up okay.*

Is there anything we can do to help Neshera? Mercy asked.

Find that little girl, the old man replied. *I pray she has the book that Piper spoke of. If the cure lies within its pages, then we need to make that cure accessible to the general population as quickly as possible.*

They severed contact as the warehouse fell into sight, and Mercy found herself squeezing the M16 with enough force to snap it in half. She made a point of loosening her grip. "Stay here," she told Piper as soon as she parked. "I'll go in first."

"Be my guest."

She left the door ajar and crept around back to the other side. She glanced up at the driver's side window, expecting to see Piper's face, but the seat was empty.

"Pssst...Parker!"

She nearly jumped out of her skin at the sound of Piper's voice. She looked across the way and there was Piper—waving from around the corner with a satisfied smirk on her face. She kept low to the ground and dashed across the dirt lot, all too aware of the broken windows overhead. A perfect vantage point from which to take someone out with a single shot to the head.

Mercy pointed toward the ambulance. "I thought I told you to stay in there!" she whispered angrily.

"Mm-hmm, you did." Piper rolled a rusty metal door aside and glanced back over her shoulder. "But I refuse to miss out on all the fun stuff just because I'm a girl."

"And I'm not?" Mercy asked, amused.

"You're a tomboy. It's different for you. You're like one of the guys." She glanced uncertainly at Mercy, seemingly trying to gauge if she had offended her. "Everyone looks at me like I'm helpless. I can take care of myself, you know."

Mercy had no doubt that she could.

"It may have slipped your mind," Piper went on, "but I went through FBI training, too." They inched their way into the warehouse. "As a matter of fact, I left the class in my dust on the long-distance runs." She tapped the weapon in her hands. "Outranked the men in marksmanship."

Mercy looked around. Dry, rotting wood surrounded them from floor to ceiling. One bolt of lightning and the entire place would spontaneously combust.

Piper continued, undeterred. "Kicked ass in defensive maneuvers. Ranked number one in hostage negotiation."

Mercy had obviously hit a sore spot. "How about I just let you hit me over the head with a blunt object and we move on?"

Piper ignored her. "Broke the record for lasting the longest during tear gas training. It may also surprise you to know that I was the only woman in my class to make it to graduation. And guess what?" She put a hand on her hip and turned to face Mercy. "I graduated at the top of my class."

"Okay, okay. Subtle, but I get it. I'm sorry."

"Took you long enough. Apology accepted." Piper moved to one side of an archway and signaled for Mercy to take the other.

They spun around, back to back with weapons drawn. Aisle upon aisle of neatly organized junk stretched out for as far as the eye could see. Sweeping the warehouse slowly from left to right, they listened in absolute silence.

The hair on the back of Mercy's neck stood on end. Shadow could be anywhere.

❖

Shadow didn't bother signaling. There wasn't any traffic around for miles. He turned on the dirt road that led to his warehouse. The van's noisy objections to the lack of pavement annoyed him as he fought to keep control of the steering wheel. The only reason he'd stolen the van in the first place was to transport his two little hostages. Dog dander and kid cooties had no place inside his spotless Hummer.

He'd visited a dealership in New Hampshire a few days ago. After being haggled to death by the salesman, he'd finally agreed to take the van for a test drive.

The salesman that accompanied him—Keith something or other—went on and on about what a great deal he'd get if he made the purchase that day. Shadow nodded politely and feigned enthusiasm at the prospect of being taken for a fool, silently counting down the minutes until he could shut Keith up for good.

Five highway exits later, he was giving Keith the Thief the choice of a lifetime: castration or mutilation? It came as no surprise when he opted for the latter. Men always behaved the same when it came to the family jewels. Well aware of the alternative, Keith the Thief did everything that Shadow asked without question, opening his mouth wide enough to let Shadow cut out his tongue with an ancient pair of black-handled scissors. The same scissors he'd used on Amber's bangs, in fact.

He'd left Keith crying and bleeding on the side of the road with promises that he would be reunited with his tongue as soon as the postal service got around to delivering it. Shadow had even kept his word, driving straight to the US Post Office where he sealed the dried-out tongue in a cardboard envelope lined with bubble wrap.

He followed the dirt road and tapped on the brakes as he rounded the last bend. An ambulance sat in the parking lot. He slowed to a stop, considering the implications of this new development.

Could Mercy have found his hideaway so quickly? He shook his head. Impossible. Even if Mercy *had* figured out where to look and flew to Arizona overnight, there was no way she could have made it out of the airport.

More than likely, some kid had made a prank call to 911, thinking it hilarious that an ambulance crew would drive to the middle of nowhere for nothing. Shadow sighed, eased his foot from the brake, and nudged the van forward.

❖

Mercy walked to an aisle and read the metal sign aloud. "Destruction, aisles one hundred thirty-nine and forty." There was no time to waste in their search for Emily, but she sensed the importance of taking a quick look around. She raised the binoculars and scanned the aisle all the way to the end. "This thing must be a quarter mile long. The shelves are filled with…" She lowered the binoculars. "What *is* all this stuff?"

Piper crossed her arms and shivered. "I don't know, but I'm not getting a good feeling here, Parker."

Aisle 139 held nothing but burned clothing. There were shelves upon shelves of neatly folded clothes, all blackened by smoke or fire. Mercy held up denim overalls that were sized for an infant. The left pant leg had been singed off completely.

Without warning, flames erupted all around her. A young woman was curled on the floor, her colorful sundress afire. She was trapped inside an elevator, clutching an infant tightly against her breast. Mercy bent down and brushed the woman's long chestnut locks away from her baby's face. Their lips and noses were stained with black soot from breathing in the poisonous air. Tear streaks lined their sooty faces as the sightless eyes of mother and child stared back at her.

Red shoes in the corner of the elevator suddenly caught Mercy's eye. Gagging, she glanced up as a dark figure stepped forward and peered down at the pair of scorched bodies. Shadow poked at the woman's lifeless arm with the toe of one shoe, parted the elevator doors with a wave of his hand, and strolled out from the fire like he couldn't care less.

Mercy released the overalls. They fell to the floor.

"Parker?" Piper knelt down beside her. "What's wrong?"

She opened her mouth to say something, but all she could manage was a shake of her head. She wiped at her eyes and stood. The mother's charred sundress lay folded on the shelf, but she didn't dare touch it.

Instead, she picked up the remnants of a work boot from a shelf on the opposite side and knew instantly that it had belonged to a coal miner. She saw the young man's body as it was tossed forty feet in the air...heard the sickening *thud* as it landed on hard-packed earth.

Mercy set the work boot back on the shelf and continued on down the aisle, counting aloud until she'd reached the very last boot. "There was a methane gas explosion in Castle Gate, Utah in nineteen twenty-four," she whispered. "He killed a hundred and seventy-two coal miners that day."

Piper laid a hand on his shoulder. "Who did?"

"Who do you think?" she snapped, pulling away from Piper's touch. Rage welled up inside her like a tidal wave as she exploded down the aisle, tearing things from the shelves and throwing them to the floor. Bits and pieces of different images came to her. Unfathomable agony. Desperate pleas for quick release from torn and ravaged bodies. Prayers for loved ones left behind.

Neither the young nor the old had been spared from Shadow's wrath.

Mercy stopped short. Something felt oddly familiar. She spun around, scanning the concrete floor for the train conductor's cap that she had just held in her hands. She bent down to pick it up, and her stomach somersaulted when she saw her parents' faces. Seeing her father was like looking at Raze. Her mother was just as young and beautiful as she remembered. She was trapped beneath a heavy cable while other passengers had escaped through the boxcar's broken windows. Refusing to leave his wife, Mercy's father had stayed behind.

Flames lapped at the boxcar's ceiling as her father pushed at the cable with all his might. Calls for help went unanswered, and his shoulders finally sagged in defeat.

The woman placed her hand over the top of her husband's. "I love you, James," she whispered, "but it's time for you to go. The twins are waiting for you. They need their father."

Mercy searched her father's sweat-streaked face as he gave up and settled down beside his wife. "No, we'll face this together," he said, holding her in the crook of his arm. "Close your eyes, Maggie. Don't be afraid."

Mercy carefully set the cap on the shelf as Piper pointed overhead. "Parker, look."

There, nailed to the wall, was a giant metal sign:

Sacrifice (Aisles 1–36)
Hatred (Aisles 37–72)
Aberrations (Aisles 73–108)
Destruction (Aisles 109–144)
Obsession (Aisles 145–180)
Wrath (Aisles 181–216)

"It spells *Shadow*," Piper said. "I get it now. I know what the names mean." She turned to face her, a look of pure terror in her eyes. "We can't let your brother end up like this. There has to be a way to stop it."

Mercy squeezed her eyes shut, the image of her parents' final moments still fresh in her mind. "What are you talking about?"

"Don't you see? Think about the names and what they mean. Take Lucent and Shadow…"

She studied Piper's face, trying to figure out where she was going with this. "Lucent means *glowing with light*."

"And the word *shadow* is literally and figuratively *a dark figure*."

"So?" Mercy put her hands on her hips. "What does that have to do with my brother?"

"Don't you remember the other two names Lucent mentioned?"

"Names I'd never heard before." She thought back to their discussion in front of the fire. "Candor and—"

"Cozen," Piper finished impatiently. "Think about it. Candor means honesty. Cozen means deception." She stared at her. "You obviously know what your own name means."

Mercy gave her a half-hearted smile. "It means I was teased a lot as a kid."

"Compassion." Piper touched her arm. "It's a beautiful name, Parker."

She had never thought about her brother's name before. It was always just a name. "Raze…" she whispered, unable to finish.

"Means *destruction*." Piper took her hand. "Like I said, we can't let your brother end up—" She let go and turned.

"What's wrong?"

"Do you smell that?"

Mercy sniffed the air as tires peeled out of the driveway. Smoke!

CHAPTER TWENTY-NINE

Shadow could hardly believe his eyes. He parked the van and walked over to just one of many glowing footprints. One set started on the driver's side of the ambulance and trailed off toward the warehouse. A second, larger set of footprints wound from the passenger's door to the back of the ambulance, and then out to the warehouse entrance.

He hunkered down and studied the ground. His mind still couldn't believe what his eyes were seeing. Mercy and Dr. Vasey had found the dragon's lair, but how?

Mercy's psychic abilities were still in their infancy. They had begun to develop, but only slightly. Dr. Vasey was psychic to some extent, though her gift was limited to looking at a photo and talking to the dead. It struck him as rather odd that someone could actually communicate with a corpse. He failed to see the benefits there.

On second thought, his former child prodigy was dead. He thought back to the moment of Amber's impact on the sidewalk ten floors below him and smiled.

Rubbing his new goatee, he thought for a moment. Amber's college graduation photo also happened to be splashed across the front page of every major newspaper in the country. Had Dr. Vasey seen Amber's photo and conjured up her spirit somehow? Had she also found out about the book and told Mercy?

Shadow returned to the van and checked underneath the passenger's seat. Amber's book was gone. He ripped open the glove compartment. Nothing. He scoured the cargo space in the rear, finding fast food wrappers aplenty from the little warrior and her mongrel. Still no book.

He was certain he had placed Amber's book under the passenger's seat for safekeeping, which could mean only one thing. The little warrior had stolen it.

Why she would steal a book that she couldn't even read was beyond his comprehension. He couldn't afford to waste his precious time trying to figure out the mind of a ten-year-old kleptomaniac. What mattered now was whether or not Mercy and Piper were aware of the *existence* of the book.

He walked to the ambulance and knelt beside their footprints. His heart picked up speed. Beads of sweat dotted his forehead and dripped down his face. He needed to find out what Mercy knew.

He reached out and dipped the tip of one finger inside the glowing footprint. Vibrant shades of yellow and purple whirled across his skin for several seconds before disappearing beneath the surface. He yanked his hand away and bit down on his knuckle to stifle his scream.

The colors burrowed into him with such ferocity that he feared he might pass out. His arm grew cold as the blood inside retreated like a vampire from sunlight. Indescribable pain gradually eased to a dull throb. He raised the sleeve of his sweater. Fluorescent purples and yellows glowed through his skin from his fingertips all the way down to his elbow.

Coming into contact with the colors of someone who worked for The Other Side always carried an element of risk. He never knew exactly how they were going to affect his body. It was a crapshoot every time.

Fortunately, the damage to his body was minimal this time. He hugged his arm to his chest, closed his eyes, and leaned back against the ambulance, waiting for the information he needed to come to him.

No doubt about it, Mercy knew about the book. She had also figured out somehow that the little warrior had it in her possession.

Furious, Shadow staggered to the warehouse. Taking great care to step around the glowing footprints, he headed off in the opposite direction to make sure the warrior and her mongrel were still locked up tight.

He turned the corner and stopped short. A wide grin spread over his face. The chair was propped underneath the doorknob exactly as he had left it. Still cradling his arm, he retraced his steps to the warehouse entrance, where he stood and listened.

"What *is* all this stuff?"

He recognized Mercy's voice at once.

"I don't know, but I'm not getting a good feeling here, Parker."

Shadow peeked around the corner at Dr. Vasey. She was naked and tied to a tree the last time he saw her. Thinking back, he wished he'd taken the time to have his way with her. He watched as she disappeared down the aisle, feeling himself swell at the thought of her squirming and fighting beneath him.

He turned away. He needed to stay focused. Fate had blessed him with the opportunity to rid himself of all his problems in one fell swoop. He wasn't about to trade that in for a few minutes of carnal pleasure with a woman who couldn't even appreciate him.

He returned to the van, climbed inside, and pressed a button. All four doors locked with an audible *click*. Reciting the ancient language of his ancestors, he waved his good hand in the air.

"A dog and human soul times three
will fail in their attempt to flee
in warehouse under lock and key
remaining for eternity."

He reached out with his mind and felt as the warehouse obeyed him. All its doors and windows were now tightly sealed.

"Good-bye, little warrior. Adios, Mercy. Arrivederci, Dr. Vasey." He kissed the palm of his hand and blew it out the window. The entire perimeter of the warehouse lit up in flames. Too bad he couldn't stay and watch the flesh peel from their bones. That was always his favorite part.

He felt his body weakening as the colors inched farther down his arm. Gritting his teeth against the pain, he sped off.

The thought of parting with his collection was intolerable. Tears blurred his vision as the burning warehouse faded in the side-view mirror. When he turned the corner on the dirt road, his beloved warehouse vanished from sight completely.

He pulled over, killed the engine, and weighed the risks of returning to salvage what he could from the fire. Adjusting the rearview mirror, he forced a smile at his own reflection. Hospitals would soon be so overcrowded that they would start turning people away. He envisioned the overflow of dead and dying bodies in the city streets.

Yes, that was it! The perfect spot from which to witness the extermination of the human race. Camping chair, popcorn, and binoculars in hand, he'd perch himself atop Good Samaritan Hospital in Phoenix like a vulture waiting for the feast to commence.

With a clear destination in mind, he restarted the engine and turned on the radio. Karen Carpenter was singing, in that sultry voice of hers, "On Top of the World."

He sang along, laughing at his own shortsightedness. He didn't need his old trophies anymore. The dawn of a new collection was about to begin.

Mercy and Piper sprinted up the aisle. They passed through the archway, found the metal door, and tried rolling it aside. The metal was hot to the touch. Smoke seeped in through the broken windows above.

The door wouldn't budge.

Piper motioned at the long stretch of hallway behind them. They ran its length, throwing open every door. Closets, bathrooms, abandoned offices—the place was huge. But there were no exits in sight.

The smoke was starting to thicken. It was getting difficult to breathe. They came to a door with a chair wedged underneath the doorknob, the deadbolt engaged. Mercy kicked the chair away, slid the deadbolt aside, and flung the door open. "Emily!"

"Bobby!"

No reply. They were probably long gone by now. In her vision on the plane, Emily and Bobby had already fled to the desert.

She and Piper lowered their bodies to the floor where it was easier to breathe. Paw prints and small footprints overlapped one another on the dirt-covered surface. If Emily and Bobby had found a way out, then it would stand to reason they could, too.

Mercy scanned the room. The Arizona sun beat down on them through a gaping hole in the roof about thirty feet up. Flames lapped at the hole's edges.

The only window in the room was about twelve feet off the ground. There was no way a dog and a little girl could have climbed out by themselves. Her eyes traveled down to the file cabinet directly beneath the window. "I'll be damned."

"You thinking what I'm thinking?" Piper asked, staring at the window, mouth agape.

"That Emily's one amazing kid?"

"No." They started crawling along the floor. "That you and I are way too big to fit through that window."

Mercy looked up and studied the window's dimensions. "Agreed. Window's out. I'm open to suggestions."

"The wood's pretty rotted. Maybe we can kick our way through the wall."

"Or"—Mercy nodded toward the hallway—"we cut our losses, keep looking for another exit."

Creak. A huge metal beam snapped in half, landing directly in front of the door with a floor shaking boom.

Piper looked at her. "Well, your idea's out."

They slid to their stomachs where the air was still clean. She spotted the golf cart, motioned to Piper, and they slithered over.

Planks of wood rained down all around them. "Get in," she shouted, taking the rifle from Piper's shoulder.

Piper slipped out of her tank top and tied it around her face, effectively covering her nose and mouth. Clad in nothing but a black sports bra and shorts, she hoisted herself into the golf cart. Mercy did her best to keep her mind out of the gutter and followed on her heels as another piece of roof thudded to the floor behind them.

She sat behind the wheel and set both M16s on the floor under their feet. The smoke was thick and black as night. Tears wrung from her eyes. She glanced to the right, barely able to discern Piper's shadowy figure. She knew they could only hold their breath for so long.

Debris clanged on the golf cart's roof. Mercy gripped the steering wheel and, out of pure desperation, *willed* the motor to start. Tiny sparks of electricity coursed through her arms and shot out from her fingertips.

Gloves of blue light cut through the smoke where her hands should have been. Instinctively, she touched her index finger to the ignition and heard the engine turn over at once. *Did I just do that?* she wondered, reaching out to make sure Piper was still seated beside her. Shaking her head in disbelief, Mercy threw the golf cart in drive and pressed the gas pedal all the way to the floor.

The golf cart surged forward, and the engine screamed. Mercy had no idea how close they were to the wall. The smoke was too thick to see anything. She reached out and held her arm against Piper to brace her for the impact.

The crash knocked the breath out of Mercy. Her knees smacked painfully against the dashboard, but the wall held.

She looked up. The golf cart's roof was on fire. She threw it in reverse and sped backward. Every breath felt like poison in her lungs. Piper was choking on the seat beside her. They hit something, and the wheels spun. She shifted back and forth between gears until the golf cart finally broke free.

The smell of burning rubber assaulted her senses. Flames lapped at the windshield. Wood splintered and cracked as the golf cart muscled its way through the wall. With one final heave, the engine sputtered and died.

They coasted to a stop a safe distance away. An eerie howl floated across the desert, almost as if the warehouse was crying out from the hole in its flesh.

"You okay?" Mercy wheezed.

Piper stepped down from the golf cart, pulled her tank top from her face, and then slipped it on over her shoulders. Regarding her with narrowed eyes, she adjusted her *Life Is Good* cap. "What is it with you and fire?"

Mercy bent to retrieve both M16s from the golf cart. "Admit it, I'm just too hot for you to handle."

"You?" Piper laughed. "My hair dryer runs hotter than you."

"Ouch." Not sure when she would get the chance again, she leaned in for a kiss. Piper's lips felt warm and soft against hers. Piper opened her mouth ever so slightly and invited her inside. The feeling was exquisite.

They jogged around the building to the ambulance. Piper threw open the rear doors and tossed out their gear. "So let me get this straight," she said, shrugging into her CamelBak. "All I have to do is insult you if I want you to kiss me?"

"You're irresistible when you pretend not to like me." Mercy climbed inside the ambulance, started the engine, and parked a safe distance from the fire. It would definitely save them a lot of time, but driving through the desert just wasn't an option. Saguaros, chollas, and prickly pears were plentiful here. Their thorns were lethal to tires.

"Just dawned on me how big the desert is." Mercy looked around, trying to determine in which direction Bobby and Emily had traveled. "I have absolutely no idea where they are."

"What about your vision?" Piper asked.

"What about it?"

"Well, does anything look familiar?"

"Let's see. Saw a few rocks, some dirt, but mainly, I was focused on the rattlesnake."

Piper studied the ground and started walking toward the rear of the building. "Then we'll look for footprints."

She followed behind her. "Any sign of them would've been washed away by the rain."

Piper shrugged. "Maybe we'll get lucky."

"Maybe…if one of them happens to weigh five thousand pounds and left a nice deep impression in the earth." She sighed. "By any chance, does Bobby weigh five thousand pounds?"

"I won't even dignify that with an answer."

"Well then, like I said, chances are good their footprints were already washed away."

"Quit being such a pessimist, and start looking."

Mercy bent down.

"Find something?"

"Does rat poop count?"

"Focus, Parker."

She did. Child-sized footprints started forming in the sand directly in front of her. They trailed out in hues of red, orange, yellow, green, purple, and blue, as if someone had stepped on a rainbow and went running barefoot through the desert. Silver-gold paw prints soon rippled on the ground alongside them. She removed her sunglasses and stared down in disbelief.

"Parker?"

She blinked, looked away, looked back. Still there. "Do you see them?"

"See what?"

"Come on," she said, already on the move. "They went this way."

CHAPTER THIRTY

Mercy and Piper maintained a steady clip. They were both silent as they ran, their footfalls quiet on the hard-packed earth. Mercy guessed they were running about a seven-minute mile, but she had no way of knowing how far Emily and Bobby had traveled. Fortunately, their colorful footprints were like beacons in the sand.

Piper crashed into her when she stopped short. "Sorry," Mercy said, reaching out to steady her. "Something's heading this way." She brought the binoculars up and zoomed in. "Get behind me," she ordered.

Piper didn't budge an inch. Instead, she ripped the binoculars from Mercy's grasp and peered into them. "Mountain lion. Coming this way and moving fast."

"Yeah, saw that." Mercy raised the M16. "So unless you want to be buffet-a-la-Piper, I suggest you get behind me."

"It's carrying something in its mouth."

She clicked the safety off and watched as the mountain lion drew closer.

A hundred yards...

Seventy-five yards...

Fifty yards...

She placed her finger over the trigger.

"Don't shoot, Parker." Piper lowered the binoculars. "She's carrying a cub."

She eased her finger off the trigger but kept the rifle steady against her shoulder. "How do you know it's a she?"

"Because I can see her belly."

"Okay, so why isn't she stopping?"

"I don't know." Piper scanned the ground at their feet. "Maybe we're standing near her den site."

Thirty yards out, the mountain lion slowed from a gallop to a trot. Her chest and neck muscles rippled in the sun. She stopped just twenty feet from them and set her dead cub on the ground.

Without giving it a second thought, Mercy handed the weapon to Piper and started toward the mountain lion.

"Parker, what are you doing?"

The mountain lion stared her down. Pupils dilated, she flattened her ears and hissed.

But Mercy couldn't help herself. She kept moving forward. Vaguely aware of Piper shouting her name, all she could focus on was the little cub. The stillness of its body called to her. Its head was bent at an unnatural angle, the fur darker where it had been stroked in vain by a mother's tongue.

She knelt in the dirt and placed her hand over the cub's black-spotted belly. A boy. His neck had been snapped by a coyote. Golden light spilled from Mercy's palm. She watched as the spinal cord magically knitted itself together and started firing off synapses to the brain.

His heart began pumping at once. He shuddered with his first intake of breath. His paws twitched. He lifted his tiny head, and bright blue eyes blinked up at her.

The mountain lion stepped forward, gingerly wrapped her jaws around the cub's shoulders, and trotted off in the opposite direction, halting just long enough to glance back with a mouthful of cub.

Piper came up alongside her, slid her hand inside Mercy's, and gave it a gentle squeeze. They were silent as they resumed their trek through the desert. Mercy couldn't think of anything to say. Whether she wanted to or not, she was changing. They both knew it. And for the first time in her life, she had no idea who she was anymore.

❖

Emily couldn't walk another step. She knew that the rattlesnake venom was wreaking havoc on her body. She had never felt so sick before in her life. Defeated, she sat in the dirt while Bobby stood guard.

A pack of coyotes had been following them for a while, driven by their curiosity and hunger. With a sinking feeling in the pit of her stomach, Emily watched as the alpha male edged closer. Much larger than the others, he always held his tail high to show his dominance.

She hated him in five seconds flat. He was an unfair ruler, a terrible bully who was used to getting his way because of his size and strength. She sensed that the other pack members lived in constant fear of him.

Every muscle in Bobby's body was poised to attack as he focused on the alpha male.

Please, I don't want you to fight him, Bobby! She grabbed a handful of rocks and started chucking them at the alpha male as hard as she could. "Go away!" she screamed. One of the rocks nailed him in the middle of his forehead. Teeth bared, hackles up, he came at her.

Bobby cut him off by slamming into his ribcage. A cloud of dirt churned up around them. The alpha male yelped and skidded to the ground. He was back on his feet within seconds and turned to face Bobby.

Before she knew it, they were thrashing against each other, snarling and growling in a tangled mass of fur and teeth. She felt Bobby's rage explode to the surface like a volcano. He let out a high-pitched squeal as the alpha male tore into the skin on his back and ripped it open.

Bobby sank his teeth into the male's hind leg and shook his head violently back and forth, separating flesh from bone.

Each kept trying to go for the throat, but they were too strong and evenly matched to fall prey to the other's advances. Everything was happening so fast. There was no turning back now. Emily knew they were fighting to the death.

She felt helpless. She wanted to do something. Anything. Movement in the distance caught her eye. Two women were jogging toward her. Black rifles swung from straps on their shoulders. She rubbed her eyes and looked again. Nope, it wasn't a mirage. They were running faster now, shouting something that she couldn't quite make out. She could hardly believe it. They were going to be rescued.

She turned her attention back to the fight just as Bobby was being pinned to the ground by the throat. "No!" She hobbled to her feet and leapt onto the alpha male from behind. He released Bobby, and they both tumbled to the ground.

She locked her feet around the alpha male's hind legs and held on to his chest with all the strength she could muster. They rolled in the dirt, end over end, until she was beneath him with his tender belly exposed. She shut her eyes and tucked her head. *Now, Bobby. Get him!*

Bobby tore into the coyote's throat more savagely than she expected. Hot blood stung her face and neck. The alpha male thrashed and kicked and tried to break free, but she hung on so tight that her muscles started to shake.

Long seconds passed, and he finally went limp. She let go and pushed the dead coyote aside as Bobby collapsed in her arms.

Blood bubbled at his throat as he struggled to take another breath. He peered into her eyes.

I'm okay, Bobby. She cradled his head in her lap, stroked his cheek, and kissed him on the nose. *You saved my life.* Tears spilled down her cheeks. *You're the best dog a kid could ever ask for.* He wagged his tail in the dirt.

I love you, too, Bobby.

And then, before she could say anything more, he was gone. The void he left inside her was unbearably dark and lonely.

A woman's arms closed around her, lifting her from the ground. But she didn't care anymore that the adults had found her. All she wanted was for Bobby to be alive, and if that couldn't happen…then she didn't know how she would go on living at all.

❖

By the time Mercy got to them, both Bobby and the coyote were dead. "Emily?" She didn't answer, didn't even look up. Mercy squatted beside her. "My name's Mercy. I'm an FBI agent. I'm here to help."

The girl had obviously gone through hell. Her pajamas were torn and filthy. Her left leg had swollen to twice the size of her right, and her foot was an unnatural shade of black. She had several deep gashes in her arm and scrapes and bruises all over.

Mercy carried her to a large flat boulder, set her down, and knelt in the dirt. "Emily?"

Her face was stained with blood and tears, but she kept her eyes on Bobby.

Mercy wiped at some of the blood on her neck, felt around for a puncture wound, and breathed a sigh of relief when she realized the blood wasn't hers. "Please look at me, honey."

Haunted brown eyes settled on Mercy's. "He's dead," Emily blurted. Fresh tears spilled down her cheeks. "Bobby's dead."

Mercy glanced over her shoulder at Piper. She was kneeling beside Bobby. "Let's focus on you right now." She popped the tube from the clip on her CamelBak and held it out. "You must be thirsty."

Emily shook her head, her eyes still locked on Bobby.

"I need you to help me out here, kiddo. Can you take my hand?"

"Why?"

"You're hurt. I'd like to try and help you feel better."

"I just want Bobby back."

"Okay." She sighed. "How about if we just sit together for a little while?"

Emily shrugged, her indifference made clear by that one small gesture.

Mercy placed her hand on Emily's foot. Her skin felt rubbery and cold to the touch. The rattlesnake venom had already damaged parts of her liver and kidneys. The need to heal Emily manifested itself so strongly within her that she couldn't hold back any longer. Golden light burst from her palm and fanned out over the surface of the small, beaten body. The light was looking for a way inside, but Emily's body wasn't absorbing it like the cub's had. In fact, she seemed to be repelling it.

She called to Piper. "It isn't working."

Piper reluctantly stood from Bobby's body and looked over. "How come?"

She balled her hand into a fist. The light faded. "Hell if I know." Mercy turned her hands over and stared down at them. How could they fail her at a time like this?

"Maybe you're dehydrated?" Piper handed her the tube from her CamelBak. "Drink some water. Try again."

She did. Same result.

Emily watched them with sad brown eyes. "You're trying to heal me, aren't you?"

Mercy nodded. Kids had amazing powers of perception, but something told her this one was exceptionally bright.

Emily jumped down from the rock and limped over to Bobby. "He saved my life. I'm not leaving him!" she screamed. "You can't make me!" She collapsed to the ground beside Bobby and started sobbing into his fur.

Of course, Mercy thought, it made perfect sense. The light couldn't find a way in because Emily didn't *want* to be healed. She stood, walked over, and tapped Emily on the shoulder.

"Go away!"

She hesitated, still unsure of her own gifts. "What if I can make Bobby better, too?"

Emily sat up and studied her with swollen eyes, a ray of hope unfolding in her freckles. "You can bring him back to life?"

Mercy smiled, trying to convey the confidence she didn't feel deep down. "Will you let me help you if I do?"

Emily wiped her tears and regarded her warily. "Help Bobby first. Then we'll talk."

Great, now there were *two* stubborn women in her life. She knelt beside Bobby. Patches of fur and skin were missing all along his bloodied body. Dark crimson blood was still pooling in the dirt beneath his throat as his eyes stared blankly ahead.

She laid both hands on Bobby's chest. They ignited with the same golden light. Skin and fur folded down and grew together in seamless perfection. The jagged wounds around his throat closed as the carotid artery started swelling in rhythm with his heart. Bobby blinked and lifted his head. Blood had congealed along the right side of his face.

"Bobby!" Emily threw her arms around the dog and hugged him tight. "You're alive!"

He wagged his tail and looked from Emily to Mercy.

"He wants me to say *thank you*." She shook her head. "I told him you wouldn't believe we can talk to each other, but he wanted me to tell you anyway."

Piper stepped forward and knelt in front of Bobby. "Hey, fur face."

He shot off the ground and licked Piper's face with such enthusiasm that he knocked her to the ground, his tail low and wagging furiously the whole time.

"Okay, okay." Piper grabbed his snout and held it shut. "A simple *I missed you* would have sufficed."

Emily giggled. "Yeah, that's pretty much what he's saying, like, over and over and over."

Bobby suddenly grew very serious. He sat in front of Piper and looked to Emily, his eyes beseeching.

"He wants me to tell you that you're very sick," the girl said, frowning.

Piper let go of his snout. "He said that?"

Bobby whined and pawed at the air. "He says you have something inside your body from the bad man…" She paused, her eyes locked on Bobby's. "And you can only get better with Amber's book."

Mercy shook her head, amazed. Emily knew about the book, even knew Amber's name. So it was true. Piper had been right all along. Amber was trying to lead them to her research for the cure to this plague.

Piper hugged Bobby one last time and whispered something in his ear. She rose and moved to the girl's side. "We've been really worried about you, honey. I'm glad Bobby was here to keep you company. I'm Piper."

"I know who you are. Bobby talked about you a lot."

Piper turned the girl's arm. "Parker, look." There, on Emily's wrist, was a colorful friendship bracelet with a small oval stone in the shape of the yin-yang symbol.

Mercy's eyes darted from the girl's bracelet to the yin-yang pendant around Piper's neck. She rubbed the scar on her own shoulder, once a tattoo. What did it all mean? The scar burned as if in answer.

The girl reached up to finger Piper's pendant. "Wow, you have one, too. So did the bad man, except his were cuff links, and they were red and gold." She frowned, her eyes returning to the symbol on her bracelet. "Are we in some kind of secret club?"

Piper looked to Mercy, but she couldn't think of how to answer that. She didn't want to lie to the kid, but she wasn't sure yet just how much they should tell her.

"Mine burned me once," Emily went on, seemingly happy to fill the silence. "Right through the pocket of my jeans. It happened when I was in math class." She glanced up at Piper. "Has yours ever done that?"

Judging from the look of shock on Piper's face, it had. Mercy made a mental note to ask her about that later.

The girl finally shrugged, looked over at Mercy, and pointed to her blackened foot. "Hey, think you could help me out now with some of that healing stuff?"

Mercy reached out for her small freckled hand. "Thought you'd never ask."

The swelling in Emily's leg subsided as fluids dispersed throughout her body. Freshly oxygenated blood circulated in her foot, restoring the blackened tissue to its original fair complexion. Finally, the damage to her liver and kidneys was reversed, and the rattlesnake venom diluted until it was no more potent than water.

"There." Mercy gave her hand a gentle squeeze. "That should do it, kiddo."

Emily climbed to her feet and walked around behind her. "Where are your wings?" she asked.

"What?" Mercy said, turning to face her.

"Angels are supposed to have wings." Emily stepped around behind her again and ran her hands along Mercy's shoulders and back. "But I don't see any here. Aren't you an angel?"

She smiled. "No, honey. I'm an *agent*."

Emily was silent for a long moment. "The agent of good fighting against evil?"

She shook her head. "Sorry to disappoint you, but I'm just a regular FBI agent."

"Oh. Can all FBI agents heal kids and bring dogs back to life?"

Hmm, the kid had a point.

"There's a magic light inside your hands that makes people better, so you're an FBI agent with superhero powers." Satisfied with her own explanation, she skipped around them in a circle. Mercy was happy to see that even the color in her cheeks had returned.

"Everything seems to be working okay," Emily reported. She flexed her fingers, rotated her shoulder, and threw a mischievous grin in Mercy's direction. "Bet I can run and pitch even faster now. Thanks."

Mercy stood, brushed the dirt from her shorts. "Baseball player, huh?"

"And soccer, basketball, hockey." The girl shrugged. "I like every sport I've tried so far."

A kid after her own heart. She was liking her more by the minute.

Piper slid the elastic from her own hair to pull Emily's back in a ponytail. "Honey, you mentioned the name Amber. Who is she?"

"Well, I never actually met her. Bobby just showed me what she looked like." She looked solemnly at the ground. "I think the bad man killed her, so we stole Amber's book from his van. Bobby made me carry it wherever we went. He never told me why, but now I understand." She looked up. "He knew you needed it to get better."

"Do you have the book with you now?" Mercy asked.

She shook her head and pointed to the small mountain behind them. "I left it up there...in a cave."

CHAPTER THIRTY-ONE

B obby pranced ahead like he already knew where they were going. Then again, he probably did. Mercy had to remind herself that he was no ordinary dog.

Emily and Bobby arrived at the base of the mountain first. With a quick glance over his shoulder, Bobby started the ascent.

Small rocks bounced and rolled down the mountainside as he dug his claws into the loose desert sand. Mercy and Piper stood by Emily's side, and they all watched as Bobby clambered up with surprising speed and agility.

The girl didn't take her eyes from the chocolate figure. "He says he'll get the book and bring it right back."

Bobby disappeared inside the cave and reemerged seconds later, tail wagging, book in mouth. He climbed down and dropped the book at Mercy's feet.

Mercy reached out with her mind to Lucent and Raze, speeding through the day's events. This mind-to-mind communication thing was pretty handy.

She learned that Lou and Raze had escaped from the airport. Lucent and Neshera had also managed to get away and were now resting safely in a motel.

May I see the book? Lucent asked.

The leather cover was scratched and dirty. Mercy flipped it open. Tiny, neat print filled each page. She did her best to relay the symbols and images before her. *Do you understand any of this?* she asked and felt the old man concentrating.

I'm afraid I don't, came Lucent's response.

Raze chimed in. *Lou says you should take it to Galveston National Laboratory and have someone there take a look. We'll start heading out that way and meet up with you.*

From the sounds of it, GNL is pretty huge, Mercy said, recalling what Lou had already told them. *Probably employs hundreds of people. How do we know who to trust?*

Guess we'll just have to figure that out when we get there, sis.

They parted ways with the understanding that they would all meet up in Texas as soon as possible.

Mercy looked down at the book. No point in trying to decipher it herself. Her notes from college science consisted mostly of keeping a running tally of the professor's *ums*, though her time hadn't been totally misspent. She had also kept detailed notes on the number of spitballs she could fire into the professor's coffee during the course of any given lecture hour. Her personal best was twenty-nine.

Fearing the onset of a biology flashback, she slapped the book shut and turned to Piper. "Now we just have to find someone who understands this sh—" She felt Emily's eyes on her. "Sheaf of papers," she finished quickly.

"Nice recovery." The kid pointed behind them. "I think he's thirsty."

Bobby sat a few feet away, eyes closed, jaws wide open, patiently waiting for some water to be squirted into his mouth.

Piper popped the tube out from her CamelBak, squirted him in the head instead, and then took a long drink for herself. Still waterless, Bobby opened his eyes and watched her drink while she pretended to ignore him. He finally trotted around behind her, got a running start, and head-butted her in the rear end. After that, he just stood there, wagging his tail and looking pretty darned pleased with himself.

Piper spit out the tube and lunged for him. He leapt just out of reach and took off at a full gallop with Piper close on his tail. Emily giggled and followed suit. Before she knew it, Mercy was chasing after them, the events of the past few days all but forgotten.

They ran in the direction of the warehouse. It felt good to play. Mercy needed the break. They all did.

Bobby finally allowed himself to be caught, and Mercy held him down while Piper doused him with water. Emily sidled up beside them and sprayed cold water down the back of her shirt.

Two FBI agents against a dog and a little girl—Mercy had known all along her training would come in handy one day. She swept Emily off her feet in midspray and plunked her on the ground next to Bobby where they both got the royal dousing treatment. The blood from Bobby's coat was rinsed away, and even more of the girl's fair, freckled skin was revealed.

Eventually, to save what little water remained, she and Piper let them up. Mercy hitched the tube back in the clip and stood as two drowned rats gaped up at her. Hands on hips, she looked at Piper. "Well, I think we've made our point."

Emily wiped the water from her eyes and sat up, a smile still tugging at the corners of her mouth. "Ran out of ammo, huh?"

The sun was just beginning to set on the horizon. Mountains took refuge in the shade and hunkered down for the night, their jagged peaks black against the fiery heavens. Piper handed out protein bars, and they trekked across the desert in silence, all eyes glued to the spectacular display of color.

Mercy halted them a few hundred yards from the warehouse. Black smoke billowed up into the darkening sky. Only a charred skeleton of the warehouse remained, its corpse gutted by fire.

Shadow was probably long gone by now, but Mercy wasn't in the mood to take any chances. Piper hung back with Emily and Bobby while she ran ahead to see if the coast was clear.

M16 at the ready, she scanned the area. She circled what remained of the warehouse and checked, double-checked, and triple-checked the ambulance. No evidence that the engine had been tampered with. No bombs strapped to the undercarriage. Tires weren't flat. She raised the binoculars and studied the surrounding landscape. No sign of Shadow anywhere, so she finally signaled to Piper.

Night was fully upon them by the time Mercy pulled out of the driveway and onto the dirt road. Piper turned in her seat. "Have you always been able to talk with animals, honey?"

"No," the girl replied. "It started with Bobby."

"Can you talk to all animals?"

Mercy watched from the rearview mirror as the girl shrugged her small shoulders. "I don't know. So far, it's only been Bobby."

Part of Mercy couldn't believe what she was hearing. Another part of her knew Emily had this gift for a reason.

Piper chewed her lip, her face troubled. Mercy knew exactly what she was thinking because she was thinking the same thing. She was worried about Emily having to go through life being so different.

As if listening in on their thoughts, the girl spoke up from the back. "I'd appreciate it if you guys didn't tell anyone. People would probably think I was pretty weird."

Knowing the girl's words had hit close to home, Mercy stole a glance at Piper. Neither of them said anything. Hiding such a wonderful gift would mean cheating the world of its benefits. But Emily had a point.

"Hey, did you find my dad?"

And there it was. The dreaded question. Mercy pulled to the side of the road, cut the engine, and turned in her seat. The lump in her throat felt like a supersized gumball. "Emily, I have some bad news."

"I already know," she said sadly. "The bad man killed him. I didn't see it happen, but I know he's dead. I just wanted to know if you found my dad, that's all."

Piper moved to the rear of the ambulance and sat down beside Emily. "Yeah, honey. We found him."

"What about Aunt Dana and Bubbles? I'm pretty sure he killed them, too." Mercy saw that she was trying her hardest to keep it together. Emily stuck out her chin when they didn't answer. "You're gonna try and break it to me easy because I'm a kid. Go ahead. Just tell me."

Which is exactly what they did, leaving out all the gory details.

Emily's chin quivered. "So what's gonna happen to me now? I don't have any family."

"You have me," Mercy said, reaching out to take her hand.

"Me, too," Piper said, reaching for her other hand.

Bobby scooted closer and laid his head on Emily's knee.

Piper brushed the girl's bangs out of her eyes. "I can't hear what Bobby's saying, but I think that officially makes three."

Emily wiped her wet cheeks with the back of her sleeve. "We should get going. A lot of people are sick. They need our help."

They drove to a hotel and reserved two adjoining rooms. Mercy desperately needed some sleep. She had been awake for so long that she couldn't remember what day it was. They were all exhausted. Even Bobby couldn't stop yawning.

She dropped off three tired bodies and headed out to pick up some groceries and a fresh change of clothes for everyone. The room smelled like soap and shampoo by the time she returned. Emily and Bobby were watching TV in bed. Piper was towel-drying her hair in the mirror, looking all cute and cozy in the hotel's fluffy bathrobe and slippers. Mercy dumped the bags on the bureau, made a second trip, and reappeared with two large pizzas in hand.

She opened the door to find Emily, Bobby, and Piper already seated at the table, paper plates in hand. "How'd you know I had—"

"Pizza?" Piper finished, prying the boxes from her grasp. "Another one of my gifts. I can smell it a mile away."

Mercy watched as Emily served two slices of the hamburger and sausage to Bobby and then took a plain cheese for herself.

"Speaking of smell," Piper said, "*we've* all showered."

Mercy's eyes darted around the room. Emily did, in fact, appear freshly scrubbed. Wrapped in a towel, strands of wet hair clung to her forehead. She grinned back at her with chipmunk-stuffed cheeks. Even Bobby was still damp from his bath.

Before Mercy had the sense to start stuffing her own cheeks with pizza, Piper herded her toward the bathroom. "Your turn."

"Wait a minute," she pleaded. "Can't I eat first?"

Piper shut the door on her and, "Nope," was all she heard from the other side.

"Will you at least save me a slice?" she called out through the crack.

"Depends on how you smell when you come out of there."

Twenty minutes later, Mercy emerged from the bathroom a new woman. Lights dimmed, TV lowered, Emily and Bobby were curled around one another in bed, fast asleep. She leaned against the doorjamb and watched as Piper draped a blanket over the sleeping duo. She kissed each of them on the forehead and motioned for Mercy to join her in the next room.

A pine-scented candle flickered in the center of the table. "Amber visited me when I was in the shower," Piper confessed around a mouthful of pizza.

"That must've been awkward."

"She was considerate enough not to come *inside* the shower. She just sat on the vanity and we...talked."

Mercy grinned. "Can't say I would've been that considerate."

"She wants you to see a young man by the name of Mark Zamoida. From what I could gather, they worked together at GNL." Her eyes wandered to the book on the nightstand. "He'll know what to do with that." She hesitated. "But I think there's a small glitch in our plans."

Mercy raised an eyebrow.

"Amber said everyone at GNL has already contracted the virus, including Mark. So you have to find him fast, Parker. I don't think we have much time."

Finished eating, Mercy checked on Emily and Bobby, closed the adjoining room door, and went to use the bathroom. Brushing her teeth, she caught sight of her wedding band in the mirror and marveled at how much her life had changed in the past few days. She leaned against the vanity and gave the ring one final twirl with her thumb before slipping it off.

Piper was sitting on the only bed in the room by the time Mercy came out. She patted the bed beside her, a knowing look in her eyes. "We need to talk about a few things, Parker."

"It's okay, I'll take the floor," Mercy volunteered, grabbing a pillow from one side of the bed. "I'm so tired, I could sleep anywhere."

Piper reached out and pulled her onto the bed with surprising strength. "That's not what I had in mind at all," she said seductively.

"I just wanted to tell you…" She bit her lower lip uncertainly. "I've never been with a woman."

Seeing Piper nervous like this was cute.

"I've never even felt attracted to a woman before," she blurted.

"Never?"

Piper shook her head. "It never even occurred to me…until you."

Mercy had a joke at the ready but thought better of it. Felt like their conversation was heading in a more serious direction. "Have you been with anyone since Tim?"

"No, not since Tim. I could never imagine sharing myself with anyone else."

Mercy hesitated. "And now?"

"And now"—she laced her fingers through Mercy's—"I can't imagine being with anyone but you." She lifted Mercy's hand, turned it over. "Your wedding band is gone."

"I took it off." Mercy looked down at their intertwined hands. "It was time for me to let go." Like Anna had said during her visit from The Great Beyond, loving Piper would never change what she had shared with Anna.

"I guess that means we're on the same page."

Mercy nodded, unsure of what to say. She felt drawn to Piper in a way she couldn't understand, let alone explain. It was nice to know the feeling was mutual.

"About tonight…" Piper said.

"I don't expect anything from you tonight," Mercy assured her. "There's no pressure. We can take things as slow as you want."

"That's just it," Piper said with a wry grin. "I don't want to take things slow with you. I just wanted to give you fair warning that you might not be able to keep up." She pushed Mercy down hard and climbed on top of her. "I'm pretty feisty in bed."

Not to be outdone, Mercy flipped her over in one fluid motion. "Don't worry." She pinned Piper's arms above her head. "I can hold my own just fine."

They took turns kissing, teasing, laughing, and getting to know the feel of a new partner. They undressed one another slowly. With the last barriers of clothing finally shed, Piper guided Mercy's hands and mouth along her body, eventually begging for release with throaty whispers in the night. Their unhurried rhythm was kicked into high gear by raw, fervent need. Piper was a quick study, pleasing Mercy in ways that left her light-headed and aching for more.

They made love quietly, passionately, with a sense of belonging and urgency Mercy had never before known. Her hands glowed under the sheets with every caress. It dawned on her that she was still trying to heal this beautiful woman from the virus that was already inside her body. Deep down, Mercy knew she could never heal Piper completely because she couldn't undo Shadow's work. Only the cure from Amber's book could help her now.

Mercy woke up five minutes before the alarm was set to go off. She cracked open the adjoining room door to look in on Emily and Bobby. Snuggled up in a tight little ball of dog and child, both were sleeping peacefully.

It was still dark outside when Mercy showered and dressed. Piper sat up in bed and watched in silence as she gathered her gear. Ready to go, Mercy sat on the edge of the bed. "Regrets?" she whispered.

Piper shook her head. "You?"

"Nope. Last night with you"—Mercy leaned in for a kiss—"was *way* better than sleeping on the floor." Making love with Piper only made it more difficult to leave. She felt like she was leaving her family behind.

"We'll be fine, Parker." Piper must have sensed her ambivalence. "Just find Mark, give him the book, save the world. Easy-peasy."

"Cakewalk," Mercy agreed. She gave Piper one last dose of healing light, kissed each eyelid, and walked out of the hotel room counting the minutes until they could reunite.

CHAPTER THIRTY-TWO

Mercy used the ambulance's navigation system to map the quickest route from Chandler, Arizona, to Galveston, Texas. It was a seventeen hour drive. Time she didn't have.

A plane could get her there in just over two hours, but she couldn't very well return to Sky Harbor Airport and request use of the colonel's private jet. The closest airstrip was Chandler Municipal Airport. Maybe she could hitch a ride with someone there.

Colors were just beginning to seep into the eastern sky as she turned right on Gilbert Road and pulled up alongside the airport security booth. The booth was empty, so she got out, lifted the black and yellow bar, and drove right on in.

The tarmac was eerily quiet. She'd always been under the impression that pilots were early creatures. It was already five thirty. The day was a-wastin'. Where was everyone?

Anchored on the tarmac, single- and twin-engine aircraft waited for their chance to take to the sky. She didn't know much about planes, but she knew enough to be able to recognize a few. Cessna Skyhawk. Beechcraft Baron. Mooney Ovation. She eased to a stop in front of a '67 Piper Comanche. Red-tipped nose and wings. Stout white body with thickly painted red lines. A *For Sale* sign hung crookedly in the cockpit window on a piece of cardboard.

A friend of her uncle's had taken her and Raze for a ride in a '67 Comanche when they were kids. She would never forget that day. Her first time in a plane had felt like magic.

She smiled, reflecting on the innocence of youth. She had never told anyone that this very plane was what prompted her chosen career path. Her uncle's friend, Bob Reed, was an FBI agent. Since Mercy was just nine when she met Bob, she'd mistakenly thought that she had to be an FBI agent, too, if she wanted a plane like the one Bob had.

Couldn't be the same plane, could it? Bob was retired now. Mercy hadn't laid eyes on the guy in over twenty-five years.

She climbed down from the ambulance to peek inside the Comanche's windows. Same tan vinyl seats with dark brown corduroy. Same shaggy pee-yellow carpet. She mashed her nose against the glass and couldn't say for sure, but she could almost make out the stain on the floor in the back where Raze had barfed his brains out.

"You in the market?" a gravelly voice called out from behind her.

Mercy spun around. It was him all right. Older, grayer, fatter, less hair—but definitely Bob.

"Simple yes or no question."

"It's been a while, Bob. You might not remember me. You knew my uncle, Chief Hamber."

Bob's eyes narrowed. "You're one of the twins."

She stepped forward and extended her hand. "Mercy Parker."

Bob declined the handshake. "You the one threw up in my plane?"

"No, sir. That was my brother, Raze."

Bob's face softened. "In that case, good to see you again." He gripped the offered hand, all the while eyeing the ambulance. "What brings you out this way?"

"I'm with the bureau now."

"Which department?"

"UCH."

"Tough department. Working a case?"

"Something like that. Listen, Bob. I need to fly to Texas."

"And Sky Harbor's closed, so you came here."

She nodded, watching as Bob assembled the pieces with a quick mind. No doubt he already knew about the virus. The media blackout had ended and they had dubbed the virus Air Abroad. So far as the media could ascertain, the source of contagion seemed to stem from aircraft.

"What part of Texas?" Bob asked.

"Galveston."

"As I recall, there's a Level Four biosafety facility out that way. What the hell's the name of that place?" Bob stroked the scruff of his beard and finally looked up, his eyes narrowed in silent accusation. "Galveston National Laboratory."

"Don't mean to be evasive, but—"

"Of course you mean to be evasive." Bob turned and skulked away.

"Hate to impose on you like this," she said, jogging to catch up, "but is there any way you could fly me there?"

"Nope." With the push of a button, Bob raised the metal door of a huge hangar. Hushed voices drifted out. About a hundred gray and balding heads turned in her direction, all dressed to the hilt in suits and ties and seated in chairs around a podium. "But maybe one of these fine gentlemen can." Bob puffed out his chest proudly. "All retired FBI from back in the day."

Mercy glanced down at her own shorts and T-shirt. *Got balls?* was written across the front with a picture of a golf club. "Funny," she said looking up. "And I thought the Old Farts of the FBI gala wasn't until next month."

Indignant, Bob strode to the podium and tapped the microphone. Men straightened in their chairs. "Allow me to introduce our newest member, Agent Mercy Parker. As some of you may recall, she's the kid who threw up in my plane."

Mercy shouldered him aside. "Let me set the record straight, gentlemen." She placed her hands on either side of the podium. "I did *not* throw up in Bob's plane. That was my brother, Raze Parker. He ate enough Doritos that day to feed a third-world country."

"Would you be willing to take a polygraph to that effect?" a voice from the left called out.

Bob reached over, closing his hand around the mic. "Careful," he whispered. "That's Harold, the Bureau's polygraph examiner, over thirty years."

Mercy thought for a moment while her audience sat in rapt attention. "I'll do you one better." She withdrew her cell and dialed Lou's number. "Put Raze on," she said when Lou answered.

"Yo, why the old-fashioned pipeline?" Raze asked.

Mercy pressed the button for speakerphone and held it up to the mic.

"Remember flying in that Comanche when we were kids?"

"You gonna ask if I can hot-wire a plane now? I'm good, but not that good, sis."

She felt as everyone's eyes bored into her skull. If there was a less convenient time to mention her aptitude for grand larceny, she sure couldn't think of one. She cleared her throat. "Remember how you threw up just after takeoff?"

Raze laughed. "Doritos," he snorted. "I was blowing orange snot for two days!"

Mercy clicked the End button without another word. "Any questions?"

Not a one.

"Okay, then." She rubbed her hands together. "Who's got enough gas in their plane to fly me to Texas?"

❖

Mercy learned that the old farts had assembled at Chandler Municipal Airport shortly after news of the virus spread. She recognized many of their faces. These were men of integrity with powerful contacts.

She listened to what they had to say and answered as many of their questions as she could, but it was approaching seven o'clock. Time was ticking. Something told her these men weren't going to let her off the hook. She had to give them something.

"What I'm about to tell you doesn't leave this room." She unzipped the backpack, pulled out Amber's book, and held it up.

"I need to get this to Galveston National Laboratory as quickly as possible. It's the cure for Air Abroad."

"You're sure about that?" someone called out.

"Yes, sir. One hundred percent."

A former director of the FBI stood. "You could have saved us all a lot of time by sharing that information up front. Who's your contact at GNL?"

"Mark Zamoida." She couldn't believe she was actually speaking to William H. Merriam. The man was a legend. Terrorism, espionage, and police corruption were just some of the issues he'd tackled during his tenure at the bureau.

Merriam turned to the gentleman seated beside him. "Gagnon, you're with me. Everyone else, meet at Galveston City Airport at oh nine thirty hours."

Mercy cleared her throat. "With all due respect, sir, is it really necessary for everyone to make this trip?"

"Once GNL manufactures this cure, how do you suppose it's going to make its way into the hands of the American people before they succumb to the effects of the virus?"

Mercy hadn't thought that far ahead. Let's see. One hundred retired agents plus one hundred airplanes equaled…

Duh.

Merriam opened his arms and smiled. "We're back from retirement, boys."

Twenty minutes later, Mercy found herself aboard the former director's very own SJ30-2 at a cruising altitude of thirty thousand feet. Merriam put the plane on autopilot, left Gagnon in charge, and stretched out on the seat opposite Mercy. "She's the fastest little jet in her class," he gloated. "We'll land at least thirty minutes ahead of everyone else." He handed Mercy a slip of paper with a phone number. "Call me if you run into any trouble."

"Aren't you coming, sir?"

"Negative." Merriam withdrew a laptop from a nearby compartment and flipped it open. His fingers flew over the keyboard.

Mercy still pecked at the keyboard like a third grader. She looked down at her hands. Who was she kidding? Even a third grader typed faster than her.

"You'll show up at GNL, meet with Zamoida, and see that the vaccine is manufactured as quickly as possible. In the meantime, I'll prepare a flight plan to make the distribution." Merriam glanced up from the screen. "Assuming you do, in fact, have this cure in your possession."

Mercy nodded.

"I'd sure like to hear how that cure landed in your lap." Merriam turned his attention back to the screen. "You can tell me the story someday over a few beers, once we're done kicking this thing to kingdom come."

A black limo was waiting on the tarmac when they touched down. Mercy reached out to Raze and Lucent with her mind. *I'm about fifteen minutes from the lab.*

Neshera and I are close, came the old man's response.

We're thirty minutes out, said Raze. *Well, twenty with my driving.*

Mercy opened the sunroof and rolled down her window for some fresh air. The morning was warm, and she was glad to be wearing shorts. The driver made a right on Eighty-First Street and hung a left on Seawall Boulevard. "Pull over here," she told the driver as soon as the sign for Sixth Street came into view.

They waited on the side of the road for several minutes until a Lincoln Town Car pulled up behind them.

Neshera is not well, the old man said in a shaky voice. *I fear she has taken a turn for the worse.*

Mercy hurried to the Lincoln and threw open the passenger's door. Neshera was curled up on the seat beside Lucent. Blood dripped freely from her nose and pooled on her chest. A dark crimson stain was still spreading across the front of her blouse. Mercy brought a hand to her cheek. Her skin was ice-cold.

Golden light did not spill from her palm this time. Neshera had been dead for too long. There was nothing she could do.

Mercy heard Metallica blaring from the speakers before the Jeep even rounded the corner. The top was down, and Lou was holding on to the safety bar for dear life. Raze pulled off the road, screeched to a stop, and jumped out without even bothering to open the door. Still in his torn jeans and leather boots, he'd traded his Harley T-shirt for a sleeveless white tank. He tossed his leather jacket over one shoulder and strode over. "What are we waiting for?" His eyes lowered to Neshera. "Holy shit, she okay?"

Mercy grabbed the old man's cane off the back seat, went around to the other side, and opened his door.

Lucent's hand trembled as he stroked Neshera's cheek. "I am so sorry, dear child. So very sorry."

"Lucent." Mercy reached in and squeezed his shoulder. "We need to go."

"I wanted nothing more than to help her, but she would not allow it. Neshera was stubborn and selfless to the end. She refused to let me use the last of my healing on her." The old man looked up, his wrinkles wet with tears. "I cannot leave her like this, Mercy. She deserves so much more."

"I'll make sure she's taken care of." She held out the wooden cane. "You have my word on that, old man."

Quiet with grief, they all climbed inside the limo. An enormous black-marbled sign soon welcomed them to the University of Texas Medical Branch.

CHAPTER THIRTY-THREE

Mercy was worried about Piper. Neshera and Piper had contracted the virus around the same time. Since her healing abilities were only able to provide temporary relief from the symptoms, Piper was still at risk. She didn't realize people were dying so quickly after exposure. Maybe leaving her behind at the hotel wasn't such a good idea.

Lou was sitting across from her in the limo. She studied him discreetly. An angry rash covered the entire surface of his neck and both hands, his cheeks were red with fever, and dried blood clung to one corner of his moustache.

As soon as Lou turned to gaze out the window, Mercy unfolded her hand and let the light spill from her palm. She dulled Lou's fever, headache, and nausea to make him more comfortable.

Lucent looked on from across the way, nodding his approval. *Well done, Mercy. You are getting stronger.*

It might be wise to ask the old man some questions while she still had the chance. *Is there any limit to this...healing?*

Yes, replied Lucent. *Two steadfast laws exist. No matter how hard you try, you cannot heal someone who does not wish to be healed. You also cannot heal someone who was maimed or sickened by your counterpart. That is why you are unable to heal those around you from this virus.*

By my counterpart, do you mean Shadow?

For now, yes. As soon as my brother and I pass from this world, your counterpart will be Raze.

Raze was busy searching for the stereo controls in the limo's numerous compartments. He didn't have a clue that Mercy and the old man were talking. *Can other people see the light in my hands when I heal someone?*

Most cannot, though there are exceptions.

Emily had seen the light. *What does it mean if someone can see the light?*

It is usually a sign that they are exceptionally blessed with their own supernatural gifts.

She thought about Bobby and the mountain lion cub. *Have you ever brought someone back from the dead?*

Yes, many times, though there are limits to that, too. No more than fifteen minutes can elapse from the time of death to the time of healing.

I'm so sorry about Neshera, Mercy said after a long, thoughtful silence.

As am I, came Lucent's response. He gazed out the window with a longing that tore at Mercy's heart.

Deciding to take a moment to check in on Piper, she called her cell and held the phone to her ear. When Piper picked up, she tried not to sound worried. She told Piper that her uncle's friend, Bob, would be there shortly to pick them up and fly them out to Galveston.

The limo pulled alongside the university's security checkpoint. Two armed guards in yellow PPE suits waved them through. They parked at the main entrance and climbed out.

Someone was already waiting for them at the curb. A DOD identification tag swung from a cord around his neck. "Which one of you is Agent Parker?" he shouted through the face mask.

Mercy raised a hand and dug her badge out from the pocket of her shorts.

The DOD employee handed her a packaged suit and breathing apparatus. "The lab's air filtration system has been compromised. Full protection is recommended for your own safety." He glanced at Lucent, Raze, and Lou. "We were expecting only you. I'll call up and get three more suits sent down."

"Don't bother." Mercy handed the suit back. "We've already been exposed."

By the time they'd passed through the double-door airlock, stepped off the elevator, and made their way down the corridor, Mercy was wishing she'd brought her sunglasses. Bright yellow suits darted in and out of offices. They hurried along the corridors in groups of twos and threes and all but oozed out of every building orifice.

Thankfully, Mark Zamoida was not disguised as a human corn on the cob. Dressed in jeans and a green Old Navy T-shirt, he rose from the table as soon as they walked in the room. He was younger than Mercy expected. By about twenty-five years.

"Is it true?" Mark asked excitedly, motioning for each of them to sit. "You have the cure?"

Taking the chair across from Mark, she decided this kid couldn't be more than twenty. Tan, lean, blond, he looked like he'd just stepped out of a Gap ad. "Do you work here, Mark?"

"Yes, ma'am. Started last year after I graduated."

"From what?" Raze snickered. "The Boy Scouts?"

"Stanford Medical School." Mark picked at the leather band on his wrist. "My colleagues give me grief about my age all the time. I'm twenty-two. Sort of jumped ahead in school."

Interesting, Mercy thought. Both Amber and Mark were child prodigies, attended Stanford, and worked at GNL. "Did you know Amber Morrison?"

Mark crossed his arms, his face guarded. "I read about the Golden Gate Bridge bomb, but I don't care what the papers say. Amber would never hurt anyone."

Mercy unzipped her backpack. "I believe you," she said, withdrawing Amber's book.

Mark reached behind him, hefted an overstuffed book bag into the chair beside him, and withdrew an exact replica of Amber's leather journal. "We each kept one," he explained. "This is where we recorded our findings on BCV-114." He gestured to the book in front of Mercy. "Can I see that, please?"

"We were hoping you could help us decipher what's written inside." She slid it across the table and watched as Mark scanned the last few pages.

"Amber and I came up with a code for recording data." Mark finally looked up. "This wouldn't make sense to anyone else. How'd you know to bring it to me?"

"Call it a hunch," she said dismissively. "Tell me...what's BCV-114?"

"The government's new pet project. BCV stands for bio-chemical virus. Made right here in America." Mark shook his head, frowning. "It always bothered Amber that the government created lethal pathogens without cures. That's how she convinced me to work here. We both had offers from top private institutions, but in the end, we decided we could make the biggest difference here."

"By doing what exactly?"

"By formulating cures for the man-made stuff that the government pays people like us to come up with in the first place. One of the perks to working in a place like this is you always have access to a lab. Amber and I came here in our spare time to work on finding cures for some of the more lethal BCVs." He held up both hands so the rash was visible on each palm. "In case something like this ever happened."

"When were you exposed?"

"Two days ago. I was one of the first teams that responded to Sky Harbor in Phoenix. Turned out my suit was defective."

Lou leaned forward. "Don't those suits come equipped with an internal alarm system?"

"Yeah, well." Mark ran his fingers through his hair, sat back, and sighed. "They're supposed to."

"That sucks." Raze leaned back, precariously balancing his chair on two legs. He laced his fingers behind his head. "How'd the virus get around so fast, anyway?"

"BCV-114 is an airborne pathogen. So far as we can tell, the air filtration systems aboard commercial aircraft were heavily contaminated with the virus."

Lou removed his glasses and wiped at each lens with a tissue. "I thought passengers were safeguarded against airborne pathogens by HEPA filters."

Raze looked over at Lou like he had three heads. "What the hell is a HEPA filter?"

"It stands for high efficiency particulate air filter." Lou slid his glasses back on. "It's a type of air filter that—"

"How do you know all this shit?" Raze grabbed a handful of peanut M&M's from a glass bowl and tossed them in his mouth, his eyes still on Lou.

"I read it in—" Lou cut himself off, waving a hand in the air. "Forget it. Sorry, Mark. Please continue."

Mark didn't skip a beat. "It looks like whoever's responsible for this knew the filters wouldn't stop it. Basically, the HEPA filters currently being used on commercial aircraft can remove particles 0.3 micrometers in size. To give you an idea of how small that is, a pencil point is about 1,000 micrometers in diameter. BCV-114 was specifically engineered to evade HEPA filters, at 0.1 micrometer."

"Making it small enough to pass through the HEPA filters and infect an entire passenger list," Mercy finished.

Lucent ran his thumb back and forth over the top of his cane. "How long does it take for this virus to run its course, son?"

"Hard to say. It's a little different for each person, but on average"—he shrugged—"about five days."

Lou pointed to the book in Mark's hand. "And how long until the cure can be transferred from those pages into something we can use?"

"Anywhere from twelve to twenty-four hours. I'll work as quickly as I can." Mark stuffed both books inside his bag, stood from the table, and slung the bag over one shoulder. "On one condition."

Mercy pushed her chair away from the table and stood. "What's that?"

"Promise me you'll clear Amber's name."

"Consider it done." They shook hands, and Mark slipped out of the room in a hurry.

❖

Mercy, Lou, Raze, and Lucent waited in the third floor lobby. They passed the time with countless games of Rock-Paper-Scissors and I Spy until finally—bless her soul—the receptionist took pity on them and pulled out a deck of cards from her desk drawer.

They were in the middle of a heated game of war when a yellow suit came rushing over. Mercy looked at her watch: 11:50 a.m. Something was wrong. Just three hours had passed since Mark took to the lab.

"Dr. Zamoida is very ill," he shouted through his face mask. "He's asking for Agent Parker."

Mercy stood and followed him down a long hallway to an unmarked door. It took him a few tries to scan the ID card around his neck. The gloves looked bulky. Then finally—*click*—an interior door lock sounded. He unlatched the door, held it ajar, and then let it fall shut behind her.

Mark was lying in a twin-sized bed. Save for his blue boxers, he was naked. The sheets lay in a tangled mass at his feet, his lean, sinewy body slick with sweat. Blood trickled from his ears and nose. He was shivering, and his teeth chattered as he spoke. "This thing is k-kicking my ass."

Mercy pulled up a chair beside the bed.

"Sorry. Didn't f-finish."

"You did the best you could, Mark." She felt bad for the kid. No one should have to suffer like this. "Were you able to decode the book so one of your colleagues could take over?"

"Tried. N-not enough time." Mark's eyelids fluttered until only the whites of his eyes were visible. Violent spasms wracked his body. The blood from his ears and nose splattered across the white sheets like an artist flinging paint at a canvas.

Mercy placed her glowing hands on Mark's chest. The young man quieted at once and began breathing deeply, rhythmically. In a comatose state, at least Mark wouldn't feel any more pain.

She untangled the sheets at the foot of the bed, pulled them up, and cleaned the blood off Mark's face.

Sometime later, she let herself out of the room with Mark's ID and made her way back to the lobby. Lou, Raze, and Lucent looked up from a game of rummy. With aces, kings, and queens laid out before him, it looked like the old man was kicking butt.

Mercy cleared her throat. "Mark just died." She shook her head, still haunted by the images of the young man's gruesome death.

No one asked what from. They put down their cards.

"The really ironic part is that he didn't have time to finish decoding the book."

Raze ran a hand over his stubble. "So we have the cure, but it's in a book no one can freaking read?"

Lou stood and slid his hands in his pockets. "Call Piper. Tell her to get over here as soon as possible."

"What good is that gonna do?" Raze asked. "She can't read the damn thing, either."

Mercy met Lou's eyes and nodded. "But Mark can," she said. "All Piper needs is a photo."

❖

Bobby jumped out of the limo first and barked as if to say hello. Mercy crouched down and gave him a good scratch behind the ears. "Hey, boy, how's Piper holding up?" she whispered.

Bobby whined and pawed at the air as Piper slid from the limo. "Things must be bad if you've started talking to my dog."

Mercy stood, wrapped her arms around Piper, and bent down to give Emily a big hug. "I really missed you guys."

"Are you always this mushy?" the girl asked, patting Mercy on the back like a little mother hen. "You haven't even been gone that long."

A small black furry head popped out from the backpack on Emily's shoulder, coming nose to nose with Mercy. She jumped back reflexively. "What the—"

"Oh, that's Ansel. He's a baby skunk. He was run over by a truck, and now I'm pretty sure he has a broken leg."

"A skunk?" She turned to Piper. "You let her have a skunk?"

Emily carefully plucked him from her backpack. He was about the size of a six-week-old kitten.

"He's been waiting to meet you," the girl stated emphatically. "Can you heal him before we go inside? Oh, and don't worry. He's already agreed not to spray you."

"You sure about that?"

The girl shrugged. "Pretty."

"You're not afraid of a little baby skunk now," Piper said, grinning. "Are you, Parker?"

Emily set the skunk in Mercy's arms and gazed up at her with big brown eyes. Mercy's future looked pretty bleak if she couldn't learn how to say no to this kid.

"Well? Are you gonna heal him or what?" Emily put her hands on her hips. "He's in a lot of pain, you know."

Mercy handed the baby skunk over and winked.

"Wow!" The girl's eyes grew wide. "You already healed him? I didn't even see it this time." Emily skipped away happily and set the baby skunk in the grass.

"So"—Piper stepped closer and kissed Mercy sweetly on the lips—"what's going on?"

"The man Amber told us to see—"

"Mark Zamoida?"

"He died about thirty minutes ago."

"There must be hundreds of qualified—" Piper hesitated. "What do you call those virus people again?"

"Virologists?"

"Right. There must be hundreds of those people in this place, so why not just give the book to one of them?"

"Good idea, except it was written in a code only he and Amber understood." Mercy swore she could literally see the light bulb blinking on above Piper's head.

"Oh. You want me to have a little chat with Mark from The Great Beyond to help decode the book."

"Do you mind?"

"Fine." Piper sighed. "But I'll need a recent photo."

"Funny you should mention that. I just happen to have one right here." She withdrew Mark's ID from a back pocket.

CHAPTER THIRTY-FOUR

Mercy made introductions and left Emily, Bobby, and Ansel in Lou's care while Piper accompanied her to the building's west wing. They followed Dr. Howard down a long series of corridors to another door that, under normal circumstances, would have required a Level Four security clearance to unlock.

She and Piper were led to a room with a large glass window overlooking a huge lab. Computer terminals and shiny, sterile surfaces reflected the harsh glare of fluorescent lights. About forty yellow-suited lab personnel were gathered in the middle of the room.

There was a modest walnut-veneered table, a black microphone that was mounted to the wall, and a chrome stool in front of the window. Someone had copied the leather journals, condensed them into a spiral-bound notebook, and affixed it to the wall with a chain.

Dr. Howard stepped over to the mic and pointed to a black switch. "Just turn this on and begin speaking into the microphone whenever you're ready. It's a two-way communication system." He pointed to the overhead speakers. "We may ask you to clarify something or repeat yourself from time to time. I'll be joining my staff down below. Please, Dr. Vasey, take a seat, make yourself comfortable." Then, flashing a ghost of a smile behind his face mask, he promptly turned and exited the room.

"Make myself comfortable," she muttered, sliding onto the shiny metal stool. "They could've at least set me up with an armchair, beer, and some pizza."

"Good thing you didn't wear a skirt," Mercy said, looking from her legs to the glass, and then out to the room below.

Piper adjusted the mic. "I guess now would be a bad time to tell you that I suffer from severe anxiety when it comes to public speaking?"

"That's unfortunate." She slid Mark's ID from her pocket. "Ready?"

"Ready as I'll ever be." Piper took a deep breath, opened the notebook, and set Mark's photo beside it. Her eyes glazed over, and her lips began moving at once. Nodding, she pierced Mercy with a faraway gaze. "Mark says he didn't die alone. He wants to thank you for staying with him at the end."

The hairs on the back of Mercy's neck stood up.

Piper turned on the microphone and began the translation for the scientists below.

Mercy hung around for another twenty minutes, watching the way Piper glanced over her shoulder at the unseen presence beside her. Amazed, she finally unlocked the door and headed back to the lobby.

She found Lucent asleep in a chair, knees primly together. He held his wooden cane across his lap. His wrinkled mouth hung open, forming a perfect O.

Raze, on the other hand, was snoring. He'd kicked off his black leather boots to prop his feet on the table. Several hairy toes poked through the holes in both socks.

Lou rose from a chair on the opposite side of the room and slid his hands in his pockets when he saw Mercy approaching. "Your brother's a pig."

"I know." They both stood in place, mesmerized by the long line of drool that finally broke free from Raze's lip to land on the front of his Harley T-shirt.

"I don't mean to alarm you, Parker, but I think there's a creature living inside Emily's backpack. It bears an uncanny resemblance to something from the *Mephitidae* family."

"The who family?"

"A skunk, Parker. I think the girl may have Pepé Le Pew in her bag."

She scanned the lobby. "Where is she?"

"Bathroom." Lou pointed. "Down the hall and to the right. She has an escort, by the way."

"Brown, furry, cold wet nose?"

Lou nodded. "That would be him."

Mercy turned the corner and knocked on the door to the women's bathroom. She heard a toilet flush as Bobby barked once from inside, but she didn't know if that was an invitation to come in or a warning to stay out. Bobby finally nudged the door open, peered up at her, and whined.

Mercy poked her head inside. "Emily?"

"In here," a little voice replied.

She found her huddled on the floor of the first stall. Vomit clung to the edge of the toilet. She was so pale. "Sorry." Emily looked up. "I'm not feeling so good."

Not her, too. Hadn't this kid already been through enough? Mercy bent to pick her up. Her skin was cool and clammy.

"There are so many of them here," the girl whispered.

Mercy set her on the counter, smoothed back her hair. "So many what, honey?"

"So many animals."

Poor kid was probably hallucinating. She pressed a hand to her forehead, feeling for a fever. "Just you, me, Bobby, and Ansel in here," she assured her. At the mention of his name, Ansel's head popped up from the backpack on the counter.

"No, not them. The *others*. They're in so much pain." She started to cry. "From being experimented on."

Mercy thought about it for a moment and realized she was probably right. This was a lab, after all.

"I reached out to them with my mind, and now I feel how sad and hurting and lonely all of them are." Emily shook her head. "It's too much. We have to save them."

"Honey, those animals are here for a reason. We can't—"

"We have to." She shuddered. "You can make them better. Please, Mercy? Oh, please don't let them suffer."

"Emily, those animals are very important. They allow us to find cures for diseases that afflict people all over the world. The lab needs those animals so they can test their medicines." She sighed. "They have to make sure that the medicines are safe for people like you and me."

Emily chewed her lip and gazed up. There they were…those big brown eyes. The only difference was that they were bigger, browner, and sadder this time.

❖

Convinced that Emily was made sick by her empathic ability and not the virus, Mercy finally gave in and agreed to search for the lab. She refused to make any promises beyond that. At least, that's what she told herself to make herself feel better. Maybe the bureau offered some type of training on how to resist the puppy dog eyes of little girls. She made a mental note to look into that as soon as all of this was over.

She helped Emily down from the bathroom counter. "You okay to walk by yourself?" she asked.

"I think so. It's just that"—fresh tears welled up in her eyes—"I feel what those animals are feeling, and I don't know how to turn it off."

She knelt and took both of Emily's hands. "Just like with anything new, it'll take some practice. On the bright side, maybe you can learn from this."

Emily wiped her nose on the back of her hand. "What do you mean?"

"Well, if I were you, I probably wouldn't reach out to so many animals at once. Maybe focus on talking to just one at a time from now on."

Bobby nipped at the edge of Emily's T-shirt and started tugging her toward the door, eliciting a small smile through the tears. "Bobby wants to take us to the lab. Like, now."

Before Mercy knew it, she found herself marching through the corridors with a little girl on one side and a chocolate Labrador on the other. Ansel was still hiding in Emily's backpack, his twitching whiskers barely visible to the untrained eye. When a guard glanced up from his post as they passed, Mercy nodded and pretended like she knew where she was going. Admittedly, they might have looked a little out of place.

The yellow suits were concentrated in the west wing. Bobby was leading them to the east wing. They turned the corner and continued down a deserted stretch of corridor.

Mercy could hear her own heartbeat as Bobby's nails clicked on the tile. The place was unnervingly quiet. Bobby halted at the last door and stared at the doorknob intently.

"He says this is the place." Emily reached out to brush her hand across the door's surface. "I can feel it, too. The animals…they're waiting for us," she said, almost trancelike.

Mercy glanced over her shoulder to make sure they hadn't been followed before swiping Mark's ID. The light turned green, and the door unlocked. She turned to Emily. "You and Bobby wait here. Let me go in first and make sure the coast is clear."

Emily set her hands on her hips. "No one's inside," she said. "I know you're trying to protect me from seeing what's in there, but the animals already showed me what those doctors did to them, and I should warn you"—she looked down, shaking her head—"it's really awful."

The pungent aroma of urine, feces, and bleach assaulted her senses as they stepped inside. Glass aquariums and metal crates lined the walls with assorted mammals: rabbits, ferrets, dogs, cats, mice, guinea pigs, rats, gerbils—even a pig and a chimpanzee. Mercy wandered past each cage, horrified. Many of the animals were already dead and far beyond the realm of her help. Each cage was marked with a sign that read *Terminate* in bold red letters.

Emily asked, "What does that mean, Mercy?"

She deserved to know the truth. "It means these animals are going to be destroyed."

"Oh, *terminate*. Like in *The Terminator*. The doctors want to kill them." She tugged on Mercy's shirtsleeve. "But we're not gonna let them, right?"

She tried not to look at Emily. She really did. But the pull from those brown eyes was just too strong.

Thirty minutes and numerous healings later, they were making their way to the rear of the lab with a herd of nineteen rats, seventeen mice, six rabbits, five guinea pigs, two cats, one ferret, a shy beagle named Rosie, a baby pig named Lipstick, and a chimp named Nana—short for Banana. Emily had them all named and standing, single-file, between her and Bobby in the span of a minute.

Mercy paused at the door's threshold and turned to say something, but the girl interrupted her. "I told them to meet up with us later. They promised to stay out of sight."

She stood there gawking at the unlikely group. "Where?"

"Where what?" Emily asked.

"Where are they going to meet us?"

"Oh." She shrugged. "I'm not sure yet. But don't worry, Mercy." She patted the back of her hand reassuringly. "We'll figure it out."

The animals waited patiently in line. Impossible. "Aren't the cats going to eat the mice?" Mercy asked.

"Nope."

"How can you be sure?"

"Because I asked them not to."

Maybe it would be better if the rats ate the mice, the cats ate the rats, and then the dog ate the cats. It would definitely be fewer animals to cart home at the end of the day.

Shaking her head, and against her better judgment, Mercy scanned the keycard and waited for the light to turn green. She watched as nineteen rats, seventeen mice, six rabbits, five guinea pigs, two cats, one ferret, a beagle, a pig, and a chimp filed outside, one by one. They trotted off to a line of trees and expertly scattered until not even a pink mouse tail could be seen.

"This is the first time they've ever been out of their cages." Emily hugged herself and smiled. "They're all so happy right now."

Raze and Lucent were still asleep when they made their way back to the lobby. Emily sidled up next to Lou and grinned.

"Well, don't you look like the cat that just ate the canary?"

She tugged on his sleeve, cupped her hand, and whispered in Lou's ear. Mercy watched as Lou's caterpillar eyebrows rose above the frame of his glasses and almost jumped clear off his face.

Mercy slid her hands in her pockets and started backing away. "Why don't the two of you get started on a game of Go Fish? I'll check on Piper." She turned and fled down the hall, feeling the fire of Lou's disapproving gaze as it burned a hole in the back of her skull.

She swiped Mark's ID and stepped inside the observation room. Piper was still perched on the stool in front of the window. The book was closed, the mic turned off. Obviously finished with her part, she was now watching the scientists below as they scurried from one workstation to the next. Their excitement was nearly palpable through the glass.

It wasn't until Mercy stepped up beside her that she realized Piper was sweating and shaking. The notebook's black cover was speckled with blood.

Catching movement out of the corner of her eye, Piper turned and then quickly buried her face in her hands. "Parker, go away. Don't look at me." Blood dripped from her ears and trickled down the sides of her face. She was using her T-shirt to staunch the flow of blood from her nose. The entire front of her chest was covered with a dark crimson stain.

Mercy felt a rising panic but refused to stand by and watch her suffer. There was only one thing she could do for her now. Tears blurred her vision as her hands filled with light and rose, almost on their own accord, to make contact with Piper's body one last time.

She placed her hands on Piper's shoulders, filling her body with light and inducing a coma just as she had done with Mark. She set Piper gently on the floor and stood, unable to stop her own tears. This wasn't supposed to be happening.

She clicked on the mic. "This is Agent Parker. Where's Dr. Howard?" She watched as a yellow-suited figure parted from a small group of huddled suits and ambled to the microphone in the room below.

A voice came over the speaker a few seconds later. "This is Dr. Howard."

"How close are you?" she asked.

"I beg your pardon?"

"To making the goddamn cure?"

The masked figure looked up at the glass. "We'll need about six hours to develop the first batch of the vaccine."

Mercy clicked off the mic and slammed her fist into the table. If Mark's passing was any indication of how fast the virus progressed at this stage, she doubted if Piper had an hour—much less six. Her mind grew fuzzy. She could bring an animal back from the dead but couldn't heal the woman she loved? It felt like a cruel joke.

She thought back to something Lucent had said in the limo. *You cannot heal someone who was maimed or sickened by your counterpart. That is why you are unable to heal those around you from this virus.*

Mercy startled the old man awake with a telepathic tap on the shoulder. *Lucent.*

She felt as the old man opened his eyes to reacquaint himself with his surroundings. *Yes, Mercy.*

Shadow isn't my counterpart. Raze is. So why can't I heal Piper from this virus?

The old man sighed wearily. *Because Raze has not yet accepted who he is. Until that happens, Shadow's position will remain unchallenged.*

Why didn't you tell me this before?

Your brother must accept who he is on his own terms, Mercy. It is futile to try to force it upon him before he is ready.

Great. Saving the woman she loved meant condemning Raze to a life of misery. How could she ever ask that of her own flesh and blood? She shook her head and choked back a sob. She couldn't. She wouldn't.

You don't have to, Raze interrupted. *I accept.*

Raze, no! I won't let you do this.

Not your choice, sis. Doesn't matter anyway. It is what it is. I can accept it now or I can accept it later. Isn't that right, old man?

I'm afraid he is correct, Mercy. This burden was his to assume from the day he was born.

Mercy felt her own rage bleeding to the surface. Raze had never done anything to deserve the life he was being sentenced to. *Wait a minute. Who says Raze is the one to walk in Shadow's footsteps? Why not me?*

Your roles were preordained long ago, Mercy. I'm sorry. I know you love your brother, but you cannot walk his path for him.

This conversation is getting a little too touchy-feely for me, Raze said. *Peace out.* And then, just like that, he was gone.

Don't do this, Raze! Do you hear me? But the door in his mind had already shut, and Raze was denying her entry. *Where is he, Lucent?*

He just needs some time, Mercy. Let him be.

There was a part of her that wanted to go after her brother—to knock some sense into him, convince him to change his mind. There was another, even deeper part that knew it wouldn't make a bit of difference.

She stared down at Piper and watched as her hands filled with light once again. If she allowed herself to heal Piper, she sensed this would seal the deal and condemn Raze to a life he didn't deserve.

On some level, she knew Raze was right. It had to happen sooner or later. By choosing not to heal Piper, she was just putting off the inevitable. If she let Piper die, she knew she would never forgive herself.

Her hands ached with the need to heal. *Raze, I'm so sorry.* She hung her head in defeat. Defeated by the love she felt for a woman she'd just met. Defeated by the love she felt for the twin brother she'd known her whole life. She finally knelt on the floor, allowing her hands to find the body that would be forever changed after this moment.

Light spilled from her palms, bright enough to illuminate a football field. Not only was she healing Piper's body, but she sensed she was somehow extending her life, as well. Piper would grow old with her, but not for many years to come. She caught glimpses of their future together and smiled.

Piper's eyelids fluttered open. "Did I finally kick the bucket?"

Mercy couldn't speak. Her throat tightened. She just shook her head and hugged Piper as tight as she dared. Piper felt good in her arms. Her skin was warm, her heartbeat strong, and Mercy never wanted to let her go.

CHAPTER THIRTY-FIVE

Mercy sat at the edge of the hotel pool and dangled her legs over the side. Not a cloud in the sky. The Texas sun felt good. She watched as Raze and Emily competed to see who could do the best cannonball.

The girl took a running leap and expertly tucked her legs against her chest, hitting the water with a sizeable splash. She popped to the surface with a grin. "Well? How was that?"

Raze shook his head. "I'm afraid this competition is over."

Her grin faded. "Why?"

Raze gave a theatrical bow. "Because you, my young friend, are the cannonball *master*."

Bobby nudged Mercy from behind, plopped a wet tennis ball in her lap, and peered at her expectantly. "Okay, buddy. One more," she promised, chucking the ball in the deep end for the thousandth time.

Bobby belly flopped in the shallow end, doggie-paddled the length of the pool, and was back at her side in less than a minute.

Mercy plucked her watch out of her sandal. Four o'clock. Time to round up the gang and get ready for dinner. She towel-dried Bobby, and they all squished down the walkway in their flip-flops to take showers and change.

Everyone met in Lou's room an hour later. Piper greeted them at the door, and they followed their noses inside. Aromas of garlic and fresh baked bread filled the room. With Lou cooking three square meals a day, everyone had put on all the weight they'd lost the week prior. Even Bobby was starting to look a little round in the middle.

Piper shut the door behind them. "We're running late," she confessed. "I kind of set something on fire."

Raze's brow creased in worry. "You burn any of our food?"

She turned away and winked at Mercy. "Just yours, Raze."

Lucent was watching TV from a leather armchair, running his thumb back and forth over the top of his cane. All television broadcasts had been preempted by 24/7 news updates on Air Abroad. CNN reported that the virus now seemed to be under control. The CDC had successfully manufactured the vaccine in mass quantities, and it was now being distributed around the globe.

Sadly, the CDC put the death toll at a staggering twenty-five million. And that was just in the United States.

They had been recuperating at the hotel for the past six days. As far as Mercy could tell, they were the only people there, staff included. At first, it had seemed like they were the only people in Galveston, though the city was slowly waking up from its dark slumber, made evident by the occasional passing car.

Lucent clicked off the TV. He stood with the help of his cane and looked around the room at each of them. "I think tomorrow would be a good day to embark on our travels back home."

Mercy had been thinking the same thing. In fact, she had already made arrangements to rent an RV for the cross-country drive.

Lou circled the table, spooning huge helpings of pasta onto each of their plates. "Okay, everyone. Take your seats. Allow me to present one of my favorite dishes. Brought to you all the way from Naples, this one's called *spaghetti con aglio, olio e diavolicchio*."

"And for those of us who don't understand whatever the hell language that was?" Raze asked.

"Allow me," Lucent said, seating himself beside Mercy. "Lou is serving spaghetti with garlic, oil, and homemade chili." He propped his cane against the wall. "I spent a summer studying Italian cuisine in college. This dish is exquisite."

Lou covered each of his hands with an oven mitt, gripped a small casserole dish from the stovetop, and set it in front of Emily.

"And for you, Miss Emily, a special dish—*pasticcio di pasta vegetariano.*'"

"I can't pronounce it," she said, "but it sure smells good."

Lou fretted in front of the table, oven-mitted hands on hips. "Guess that does it, then?"

Bobby padded over with his bowl between his teeth. He looked up solemnly at Lou.

"Oh! My apologies, Bobby. I made something extra special for you." He peeled some foil from a steak, cut it into bite-sized pieces, and threw some steamed vegetables on the side.

They ate, laughed, and thoroughly enjoyed one another's company. It was decided later over hot fudge sundaes that they'd start on the long drive back home in the morning. They cleared the table, washed the dishes, and ended the night. Mercy closed the door to Lou's room, grateful to have a family—a real family—for the first time in her life.

❖

Mercy opened her eyes and looked at the clock: 5:40 a.m. Something wasn't right. Careful not to disturb Piper, she quietly slipped out of bed, checked the door and windows, and then crept into the adjoining room. Emily, Bobby, and Ansel were snuggled up together on one bed, sound asleep.

She threw on a pair of shorts and stepped outside. The sun was gently prodding the nighttime sky from its slumber. Dusky blues and purples held promises of brighter colors to come. She took a deep breath, savoring the sweet scent of orange blossoms, and stood in her bare feet while she tried to decide on a course of action. Everything *seemed* fine, but something felt…off.

This past week at the hotel had done them all an enormous amount of good. Lou, Raze, Piper, Emily, Lucent, and even Bobby seemed relaxed and happy. Maybe the nagging feeling she had now was a simple case of waiting for the proverbial shoe to drop.

She yawned and stretched. Crawling back into bed with Piper and sleeping for a while longer sounded fantastic. With one hand on the doorknob, she hesitated. There was probably no basis to this newfound paranoia. Still, it couldn't hurt to check.

She knocked softly on Lucent's door before letting herself in. The bed was empty. She checked the bathroom and jogged down to the pool, but the old man was nowhere to be found. She reached out with her mind. *Lucent, where are you?*

There is no need to worry, Mercy. It was time for me to go.

Are you okay?

Yes. As I mentioned before, my time on this earth is drawing to a close.

Mercy felt a lump in her throat. She'd thought they had more time. *Lucent, come back. I can take care of you.*

I cannot. I'm sorry, Mercy.

She sat in one of the poolside chairs and watched as the first light of day danced across the water. *I don't understand. You're going off to die alone?*

The old man hesitated. *I must find my brother.*

Mercy's blood pressure skyrocketed at the thought of Shadow. *To make him accountable for what he's done?*

On the contrary, Lucent replied. *I seek only to bring him comfort.*

Mercy stood so abruptly that her chair went skidding across the pavement. *He killed millions of innocent people, Lucent! What the hell are you thinking?*

Please calm down, Mercy. This is between me and my brother. You, of all people, should understand that.

Like hell I should! I would never let Raze off that easy.

The old man sighed. *Is it your wish, then, for our last conversation be one of conflict?*

No. Mercy righted the chair, sat, and took a deep, cleansing breath. *What do you want me to tell everyone?*

The truth, Mercy. Lucent went on to share his parting gift. Emily and Bobby's unique connection and love for one another had left a lasting impression on him. Knowing that a dog like Bobby had an average lifespan of only ten to twelve years, he'd decided to use the last of his magic to extend Bobby's life to match Emily's.

The more the old man talked, the harder it was for Mercy to fight back the tears. They had known one another for such a short time, but she would remember his generous spirit for the rest of her life.

❖

"Slow down. We are close." Lucent leaned forward and watched the passing tree line carefully. This place had changed a great deal over the last century. He caught sight of the monstrous pine tree with *L+S* carved into its belly. "Stop here," he called out to the driver.

The driver pulled over and promptly opened his door. Lucent slid his cane across the seat and climbed out. "That will be all."

"You sure you want me to leave?" the driver asked uncertainly. Giant pines stared back at them from every direction. "There's nothing out here for miles."

Lucent smiled. "I assure you, I will be fine. This"—he waved a hand in the air—"is *exactly* what I came for." He withdrew the cash from his gold money clip and handed it to the driver.

"Sir, this is too much. I can't take—"

"Hush now, I won't hear of it," Lucent said gruffly. "Use this for your granddaughter's surgery."

"What?" The driver's eyes welled up. "How do you know about my Gracie?"

"The money in your hand will not cover all the expenses for her bone marrow transplant, but this will." He slid a check from his suit pocket, placed it in the man's hand, and turned to walk away. "I know you'll use it wisely," he called back over his shoulder.

Lucent took his time on the overgrown path, ambling along until the sound of crunching leaves made him turn in surprise.

The driver stepped out from the shadows and handed him a bottle of water. They stood together in silence, watching as a woodpecker pecked his little heart out overhead.

The driver stuffed beefy hands in his pockets. "I can't just leave you out here."

"You must." Lucent took a long drink. "This is my home."

The driver opened his mouth, hesitated, and finally asked the question Lucent had come to expect. "Who *are* you?"

"I am simply a tired old man." He took another long drink and handed over the empty bottle. "It is time for us to part ways, I'm afraid."

Lucent waited until the limo's engine faded in the distance before resuming his journey. He inhaled the sweet aromas of Mother Nature with each step. Traces of rainwater, sunshine, and wet maple leaves lingered in the air. Moss-covered rocks, mushroom-lined tree stumps, and sodden, insect-riddled logs smelled just the way he remembered. And there was still just the slightest hint of seawater from the nearby Pacific. In all his travels throughout his life, nothing had ever smelled so heavenly.

He hiked for hours, mesmerized by the intoxicating beauty around him. Trees cast long, dark shadows on the pine-needled earth. Turtles poked their heads out and blinked up at him as he passed. Rabbits scampered from their burrows and followed in his footsteps. A small female bobcat kept pace alongside him for a mile or more, her glorious spotted coat rippling with each stride. Cougars, elk, black bears, even the deer drew close enough to touch, their white tails flicking from side to side. He trekked across the forest for hours in their presence, touched by their concern for him. He spoke aloud to each of them to put their minds at ease.

The sun wrapped itself in a dusky cloak, leaving the forest shrouded in nighttime mystery. At last, a saltwater breeze drifted over him. The animals looked on from the safety of the trees as he stepped into a clearing where the land surrendered to the power of the ocean.

Cliffs with serrated edges jutted out along the coastline. The moon was full, the night sky dotted with tiny pinpricks of light. His suit jacket flapped wildly about as he nudged his cane forward and peered into the darkness.

There Shadow stood, arms outstretched, looking boldly into the ocean depths below.

"I am here, brother." His words must have carried on the wind as Shadow turned in his direction.

"Come," Shadow mouthed, extending his hand.

Lucent limped over and stood beside his brother to gaze at the stars as they had done countless times in their youth from this very spot. He was the first to break the silence. "There is still goodness in your heart."

Shadow sighed. "No, brother. There is only darkness in me now."

"You once possessed an abundance of kindness and decency. I will honor you by keeping those memories close to my heart."

"Aren't you going to ask me why I killed all those people?"

"I already know."

"Then why did you come here?" Shadow's tone had turned to one of anger.

Lucent rubbed his thumb over the top of his cane. "I journeyed here to give you the comfort of companionship."

"I don't need your damn companionship." Shadow wrenched the cane from Lucent's grasp. "My own hatred is company enough."

He met Shadow's gaze and saw that he was right. His eyes were flat, empty, hard, and mean. There was nothing left of the brother he once knew.

Shadow's eyes suddenly narrowed. The corners of his mouth lifted into a frightful grin.

As children, that very same expression would fall over Shadow's face when he was about to do something he shouldn't. Lucent reached out to caress his brother's cheek with a bony, trembling hand. "I forgive you, dear brother."

Shadow smacked his hand away with the wooden cane and, without another word, shoved him over the cliff's ledge.

Lucent heard the animals cry out from the trees as he soared through the air. He tasted saltwater on his lips as it misted his face, felt the ocean's compassion as it reached up to cushion his fall. Weighing him down most heavily, however, was the lack of remorse in his brother's charred, black soul. Filled with grief deeper than any he had ever known, he halted the beating of his own heart before allowing the ocean to swallow him whole.

CHAPTER THIRTY-SIX

Mercy jerked awake and sat up in bed. The clock read 4:59 a.m. Her cat, Bad Ass, leapt off the bed in a huff, clearly inconvenienced by the early morning disturbance.

Piper reached over to click on the bedside lamp. She sat up beside Mercy, their shoulders touching. "Same dream?"

Mercy rubbed her eyes and nodded. "Same dream." But she knew it wasn't a dream at all. She had no doubt that Lucent had been murdered by his twin brother, Shadow. Thrown from a cliff into the ocean, Lucent's final thoughts had been about forgiveness and love. He was truly a remarkable man. She missed him dearly.

She and Piper had been living together for the past three months. Deciding it made more sense to stay in New York to be close to the office, Mercy had sold her house and they'd bought one together. Piper had even returned to working as a profiler for the FBI, but she didn't feel the need to keep her psychic abilities secret anymore. She was no longer ashamed or afraid of what people would think. Colleagues accepted her gifts and quickly came to depend on them.

"It's Saturday," Piper said. "We don't have to be at the restaurant until twelve." Lou had taken his late wife's advice and opened his own restaurant. Wanting to be closer to Mercy, Piper, and Emily, he'd moved into the in-law-apartment attached to their house. The restaurant's grand opening was tonight.

"Is Raze still coming to watch Emily?" Mercy asked.

Piper nodded. "Said he'd be here at eleven."

"School is starting in a month. We should get her registered soon."

"I've been thinking." Piper laced her fingers through Mercy's. "One of us should adopt her, make it official. With her blessing, of course."

"Only one of us?" Mercy asked, incredulous.

"Well"—Piper bit her lip uncertainly—"we can't both adopt her."

"Why not?"

We're not married, Parker."

"Funny you should mention that." Mercy leaned over, slid open the nightstand drawer, and withdrew a white velvet box that fit perfectly in the palm of her hand.

Piper's eyes grew wide. "Hold that thought." She leaned over, slid open the nightstand drawer on her side of the bed, and withdrew an identical white box.

They looked at each other, laughing. "On the count of three," Piper said. "One...two..."

"Marry me," they said in unison.

Mercy decided to stop at the store on her way home from work and pick up some ice cream. A year had passed since the Air Abroad disaster. Their lives were finally returning to normal. Better than normal, actually. Mercy realized she was the happiest she had ever been in her life.

For the first few months after Lucent disappeared, she awoke each morning with a feeling of dread—dreading the fate that awaited her, dreading the tasks she and her brother would be required to perform. But all that dread eventually passed, because nothing ever came of it.

No more shiny footprints. No more healings from the mysterious light in her hands. No more mind-to-mind conversations with Raze. Nothing. Nada. Zip. If it wasn't for the fact that Emily and Piper still had their abilities, she'd be wondering right now if all of it was just a bad dream.

Mercy was standing in line at the grocery store when a skinny man in front of her caught her attention as he smiled at the cashier with pale, pockmarked cheeks. She knew in an instant that this was the man who shot up the deli three years ago.

The scumbag who murdered her wife.

Anna. Sweet Anna.

She abandoned her grocery cart and followed Anna's killer. Ten minutes later, she found herself sitting across from a crack house, watching as the skinny man carried his groceries inside.

Mercy unsnapped her leather holster, slid out her 9 mm, and checked to make sure it was loaded. She had been waiting for this day for three long years.

She waited for a truck to pass, pushed open her car door, and stepped onto the cracked, uneven pavement. She was halfway across the street when a motorcycle peeled around the corner and came to a dead stop two inches from the toes of her shoes.

"Get back in the car, sis."

"What are you doing here?"

Raze nodded toward the house. "Old buddy of mine lives there. I came to settle a debt."

Mercy knew he was lying. Somehow, her brother had picked up on her thoughts. "I can't let you do this, Raze."

"You don't have a choice." Raze revved the bike. "Get back in the goddamn car."

A slew of police cruisers had parked along the street in front of the crack house when Mercy drove past the next morning on her way to work. She had tossed and turned all night long. There was a brick in her stomach where her breakfast should have been. *Oh God, Raze. What did you do?*

My job, Raze said without the slightest hint of remorse. *Now it's time for you to do yours.*

Mercy parked, got out, and held up her badge to an approaching officer. "What happened here?"

"Crack dealer got his head bashed in."

"Any leads?"

"Pick any freakin' junkie off the street."

"Is Sergeant Sloan inside?"

"That's his black-and-white behind you." The officer looked down and frowned. "You know you got your shoes on the wrong feet?"

"Yup, thanks." She had been forced to plunge into the depths of The Box when she showed up late for yesterday's steady room meeting. "Mind if I take a look around?"

The officer tried to stifle a snicker and failed. "Be my guest."

Mercy crossed the dirt lawn and stepped inside. Crime scene photographers were still taking photos of the body on the kitchen floor. The refrigerator door hung open like an unfed, hungry mouth. Plastic grocery bags spilled their contents onto the stained tile floor. And there, all around the body, were Raze's bloody footprints. As clear as day. Mercy could pick her brother's footprints out of a lineup if she had to. A distinct pattern was worn into the sole of each boot from the way he rode his motorcycle.

She ventured into the living room and found a photo tucked into the cushions of an armchair. A mother and young boy smiled at the camera. The boy was the dead man on the floor, and the woman was his mother.

Mercy knew—without wanting to—that the dead man had wiped out his mother's savings, periodically beating her until she surrendered more money. She was now seventy-two and living out of a cardboard box on the Lower East Side.

The woman had a granddaughter, Gracie, who didn't even know she existed. Gracie was in desperate need of a bone marrow transplant, and her grandmother was a perfect match.

Mercy looked up when she saw her old friend marching toward her. "Hey, Bug."

Bug narrowed his eyes and reached for his gun.

"My bad." Mercy threw her hands up in mock surrender. "Sergeant Bug," she corrected herself, pocketing the photo.

Bug eased off his weapon and shrugged. "All I want is a little respect."

"Just a little bit," they said in unison.

Mercy tried to sound nonchalant. "Any leads on the footprints?"

"What footprints?" Bug asked, scanning the tile. "You find something I missed?"

She thought Bug was pulling her chain but soon realized her friend seemed genuinely baffled. Mercy took one last look at the footprints and shrugged. "There's a lot of blood. Just figured there might be one around here somewhere."

"Your shoes are on the wrong feet," Bug said casually.

"So I've been told."

"What brought you out this way?"

"Passing through. Heard the call over the radio and wanted to see what was up." She slid her hands into the pockets of her coat. "Tell the chief I'll stop by later for lunch."

"Will do."

Her feet were starting to ache, but she did her best to limp with as much dignity as possible back to the car. She climbed in, started the engine, and called the office to let them know she was going to be late…again.

She had an old woman in a box to find.

About the Author

Michelle lives in the Boston area with her two young sons and dog. She garnered material for her stories while working as an EMT, dog trainer, inventor, entrepreneur, and business owner. Her days now consist of changing diapers, chasing the baby (who travels at the rate of a speeding torpedo), kissing boo-boos, and writing in the wee hours when the kids are asleep—a life she couldn't have dreamed was even possible and wouldn't trade for anything. *Mercy* is her debut novel.

Books Available from Bold Strokes Books

A Call Away by KC Richardson. Can a businesswoman from a big city find the answers she's looking for, and possibly love, on a small-town farm? (978-1-63555-025-2)

Berlin Hungers by Justine Saracen. Can the love between an RAF woman and the wife of a Luftwaffe pilot, former enemies, survive in besieged Berlin during the aftermath of World War II? (978-1-63555-116-7)

Blend by Georgia Beers. Lindsay and Piper are like night and day. Working together won't be easy, but not falling in love might prove the hardest job of all. (978-1-63555-189-1)

Hunger for You by Jenny Frame. Principe of an ancient vampire clan Byron Debrek must save her one true love from falling into the hands of her enemies and into the middle of a vampire war. (978-1-63555-168-6)

Mercy by Michelle Larkin. FBI Special Agent Mercy Parker and psychic ex-profiler Piper Vasey learn to love again as they race to stop a man with supernatural gifts who's bent on annihilating humankind. (978-1-63555-202-7)

Pride and Porters by Charlotte Greene. Will pride and prejudice prevent these modern-day lovers from living happily ever after? (978-1-63555-158-7)

Rocks and Stars by Sam Ledel. Kyle's struggle to own who she is and what she really wants may end up landing her on the bench and without the woman of her dreams. (978-1-63555-156-3)

The Boss of Her: Office Romance Novellas by Julie Cannon, Aurora Rey, and M. Ullrich. Going to work never felt so good. Three office romance novellas from talented writers Julie Cannon, Aurora Rey, and M. Ullrich. (978-1-63555-145-7)

The Deep End by Ellie Hart. When family ties become entangled in murder and deception, it's time to find a way out... (978-1-63555-288-1)

A Country Girl's Heart by Dena Blake. When Kat Jackson gets a second chance at love, following her heart will prove the hardest decision of all. (978-1-63555-134-1)

Dangerous Waters by Radclyffe. Life, death, and war on the home front. Two women join forces against a powerful opponent, nature itself. (978-1-63555-233-1)

Fury's Death by Brey Willows. When all we hold sacred fails, who will be there to save us? (978-1-63555-063-4)

It's Not a Date by Heather Blackmore. Kade's desire to keep things with Jen on a professional level is in Jen's best interest. Yet what's in Kade's best interest...is Jen. (978-1-63555-149-5)

Killer Winter by Kay Bigelow. Just when she thought things could get no worse, homicide Lieutenant Leah Samuels learns the woman she loves has betrayed her in devastating ways. (978-1-63555-177-8)

Score by MJ Williamz. Will an addiction to pain pills destroy Ronda's chance with the woman she loves or will she come out on top and score a happily ever after? (978-1-62639-807-8)

Spring's Wake by Aurora Rey. When wanderer Willa Lange falls for Provincetown B&B owner Nora Calhoun, will past hurts and a fifteen-year age gap keep them from finding love? (978-1-63555-035-1)

The Northwoods by Jane Hoppen. When Evelyn Bauer, disguised as her dead husband, George, travels to a Northwoods logging camp to work, she and the camp cook Sarah Bell forge a friendship fraught with both tenderness and turmoil. (978-1-63555-143-3)

Truth or Dare by C. Spencer. For a group of six lesbian friends, life changes course after one long snow-filled weekend. (978-1-63555-148-8)

A Heart to Call Home by Jeannie Levig. When Jessie Weldon returns to her hometown after thirty years, can she and her childhood crush Dakota Scott heal the tragic past that links them? (978-1-63555-059-7)

Children of the Healer by Barbara Ann Wright. Life becomes desperate for ex-soldier Cordelia Ross when the indigenous aliens of her planet are drawn into a civil war and old enemies linger in the shadows. Book Three of the Godfall Series. (978-1-63555-031-3)

Hearts Like Hers by Melissa Brayden. Coffee shop owner Autumn Primm is ready to cut loose and live a little, but is the baggage that comes with out-of-towner Kate Carpenter too heavy for anything long term? (978-1-63555-014-6)

Love at Cooper's Creek by Missouri Vaun. Shaw Daily flees corporate life to find solace in the rural Blue Ridge Mountains, but escapism eludes her when her attentions are captured by small town beauty Kate Elkins. (978-1-62639-960-0)

Somewhere Over Lorain Road by Bud Gundy. Over forty years after murder allegations shattered the Esker family, can Don Esker find the true killer and clear his dying father's name? (978-1-63555-124-2)

Twice in a Lifetime by PJ Trebelhorn. Detective Callie Burke can't deny the growing attraction to her late friend's widow, Taylor Fletcher, who also happens to own the bar where Callie's sister works. (978-1-63555-033-7)

Undiscovered Affinity by Jane Hardee. Will a no strings attached affair be enough to break Olivia's control and convince Cardic that love does exist? (978-1-63555-061-0)

Between Sand and Stardust by Tina Michele. Are the lifelong bonds of love strong enough to conquer time, distance, and heartache when Haven Thorne and Willa Bennette are given another chance at forever? (978-1-62639-940-2)

Charming the Vicar by Jenny Frame. When magician and atheist Finn Kane seeks refuge in an English village after a spiritual crisis, can local vicar Bridget Claremont restore her faith in life and love? (978-1-63555-029-0)

Data Capture by Jesse J. Thoma. Lola Walker is undercover on the hunt for cybercriminals while trying not to notice the woman who might be perfectly wrong for her for all the right reasons. (978-1-62639-985-3)

Epicurean Delights by Renee Roman. Ariana Marks had no idea a leisure swim would lead to being rescued, in more ways than one, by the charismatic Hudson Frost. (978-1-63555-100-6)

Heart of the Devil by Ali Vali. We know most of Cain and Emma Casey's story, but *Heart of the Devil* will take you back to where it began one fateful night with a tray loaded with beer. (978-1-63555-045-0)

Known Threat by Kara A. McLeod. When Special Agent Ryan O'Connor reluctantly questions who protects the Secret Service, she learns courage truly is found in unlikely places. Agent O'Connor Series #3. (978-1-63555-132-7)

Seer and the Shield by D. Jackson Leigh. Time is running out for the Dragon Horse Army while two unlikely heroines struggle to put aside their attraction and find a way to stop a deadly cult. Dragon Horse War, Book 3. (978-1-63555-170-9)

Sinister Justice by Steve Pickens. When a vigilante targets citizens of Jake Finnigan's hometown, Jake and his partner Sam fall under suspicion themselves as they investigate the murders. (978-1-63555-094-8)

The Universe Between Us by Jane C. Esther. Ana Mitchell must make the hardest choice of her life: the promise of new love Jolie Dann on Earth, or a humanity-saving mission to colonize Mars. (978-1-63555-106-8)

Touch by Kris Bryant. Can one touch heal a heart? (978-1-63555-084-9)

Change in Time by Robyn Nyx. Working in the past is hell on your future. The Extractor Series: Book Two. (978-1-62639-880-1)

Love After Hours by Radclyffe. When Gina Antonelli agrees to renovate Carrie Longmire's new house, she doesn't welcome Carrie's overtures at friendship or her own unexpected attraction. A Rivers Community Novel. (978-1-63555-090-0)

Nantucket Rose by CF Frizzell. Maggie Jordan can't wait to convert an historic Nantucket home into a B&B, but doesn't expect to fall for mariner Ellis Chilton, who has more claim to the house than Maggie realizes. (978-1-63555-056-6)

Picture Perfect by Lisa Moreau. Falling in love wasn't supposed to be part of the stakes for Olive and Gabby, rival photographers in the competition of a lifetime. (978-1-62639-975-4)

Set the Stage by Karis Walsh. Actress Emilie Danvers takes the stage again in Ashland, Oregon, little realizing that landscaper Arden Philips is about to offer her a very personal romantic lead role. (978-1-63555-087-0)

Strike a Match by Fiona Riley. When their attempts at matchmaking fizzle out, firefighter Sasha and reluctant millionairess Abby find themselves turning to each other to strike a perfect match. (978-1-62639-999-0)

The Price of Cash by Ashley Bartlett. Cash Braddock is doing her best to keep her business afloat, stay out of jail, and avoid Detective Kallen. It's not working. (978-1-62639-708-8)

Under Her Wing by Ronica Black. At Angel's Wings Rescue, dogs are usually the ones saved, but when quiet Kassandra Haden meets outspoken owner Jayden Beaumont, the two stubborn women just might end up saving each other. (978-1-63555-077-1)

Underwater Vibes by Mickey Brent. When Hélène, a translator in Brussels, Belgium, meets Sylvie, a young Greek photographer and swim coach, unsettling feelings hijack Hélène's mind and body—even her poems. (978-1-63555-002-3)